PALATINE

The Four Emperors Series

PALATINE

Book I of the Four Emperors Series

L. J. Trafford

KARNAC

First published in 2015 by
Karnac Books Ltd
118 Finchley Road
London NW3 5HT

British Library Cataloguing in Publication Data

A C.I.P. for this book is available from the British Library

ISBN-13: 978-1-78220-264-6

Typeset by V Publishing Solutions Pvt Ltd., Chennai, India

Printed in Great Britain

www.karnacbooks.com

For JA

CHARACTERS

The Imperial Family
Emperor Nero*
Empress Statilia Messalina*

The Staff—Freed or Freeborn
Tiberius Claudius Epaphroditus—the emperor's private
    secretary*
Tiberius Claudius Philo—the emperor's private secretary's
    secretary
Calvia Crispinilla—mistress of the wardrobe*
Phaon—head of the messenger section*
Ofonius Tigellinus—Praetorian prefect (the drunk one)*
Nymphidius Sabinus—Praetorian prefect (the sober one)*
Felix—head of slave placements and overseers

The Staff—Slaves
Artemina (Mina)—keeper of the towel
Alexander (Alex)—messenger
Sporus—part time empress*

Straton—an overseer of exceptional skills
Lysander—announcer
Daphne—a seamstress
Erotica—a girl of obvious talents

In Spain
Galba—would-be emperor*
Titus Vinius—Galba's second in command*
Cornelius Laco—Galba's second, second in command*
Icelus—Galba's freedman*
Marcus Salvius Otho—a skilled courtier*

*Historical personages

PART I

NERO
SPRING AD 68

*"He looked forward cheerfully to a ripe old age
and an unbroken run of good luck"*
—Suetonius, "Life of Nero",
The Twelve Caesars

ONE

It was Julius Vindex who started the revolt against Nero. The idea hit him with the force of a slingshot between the eyes: the emperor must go.

So obvious was this thought that Vindex could not believe that everyone else did not share it, and he eagerly scrawled out letters to the governors of the provinces neighbouring his own. Then he waited for the support he knew he would be offered.

When it did not come, when Vindex was left with silence from his contemporaries, he was puzzled rather than downhearted. But such was his conviction, his itching impatience, that he burst into action anyway.

TWO

Tiberius Claudius Epaphroditus was an important man. This was evident by the lavishness of his office. It lay in what the imperial workforce referred to as the old palace. The new palace, built by Nero after the great fire wiped out vast tracts of the city, was a study in opulence: the golden ceilings rotated, blossoms rained onto visitors, and perfume misted from the walls. This was the home of the large-scale imperial entertaining that Calvia Crispinilla, Nero's mistress of the wardrobe, commanded.

The old palace, dating back to Emperor Tiberius, a muted affair in comparison, stood imposingly over the forum with high arches and a distinct lack of glamour. A dull, sturdy, but commanding and visible presence of imperial might for all those shoppers who happened to glance upward; it teemed with energetic slaves and heavily armed guards. Here the real work went on, in the home of the extended bureaucracies headed by the freedmen, those former imperial slaves who ran the empire.

Epaphroditus held the title of private secretary, which was misleading in its humbleness, for Epaphroditus was as high as it got. His path from imperial slave to pre-eminence had been a treacherous one. He'd survived by successfully skidding between palace factions, keeping his head down when others were literally losing theirs, and by being really quite good at his job.

Now aged a trim forty-seven, he sat in his enormous office behind a large ivory-adorned desk, signing scrolls, arranging meetings, making copious notes, undertaking a little light filing, and generally being damn useful. He was scanning some important documentation when his assistant, Philo, slipped in through the door.

Noting the worried expression on his face, he asked, "What is it, Philo?"

The young freedman cleared his throat. "It is Tigellinus to see you, sir."

"Tigellinus?"

"Yes, sir."

Epaphroditus leaned his chin onto linked fingers. Now this was unusual: at this hour he would expect Tigellinus to be sleeping off the previous night's entertainments. Epaphroditus could not remember the last time he had seen the prefect in daylight hours.

"You had better send him in."

Tigellinus strode in, his unsteady gait betraying his unusual wakefulness; he was drunk, roaring drunk. He did not wait for permission to sit, plonking himself down, removing his purple-plumed helmet and placing it on the floor beside his chair. Chestnut, gold-flecked eyes met Epaphroditus' shrewd green ones.

A click of fingers produced Philo with a tray of drinks. Tigellinus reached for his, downed the liquid in one, and replaced the beaker on the tray without once removing his eyes from Epaphroditus. The secretary ignored this bravado, taking gentle sips and waving Philo away.

One thing Epaphroditus learnt as a slave was patience, so he sat quietly and waited for Tigellinus to begin.

"Some slave handed me this."

He waved a scroll in Epaphroditus' direction. The secretary followed its movements trying to identify the seal.

"Apparently there is trouble in Gallia Lu … Gallia Lug … Gallia something or other."

"Gallia Lugdunensis?" supplied Epaphroditus.

Tigellinus showed his teeth. "You are well informed. I had to ask a slave where in Hades it was. They've rebelled or are rebelling, something of that kind."

Epaphroditus noted the prefect's bloodshot eyes wandering, the stench of last night's stale wine wafting from every pore. Tigellinus had changed. No longer the lean horse trader Epaphroditus had first encountered as the young emperor's new and greatest friend. Tigellinus had been a skilled and clever courtier then; now he was a lumbering embarrassment.

A year or two older than the secretary, he was showing the signs of ageing very badly. A pot belly hung over his belt and seemed destined to expand; his unusually large head with its chestnut curls was red veined; and his eyes bleary. Dissipation could do that to you, noted Epaphroditus, and reassuringly patted his own flat, toned stomach.

"What is the scale of the rebellion? How many tribes?"

The prefect waved his hand. "Oh, I don't know. Some. The ones you can't pronounce. But that's not important."

Epaphroditus held back from suggesting it might be of some help in the ensuing crackdown, asking lightly, "Perhaps if I could examine the document?"

Tigellinus gave a belch, a fist held in front of his mouth as he swallowed with a gulp. "Excellent idea. I'll leave this to you."

He handed over the scroll then pushed himself to his feet, staggering and grabbing onto the edge of Epaphroditus' desk in an attempt to right himself. The desk wobbled, two stylos rolling off the end with a clatter. This brought in Philo, who quickly scouted round and picked them up.

"You'll deal with this then, Epa … Epa … Epaphro …"

"Certainly," smiled the secretary serenely.

Tigellinus bent down to retrieve his helmet, a motion so alarming in its wobbling precariousness that Philo sped forward and picked it up for him.

"Thank you, boy," grinned Tigellinus, patting the thirty-year-old Philo on the head with a large palm.

He exited with an attempted salute, a flabby hand whacking him on his forehead.

Epaphroditus broke the seal and unfurled the scroll, quickly scanning the content.

"Trouble, sir?" asked Philo nervously, his black hair flattened by Tigellinus' pat.

Epaphroditus gestured to the chair that Tigellinus had vacated. Philo sat down, placing his wax writing tablet on his knees, a stylus held in one hand in anticipation.

As Epaphroditus read, his brow furrowed. He carefully wound up the scroll and placed it down, resting his elbows on the desk.

"Well," he told Philo, "The tribes of Gallia Lugdunensis have united and are causing trouble. Their estimated strength is 100,000 men."

"The legions overcame a much larger force in Britannia," offered his assistant. "Well over 200,000 men. Ten times the number of legionaries."

Epaphroditus gave a tight smile at the reference. They had almost lost the province, Londinium had been burnt to the ground, and tens of thousands of Roman citizens had been butchered. Yet Philo was right, Rome had, as ever, prevailed.

"They are being led by Julius Vindex, the governor of Gallia Lugdunensis."

"Oh," said Philo chewing the end of his stylus. "Odd."

"Isn't it? Vindex is a Gaul by blood; we considered him Romanised, advanced him. Apparently we were wrong. Let us hold off from informing the emperor until we have more details."

Philo's stylus flew quickly across his tablet as Epaphroditus spoke.

"I see no need to inform the senate at this stage either, not when we know so little. Can you talk to Phaon in the messengers section and get him to send one of his boys up to Gaul to gather facts? Once we have the full report we'll set up a briefing with the emperor. Oh, and let's also send missives to the other western governors. Give them a chance to declare their devoted allegiance to the emperor. They love any opportunity to crawl."

He paused, and sensing a dismissal, Philo got to his feet.

Epaphroditus pointed to the chair. Philo sat down again. His boss fixed his eyes on him and gave a genial smile.

"I have been meaning to have a chat with you. Freedom seems to be suiting you Tiberius Claudius Philo."

Philo gave a shy smile and fiddled with the hem of his new blue tunic, pulling it over his narrow knees.

"Are you enjoying your new status?" Epaphroditus asked him.

"Yes, sir."

"Good, good. It does bring more responsibilities. You have a name now. Tiberius Claudius is a proud name, the emperor's own forenames, which he has bestowed upon you. You must do your very best to live up to such a distinction. Everything you do now, Philo, will stick to that name for better ..." he paused for effect, concluding, "or for worse."

Philo shifted slightly on the chair.

"You have a blank tablet, your past life is over, and you are starting afresh. It is a fantastic position to be in: use this opportunity wisely."

There was a pause which Philo felt he was expected to fill, "I will, sir."

Epaphroditus rubbed his hands together. "Excellent. I have high hopes for you Tiberius Claudius Philo."

"I hope I shall fulfil them, sir."

"I am glad to hear that," Epaphroditus smiled.

This was a speech he had given many times. So far no one had let him down and his former assistants littered the palace in high positions, where they naturally fed back information to their former boss on a regular basis; at least one reason why Epaphroditus was so well informed. Turning his attention back to a scroll on the desk, Philo saw this as a dismissal and took his leave. He was at the door when Epaphroditus made his final point.

"Oh, and Philo," he called. "As a freedman there are certain practices that are now unacceptable."

Philo, who was not to know that this was simply part of the speech, felt the heat rush up his neck as he quickly closed the door behind him. Epaphroditus leaned back in his chair, lacing his fingers behind his neck. Julius Vindex was a foolish man: Gaul had to be the very worst place to start a revolt. It was within a few days' marching of Germania, where the toughest, hardest, meanest of the legionaries were posted. They were in prime position to crush Vindex and his trousered pals into mushy corpses.

No, if Epaphroditus were staging a rebellion he would choose North Africa. From there one could intercept the grain ships bound from Egypt to Rome and starve the populace into deposing the emperor for you. The Roman mob had a long history of expressing its displeasure with grain famines. Old Emperor Claudius had been physically manhandled during one such protest.

Epaphroditus drifted off, contemplating the sheer brilliance of such a scheme, working out the exact number of days it would take to demolish the grain supply held in the Aventine silos, when he realised with a jolt the treasonous nature of such thoughts. He picked up the scroll again and said out loud: "Vindex is an idiot!"

THREE

It was typical, steamed Nymphidius Sabinus, absolutely
typical.

"Are you sure?" he demanded of his slave.

"The meeting is taking place today in the garden room."

Sabinus was on his feet. The slave winced, expecting a
kicking.

"How am I supposed to ensure the safety of the emperor
if I am excluded like this? I am a Praetorian prefect! I need to
know of such threats. I shall attend," he decided briskly. "Let
Epaphroditus dare to bar me!"

The garden room was located in what had once been Nero's
great-grandmother Livia's house. Though a separate building standing behind the Temple of Apollo, it was linked to the
newer parts of the palace by a series of tunnels allowing slaves
to move quickly and discreetly to their positions. Most visitors
to the palace were unaware such tunnels existed, for they were
guided through the gardens or wonderfully decorated corridors instead.

The garden room, compared to most chambers in the
palace, was rather basic. Harking back to Augustus' belief in

old fashioned family values and austerity; values which had not been passed down the generations. It was called the garden room for the frescos, which depicted lush vegetation with exotic birds dotted about here and there. It also opened out onto a small courtyard, the skill of the artist, and indeed the current gardening team, shown by the difficulty of deciphering where the garden finished and the wall began.

The only furniture was a white bench and a low round table. Livia, it was said, had sat on this very bench watching her grandchildren play, Nero's mother Agrippina amongst them.

Epaphroditus was just old enough to remember Livia, though not her husband the Emperor Augustus. If asked to recall he offered some vague waffles, infected by the freedman's insistence that his life began on the day of his manumission from slavery. This was a shame since he possessed the type of tip-top stellar imperial gossip that sadly never makes the history books.

He had chosen the garden room for the Vindex briefing as he did most things in life, carefully. Nero had an extremely short attention span and was likely to be distracted by the gimmickry in the new palace rooms, which he loved to show off alongside the plans for its extension. This was ongoing and nearly bankrupting the city. The garden room was also sufficiently small and private to address the subject of Vindex's ongoing rabble-rousing.

Epaphroditus did not want a room full of Nero's flunkeys and hangers-on gasping with shock when he broke the news of the revolt. He wanted it low key, casual, and he wanted Nero relaxed, but not too relaxed. Hence the meagre selection of a single jug of wine and water laid out on the low table. Philo positioned himself on a low stool in a discreet corner of the room, ready to take notes if required.

A slave announced Tigellinus. He sauntered in with a slight swagger, no doubt wine induced.

"This about Gallia whatever it is?" he slurred at Epaphroditus.

The secretary nodded. "I've got the full report back from Gallia Lugdunensis," he pronounced effortlessly. "The emperor needs to know the basics."

"How are we playing this?" asked the prefect.

"Like the foolish enterprise it is."

Tigellinus helped himself to a cup of wine, taking a long draft.

"Why do I feel like I've been here before" sighed the Praetorian prefect. "I don't understand it, I really don't. You have this emperor who is just the best thing that has ever happened to this damn city. He erects fabulous buildings, puts on marvellous shows, the people love him. Yet these worms keep crawling out. What do they want?"

It was rhetoric, so Epaphroditus simply shrugged.

He was right though, the worms did keep crawling out. Three years earlier, Epaphroditus had helped suppress the strongest of these attempts to rid Rome of Nero. Gaius Calpurnius Piso, distinguished senator and traitor, had put in place a scheme of such audacity and scope that nineteen men had been executed with a further thirteen exiled for life.

Among the dead were Nero's former tutor, Tigellinus' fellow Praetorian prefect, the master of the wardrobe, and several close friends of the emperor. The worms were higher placed, better connected, and harder to squish. All of which accounted for Epaphroditus' long hours.

The announcer slid in and pronounced, "Gaius Nymphidius Sabinus, Praetorian prefect."

Tigellinus and Epaphroditus shared a joint groan as Nymphidius Sabinus marched in.

"This business in Gaul …" he addressed the secretary rather than his own colleague. It was well known that Tigellinus and Sabinus loathed each other.

"Some trouble in the provinces. Gallia Lugdunensis. It is under control," smiled Epaphroditus. "This is merely information sharing. You need not stay, Sabinus, if you have other matters to attend to."

The prefect crossed his arms and did not move.

The two Praetorian prefects were as different in temperament as they were in appearance. Sabinus, a tall, grim-faced man with a large grinding jaw and overhanging brow. Fussy in both appearance and manners, he held himself like the soldier Tigellinus had never been.

For all that, Epaphroditus knew who he would rather turn to in a crisis. There was something that unnerved him about Sabinus, always had. It was not that the prefect could deflate the cheerful atmosphere of a room merely by entering it, nor was it the brutal zeal that he had installed in his guards, rather it was the prefect's frigid nature that nagged.

It was rumoured that Sabinus possessed a private life more barren than the Arabian desert. Epaphroditus had never known him to have a mistress or an attractive boy or to use any of the thousands of slaves available to him for his pleasure. Perhaps this was due to discreetness, though he doubted this: his spies littered the palace and none of them had anything juicy to report about Sabinus.

It was this coldness to normal everyday behaviour that unnerved Epaphroditus. A man with no secrets could not be blackmailed, and if Sabinus were only half as upright as he pretended, he could not be bribed either. This was frighteningly subversive behaviour for a palace official.

You could always tell when Nero was about to enter a room. The air was sucked out, there was a momentary silence, and then you were hit in the face with a full-blown typhoon. It was, Epaphroditus imagined, like hearing the whistle of a ballista-fired bolt above your head just before it obliterated you off the face off the earth.

Epaphroditus, Tigellinus, and Sabinus positioned themselves and waited in unnatural stillness until … in danced a small troop of bejewelled girls wearing indecently short saffron tunics. They threw long overarched arm stretches depositing red rose petals on the ground. Light on their feet, they gave the garden room two circuits before dancing out again, leaving the mosaic floor completely obscured. Epaphroditus' and Tigellinus' eyes followed their cute little rears out of the door. Sabinus fiddled with his sandals, removing a couple of petals that had lodged between his toes.

The pipers were next, and were inexplicably sporting the hairy legs of a faun. Even in hooves, they gracefully gambolled and frolicked and held the tune pretty well. Two enacted a play fight, throwing handfuls of petals at each other. One ducking behind the bench and popping his head up, accompanied by a long "ooh" on his pipe.

Tigellinus, who loved a show of any sort, clapped his hands in time to the music and laughed at their mimes, which only encouraged them. Having exhausted every possible jump and frolic they skipped out, hairy buttocks high and proud, to a suitably jaunty melody. Epaphroditus gazed upwards and silently prayed to Jupiter that they would be spared a poetry recital.

A short display of acrobatics was mildly amusing given the proportions of the room. The eunuch had sung tolerably well but the jugglers, oh the jugglers! At exactly the point Sabinus was wound to breaking point, a fact betrayed by his purple face and grinding jaw, three trumpeters entered and gave a short burst that bounced off the walls and nearly deafened them.

A tall, elegantly proportioned slave entered and announced the divine (a word which made Sabinus wince) Nero Claudius Caesar Augustus Germanicus. Audible sighs all round.

For such a build up, the appearance of the emperor was anticlimactic. He was not an imposing figure. Medium height with a dry thatch of limp blonde hair, which grew long over his neck, culminating in a pair of tirelessly teased bushy sideburns.

His eyes were a watery blue and protruded from his head as if constantly surprised. His legs, which had been good in his youth, were overwhelmed by his enormous stomach, making them appear spindly in comparison. He was dressed in a purple tunic covered by a long dressing gown, which flapped round his ankles. A white scarf was tied around his neck and flicked casually over his right shoulder.

Hanging off the emperor's arm was at first glance an extremely beautiful, glamorously attired woman. A peach gown floated on her form, skimming over the flesh. Red hair piled high above an unlined brow in gravity-defying rolls, cushioning a glittering diamond-studded tiara matched with chunky necklace, bracelets, and rings on each finger of both manicured hands.

At second glance, the overt posturing of her walk and gait was noted: the overemphasis of every gesture. The conscious way she held her body was studied rather than natural, and then there was the heavy make-up that disguised rather than accentuated.

She, of course, was not a she. Neither was she a he. It was a eunuch named Sporus and he (for grammatical clarity we shall stick to he, for Sporus had indeed once owned the correct anatomy for such a description) made a very passable and attractive woman.

On sight of the eunuch, Sabinus' large jaw clenched.

The head of the known world plumped his ample buttocks down on the bench. Sporus, curling himself next to Nero, let a decorated ankle drape suggestively over the edge. Sabinus glared at the eunuch, who smiled back, running his tongue across his lips. His existence was enlivened by finding an increasing number of ways to wind up the prefect.

"What ho, friends!" cried Nero clapping his hands. "What news? What am I doing here?"

Epaphroditus opened his mouth but quickly snapped it shut as Nero continued, "It had better be quick. There is a stunner of

16

an athletic competition I want to see. There's this wrestler, they call him The Ox. Did you hear that, The Ox?"

"Fancy."

"Can you guess why? I bet you can't. What say you Tigellinus? Why do you think they call him The Ox?"

The Praetorian prefect was game to play along. "An ox is a large, muscled creature. Apt for a wrestler, Caesar."

"Aha," snapped Nero. "You're wrong Tigellinus. Completely wrong." He sat back satisfied.

"Oxen are slow, slovenly," mused Tigellinus.

Nero shook his head vigorously to each suggestion. Patting Sporus on the knee, he said, "He'll never get it. Never."

"Oxen are able to pull twice their body weight. Does The Ox do the same?"

"No, no, no."

"He has a tail?"

"No," giggled Nero. "Do you give up yet, Tiggy?"

"Never. I shall never surrender."

This amused Nero greatly. He turned to Epaphroditus. "You will have to arrange for my bed to be moved to this room because we are going to be here for *days*!"

"He lives on a diet of turnips?"

A head shake.

Epaphroditus affected his most genial smile. "I think that you are going to have to tell him, Caesar. I doubt he will even blunder onto the solution."

"No he won't, will he? Then I shall have to divulge. They call him The Ox because he has this absolutely enormous tongue. It flaps out of the corner of his mouth when he wrestles like some huge, horrible, purple ox tongue."

"I would never have got that."

"No you wouldn't. You wouldn't have got it at all. We would have had to live here in this room, all of us together. Do you snore Epaphroditus?"

"My wife has never commented, so I assume not, Caesar."

17

"My darling snores, just a little," he confided. "I find it sweet, she snores like a tiny little bird."

Sporus gazed up from under false lashes, giving them a quick flutter. Emperor and eunuch squeezed hands.

Sabinus' jaw audibly clicked into place.

Nero looked up. "Sabinus, why so grim? You are always so grim. You remind me of my uncle Caligula in your grimness. You lower my spirits. I feel out of sorts."

"If we could move to the matter now, then Caesar could regain his spirits at the athletics," Epaphroditus suggested smoothly.

"Yes, let's. Let's get this whatever out the way so I can go and see my wonderful Ox."

He gestured to Epaphroditus.

"Nothing to concern you, Caesar. Just a small matter that you should be informed of. A disturbance in Gallia Lugdunensis."

"Gallia what?" asked Nero, who was losing interest already.

"Gallia Lugdunensis, Caesar. There has been a small revolt."

"Revolt?"

"A local stirring up of trouble by a man who should know better. It is being dealt with."

Nero snapped back to attention "Oh, it is, is it? That is good."

He heaved himself off the bench. "Thank you for telling me, Epaphroditus."

"I will keep you informed of any developments."

"Good, good. Ask the legions to capture him alive will you?"

"Certainly, Caesar."

"I will have a triumph. I shall ride in a golden chariot pulled by a dozen, no two dozen camels. Do they have elephants in Gallia whatever it is?" he enquired.

"Sadly no, Caesar."

"Shame, shame. Never mind. Here's an idea though, Tiggy. I shall write an ode to the vanquished ... what's his name?"

"Vindex."

"Oh, that's good. The Vanquished Vindex. I like it. I shall start it right away."

Sporus nudged Nero slightly, "The Ox, husband?"

"Oh yes, of course. My darling wishes to see The Ox in action and who am I to refuse? Ox first, ode second. Epaphroditus, can you make sure my lyre is ready for composing."

"Of course, Caesar."

"Excellent. Tiggy, let's go see this athletics!"

They departed to another burst of horn, leaving Epaphroditus and Sabinus.

"A little local trouble?" said Sabinus in his usual monotone. "100,000 men? Hardly little."

"Untrained men," replied Epaphroditus lightly. "Barbarians."

"You should not underestimate them. You will keep me informed of the situation," Sabinus instructed.

Epaphroditus shrugged non-commitedly, "There is nothing to tell. Vindex is probably dead already."

"Then you will inform me of that," insisted Sabinus. "I am in charge of the emperor's security and safety. I must know such details."

Then he marched out, for Sabinus never merely strolled or ambled. He moved as if permanently under the watch of a cudgel-happy centurion.

"Cock," swore Epaphroditus under his breath. "Did you get all that?" he asked Philo, who had been quietly taking notes.

"Yes, sir," replied the scribe, tying his tablet shut with leather ribbons.

Epaphroditus gazed into space, "Did you ever know his mother?"

"Sir?"

"Nymphidia Sabina," he said with a sigh.

"I don't think so, sir."

"A truly beautiful woman, a real pleasure to spend time with. You would not believe he was her son."

"Perhaps he takes after his father," suggested Philo.

His boss shrugged off some rather pleasant memories replying, "Whoever he may be. Sabina was rather liberal in her favours."

Liberal enough for the prefect to take her name, screaming his illegitimacy to all.

FOUR

The soldier lay face down on the floor, his colleagues in arms standing in a circle around the figure. Nymphidius Sabinus stood to one side, his expression hard.

"Guard Paulus has committed a crime. He has let himself down. He has let you, his fellow soldiers, down. He has let down the great name of the Praetorian Guard. This cannot be allowed. Nothing should tarnish the Guard, nothing and nobody."

Such was his emphatic rhetoric that there was a general run of nodding heads.

"What say you, Paulus?"

Lying face down was not a conducive position for an eloquent reply and Paulus' utterances were inaudible.

"And that is all you have to say?"

Another mutter.

"Paulus was caught gambling whilst on duty. This is unacceptable and excuses are not valid," stated Sabinus. "You will be punished by the very colleagues you have let down with your conduct."

A shudder ran through Paulus' body.

Sabinus gestured to the soldiers. They approached their colleague and began to kick the figure, ten of their sharp-booted kicks. Kicks that were meant. The first hit Paulus on his right side and he twisted to evade, only to receive a sharp blow to the left and then another and another.

At first he could identify single blows, but soon the pain was such that he was no longer aware where and when they struck, his whole body was a pulsating throb of hurt.

Sabinus watched satisfied as Paulus cried out. Faces, who a moment before had been friendly, stared down at the unfortunate guard with sheer loathing.

"Please, please," Paulus was groaning.

Sabinus let a few more blows strike before giving a sharp whistle. The soldiers stood back, breathing heavy from the exertion, splatters of blood on their sandals and legs.

"Help him up."

Two guards grabbed Paulus under the armpits and raised him up. He attempted to put his feet on the floor but slipped and fell to the floor again.

"Keep him upright."

They struggled with him so that his face was level with Sabinus'.

Both Paulus' eyes were swollen shut, his nose bent at an odd angle, he shook his head and then spat out two teeth onto the bloody floor.

"Look at me."

Paulus opened one eye, seeing a blurred image of the prefect.

"Let this be a lesson. Your colleagues will not tolerate you tainting their good names with your antics. I am a Roman and it is a good Roman's duty to show clemency, so I will allow you to live this time. And because I am merciful, I will let you rest for today. But I expect you on duty tomorrow. Is that understood, Paulus?"

Paulus murmured something that could be construed as "Sir". It was certainly what Sabinus heard because he nodded and ordered Paulus to be dragged off to the mess hall for recuperation.

Stepping over the pool of blood Paulus had left behind, Sabinus deliberated. He was right to show mercy. Paulus was a good recruit but ill willed. A quick, hard dose of his colleague's contempt coupled with his own humiliation should smooth out those rough edges. And, if not, then his mercy would be withdrawn.

Sabinus had no time for malcontents. He had brought the Roman army's own peculiar brand of brutality to the palace.

Returning from hard action on the German borders to take up the mantle of Praetorian prefect, Sabinus had been horrified by the state of the guards who faced him. They had never been drilled, they partook in little physical exercise, and frequently showed up for duty unshaven. They were a shabby mess and Sabinus was thoroughly ashamed by his association with them.

Foolishly he had voiced his concerns to Tigellinus; eager for the prefect's opinion on how the two of them could reform the Guard; picturing them as a team, working together, co-ordinating and providing infallible leadership. As the younger partner, he was prepared to bow to Tigellinus' greater experience and knowledge.

Listening to the litany of complaints that fell off Sabinus' tongue, Tigellinus heard him out and simply shrugged. Sabinus goggled at such nonchalance.

"The Guard are a mess," he insisted. "They are in no shape to protect the emperor!"

"Why would they need to? The emperor's the most popular guy in town," Tigellinus said, hands spread wide.

In time Sabinus had learnt where the laxity lay. It was Tigellinus, hung over each morning, who failed to ensure a drill. It was Tigellinus, caught up in the emperor's perverted pastimes, who turned a blind eye to his troops' proclivities.

It was Tigellinus who had allowed them to get flabby and lazy.

Sabinus, enthused with righteous anger at such dereliction of duty, took himself to see Epaphroditus. He would have asked to see the emperor, but didn't wish to panic the sovereign by laying forth the deficiencies in his own personal safety.

Epaphroditus listened with more patience than Tigellinus. Though he did not shrug, he offered the verbal equivalent of a brush off.

"You are the Praetorian prefect," he had said.

"I am," replied Sabinus, not understanding.

Epaphroditus laced his fingers and spoke very slowly. "It is your job to discipline and order the troops."

There was a pause. "You're saying I should deal with the troops? That I should resolve these problems?"

"Exactly. It is your job."

"It is," said Sabinus, feeling brighter in spirit. Though looking at him from the outside one would never know, for he appeared as dour as ever. "And Tigellinus?"

Epaphroditus forced a tight smile, "Is free to do whatever he sees fits. Though I doubt he will stand in the way of your improvements."

So Sabinus had instituted a new tougher regime, moving into the Praetorian camp in an attempt to instil the camaraderie he remembered from the army and to keep an eye on the Guard's activities. Though he had separate quarters, he made sure that they greatly resembled his men's own mess and contained no additional luxuries. He shared the same basic rations and threw himself with vigour into the new, harsher training schedule.

They came in time, if not to like him, at least to respect him. For although he was tough, he was fair, and rewarded good work as often as he punished bad. Tigellinus was happy to let

Sabinus manage the troops on a day-to-day basis. The novelty of command having long worn off, he relished the additional free time now allotted and he filled it with increased drinking and fornicating.

Sabinus cracked his knuckles, sitting down at his desk ready to fill in the Guard's daily log, an additional administrative layer he'd introduced. Unlocking the top drawer of the desk and pulling it open carefully, he selected a suitably sharpened pen. He delayed shutting the drawer, snaking an arm in and reaching to the very back, his fingers clasping around the desired object.

It was a small ivory sculpture, half the size of Sabinus' fist, depicting the head and shoulders of a man resting on a darker plinth. He placed it on his desk. It was an example of good Roman craftsmanship. The sculptor, working in miniature, had managed to depict the heavy fringe, the large forehead and the stern countenance of the man. The prefect traced his little finger along the jaw line, running a forefinger across his own at the same time.

So caught up was he in this act that he didn't hear the slave enter until he announced, "There is a man to see you, sir."

Sabinus threw the bust back in his drawer, slamming it shut and locking it, swinging round and fixing his slave with his most intimidating of glares. "What man?" he demanded.

These slaves never gave you the full information.

The slave, knowing his master's ill temper, lowered his head, cringing from imagined blows. "The gentleman declined to state. Only that it was of the utmost importance."

That phrase elicited Sabinus' attention. A security issue? Action needed from his troops?

There was scarcely any other reason why someone would seek Sabinus out. He was hardly good dinner party material and as far as anyone knew, he had not a friend in the world.

"Bring him in."

The slave returned with a poor specimen in Sabinus' eyes: a bald-headed man with heavy black eyebrows and a thin wrinkled neck with protruding bulge, which bobbed up and down as he swallowed nervously.

"Nymphidius Sabinus, may I have a word?" he asked.

Sabinus gestured with his hand to a chair.

The man glanced round at Sabinus' slaves dotted around the room.

"Alone."

Sabinus angled his head slightly and the slaves trotted out. His visitor sat down awkwardly on the edge of the chair.

"Speak," commanded the prefect.

The ball in his neck plummeted downwards and then back up again. "My name is Icelus."

"You have information for me," interrupted Sabinus.

Didn't this creature know that he had duties to attend to? Troops to drill, paperwork, endless paperwork that Tigellinus would never deign to complete.

"My name is Icelus," he repeated. "You will have heard of my master, Gaius Servius Sulpicius Galba. My master is the governor of Spain."

"I am aware of that," stated the prefect.

"Are you also aware of the current situation in Gaul?" queried Icelus carefully.

"Vindex's revolt? Certainly. I am fully informed," he replied tetchily, Icelus unknowingly touching upon a sore point.

"Vindex has written to my master in Spain."

"You have these letters?" Sabinus held out a hand. "I will pass them on to the emperor. The other governors are merely posting their allegiances. Your master's attention to detail will be noted."

"Vindex's letters to my master were different to those that were sent to the other provincial governors," stressed Icelus. "They held a proposal."

"Indeed. To offer Vindex military support, that is what was in the other letters."

Sabinus tapped a finger on his desk. Why was this slave grovelling to him? It was Epaphroditus' job to listen to their pathetic cries of loyalty.

"If you will give me the letters, I will ensure that the emperor hears of your master's loyalty."

He clicked his fingers, held out a hand, eager to dismiss this bald creature. Icelus glanced back over his shoulder before facing Sabinus again and lowering his voice. "My master has heard good things about you, Nymphidius Sabinus. He admires the way you have taken control of the Guards; he feels it is a shame that you must share your command with one so inferior in his abilities."

A statement that Sabinus fully concurred with.

"Your master no doubt remembers a time when court positions were handed out on merit. Sadly that is seldom the case these days."

"Tigellinus—"

"Is a despicable, debauched courtier of the most disgusting habits and corrupt character," supplied Sabinus, sitting back in his chair and crossing one leg over his knee.

"Quite," smiled Icelus. "It is a shame that such men should flourish, should be prized by the emperor. My master feels it is a pity that the emperor has been led by such men as your colleague and the likes of Calvia Crispinilla."

"A woman who had defiled a good name," spat out Sabinus on mention of Nero's mistress of the wardrobe.

"And Epaphroditus—"

"A slick slave, as slippery as a lamprey."

"And this Sporus."

"He calls himself Nero's wife and poses as the empress at public events in full view of decent men and their wives and children," continued Sabinus, rapidly turning purple, his fists clenched tight.

Icelus leaned forward and said quietly, "My master shares your concerns. He worries too about this decadence, this immorality. He worries for the emperor's character. He worries that the emperor is too corrupted by these parasites to be saved. He worries that the empire will be infected, that it will totter under such disrespect. In the provinces the legions mutter—"

He paused at this dark premonition, giving Sabinus the chance to digest his words.

"You estimate the legions will join Vindex's endeavour?" asked Sabinus, his heavy brow furrowed.

Icelus had said enough to be convicted of treason: Nero would not accept the slightest criticism or jest, no matter how well veiled. Men had opened their veins for less. However, Sabinus felt no urge to denounce him. He was surprised to find himself intrigued by this thin-necked, reedy slave. He spoke sense, his eyes were open. He and his noble master saw what Sabinus had seen ever since his return to Rome.

"The legionaries sing ditties as they march to the detriment of the emperor. They sing that he murdered his brother, his mother, and his wife."

"Wives," corrected Sabinus. "His first wife Octavia was forced to commit suicide and then the second, Poppaea, he kicked to death. Statilia Messalina, his third wife, is unharmed, so far."

"The point is that they are openly disrespectful. The emperor has not visited the army recently."

"Ever," corrected Sabinus again.

"And they hear too of unmanly practices by the emperor. Vindex has used such feelings to his advantage. To our advantage," he stressed heavily and continued quickly before Sabinus could interrupt again.

"Vindex wrote to my master. In fact he has written many times expressing his contempt for what has become of the empire. My master naturally advised caution, advised him to keep quiet his doubts as we heard of senator after senator facing trial for so much less. But Vindex was beyond caution. He could no longer bear 'that man', as he calls the emperor, ruining his Rome. He took action and he wrote to my master one final time. In this letter he made my master an offer."

Icelus stopped and produced a scroll which he handed to Sabinus. "Here is the letter. Read it for yourself. Digest its contents and then come find me at my master's home, for ill or otherwise."

He stood, "I leave the fate of the empire in your hands."

Which was exactly the sort of nationalistic, empty phrase that was guaranteed to appeal to the prefect.

After Icelus' departure Sabinus sat by the light of a single lamp holding the scroll in his hands. He dismissed his slaves and told his tribune that he was not to be disturbed in any event. Then he sat alone in his chair and stared at the scroll.

Sabinus considered himself a loyal subject. He had served emperors in the wild provinces, fighting barbarians and spreading Roman values. He returned to the city appointed Praetorian prefect with the express aim of protecting the imperial family, and that he had done.

He had no doubt from Icelus' carefully chosen words that this scroll contained some kind of treason. If he opened it, if he read it, he was complicit. Yet that bald slave spoke truths.

He too was disgusted by Rome. By the cesspit it had become, the men of good name debasing themselves to gain favour from a depraved emperor. All those eunuchs and dancing boys that surrounded Nero, that huge new palace sprawling across a third of the city, sucking up funds that should have been used for the good of Rome. The parties held there were of such notoriety that even in the decadent East, Parthian kings sighed with wonder at that strange Roman king's antics. If Nero's great-great-grandfather, that noble exalted Emperor Augustus, could see what his legacy had become …

Sabinus shuddered. Then he unrolled the scroll and read Vindex's words to Galba, holding his breath until he got to the end, whereby he released it with a hiss. He placed the scroll carefully back onto his desk. It was indeed treason. One very big treason. Vindex was proposing that the Spanish Governor Galba declare himself emperor.

FIVE

Philo, he of the nimble stylus and possible hidden vice, awoke late. Cursing, he leapt out of bed and flew around his small room locating woollen underwear and sandals, pausing over the tunic selection. He owned a total of three coloured tunics so far: one blue, one red, and one brown. His plan was to acquire a range of tunics in a vast array of colours, anything but the white he'd worn as a slave.

He'd yet to decide what colour he liked best. His landlord's daughter Teretia had, only two days before, told him that he looked very smart, and he was sure that he'd been wearing his red tunic then. He held up the item and examined it for stains; red today, definitely red.

Slipping the tunic over his head, he was fastening his belt when a thought struck him: had it been the red tunic that Teretia had complimented? What if it had been the blue?

Therefore she had not said anything about the red tunic. Which surely meant she did not like it. Perhaps red didn't suit him. Not possessing a mirror, Philo was unable to assess the truth of this. He nibbled at a fingernail, a gnawing anxiousness gripping his heart.

Should he wear the red or should he wear the blue? Epaphroditus had stressed that more was expected of him now he was freed. That he had new responsibilities. Which of his tunics would communicate that responsibility?

Feeling unsure on the red tunic, he began to strip. Interrupted by a tap on the door, he pulled the tunic back over his head. Sliding back the bolt, one of his new advantages being the ability to lock himself away, he opened the door to find his landlord's daughter Teretia. She was holding a bowl of steaming porridge.

"Mother was worried when you didn't come for breakfast. She asked me to bring this to you."

"That is very kind of her," he said, taking the bowl and spoon from her.

Seeing her smile dip, he added, "And very kind of you to bring it up for me."

This visibly reassured her and a flush ran across her cheeks. She didn't, however, move. Philo stood awkwardly on the threshold of his room with the bowl in his hands. What did she want? He had thanked her, surely she should withdraw? Did she expect him to invite her in? What would happen then? Would she sit on the floor and watch him eat? Having grown up with his every move dictated, Philo was mystified by the behaviour of others.

Finally he said, "You must have a lot of chores to do."

She nodded eagerly, "Oh yes. It's washing day today." Shyly she added, "Is there anything I could wash for you?" Her cheeks reddened again.

Philo considered. He hadn't decided yet between the red and blue tunic, and the brown one was unworn. "I don't think so," he replied.

"It would be no trouble. I don't mind."

"No, no it's fine. I don't need. Nothing needs."

He nodded towards the bowl, "I should ..."

"Yes, you should, before it gets cold, Mother says."

Yet she still did not move.

"Well, erm, I should go and ..."

He ran out of words, turning and closing the door, clicking the bolt across.

Philo sat on the edge of his bed balancing his bowl on his lap, feeling its warmth on his thighs. His room was compact, his narrow bed managing to touch three of its four walls. The rest of his furniture consisted of a wooden stool on which he had laid his precious tunics, and a low table that served no other purpose than as an object on which to stub his toe. It had been his home for two whole months now.

The apartment itself was situated on the first floor of a three-storey block in a quiet street on the Viminal Hill. A very respectable area, his landlord Teretius had assured Philo, before going on to list all the streets he should avoid after dark.

The Viminal Hill, an as yet unfashionable district of Rome, contained the usual slum at the bottom, and on its cooler heights, large villas owned by moderately successful merchants who could not have afforded even a flat on the more prestigious Caelian and Esquiline Hills.

Teretius and Pompeia, parents of Teretia, lived in the middle betwixt these two extremes. Their home had been described to Philo as spacious, with three separate bedrooms linked by a narrow corridor, and a kitchen with a working stove. He'd tried to appear impressed, but since he had grown up in a palace his notions of scale were rather different.

When Teretius had mentioned the daily rent required, he'd enquired earnestly "Is that a lot?"

For Philo was new to money: growing up in the palace, everything was provided for him; he was issued with new sandals whenever the buckle cracked or the strap snapped, his white palace tunic was replaced on an annual basis, and he had, like all the palace slaves, been fed every morning and evening in the refectory. He had never worried about paying for anything before.

It was true that he had collected a bag of those strange metallic circles to buy his freedom. But he did not really understand their purpose, staring perplexed at the coins, unsure as to the value of each coloured disc.

On purchasing his red tunic, he simply handed over his wages and let the tailor pick out the amount he required. Naturally this had singled him out as a good prospect to the local shopkeepers, who fleeced him on a regular basis. Philo had yet to work out that his lack of funds was not due, as he thought, to his inability to budget, but rather to the unscrupulous nature of the Viminal Hill merchants.

In the first days of his freedom he rejoiced in the quiet that his room offered him. Locking his door each night he sat and wondered at the absolute silence, marvelling at being able to hear his own heart beat. The palace in comparison was a muddle of noise. Slaves worked different shifts depending on their role, so when you were trying to sleep there was always someone else who was just getting up, banging around.

Often there would be an impromptu gathering for a dissection of all the latest gossip, or an arm-wrestling competition with heavy bets placed on the winner, or maybe somebody would sneak in some wine from the imperial cellars for a tasting session.

However, the novelty of silence had worn off and Philo dreaded sitting in his little room at night. He missed the barrage, the bustle, the gossip, the rows, the fights, and the parties. Not that Philo had participated in any of that, his shyness hindering him in social situations.

In retrospect he supposed he must have enjoyed the spectacle, but he had failed to appreciate it. Now he spent every night in aching loneliness waiting for the sun to rise so he could go to work. It was not how he had imagined freedom.

34

Calvia Crispinilla, mistress of the wardrobe and the premier palace party organiser of Rome, glared down at the creature lying on the bed.

It was sleeping, one arm draped across its face, leading to a slender hand and taloned fingernails painted a deep purple. As it rolled over and the arm fell, Calvia noted the kohl-smudged eyes, the red blush that had crept all over its cheeks, and indeed the formerly white pillows, now a dusky pink.

Her tongue clicked. "Bloody eunuchs!" she cursed and then she grabbed it by the ankle, giving a hard tug.

"You slept in your make-up again, didn't you?" she yelled.

The eunuch Sporus opened one eye, Calvia's pinched features staring down at him.

"Didn't you," she repeated with emphasis. "I've warned you about this before; it ruins the skin."

She pinched at his cheek pulling at it, exposing his teeth. He made a grunting noise and flapped a hand at her.

"What time is it?" he asked, yawning.

Calvia turned her back and busied herself with the laying out of Sporus' garments. "Time you were up," she replied. "The emperor has requested you by his side. So I am here to dress you."

Sporus sat up very slowly. A thumping pulse was beating on the right side of his face: he must have been stupendously drunk last night. Swallowing, he noted that his mouth was entirely devoid of saliva and that his tongue seemed to be coated in some strange concoction. "Nero never wants me in the morning."

"Well, he does this morning so get your scrawny arse out of bed!"

Sporus leapt up when he saw her eyeing the curling tongs. Calvia possessed a filthy temper and a quick hand. His leap, however, was a bit too sudden and he pulled a hand over his mouth, swallowing painfully, "Aaach."

"Stand up straight," she admonished, giving the backs of his knees a quick smack with a hairbrush. "The quicker you comply, the quicker it'll be over."

Sporus stood, as was required, in the middle of the chamber with his arms outstretched, ready for the garbing ritual. Head held high he enquired, "Who am I?"

This was not a philosophical question, for Sporus held a dual identity. Some of the time he was merely Sporus, an imperial slave and eunuch of indeterminate duties. Sporus wore long colourful robes with kohl-defined eyes and a hint of rouge on his lips. He favoured bangles and had one ear pierced with a single emerald. He was to be found at imperial banquets, seated at a discreet distance from the emperor but near enough to suggest an important position in the palace. He was charming, witty, could disarm with inconsequential chatter, and was the purveyor of top-quality gossip.

And then there was his alter ego, Poppaea. Poppaea had been Nero's second wife, a snarling wildcat of a woman with a dangerous beauty and a wicked tongue. A certain resemblance between them had led to the eunuch's strange role. Though Sporus' interpretation of the deceased empress was much more demure than the living, breathing Poppaea had ever been.

His Poppaea sat next to her husband at events where she could play a moderating influence on him, gently placing her hand on his when his temper threatened to boil over. She sang softly to him when he was suffering from one of his heads, and submitted to his lovemaking with feminine grace. Poppaea wore modest flowing gowns of chiffon in pastel shades with limited jewels. Her make-up was traditional, with a white lead foundation and red rouged cheeks. Her hair was pinned into gentle rolls on her head with ringlets that flowed onto her shoulders.

Though the hair was a wig, Poppaea's toilette was a tedious trial of plucking, shaving, scraping, and polishing. So for Sporus, it mattered very much who he was on any particular day, and he failed to suppress a groan this particular morning when Calvia told him.

"Poppaea."

"Again?!" he cried. He was never just Sporus these days.

Calvia approached with a bowl of red-hot walnut shells for depilating his legs. Knowing how much Sporus despised this part of the proceedings, Calvia clicked her fingers and two burly slaves appeared either side of him. Sporus stood naked and eyed them up very slowly. He got fierce-looking glares in return, reducing him to giggles.

Calvia left the depilating to her assistants and busily pinned the Poppaea wig into a fashionable style. She would have been an attractive woman if it were not for her sour expression. For someone who created such wonder and delight, Calvia was remarkably foul. The wardrobe slaves sported impressive bruises. Sporus recalled readily the time Ligia had mistakenly cut a tress off the Poppaea wig and Calvia had flown at her cursing like a fury, stabbing her in the arm with a hair grip. Really, they should have made her a slave overseer for she possessed the required qualities of cruelty, casual brutality, and a solid work ethic of getting things done.

Sporus submitted himself to the ministrations that would transform him into Poppaea. Time being in short supply, his bath was skipped and instead he was lightly refreshed with damp sponges and sprinkled with perfume. He moved only slightly when the cold cream was smoothed onto his face, the first of many layers of make-up that Poppaea required.

A total of five wardrobe assistants administered to him, undertaking their tasks with trembling hands lest Calvia find fault. The mistress of the wardrobe produced a pair of silver sandals and a shimmering gown of light green.

"It's a bit flash," said Sporus, as he stepped into the gown.

"The emperor is unwell, he needs calming. Green is appropriate," Calvia explained, aiming a kick at a slave who had foolishly got in her way.

37

Sporus was helped into the heeled sandals and the heavy wig placed aloft his head. Calvia approached with curling tongs, reached under the wig and tightly pulled down a strand of Sporus' own hair, setting to work on it. He gritted his teeth as she pulled and teased a ringlet out of him, acutely aware of the heat from the tong.

She stood back to admire her work, pursing her lips. He looked beautiful; a gorgeous, dazzling Roman woman. He looked like Poppaea. Calvia felt a stab of sadness as she wondered how Nero stood it, how could he bear to see over and over again this approximation of what he had lost?

Poppaea, the real Poppaea, would have flipped her shawl across her shoulder, blown a sarky kiss to Calvia, and told the slaves that she was "off to provide a wank fantasy for the imperial guards". Sporus would never have her spirit; he was just a slave, a pretty slave, dressed in her clothes and answering to her name.

"You'll never be her," Calvia slipped in, betraying her thoughts.

Sporus looked into a bronze hand mirror, Poppaea smiling back at him. "Oh, I don't know. I get closer every day. Thanks to you."

Calvia sniffed, "You had better be careful then. We all know what happened to the first Poppaea."

It was an unforgivable thing to say, an unforgivable thought to express. Everyone in that chamber, from Calvia and Sporus, down to the attendants, and even the guard that stood by the door found themselves involuntarily looking at the floor. A simple black and white geometric mosaic.

If they hadn't been present that day they'd all heard about it. If you looked close enough at that black and white mosaic, you could just about see a tiny fleck of blood that remained from the day that Nero had kicked Poppaea to death in this room. Sporus gave a shudder.

Calvia took this as a triumph.

SIX

Philo was struggling to get to work on time. Still unfamiliar with Rome outside the palace he took a wrong turn on his way from the Viminal, finding himself in some kind of fish market. Walking through the old palace entrance hall, sniffing at his new blue tunic, he could detect the faint aroma of sardine.

He moved as quickly as he could without breaking into a run, such things being strictly forbidden in the corridors. The attempt gave him an off-centred, faintly comic gait. He was never going to be on time now, cursing himself for stopping to enjoy that bowl of porridge, for vacillating over his tunic, for waking up late, and for being the utterly hopeless being he felt himself to be. His lateness would be noted and it would be held against him by Epaphroditus, a distressing thought to the loyal scribe who revered his boss.

He was so distressed at the thought of letting Epaphroditus down that skidding round a corner he ran smack bang into Straton, a particularly nasty example of the species known as "slave overseer". The collision was such that Philo found himself temporarily winded. Straton, who was as wide as he was tall, was unaffected by the accident and stared down at Philo with a smirk.

He was an intimidating presence with a shaven head, pockmarked face with bristled chin, a red slash for a mouth, and small black bead-like eyes that could switch from humour to anger as quickly as he could crack his whip. An evil, raised scar ran across his neck, the origins of which had been hotly discussed by several generations of imperial slaves.

If it gave comfort that some brave soul had once stood up to Straton, the fact that he had survived such a deadly encounter had given rise to the all too plausible rumour that he was immortal.

Philo was not alone in finding Straton terrifying, but he did have one advantage now over the slave overseer, namely that he was no longer a slave, and thus Straton had no power over him. It was with this thought that he gathered himself up, chest thrust out as he said with only a slight tremble, "If you will excuse me, I have an important meeting to attend."

The overseer consciously stepped in front of him and absently fondled the whip that curled at his belt. Though Straton may have seemed like a rough customer, he was finely tuned to the intricacies of body language. His career depended on distinguishing between mere bravado and outright rebellion, and he gained great enjoyment from the expression that crossed Philo's face.

Taking the whip from his belt, he held the handle in one hand and let the other fondle the length of the leather, very slowly.

"Now," he croaked, for the slice to his throat had affected his speech and he spoke in a hoarse whisper. "You come with me."

Philo felt his knees weaken and was about to obey meekly, when he remembered Epaphroditus' speech of the previous evening.

"I have a meeting to attend," he said in a smaller voice than he had intended. In his head it had been a blistering and withering statement of intent.

Straton smirked and stepped in his way.

"I have to go," Philo squeaked, staring down at his sandals, mentally chanting, "You are free, you are free, you are free."

"You come with me."

It was a statement more than a command. Straton did not need to command, the thought of anyone daring to do otherwise was inconceivable. Philo felt his resolve weaken as Straton pointed in a direction that Philo knew well, and knew well what awaited him there. It was one thing to have free will. It was quite another thing to exercise it, and Philo found himself being led down the corridor, the overseer keeping one hand gripped firmly on the back of his neck.

No doubt this encounter would have ended up as usual. However with supreme timing, Alex, a young messenger boy, bounded round the corner with all the enthusiasm of a housewife finding a bargain at the fish market, or, if you prefer, a Praetorian guard encountering an attractive, unchaperoned girl. He clutched in his right hand a sealed scroll which he felt sure, for he was an optimistic soul, contained a message of the utmost importance. Uncannily it was addressed to Philo.

Catching sight of his quarry much sooner than he had expected, he skidded on his heels and came to an abrupt halt.

Straton's hand fell from the back of Philo's neck. Alex stood upright as a plinth, presenting his scroll.

"Message for Tiberius Claudius Philo."

"Thank you, Alexander. I shall read it on my way."

"I'm to wait for an answer, sir."

Clearing his throat and sounding much more like himself, Philo retorted, "Walk with me then."

This was most unusual but Alex shrugged and trotted beside Philo.

Straton watched his prey depart with narrowed eyes.

Philo struggled with the seal, his hands unpleasantly damp and trembling. If Alex noticed this, he didn't comment but walked alongside him in silence. He scanned the document quickly, taking in the important points. Alex, observing, asked, "And the reply, sir?"

"Report back that it will be dealt with."

Clicking his heels and saluting, Alex prepared to depart, but then added unexpectedly: "It must be great not to have to do what the overseers say, sir?"

Philo looked into Alex's eager eyes and muttered sadly, "Yes, it must."

SEVEN

"You're late," said Epaphroditus not looking up. "Again."

"Sorry, sir," muttered Philo, still traumatised by his Straton encounter. "I overslept," and then noting the stack of scrolls piled upon Epaphroditus' desk he asked, "News from the provinces?"

"Hmm, yes," muttered Epaphroditus. "Phaon dropped them off: they're the sworn allegiances from the relevant governors." Epaphroditus looked up. "Some of the panegyric is really quite touching. I could almost believe that they genuinely love their emperor. If I didn't have my informers that is," he added dryly.

Philo rubbed the sleep from his eyes and gave a yawn before saying, "So it is all in hand then? Vindex is isolated."

Epaphroditus smiled smoothly. "Indeed. A couple of omissions in the Nero adoration camp, but no one of any consequence. Verginius Rufus is marching his legions to intercept Vindex's barbarian corps. It will soon be over."

He stood up smoothing down his tunic, "I shall go inform the emperor of the good news."

For such a clement day, Epaphroditus would have expected to find the emperor in the ample new palace grounds, feeding the giraffes, enjoying a pleasant boat ride on the lake, perhaps feasting in one of the many shell-studded grottos that were specially designed for such an activity. However, a slave informed him that Nero was resting in his quarters.

The chamberlain of the bedchamber is a superior position. It requires poise and elegance and a straight face. The chamberlain on duty outside Nero's private rooms was sporting a very slight smirk.

"Interesting day?" queried the secretary.

Well trained, the chamberlain did not respond, he merely raised his eyebrow ever so slightly, denoting that His Imperial Majesty was in one of his more intriguing moods.

A forewarned Epaphroditus glided through two further levels of security until he reached the announcer, Lysander. His smirk was much more obvious than the chamberlain's; it showed a full set of teeth, and his shoulders were trembling with amusement and suppressed laughter.

"Who is in there?" asked Epaphroditus, angling his head towards the door that led to Nero's inner sanctum.

"Sporus, Sabinus—" began Lysander.

This put Epaphroditus on full alert: that combination was combustible.

"Daedulus, the emperor's singing tutor. Usual contingent of body slaves, guards, etc.," concluded Lysander, adding conspiratorially, "That's not the fun bit though."

"No?" queried Epaphroditus.

"Do you want to know or would you rather it was a surprise? I would hate to ruin it for you. It has completely made my morning."

"Prepare me." Forewarned was forearmed.

"Caesar has decided that his voice is too weak for use today, he wishes to save it for his performance tonight. Daedulus has agreed to be the emperor's mouth for the day."

44

Epaphroditus mulled this over. "The Emperor was sitting in the senate today."

"He was, but Daedulus did all the talking," advised Lysander.

The secretary was sure the senate had adored being addressed by the emperor's singing tutor. He rubbed a knuckle between his eyes. He knew he should have accompanied the emperor: he could have smoothed away this madness. If Philo hadn't been late, he would have. This was exactly what happened when he wasn't around: negating Nero's fevers was a full-time job; one could not take even a moment to breathe.

"Announce me."

The door swung open and Lysander's pleasing baritone rang out. "Tiberius Claudius Epaphroditus. Viator Tribunicius, Hastis Puris, Coronis Aureis, private secretary to His Imperial Majesty Nero Claudius Drusus Germanicus Caesar."

"Ahh, Epaphroditus."

The speaker was an upright, dignified-looking man with a prominent mole above his top lip and distinguished grey hair. This was Daedulus the singing tutor.

The emperor was laid out on a couch, covered by a blanket, and wearing a tight Phrygian cap on his head. Sporus curled on the floor beside the couch, holding onto the emperor's limp hand, playing the role of the concerned wife, wiping a damp cloth across his beloved's brow and sighing with worry.

"Epaphroditus, I am not well. I am very sick. Weak."

This came not from the emperor but rather Daedulus again, causing Epaphroditus to wonder which of them he should be addressing.

He settled on a neutral stare at the floor as he announced, "I come with good news, Caesar."

"Excellent," replied Daedulus. "Pray do reveal."

Epaphroditus gazed around the room wondering whether Daedulus was going to do Nero's thinking for him as well (not necessarily a bad option), catching sight of Sabinus standing quietly in a corner. The prefect was stood as upright as ever, so straight that you could have used him as a ruler, but to the secretary's keen eye there was a difference in his stance. It took him a moment to identify the change, a black smudge beneath his eyes as if the prefect were lacking sleep.

Epaphroditus would not have suspected the prefect of such restlessness. He had long believed that Sabinus lacked the imagination for dreaming, that his head hit the pillow and he was instantly unconscious, waking up to an ice bath and 200 press-ups. It was intriguing to wonder what was troubling him. Sabinus caught Epaphroditus' speculating gaze and stiffened his jaw, shifting his eyes towards the emperor, clearly uncomfortable.

Odd, thought Epaphroditus.

"The news?" prompted Daedulus.

The secretary smiled, "The western governors have pledged their allegiance to His Imperial Majesty and denounced Vindex in the strongest words available to them and their scribes."

This attracted Nero's attention, and he waved frantically to Daedulus' back. Epaphroditus pointed over the tutor's shoulder and the tutor sped round.

"Husband, husband," cried Sporus, wrestling with the emperor's hands. "You must not upset yourself. You must rest."

Nero mimed the motion of writing. The body slave, Juba rushed forward with a writing tablet and stylus. Nero wrote quickly and then handed the tablet to Daedulus who read out loud.

"So Vindex is vanquished?"

"Yes, Caesar," replied Epaphroditus. "The traitor will be dealt with adequately."

"Brilliant," cried Daedulus, clearly off message since it set off more gesticulating from the prostrate emperor.

The tutor was handed another message: "It would soothe my weakened soul to hear my governors' kind words on their emperor."

"It will rejuvenate him!" piped in Sporus, who had evidently squeezed out some teary concern earlier since his eye make-up was smudged down his face like errant spider trails. That the pristine eunuch had not immediately rushed to fix his face showed that this was all part of today's performance. The eunuch dipped a cloth in a bowl of water, wrung it out, and then placed it carefully on Nero's forehead. "Does that help, husband?" he cooed gently.

Nero clasped Sporus' hands in his and mouthed, "I love you."

"Me too, my great love. Me too."

This tender scene of love betwixt an emperor and his eunuch faux wife would normally have set Sabinus off into an audible teeth grind. However, the prefect remained blank faced, which belied the torment beneath his stolid exterior.

Epaphroditus concluded his summary with a nice line in which the emperor's lyre playing was reported as being much missed, "Oh, to hear such wondrous sounds once more such as Apollo could not compare."

The emperor wiped a tear from his eye, Daedulus wiped one from his in perfect symmetry, Sporus openly wept, Sabinus' lip curled ever so slightly upwards.

"I am glad that these simple words bring such joy to His Imperial Majesty," smoothed Epaphroditus.

Nero held his palms across his heart, the tears streaming down his cheeks.

Job done, thought the secretary, and was about to manoeuvre his way into the subject of a reward for being the receptacle of such joy when Sabinus suddenly interjected, "Did all the governors respond with such words?"

Epaphroditus shot him an annoyed look. Sabinus met it evenly. His expression was his usual dour one; unreadable, fixed.

Daedulus read from the latest tablet, "Did they, Epaphroditus?", adding in an imploring dramatic plea of his own, "Did they?"

Nero sat up on his couch with interest, the blanket sliding from his lap. Epaphroditus was not a violent man. He was certainly not an aggressive man. He saw anger as a facile emotion, the last retreat of the inarticulate and stupid. He much preferred to use his judgement and his cold reason. However, today he could cheerfully have punched Sabinus smack onto his large, square jaw. He would then have jumped for joy onto the prefect's genitalia and squashed for good any faint chance there was of those grim, frigid features being passed down to another generation.

Bang had gone his chance of delivering uniformly good news, bang had gone his chance of reward, and bang, Epaphroditus had decided, had gone the prefect's chances of any further promotions.

You did not lie to an emperor, not blatantly anyway, so Epaphroditus offered contritely, "There have been a couple of omissions, true, Caesar," then with hands held wide, "Postal delays."

Nero looked almost placated, until Sabinus piped in again, "Who has not responded?"

Epaphroditus, stood beside a triangular marble topped table, suppressed the urge to lift it up and fling it at the prefect.

"No one of any importance," soothed the secretary to the emperor's stricken face.

In fact there were two notable exceptions: Galba, the Spanish governor, and the governor of Lusitania, Otho. Epaphroditus knew which one he was prepared to offer up for sacrifice, "Galba, Caesar."

Nero clicked behind him and a slave shot forward. He was a nomenclator, that is he was paid to remember names and pertinent facts on behalf of the emperor.

Epaphroditus could have told Nero all he needed to know about Galba, so could Sabinus. Possibly even Sporus had a fact or two at his manicured fingertips, but this was the nomenclator's golden moment and he shot forward in a glow of expectation. It would have been a hard man indeed to puncture such glee.

"Gaius Servius Sulpicius Galba, governor of Spain. Great-grandson of Quintus Catalos Caitlin. Former governor of Aquitania, former commander of Upper Germania, proconsul of Africa, member of the board of fifteen and the priesthood of Augustus. Widowed, no issue. Galba was a firm favourite of Empress Livia, wife to the divine Augustus, and indeed he was rewarded in her will."

All very commendable, all very reassuring, such a solid individual with a lifetime of duty to the state and to the imperial family. However, the nomenclator in his eagerness to show off his prodigious memory, the very tool of his specialist position, failed to use his judgement and simply splashed out everything he knew on the man, concluding, "Galba was once suggested as a suitable husband for the lady Agrippina—"

Mistake. The lady Agrippina, Nero's mother, the one whose death he had ordered, an act so impious that it had haunted him ever since, and he forbade even the mention of her name. The emperor made a startling recovery, leaping to his feet and screaming at full force, "HE DIES!! THE FIEND DIES!"

There followed a deeply uncomfortable silence. Sporus shuffled backwards on his heels, hanging his head down, morphing from Poppaea back into a mere slave. Daedulus stared at the floor, the colour draining from his face, a hand nervously shaking by his side. The nomenclator's features were frozen in horror at this error.

"He dies," continued Nero, a little calmer. "Make it so, Epaphroditus."

"Yes, Caesar."

"An assassin, yes, an assassin, a dagger-loaded assassin. With a poisoned dagger, yes, that's it, a poisoned dagger."

The emperor began to pace as the ideas flowed. "The poison will be on the tip and before our hero delivers the fatal motion he will say, and you must, must put this into the instructions, Epaphroditus. He must deliver these words." Nero paused, fingers on his chin, "Juba, bring me my Sophocles."

The body slave dashed off and returned with the volume. Nero placed the scroll onto a table and rolled it out.

"Mmm," he traced a finger over the words. "Perhaps … but not."

He unrolled it further. "Maybe … but not."

Finally he found the correct sentiment. "Yes, here it is! Let him say: 'You here? You have the gall to show your face before the palace gates? You, plotting to kill me, kill the king— I see it all, the marauding thief himself scheming to steal my crown and power! Tell me, in god's name what did you take me for, coward or fool when you spun out your plot? Your treachery— you think I'd never detect it creeping against me in the dark? Or sensing it, not defend myself? Aren't you the fool, you and your high adventure. Lacking numbers, powerful friends, out for the big game of Empire—you need riches, armies to bring this quarry down!'"

It was rather a long speech for a killer, mused Epaphroditus. Galba, aged though he was, could have fled to Lusitania by its conclusion.

"Yes, Caesar. I shall put it in the instructions."

"Good, good," smiled the emperor, his good humour restored. "I shall look forward to the account. Oh, and he dies too." He pointed at the shaking nomenclator.

"Yes, Caesar."

Two Praetorians took the now sobbing nomenclator by the armpits and hauled him out.

The emperor, satisfied, sat back on his couch, Juba helping him arrange the blanket back over his body.

"Where is Poppaea?" Nero asked.

"She is here," soothed Epaphroditus, clicking his fingers to Sporus who was flinching in a corner.

"Come here, my love," cooed the emperor patting the couch.

Sporus crawled over and took up the position, snuggling into the emperor. "You must not be so sensitive, my great love," sighed Nero, kissing Sporus lightly on the lips. "Women feel such things deeper don't you think, Epaphroditus?"

"Yes, Caesar."

"But your husband is safe, Poppaea, the creature Galba will be dealt with. So you have no reason to worry."

Sporus snuggled in tighter and made suitably feminine noises. Harmony was thus restored, until Sabinus suddenly burst out, "What if it is a postal delay?" With such force that he had clearly been holding onto the thought for some time.

"Hey?" queried Nero, spreading kisses up Poppaea/Sporus' neck.

Sabinus took a large military step forward. "Caesar, Epaphroditus is correct. Galba's reply could be forthcoming."

Nero gave Poppaea a tickle under the chin, Sporus giggling girlishly. "Is this Galba wealthy?"

"Exceedingly," confirmed Epaphroditus.

"He dies," stated Nero.

Sabinus formed a "but" with his lips but he did not word it, his brow furrowing into lines.

"You will leave. You will all leave. I wish to spend time with my Poppaea. Rome needs an heir as everyone keeps telling me. It is my duty. Our duty."

Good luck with that one, thought Epaphroditus as he departed to the sounds of a giggling eunuch and his amorous emperor. Outside the door the secretary was addressed by a shocked-looking Sabinus, "Epaphroditus, you're not going to fulfil this order?"

"Of course."

"But Galba's letter may just be delayed—" he protested.

To Epaphroditus' mind this was no matter, but he replied evenly: "He has hesitated in proclaiming his loyalty."

"But he has been given no chance to defend himself. No trial. There is no evidence."

Epaphroditus blinked in surprise, surely he wasn't that naïve?

"Others have been offered these opportunities. It is the law. It would set a dangerous precedent," continued the prefect.

Epaphroditus blinked again. The "others" Sabinus noted had been given the appearance of a trial certainly, but the evidence had been faked. He knew this because he'd faked it, sitting down with the noble senators and carefully explaining their options. Happily for Epaphroditus they had been sensible men and had opened their veins promptly, ending the charade and negating the need for a formal trial.

"You can talk to the emperor. You are his advisor. You can rectify this mistake," Sabinus continued to plead.

Epaphroditus was amazed. Sabinus had been prefect, was it three years now? He must know how things worked. Mind you, mused the secretary, for two of those three years Nero had been on his tour of Greece. And prior to his appointment, Sabinus had been away serving with the legions. Epaphroditus clearly remembered his departure during Claudius' reign. Nymphidia had been inconsolable, though a great contingent of palace freedmen and officials had done their very best to be of solace to her.

It was quite probable that until late last year Sabinus had never even met Nero; an interesting thought.

To the prefect, Epaphroditus stated carefully, "It is my job to ensure that Caesar's will is fulfilled. It is Caesar's will that Galba dies."

"But ... but ... It's wrong!" cried Sabinus, genuinely confused.

"I will pretend that I did not hear that, Gaius Nymphidius Sabinus," stated Epaphroditus gravely. "To doubt Caesar's will is treason."

Here he left the prefect, his square jaw gaping open.

EIGHT

Alex was bored, toe-tappingly, impatiently, itchingly bored. Leant against a wall in the messengers hall he watched white tunics dash back and forth with scrolls and tablets, waiting to be noticed and assigned a delivery of his own.

So far that day he had been given two whole messages to deliver: one to Philo, who had been depressingly easy to find, and one to the laundry girls—a personal complaint from an administrator about the grey tinge to his tunic.

Since then he had been severely underemployed, watching with increasing envy as his colleagues dashed off to deliver messages outside the palace complex into the city itself, returning with tales of dubious Subura wine bars and supposed encounters with Amazonian women, who somehow or other found acne-ridden, gawky imperial messengers utterly irresistible.

Alex didn't believe a word of it, because he didn't want to. When was he going to be given a mission outside the palace? He was tired of delivering petty administrative scrolls to even pettier administrators. Where was the glory in that? They didn't even tip him! To this end he approached his boss.

"Lower Germania. Deliver to Fabius Valens. There are twenty stop points on the way. Remember your imperial pass to qualify for free hospitality."

The long-distance messenger gave a gruff reply before snatching his assignment.

"Phaon, is there anything for me?" asked Alex hopefully.

Phaon turned to his assistant, "Anything internal going?"

"Or external?"

Phaon shook his head, "You're not qualified, Alexander."

"I could do it. I spend every night studying maps of the city. I know every street, every district."

Phaon was not moved. "You have to work your way up the ranks like everyone else."

"How long will that take? I'm ready now, not in five years' time," pleaded Alex.

"There's two internal, sir," said the assistant handing over the scrolls. "One to the Department of Internal Auditors over that missing figure on last month's accounts."

Alex sighed.

"Or one to the Praetorian prefect."

Phaon handed Alex a tightly wound scroll. "There you go, Alexander, enliven your afternoon by taking this to Nymphidius Sabinus."

Alex gazed at the seal. "Really, sir?" This was a far better assignment.

"If you satisfy Sabinus, I might think about moving you up to externals."

Alex grinned and dashed off with his scroll at triple his usual pace.

"Sabinus is never satisfied," Phaon drolled to his assistant. "I've never known him yet receive a scroll without issuing a complaint about the messenger."

Nymphidius Sabinus' office lay in a quiet corridor within the guards' area of the palace. There was always one cohort of duty at the palace, some 500 men to harass visitors, terrorise the slaves, and sneer with particularly lecherous intent at any passing female. Such hard work was tiring and they were given several rest breaks on each shift. This was where they came to unwind.

It was a masculine space, reeking of leather and sweat. There were no pretty frescos here, no attractive mosaics, but rather a series of graphic graffiti scrawled up the walls. Every now and then, offended by the particularly anatomical female descriptions, Sabinus would order the walls to be painted. Yet the scribbling would always reappear even filthier than before. No doubt linked to the prefect's strict censures on fraternising with women.

The slave outside Sabinus' office was brisk in his rejection.

"The master is not to be disturbed."

"But I have a message for him." Alex waved the scroll.

"Not to be disturbed," reiterated the slave.

"I have to deliver it."

"You can give it to me."

And ruin his chance to shine before the great Nymphidius Sabinus? Not bloody likely! Alex folded his arms across his chest. "It is for his eyes only. It is very important," he hedged, adding in, "Urgent." Offering the gatekeeper determined brown eyes and a serious mouth.

An anxious look floated across the slave's features, "Wait here," he warned and disappeared inside.

Sabinus was resting his elbows on his desk, his large brow held in his hands. Epaphroditus had been correct in ascertaining that the prefect was having difficulty sleeping. Since that night when Icelus had visited him, Sabinus doubted he had enjoyed even one hour's doze.

He was fatally torn between two emotions: his absolute loyalty as a servant and his utter disgust with the man he served.

Those letters to Nero from his governors, praising that invert. No, praise was not the right word for it. Flattery it was. Sickening and toadying flattery of the most debased kind. It had turned Sabinus' stomach to listen to such honeyed lies. That provincial governors, men of breeding and standing were reduced to such dreadful verse showed how low the patrician class had sunk under this ruler.

And then when Nero had stood and screeched Galba's death sentence for no other reason than it suited him, Sabinus had felt something twist inside him. Outrage. That a governor of a Roman province, elected by the senate, appointed by law, should be murdered by that man for no reason at all!

He had to warn Galba. It was his civic duty. If all the good men died then who would run the empire? Lackeys, sexually degenerate friends of the emperor. The empire would fall under such dubious talents. All that Sabinus so passionately believed in would crumble before his eyes. The gods would desert Rome.

Galba would be warned, Sabinus decided firmly. All those sleepless nights of worry faded from his mind. Once Sabinus made a decision he stuck to it with utter resolution. He felt strong again, driven.

He would assist Galba in removing the tyrant. Had not the great Augustus been forced to arms to rescue Rome once before? It was unfortunate that such steps were necessary. But there it was. Nero must die. Rome must be reborn under an emperor who remembered the golden years, who had actual experience of government, who had years of wisdom to guide him.

But how to warn him of his intended assassination? Now Galba was out of imperial favour, the household would be under suspicion. Epaphroditus would be watching Icelus carefully. The slave would be state property soon enough when his master was gone.

The prefect began to pace his office. It was no good sending one of his guards, even in civilian wear you could not mistake the arrogant swagger of a Praetorian. One of his personal slaves? No. Sabinus did not trust his stock, he was suspicious. No, not suspicious. He knew that they spied on him and reported back to Epaphroditus.

No, his slaves were not to be entrusted with this crucial mission. He needed someone unconnected to both himself and Icelus. Where could he find such a man?

Sabinus' keen ears heard the slave shuffle in, "I SAID NO INTERRUPTIONS!"

"A messenger slave, master."

A message? From Galba? From Icelus?

"Send him in."

The disappointment to Sabinus on Alex's entrance was acute. It was just an imperial messenger, a poor specimen even for that low grade department. And the message? He recognised the seal as Tigellinus' own. Cracking it open, he unrolled it and read, with a "Ha."

"Is there a reply, sir?" asked Alex with enthused deference.

Sabinus rubbed a hand across his face, "No, there is no reply."

Bollocks, thought Alex, how was he going to shine if he were to be dismissed so soon?

"Are you sure, sir?"

Alex was supremely lucky that Sabinus was so distracted. Usually such impertinence would not have been tolerated. The prefect looked up and saw the slave properly. Seventeen, perhaps eighteen years old. In that gangly stage between boy and man. Long ginger-flecked legs with prominent knee caps. Hands that were too large for his spindly arms and a bushy red-haired head with freckled cheeks balanced above the whole rickety construction. He would grow into his extremities eventually but for now the look was distinctly awkward.

It was no wonder he'd been classed as a messenger. He didn't even look like imperial stock. Most of the slaves were of Eastern or Greek heritage, all black hair and smooth brown limbs. The boy was not unattractive but with that pale skin and that bright hair, he did not fit naturally into the accepted norms. And it was here that an idea struck the prefect.

Sitting forward on his chair, he fixed his gaze onto the boy and said, "I have an important message for you to deliver. This is a task that requires discretion."

A thrill tingled up Alex's spine.

"You must not reveal anything that I tell you now or I will know and I will take the necessary action. Do you understand?"

"Yes, sir."

"I have my spies. One word." Sabinus snapped his fingers.

"You can trust me, sir."

"I hope so, slave."

Sabinus reached behind him, producing a sealed scroll which he rolled in his palm as if undecided about handing it over. He pressed his thumb over the wax seal and a decision seemed to have been made for he handed it to Alex.

"You will deliver this to a man named Icelus. I have the directions here. You will memorise them and then I shall destroy them."

He handed Alex a scrap of parchment. The messenger scanned the contents and felt a bubble of panic. They seemed very complicated, lots of lefts and rights and looking out for particular cook shops as markers. Sabinus was waiting, tapping a foot on the floor, signalling his impatience.

Keen to seem efficient, Alex took in what he felt were the most important details: two theatres, a bridge beyond the Tiber Island, and a house, his destination, which had a large door carved with a depiction of the entwining trunks of two elephants.

He nodded his assent and Sabinus took back the parchment, holding it over a lamp until it burnt to cinders.

"You will hand this scroll to him alone and await an answer. It will be conveyed to you verbally and you will deliver it to me in person at the Praetorian camp."

Alex gave curt nods to each point, which he hoped made a favourable impression on the prefect.

"Discretion as mentioned is necessary."

Alex nodded eagerly, his brown eyes sparkling.

"You will need a disguise. A palace uniform would be a talking point in this neighbourhood," explained Sabinus. "You have another tunic beside your uniform?"

"Yes, sir," barked Alex thinking of the sludge-coloured tunic he slept in during the cold winter months.

"Excellent," smiled Sabinus. "I shall expect to see you at the Praetorian camp. Failure is not an option."

Alex was near vibrating with excitement. "I shall not let you down, sir."

"Good lad. You are dismissed."

Alex clipped his heels together and departed in a flash of white.

Sabinus sat back in his chair and smiled. If Epaphroditus had his spies placed, all they would have to report was a young boy making a delivery, perhaps the butcher's lad or the cobbler's apprentice. Most likely Alex would pass by without them considering it worth noting his arrival.

NINE

"I need an assassin," said Epaphroditus. "A good one."

Philo took out his note tablet. "Locusta?" he suggested.

"The poisoner? Not really suitable for this assignment. The emperor wishes the victim to be stabbed through the heart."

Philo chewed the inside of his cheek, "What if he survives?"

Epaphroditus stretched backwards in his chair, linking his hands behind his head. "Yes, I know. It has not proved a particularly accurate type of murder in the past. Perhaps we could combine it with a decapitation."

Philo scribbled down the instruction and then looked up, "Do you want the head sent back for proof, sir?"

Epaphroditus wrinkled his nose, "No thank you. By the time it comes back from Spain, I doubt it will be in a good enough state to be evidential. Do we have anyone who speaks Greek? The emperor is particularly keen on a recital prior to the deed being done."

"I don't know, sir," admitted Philo, furrowing his brow. "I could check."

"Please do."

Teretia was giddy with excitement when she noticed it.

"Mother, Philo has forgotten his lunch," she announced holding up an apple. Philo usually picked up his lunch on his way out in the morning, stashing it in his satchel.

"Oh dear," said her mother, who shared Teretia's concern for their lodger's constitution.

Her daughter tried to keep the excitement out of her voice as she said, "I think I should take it to him at the palace because otherwise poor Philo will have nothing to eat for his lunch! And how will he work with an empty tummy?"

"I think that is a very good idea, my dear, very considerate. You are quite right that we can't have poor Philo hungry when we can take his lunch to him. I can spare you from your chores. I'll get your father to draw the water from the fountain."

"Are you sure, mother?"

"Yes, my dear. Now why don't we go find a nice frock for you? They won't let you in the palace with your workaday dress on."

Teretia looked down at her drab brown woollen gown. She'd always imagined Philo working in the palace surrounded by the very highest ladies in society draped in silk gowns, with their hair coiffured and dripping priceless gems. They would wear peach scent and walk as if gliding on air. This was not all her imaginings, for Teretia had seen such creatures entering the Temple of Vesta and at public festivities. Not that she'd ever got so close to one, not like Philo probably did on a daily basis.

Picking up on her thoughts, Pompeia patted her on the arm reassuringly, "You're as good as any of them up at the palace. Better. You're a real beauty, a natural beauty. You don't need all that make-up and fashion to shine."

Teretia gave a tight smile, still a little unsure of herself.

"Now then my dear, let's go put on your best dress."

Teretia's best frock was a light green gown gathered below the bust and held together by two golden clasps in the shape of clam shells. For her trip to the Palatine she'd combined this with a darker green shawl for warmth, and a matching veil attached to the back of her blonde hair. Her father escorted her as far as the forum, to the bottom of the Palatine Hill. Hugging her tight, he told her, "You're a stunner, my girl, and don't you let anyone tell you different. You look lovely."

Teretia had dutifully blushed and felt her heart tighten with love for her wonderful, caring parents, tottering up the ramp that led to the great palace doors in nervous anticipation. Nervous because she had never been inside a palace before and nervously excited about seeing Philo; for she was totally, utterly, and completely in love with the scribe.

Teretia had never met anyone like Philo before. He was kind and polite. Not like the local Viminal boys who were rough and dirty. They shouted comments at her when she walked to the bakery that made her blush and scuttle along quicker, their laughter following her.

Philo had never done anything like that. She felt sure he didn't even know any of those horrid words they called at her. He was cultured, literate, and handsome. She mooned over his small delicate hands as he ate with her and her family in their cluttered kitchen. She adored the shy smile he often gave when they passed in the corridor, pressing himself against the wall to ensure that she could pass him unimpeded.

Beneath Philo's meek exterior, Teretia felt sure there lurked a passionate soul just waiting to declare itself in some perfect moment that would sweep her away.

Teretia was not alone in her romantic imagining. Her parents had similar thoughts regarding Philo. Sitting weaving quietly of a night, Pompeia would turn to her husband and witter about "the nice man from the palace".

Though Teretius would switch off from the more general inanities of their lodger's nice manners and clean habits, he was in total agreement with his wife on one factor. Philo would make the perfect husband for their daughter.

Teretia was a much-adored only child born late to her parents after the loss of seven earlier offspring. That she alone had survived made her special in both her parents' eyes and they believed that she was made for far more than what their life could offer.

Saving their coins, they sent her to a tutor who'd taught her to read and write. An unnecessary extravagance, the neighbours had said, who do they think they are? But then Philo had come to lodge with them and they knew their investment had paid off.

That Teretia evidently admired him was a bonus, but they would have pushed the match even if she had not. At fifteen Teretia was ripe for marriage. Some might say a little too ripe. For in the last year she had developed a set of breasts that made grown men want to bury their faces in them and never leave their comfort. Whenever she passed the local youth they were apt to hold aloft melons or cup their hands in mimicry of handling those luscious orbs. The neighbours with a sad shake of their heads would comment that if they didn't marry that girl off soon there was bound to be trouble.

Her parents were not unaware of this but had hoped for a son-in-law with prospects, an unlikely figure in their neighbourhood. But then came Philo; the nice man from the palace.

They decided that their only daughter should be married by next spring, that the couple would naturally continue to reside in the household and be a support to them in their increasing age, talking gleefully about grandchildren. Mostly they speculated on how green the neighbours would be.

At the top of the ramp stood two Praetorian guards. To Teretia they looked unfeasibly tall, with purple plumed helmets and leather breastplates sporting the scorpion emblem that was the Praetorian motif. They glared down at her with spears crossed over the entrance.

"Who is it you wanna see?" asked the big, beefy one.

"Philo," she said quietly, wilting under their gaze.

"Philo?" mused the thinner one. "What does he do?"

"He's …" she began, before realising she didn't actually know what position Philo held. She knew it involved writing since she had sneaked a peek into his satchel and it was full of tablets and scrolls. But he had never actually spoken about his job. Mother had elicited some answers from him, she recalled.

"He's a secretary," she settled on finally.

"A secretary," the beefy one mocked in a high pitched voice. "Philo the secretary. They're all bloody secretaries in there!" Teretia felt close to tears. What if they wouldn't let her in? She had her best dress on. She'd walked all this way especially. Her parents would be so disappointed in her.

Blue eyes welled up as she gave a small sob and explained, "I have his lunch."

The two guards, both hardened veterans of the legions, looked down at Teretia and felt, possibly for the first time in their lives, utterly ashamed.

"Missy, missy," implored Proculus, the bigger of the two. "We were just messing with you. We didn't mean nothing by it."

"We have to be careful, miss," said the other, Lucullus. "For the safety of the emperor and like. You understand, don't ya?"

Teretia gave a small nod, her bosom pleasantly heaving with suppressed emotion.

"Missy, we can sort this out. There's no need to upset yourself."

"No need," agreed Lucullus.

She attempted to compose herself but the thought of the fresh bread in her basket going stale and the dates going mushy and poor Philo sitting hungry at his desk, reduced her to a fresh bout of sobbing.

A passer-by witnessing this scene spat on the ground.

"You brutes," he said with all the contempt of the world hurled into those two words.

"We haven't touched her," Proculus declared righteously.

67

"Yeah, right. Why is she crying then?"

Proculus pointed his spear straight at the man, who feeling the tip of it press against his throat took one large step backwards.

"I think you'd better move along now, sir," he suggested with menace. "And for the record, the little lady is crying because she's brought her lunch up for her man and she can't remember what department he works in."

"And," butted in Lucullus, "we are assisting her in this matter."

"You alright, love?" the man asked Teretia.

She gave a silent nod, retaining the tragic appearance of a maiden in distress. It was a look she wore well. Hence the interference of the passer-by who'd spent his life staying out of trouble but was perfectly willing to take on two mean-looking Praetorians unarmed in order to protect her honour. It was the sort of affect she inspired in strangers. Once he was assured of her safety, the passer-by passed on by.

"Now then, missy. You say your fellow's called Philo and he works as a secretary. Now could you narrow that down a little? What does he look like?" asked Proculus.

This was a theme that Teretia could warm to. Dabbing her eyes with a cloth she had been inexplicably storing in her bosom, she began, "He has brown eyes with green rims around the iris. Delicate hands with ever so neat nails, thin narrow eyebrows but soft long eyelashes. Oh, and thick dark hair that flicks upwards on his neck."

She demonstrated the curl of Philo's hair with her finger. "Which I know he doesn't like because I often find him trying to dampen it down with water. But I think it becomes him much," she concluded dreamily.

"OK ...?" murmured Lucullus.

Eager to please, Teretia added: "He was wearing his blue tunic today, it's his favourite."

"Height?"

"A little taller than me."

"Right. So we're looking for a short, dark haired, brown eyed, delicate-handed man in a blue tunic."

"Who's a secretary. Probably."

Teretia nodded, "I have his lunch." She held up the basket.

"Hang on a mo," said Lucullus. "Isn't there a Philo who works for Epaphroditus?"

"I reckon you might be right there."

Lucullus struggled to put a face to the name. "Little Indian fellow, always standing behind his boss scribbling on them tablets."

"That's him!"

"You might have mentioned the Indian bit up front, missy. Would have made it easier to identify 'im."

"Sorry, sir, I didn't think," apologised Teretia, dabbing at her eyes to inspire a heave or two within Proculus' and Lucullus' own bosoms.

It was Proculus, much to Lucullus' frustration, who won the coin toss and thus the opportunity to escort Teretia to her destination. It was entirely a pleasure for the guard, watching as Teretia's eyes gaped at her surroundings, her pink mouth falling open as she gazed upwards to the painted ceiling.

"It's beautiful."

"This is nothing, you should see the new palace. Now that is magnificent. There's this round hall and the ceiling moves to show different pictures and that."

Teretia looked astonished. Proculus smiled. "Right pretty it is. Perhaps your Philo could take you to see it. 'Course the building work's still going on, endless it is. But there's plenty of nice bits. Nice grounds too. And a lake."

"A lake?"

Proculus grinned. "With boats bobbing on it. And fish in it. Bright, colourful things they are. The empress likes to feed them in the morning."

Teretia, gazing at a particularly fine fresco, almost walked into a pillar. Proculus lightly took her by the elbow and guided her out of the way.

"Do you get used to it? All of this?" She waved her arm in the direction of the gold-studded ceiling that arched many feet above their heads.

"Well, missy, I can't say the Praetorian camp is as luxurious as all this."

"Sorry, I'm being silly."

"Not at all, missy, not at all."

The guard couldn't help smiling, she was such a sweet girl. He had never noticed the pictures of the god Apollo and his sister Artemis that were painted at the top of the walls until she had gasped, pointed upwards, and demanded to know how they made it so colourful. Proculus didn't rightly know but he felt he had made a decent stab at it. Teretia seemed to appreciate it and listened open-mouthed to his explanation.

A nice girl, the sort of girl that was sorely missing from the palace, thought Proculus. All those scheming slave girls who'd open their legs if they thought they would gain from it. And the women the emperor surrounded himself with. High born they were supposed to be, but they lacked the sheer goodness that this young Roman girl radiated. Sabinus had it right there.

Teretia to Proculus was a fine example of Roman womanhood. She was the kind of girl who would gently rebuke you for walking mud in the house but clean your boots for you anyway and, in Proculus' opinion, entirely wasted on that skinny little Indian.

"Now then, missy, this is your stop," he told her. "I'd better go in first to announce you properly."

Teretia gave a small giggle. Proculus just managed to stop himself from clasping her in an embrace and declaring undying love for her.

Striding into the antechamber, he found Epaphroditus, moving scrolls around on Philo's desk, apparently searching for something.

He raised an eyebrow, "Guard?"

"I was looking for Philo, sir."

"Any particular reason?"

"The girl, sir," said Proculus who, faced with authority, had resorted to his usual basic soldier responses.

"Girl?"

A blonde head poked cautiously round the doorway.

"That girl, sir."

Teretia shuffled nervously into the doorway, clutching her wicker basket in both hands. Epaphroditus turned on the charm, cooing, "Hello there. Come on in, don't be shy."

Then, turning to the guard, "You are dismissed."

Proculus broke protocol before retreating. "Nice to meet you, missy."

"You too. You've been so kind."

Guardsman Proculus took that delightful smile to bed with him later that night.

"So," began Epaphroditus, gesturing for her to sit and even pulling the chair out for her, "You're here to see Philo?"

It came out as a question.

Teretia sat meekly on what was Philo's chair, her basket on her lap. The man had awed her into silence by his effortless dismissal of that nice Praetorian. He was obviously someone very important.

"He shouldn't be long," smoothed Epaphroditus. "He is running a little errand for me before lunch."

"I have it here," Teretia burst out. "His lunch." She held up her basket slightly and then placed it back down, embarrassed.

Well, this is intriguing, thought the secretary, positioning himself on the corner of Philo's desk, all the better to gaze down on those fantastic assets. For Epaphroditus, the mystery of Philo's incessant lateness was solved. If he had this beautiful girl in his bed, he wouldn't want to get up either.

"I am sure Philo will be most appreciative."

"Really?"

She looked so eager, so young, so utterly delicious that Epaphroditus had to fight off a similar urge to Guardsman Proculus a moment before.

"Most definitely. Philo always works best after lunch."

"Really?"

"Much more productive," he assured her. "I have often noted it. Now I know why."

Teretia's shoulders relaxed. "I make it for him every day," she volunteered. "Bread and dates. Sometimes cheese. Sometimes meat if we have any. But not beef. Philo doesn't eat beef."

Excessively proud of knowing this fact, if not the reason why, she lifted up the basket cloth. Epaphroditus leaned over to fully appreciate her wares. It looked much like the morsels that Sabinus was forcing on his troops these days. Yet he made appreciative noises and told her, "I think Philo is going to have a very productive afternoon."

She shone under his attention and began to babble about her mother's special bread-making system or something of that sort. Epaphroditus stopped listening fairly early on, keeping an interested look on his face as he marvelled at this exquisite creature that sat before him.

He was quite prepared to wipe clean his whole afternoon schedule to show this beauty some real attention, when he mentally slapped himself, remembering that this was Philo's girl. Steeling himself, he resolved to show platonic concern and vowed to clear his meeting with Miltiades regarding the shocking increase in stationery expenditure. He would use the free time to pay his latest young mistress, Artemina, a visit.

Philo's first view was of his boss perched on the edge of his desk nodding indulgently at an unseen guest. For a moment he assumed it was an assignation and was about to make a discreet exit when someone cried, "Philo!" And he saw Teretia.

He blinked, his eyes moving from his boss to Teretia and back again. Epaphroditus, noting his confusion and her sudden reversal to mute shyness felt he had to intervene. "Sorry, I didn't catch your name?"

"Teretia."

"Teretia," he mused. "What a beautiful name. Teretia has kindly brought your lunch."

"You forgot it," she said placing the basket on the desk.

Philo winced as she moved his precious filing in order to create space for the food.

"Oh," he said "That's …"

"Thoughtful," supplied Epaphroditus.

"Yes, thoughtful of you."

Teretia beamed. Philo pulled at the neck of his tunic. Epaphroditus, assuming it was his presence that was creating the uncomfortable atmosphere clapped his hands together, making both Teretia and Philo jump.

"Well, I have to go do some work." He thumbed in the direction of his office. "It was lovely to meet you, Teretia. I do hope I shall have the pleasure again."

She smiled at him and he was galled to note that it lacked the naked adoration with which she had greeted Philo. An Artemina pick-me-up was definitely in order.

Left alone, Philo had absolutely no idea what to say to Teretia. He muttered another thank you.

"It was no trouble," she said. "I didn't," she paused, looking down shyly, "I didn't want you to go hungry. It would have upset me."

"I wouldn't have gone hungry. There is always plenty of food rattling around. Titbits left over from meetings and banquets. They usually bring in a platter or two."

Epaphroditus, had he been listening, would have groaned.

TEN

Alex walked swiftly down the corridors, his head held high in a manner not at all slave-like. The creature who wore this sludge-coloured garment was Julius, a free-born Roman, wandering the streets minding his own business. This would be the story he would stick to should he happen to be arrested or interrogated or even tortured. Though given he was working for Sabinus, presumably this wasn't such a danger.

Julius was a builder, no, a carpenter, and he was in the Janiculum area because he had news of a good wood consignment, or something like that. Alex could improvise if necessary and he was definitely the type to have an elder brother who had run away to join an acting troop, and a sister who had married badly, decided Alex.

Caught up in Julius' fully imagined life, Alex failed to notice Artemina, or Mina to her friends, which Alex certainly was, until she grabbed hold of his arm.

"What's with the garb?" she asked, looking him up and down and fingering the arm of his tunic. "You look like a tradesman." Which gave Alex a secret rush of pleasure, good old Julius.

"I am on an important mission."

Mina was scathing, "Bollocks you are. What's really going on?"

Alex was hurt. Why shouldn't he be on an important mission? He pursed his lips shut.

"Oh go on, Alex, tell me. I've had such a lousy morning. I had to stand for hours with a towel draped across my arm, while the empress sat up to her neck in water just staring at the petals floating past her. Look, look at this." She held out her arms straight, they trembled ever so slightly. "I can't stop it."

Alex forbore from pointing out that surely as the empress' keeper of the towel, this was a minor and unavoidable industrial injury.

"Oh tell me, please, please, please." She stopped short of jumping up and down, as she had done when they were children and she was bound on Alex performing some favour for her. Today with her hair neatly tied back, her face naked of adornment, and in her simple white palace gown, Alex was strongly reminded of the little girl she had once been.

"I am delivering an important message."

She narrowed her eyes. "Why aren't you wearing your messengers' uniform?"

"Because not everybody wishes to be seen receiving a message from the palace." Which he felt was a pretty good answer.

Mina started to say, "But why wouldn't …," and then stopped, her eyes wide. "Bona Dea! Is it a call to suicide? The emperor demands you open your veins, that sort of thing? Is it?"

Alex was humbled. He'd been so excited by Sabinus choosing him for the mission that it hadn't occurred to him to wonder what the message contained. To cover up his embarrassment, he said piously, "I cannot divulge that information."

Which Mina took as a yes. "Gods" she mouthed. "Who is it? Who has to kill themselves?"

"I cannot divulge that information."

Mina punched him hard on the arm.

"Oww, cut it out."

"Tell me," she whined, mimicking pinching fingers as a threat.

"Don't," warned Alex taking a step backwards. "Don't or I'll scream and an overseer will hear and come and whip you to shreds."

"You reckon?" she asked, taking a step forwards.

Alex, having been on the receiving end of Mina's technique before, held his arms protectively across his nipples. "I do. Maybe it'll be Straton," he rasped the overseer's name in imitation. Mina shuddered.

"Truce?" he offered.

Mina shrugged, "Can I come?"

"Come where?"

"With you on your mission. I can be your cover so no one suspects your dark purpose."

"No."

"Why not?"

"It's a top secret mission. I can't tell anyone about it."

"But I already know," pointed out Mina.

Alex considered. Mina could add to his disguise, she could be Julius' wife Cornelia. Sabinus might appreciate his extra lengths to ensure the success of his mission. And it would be good to spend time with Mina; it would be an adventure, like old times.

"You'll have to lose the uniform too."

Mina smiled a devastingly sparkling smile that crinkled her eyes and near-on lit up that small corridor.

"This is going to be such fun!"

Alex pulled his cloak tighter, stood outside a palace side entrance hopping from foot to foot to keep warm, waiting for Mina. It was supposed to be spring but it didn't feel very spring-like to Alex: there was a distinct winter chill. He wanted to get there and back to the Praetorian camp before the sun began to set, for Alex had a dread of the city after dark. He'd heard all kinds of tall tales from his fellow messengers involving sabre-armed gangs and supernatural beasts that liked nothing better than to violently thwart the work of young, innocent imperial slaves.

He was beginning to get annoyed when Mina floated out, and his irritation evaporated. She was dressed in a blue gown that was belted high under her breasts, a brown cloak fixed at her neck with a butterfly brooch, her brown hair cascading down her back in a wave.

Seeing Alex's quizzical look she informed him, "The gown is one of the empress' more simple garments. She never wears it, so she'll never miss it."

She linked onto his arm, "So husband Julius, do you know where we are headed?"

"Of course," smiled Alex.

It was some hours later that the utter falsehood of that statement became clear.

"I am going to ask that man over there for directions."

"No," cried Alex, gripping her wrist tight.

Mina swung round and thumped him in the stomach.

"Mina," he gasped "Nobody can know about the mission."

"Gods, Alex! We've been wandering around for miles."

"I know we're on the right road. We passed two theatres, the instructions said I was to pass two theatres."

Mina released a frustrated howl, "We haven't passed two theatres. We've passed the same theatre twice. We've walked round in a circle! You are so unobservant. How you ever made it to messenger, I'll never know."

Alex took a deep and calming breath. "It's to the left," he stated.

Rubbing her wrist, Mina looked daggers at him. "The empress likes to bathe before her evening meal. She'll be standing there sopping wet looking for her keeper of the towel who won't be there because," her voice began to rise, "I am traipsing the city streets, gaining blisters, and do you know how blisters could affect my work? I have to stand still for hours and, thanks to you, I shall be standing on a sole of red hot, bursting blisters. It'll be torture."

"Oh, torture will it? What would you know about torture?"

Mina sighed loudly. "Not that old tale! Gods alive, Alex, when will you let that one drop?"

"If you had ever been tortured, you would not use that word so lightly!"

Mina stood on her toes to avoid her new blisters and to gain a better height to roar in Alex's face, "You lost a flipping fingernail, big bloody deal!"

Alex shook his head. "Big bloody deal, she says. If you knew!"

"If I knew what? If I knew that they brought out the extractors and you fainted and on the way down to the floor caught your finger on a table splinter and ripped out your nail. If I knew that, Alex?"

Bane of the ginger haired, Alex could feel his face reddening and knew what a sight he must look. They were attracting quite a bit of attention now: it was a quiet suburban street, the theatre was not performing, and the only entertainment available was Mina and him.

He should back down, apologise, make up with Mina, get on with his mission and satisfy Nymphidius Sabinus. But with his much-repeated adventure tale revealed as a fraud, he felt sore and retaliated with, "You want to know how I got to become a messenger? I did the proper training and learnt my role. I didn't take the easy route."

"Sorry, is that a dig at me? What I am supposed to have done?"

"I don't know, you tell me. What did Epaphroditus make you do to secure the keeper of the towel? I hear all sorts of rumours ..."

Indeed he had. Mina's affair with Epaphroditus was the hot gossip of the moment. He stood defiant, arms crossed. Mina gave him a withering glare, the sort that Medusa used to turn men to stone.

"Jealous, are we?"

Which was just a little too close to the truth for Alex. "Why would I want to perform sex acts for a wrinkly old man to get a job that I loathe and moan about constantly?"

She looked as if she were to even the score, opening her mouth and then slamming it shut. Lowering herself onto the flats of her feet she shook her head sadly and walked away.

"Mina, where are you going?" he shouted at her back. She didn't reply.

Alex watched her walk down the street and take a right turn. The moment she was out of sight, his anger subsided. He couldn't allow her to walk through Rome alone, it wasn't safe for a woman. If anything should happen to Mina, she would surely blame him. Panicked he ran in her direction, pushing people out of the way. It was lucky he was speedy on his feet for there were many who objected to such treatment.

He took the right turn and saw a long crowded street, shops with their banners down either side attracting attention. He couldn't, however, see Mina. Standing on his toes, he tried to see above the sea of heads.

"Mina!"

He caught sight of her far ahead: she was talking to a large, bald-headed man. Even from this distance Alex could make out the glint of knives that hung from the man's belt. He nodded at whatever Mina had said to him and led her through a curtain into the rooms beyond.

Alex ran. Bursting in with his dagger held in front, he found the two of them poring over an outline on the floor. The man held a piece of chalk in his hand.

Mina looked up unsurprised at Alex's dramatic entrance. "Excellent news. Portus here knows where we can find the house with the two entwining elephant trunks!"

The steward instructed them to wait in the atrium. Mina seated on the edge of an ornamental pond, trailing her hand in the water. Alex sat beside her. "Sorry."

"For what?"

"For shouting at you, for suggesting …"

"For suggesting that I slept my way into my job?" she enquired.

Alex nodded, shamefaced.

"It's true, though. I did," she admitted unapologetically.

There was a silence that Alex felt Mina should be filling. "Are you going to apologise?"

Mina wiped her wet hand on her cloak, "I thought not. You thoroughly deserved being shouted at, making me traipse all over the place, refusing to ask for directions."

Alex gave a sheepish grin, shrugged his shoulders. "Sorry. Friends?"

She smiled. "Always."

They enjoyed a platonic hug that Alex held onto a moment longer than was necessary.

"Mina—" he began, but was interrupted by the steward, a neat servant in a household uniform of green.

"Follow me, messenger."

Mina remained seated, "You go. I'll stay here."

He kissed the top of her head. She reached back and clutched his hands. "I can contemplate apologising while you deliver your message."

Icelus read the scroll, his lips moving as he did. A thin bald man, the tunic he wore enveloped him, a narrow neck and small round head peeking out at the top. He reminded Alex of the tortoises the emperor kept in the gardens for the amusement of guests.

Eventually Icelus finished reading and rolled the scroll up. Moving to a nearby brazier he held it under the flame until it caught fire, placing the flaming remains on a silver tray to burn. He turned his attention to Alex, fixing him with nervous eyes. "Were you followed?" he asked, a slight catch in his voice.

Alex thought it unlikely. Any pursuer would have got bored and given up hours before on their meandering march. He'd managed to convince himself that their getting lost was a deliberate tactic to avoid detection.

"No. I am to return with a verbal message to Nymphidius Sabinus."

Icelus' head darted back and forth, "Ssh," he warned Alex, walking to the door and glancing outwards. "Quiet down, slave. Let me think."

Given the time it had taken him to read, Alex braced himself for a long stand. Icelus rubbed a bony hand across his bald cranium, wiping away a sheen of sweat from his forehead, fidgeting with the cuff of his dark tunic. Not green, Alex noted, not a household slave then. Icelus was not a Roman name he had heard, a freedman then.

Icelus cleared his throat, "Tell him," he paused, shaking his head. "Tell him." Another pause. "Tell him that I am thankful for his warn—" he broke off. "Tell him I am thankful for this, for this, erm, message. Tell him that I will be in touch. That things will, they will move. They will definitely move."

Alex nodded, confused by the vagaries of this reply. Icelus seemed happy though. He smiled lopsidedly revealing a singular chipped tooth. Alex bit back a laugh: really he was just like a tortoise.

ELEVEN

Tigellinus lay nude on a couch, a naked slave girl kneeling on the floor passing grapes to him one by one, sparing him valuable effort. Her name, should it be important, was Erotica. Though it was difficult to say whether she had grown into the name or the name itself had defined her. She was, in short, a cracker. Tigellinus had purloined her from the emperor's harem for the afternoon, and what a pleasant afternoon it had been.

He was winding down now, stretching his toes, and feeling just nicely sleepy, which might have been to do with the discarded and very empty wineskin that lay under his arm, or might have been due to Erotica's efforts. Whichever it was, he felt pleasantly tipsy and ready for a bit of a nap.

"Enough of the grapes, come snuggle with me."

Spooning comfortably, Tigellinus couldn't resist nibbling her ear. Erotica, who was well trained, gave a girlish giggle and snuggled in closer.

A nice scene, I am sure you will agree, and it would probably have stayed that way had not Nymphidius Sabinus been announced.

"Arse," muttered Tigellinus, not bothering to move.

"Would you like me to delay him?" queried the announcer, Lysander.

Tigellinus' thought processes were not at their best. "Oh, just send him in. Let's get it over with."

Lysander raised his eyebrows ever so slightly and there may have been a twitch to his mouth, but otherwise he played it straight.

"As you wish, sir," and darted out to inform Sabinus that Tigellinus would see him now.

He could have warned Sabinus as to his colleague's state but, heck, that would have ruined all the fun.

Nymphidius Sabinus had a very fixed expression that rarely registered emotion, so it was difficult to tell if he were displeased or not. He certainly gave the girl a harsh look. But he gave that look to everybody from the emperor down to the boys who cleaned the privvies.

"Tigellinus," he stated. "Lose the girl."

"Really?" Tigellinus feigned horror.

He ran a hand slowly down Erotica's waist, across her hips and then snaked round her thighs, dipping in between her legs. Erotica gave a small gasp as Tigellinus' fingers explored.

Sabinus reached forward, grabbed her by the wrist and dragged her off the couch. She fell badly, hitting her hip on the marble floor.

"Out!" Sabinus hissed at her and near threw her across the room. Erotica did not stop to count her bruises, but scampered off as quickly as she could.

Tigellinus watched the scene impassively. "You ruin my fun."

Sabinus turned quickly and Tigellinus saw a look of sheer venom cross his face, before it settled into its usual disdainful expression. He snapped his fingers at a slave, "Chair."

A bronze stool was carried over. Tigellinus stayed lounged across his couch and gave his crotch a quick scratch. He took another swig from the wineskin though it was empty, simply because he couldn't resist an opportunity to wind his colleague up further.

Sabinus sat on the stool, his hands palm down on his knees. Tigellinus regarded him through heavy eyes. He made an effort to prop himself up on an elbow, but it was a struggle.

"Juno's arse, Sabinus, what is it?" he slurred. "Can't a man enjoy a fresh girl without you storming in and spoiling it?"

"You are officially on duty. My shift does not start for another hour."

"Which begs the question, why are you in full uniform?"

"And why are you not?" retorted Sabinus.

Tigellinus smiled; a drunkard's smile, Sabinus noted. "Nothing gets past you does it, Sabinus?"

"I am here for the duty log."

Tigellinus shifted on the couch, reached down underneath his buttocks and produced the squished scroll. He gave it to Sabinus who handled it with the kind of delicacy Tigellinus had afforded Erotica earlier. He laid the battered scroll onto his lap like a precious artefact, noting the odd stains on its exterior.

"Might want to start up a new one," suggested Tigellinus. "It might have got … erm … caught up in the action."

The left side of Sabinus' face jolted upwards. "You're a disgrace. A disgrace, to your unit, to the Guard, to yourself."

The prefect took the rebuke coolly and gave a guffaw of such volume that a glass jug on a nearby table jiggled to the edge. Perhaps it was Sabinus' stern expression, perhaps it was the last of the wine kicking in, or perhaps it was just from the sheer joy of life but once he started Tigellinus found he could not stop. He laughed long and hard until his sides ached from the exertion.

When he finally ceased, Sabinus was absolutely furious; picking up the duty log and telling the merry Tigellinus through gritted teeth, "Laugh all you can now, for the time of your kind is nearing its end."

Seeing this for the threat it was, Tigellinus got off the couch and regarded Sabinus eyeball to eyeball; Sabinus forcing himself not to recoil at having his colleague's naked form so close to him. They stared at each other, only a few inches apart, neither one wanting to be the first to blink.

They were of the same height but that was the only similarity between them. Tigellinus' body was flabby, particularly around his stomach, where it had formed a paunch of a size that nearly hid his shrivelled and damp genitals below. Sabinus, underneath his leather breastplate and skirts was as lean and hard as an Olympian, the result of a punishing exercise routine.

"My kind?" Tigellinus queried, his voice still light. "Our kind, Sabinus."

"I am nothing like you. I will never be like you."

"You think you're better than me then?"

Sabinus didn't hesitate. "Without a doubt."

Another guffaw, but this one was aimed straight at Sabinus who couldn't help but take a step back. "The son of a palace whore thinks he's better than me."

"What did you say?"

Sabinus' tone should have alerted Tigellinus that he was blundering into extremely dangerous territory. But Tigellinus was afternoon drunk. He was the Praetorian prefect. A friend to Nero. He thought himself invincible.

"You heard. You amuse me, Sabinus, with your attitude, your superior sense of being, your sneer. You sneer at me for *my* supposed humble beginnings. At least I can name my father. There must be a cast of thousands for yours; do you ever think to ask these people you work with? Phaon, Miltiades, Halotus, Rufus, Jason, Thebes, Apollodorus, Narcissus, Pallas, Epaphroditus ... they've all had her."

It was meant to wound and wound it did. Sabinus blinked. Tigellinus tottered unsteadily backwards, arms outstretched, declaring his victory. Sabinus stomped out, hearing Tigellinus' laugh way down the corridor, storming all the way to the guards' room, addressing nobody, not even his own staff when they saluted him.

It was only when he had slammed the door to his office that he allowed himself to breathe, taking deep intakes as he leaned against the back of the door. Sliding down to the floor, hugging his knees, closing his eyes tight, trying to stop the images that flashed across his mind.

He remembered being six or perhaps seven. He couldn't sleep; a nightmare of some sort had woken him. Trailing a blanket behind him, he had wandered into his mother's room. His first distinct impression had been of a sea monster, a writhing mass of tentacles on his mother's bed. He had screamed, naturally, and the creature had yelled "Bona Dea! Get that kid to shut up."

The writhing tentacles had untangled themselves to reveal his mother lying on her back, her legs spread impossibly wide. Between them was a large hairy man whom Sabinus knew to be Pallas, an important person at the palace.

He held his blanket to his mouth. His mother gazing backwards at him said, "Ssh now, darling. Go back to bed."

Pallas, glad of the quiet, regained his stride and continued his hard thrusts, his huge hairy stomach wobbling and rippling as he did.

If there were ever an image guaranteed to put anyone off sex, then it was that particular vision. Whether it was that occasion, or one of the many others where he witnessed his beloved mother in congress, that led Sabinus to be the strange, celibate man he was, who could tell. One thing was clear, he had deliberately moderated his life to be the absolute antithesis of the playful, fun creature that was Nymphidia Sabina.

The present-day Sabinus rubbed his eyes and struggled to regain his composure. He fell back on an old trick, pulling the emotion inwards and converting it into anger. Anger he could deal with. He felt it thickening his veins, his heart beating faster. Tigellinus, what was he after all? A flabby, dissipated fool. He had to be a fool not to see the way the world was turning. He was a symptom of the moral decay and baseness evident everywhere in Nero's Rome.

Well, not for long: a great wave was coming and it would wash clean the streets. It would break down the doors of the palace taking everything and everyone with it. And those that were left would be those that deserved to be. The good, the decent, the disciplined, and there to guide them through this exciting new era would be Nymphidius Sabinus.

TWELVE

After the successful completion of his assignment, Alex had expected Sabinus to seek him out personally for further missions. He saw himself as a trusted aid to the prefect, keeping important confidences and running ever more dangerous errands for him. None of which had happened. Meeting him in the corridor one day, the prefect had passed him without recognition, leaving Alex crushed with disappointment.

It didn't help that Sporus had stopped by and spent an entire evening name dropping and making out how glamorous and exciting his life was. Alex listened in maudlin silence. Eventually even a creature as self-absorbed as Sporus noticed his melancholy.

"What is up with you tonight?"

Concentrating on picking a scab on his knee, Alex shrugged and said, "Nothing, I'm fine."

"You don't seem fine. Where's Mina tonight?"

"With her lover."

Sporus leaned forward. Alex saw the concern in his face, "Is that it? Is that what's bothering you? Mina and Epaphroditus? It doesn't mean anything."

"Easy for you to say," Alex grumbled, peeling off the edge of his scab.

"It's true. You know as well as I do how much she hated working in the nursery. She wanted a way out. He got her that keeper of the-whatever-it-is job. It's a straight-off bargain."

"And he gets?"

Sporus gave a beatific smile. "Oh, I think we all know what he gets out of it," and then seeing Alex's face fall, added quickly, "Come on, she would have thrown herself at anyone if they could have got her away from those thorns and flowers."

"You excel at this cheering up lark, don't you?"

"Anyone with clout, I mean. She was aiming for Philo, it was sheer luck that she bumped into Epaphroditus."

"Still not helping," insisted Alex.

"I am trying to make you see sense. You haven't a hope in Hades of getting it on with Mina. I've told you that for years. It appears that it needs reiteration. She's too good for you!"

"Because I am just a lowly messenger!"

"No, because she is beautiful and charming and you're lanky and ginger."

Alex swung for him and got him smack on the mouth. The noise of a eunuch in pain much resembles the sound of a swine at the moment its throat is slit. The squeal that emitted from Sporus was high in velocity as well as pitch and guaranteed to prick the ears of any local overseer.

"Shut up will you," pleaded Alex attempting to grab him.

Sporus, one hand clutched against his injured mouth and a look of sheer murder in his eyes, was having none of it and nimbly evaded all attempts at capture.

"Shut up!"

Alex, leaping over the bed rather inexpertly, caught his foot, crashing into the earthenware piss pot, emptying its contents all over the floor.

Sporus stared down at his urine-spattered Persian slippers, "You oaf," he screeched, revealing a thickened upper lip.

"I suppose this is how you men treat your friends. I see it all the time with the Praetorians. Vicious slaps on the back in the name of camaraderie, sharp blows to the arm in apparent levity, all trying to out-macho each other. I find it most interesting that you, whom I thought I knew, have fallen into this use of sham masculinity."

Sporus was endlessly fascinated by men's ways. He had viewed Alex's own descent into puberty with interest, watching intrigued as his room-mate shot up in height, grew odd spouts of hair, and was afflicted with ever-stranger bodily responses. It was all a bit unnatural, in Sporus' eunuchised (a phrase he much preferred to the vulgar castrated) opinion.

Violence, he had observed, was all part of being an un-eunachised male. Sporus did not possess a violent bone in his body, for one very good reason that had nothing to do with his lack of testicles: he was a terrible coward.

Alex, seeing his friend's engorged lip winced. "Does that hurt?" he asked.

Sporus touched the wound with his finger. "Hugely, it pulsates with ache. Why'd you hit me? Most unnecessary."

"Dunno."

"You are so tetchy these days. You never used to be like this. You'd be much happier if you would just accept the Mina situation and find yourself some sweet little pastry cook."

A deflated Alex flopped onto the bed. "Sorry," he said from his prone position.

Sporus, skipping over the pool of piss, lay beside him. "I could set you up. I happen to know a sweet little pastry chef."

"Not interested."

"I think it would help."

"Help with what?"

"The extreme sexual frustration you are experiencing."

"I am not sexually frustrated."

"Alex, old friend, I am a highly trained catamite. Trust me, you are sexually frustrated. You reek of it. It's why you're so tetchy. It's why you hit me just now."

"I said sorry about that."

"I have graciously forgiven you. My lip though is throbbing, much like your frustrated manhood, but I shall survive. The pastry chef though, she is lovely."

Sporus' matchmaking attempts were frequent. If it wasn't a wonderful weaver or a terrific towel folder, it was a super seamstress or a fabulous flower arranger. Low grade slaves, within what Sporus considered Alex's grasp. Although Alex may have taken up his friend's romantic suggestions every now and then, they had never led to anything truly special, for the simple reason that they were not Mina.

Sporus paused and turned his head. There was someone approaching. He turned back, facing Alex with wide, frightened eyes, "Overseer?"

"Could be," agreed Alex, shooting to his feet.

Mina burst in to find Sporus apparently making the bed and Alex poised with broom in hand. Clinging to the door frame she announced breathlessly, "I have top gossip," before arranging herself on the bed.

"This is so good that you two should kneel at my feet to be worthy of it."

She pointed an elegant toe to the floor, sniffing and wrinkling her nose. "Is that piss?"

"Gossip first, piss later," said Sporus, rubbing his hands together.

"OK, OK. Settle yourselves away from the piss, which I shall be wanting an explanation for later, you grubby boy and non-boy."

Mina sat at the head of the bed, cross-legged and eager-eyed.

"Philo", she breathed, pausing for effect, "has a girlfriend."

"He does not," scorned Sporus.

"Does too," insisted Mina. "And if you think about it, it explains everything. Like that time he turned me down."

"He didn't turn you down, he fled in terror."

"Turned me down, fled in terror, whatever. I think we can all agree that it was a rejection."

"Agreed."

"Agreed."

"Well, clearly it was because he had this girl tucked away and he didn't want the temptation to be unfaithful to her. Hence the fact that when I made that subtle pass at him—"

"For subtle pass read pinned him against the wall and thrust your breasts at him."

Mina gave Sporus a dry look. "Hence", she continued with emphasis, "the fact that he ran away. They are raucously in love apparently."

Sporus shook his head. "No, I'm not buying it. Are you buying it Alex?"

"I don't think I am. Philo is so ... well he's ... sort of ... he's a bit ... Someone help me out here! What am I trying to say?"

"The word you are looking for Alexander is neutered," supplied Sporus.

Alex gave a nod, it pretty much summed up his thoughts on a man who on being given the chance to sleep with Mina had legged it as fast as he could.

"It is true. Epaphroditus has met her," insisted Mina.

"Ahh. She reveals her source."

"Shut up, Sporus! Do you want to know or not?"

"Go on, fabricate some more for us."

Mina pointedly addressed Alex: "She is called Teretia."

"A pleb then?"

"I doubt he could pull the queen of Bithynia. She is called Teretia and she is a stunner."

"Your words or Epaphroditus'?"

"He said stunner. He's stunned that Philo could grab such a stunner."

"I'm stunned."

"I think we're all stunned. It is stunning news."

"She's blonde, blue eyed, a little shorter than him and is possessed of a very pleasing figure with a large but rounded bosom."

"Was he taking notes? That seems a suspiciously well-drawn portrait," mused Alex.

"It's a noteworthy occasion," pointed out Sporus.

"Too true."

"How'd they meet? I can't imagine Philo chatting up some pleb girl on the street."

"She is his landlord's daughter."

Sporus and Alex looked at each other and said almost in unison, "Crafty way to keep the rent low."

Mina sat back, satisfied at being the conveyer of such hot news. "Can we talk about the piss now? And gods! Sporus, what happened to your lip?"

"This trifle? This is nothing. Alex punched me."

"Alex? What the—?," she asked waving her arms about. "You punched Sporus? *You* punched Sporus?"

Alex grinned at Sporus who grinned back, "I did. I punched him."

"A good right hook. Right in my smacker." Sporus tentatively pressed a finger to the damaged lip. "How long before it goes down do you think?"

"Screw that, why did you punch him?"

"You mean you've never considered it?" queried Alex to deflect her from the actual reason.

"All the time," confessed Mina. "He's an annoying little twerp."

"Agreed."

"Fundamentally not agreed!"

"So, let's get back to Philo."

"I wanted to ask about the piss," moaned Mina.

Sporus, grasped by a sudden thought, grabbed hold of Mina's ankle, "Mina, what do you think about Alex and that pastry chef?"

"Sybillia? Ooh yes. She's sweet. Alex, she's really sweet. You'd go great together. Sporus, wouldn't they have perfect children together?"

"That is exactly what I thought," confided Sporus smugly. "And it would deal with the tetchiness problem."

"Tetchiness problem?"

"I am finding Alexander very tetchy these days: sexual frustration you know."

Feeling his face heat, Alex said hotly, "I am not sexually frustrated."

"You are tetchy though. Remember the other day when we got lost in the city? You were really tetchy then."

"You got lost in the city?"

"The other day when we were on Alex's mission."

"You're not to talk about the mission," stressed Alex.

Mina shrugged. "Oops. It's only Sporus."

"It's only Sporus, arch-gossip of the palace."

Sporus looked put out. "How come I didn't know about your city trip?"

"Because it was a secret mission."

"Mina!"

"Sorry, sorry. Oops again."

"I wouldn't look so narked, Sporus. I doubt I'll get any more secret missions with blabbermouth here."

Mina made a point of closing her lips tight.

"So what was this mission?"

Alex folded his arms, "I can't tell you. It's a secret"

Sporus laughed, "You can tell me. I'm your best friend."

Alex was adamant, "I cannot tell you."

Sporus stood up on the bed. "You are no fun at all tonight. I don't think I shall bother with you in future."

"Don't be like that," soothed Mina. "Alex had strict orders not to tell."

"He told you."

"I wheedled it out of him."

"I'm sure. It wouldn't take much, a flash of ankle, a hint of wrist. Anything more and Alexander would self combust."

Alex gave Sporus a warning glance. He returned it with a condescending smile.

"What are you talking about?" Mina asked, exasperated.

"Nothing at all, Artemina. I shall leave you both now to your little secrets. I would so hate to be in the way of this tryst."

It was useless to try to argue with Sporus when he was in this mood. It was a sign of his condition, a compulsive need to have the last word and a flashy exit. So Alex and Mina let him flounce out and didn't say a word, even when he trailed his fine purple dressing gown through the pool of urine.

"He feels left out," said Mina.

Privately Alex smarted at this, having sat through endless debates over banquets and parties that Mina, attending the empress, and Sporus attending the emperor, had witnessed. Publicly he said, "I gathered that."

"We should have asked him along."

"You weren't even supposed to be there. And how noticeable would we have been with Sporus in tow?"

Mina laughed, "Gods! Can you imagine it? Sporus in his cherry-pink silk gown and dainty slippers wandering up the Janiculum Hill."

Alex couldn't help but smile. "He would never have made it past that cesspit. I would have had to carry him on my back."

"We should do something nice together, the three of us." She grasped Alex's hand affectionately. "Like old times."

He squeezed her hand back, agreeing, "Just like old times."

He smiled at Mina who leaned back and rested her head against his shoulder, he placing his arm around her and hugging her close.

He knew then that no little pastry chef, no matter how sweet, was ever going to distract him.

THIRTEEN

Alex was awoken the next morning in the traditional manner, an overseer kicking the soles of his feet and yelling, "Get the fuck up, you little fucker."

Mina had stayed late the night before and they had covered such diverse topics as:

Had Sporus been that flouncy before his operation?

Alex was of the opinion that he had not. Mina argued that Sporus had always been an infuriating twerp, even when he was intact. They reminisced over those bleak first days of Sporus' eunuchisation, watching the new eunuch twist in his bed, sweating and crying, as they held tight onto his hands and entreated every god they could think of for his survival. They did both agree though that Sporus made a better eunuch than he ever would a man.

Did the empress loathe the emperor?

Mina thought so, sharing that the empress looked like thunder before a scheduled conjugal visit.

How could Phaon afford his fabulous new country villa?

Mina thought bribery. Alex, through loyalty to his boss, claimed that he was simply a careful saver.

What was Epaphroditus' wife like?

Neither of them had met her so she was game for Mina's vicious tongue, Alex did not dare disagree.

It was the usual sort of evening for them, voices kept low to avoid attracting overseers, an animated Mina grabbing at his arm with excitement as Alex drolly offered his insights. All it needed for a perfect session was Sporus. They both agreed that he would get over his hissy fit and was probably right now regretting the scene he had caused. Alex had gone to sleep smiling, secure in his friendship with Mina.

This morning he felt melancholic, pulling his uniform on slowly and struggling over the strapping on his sandals. He was standing still. That was the problem. That was why he enjoyed such evenings, they reminded him of his childhood and he hung onto them as something precious. In his heart he knew they would not continue much longer; Sporus and Mina had far too much going on in their lives to visit him.

The gap between them was growing. His friends had daily contact with the imperial family, intimate contact in Sporus' case. Alex had never even set eyes on the emperor in all his seventeen years. And though Sporus may have stomped out feeling excluded, it was Alex who was left out: Sporus and Mina frequently talking of events he had not attended and people he did not know. They would laugh and gossip as he sat on the sidelines unable to participate, a state that was increasing in frequency.

That was why he felt so crushed by Sabinus' indifference. He'd seen it as his chance to equal himself, to close the gap between him and his friends.

Sighing, he pulled a comb through his hair, breaking two teeth off as he did so. He gazed at himself in the round, bronze mirror that Sporus had left behind. A freckled face looked back, brown eyes and that bushy red hair that grew vertically above his brow. He saw nothing appealing in that face, and neither did anyone else.

He'd been rejected from the breeding programme that Apollodorus ran to replenish the imperial stock with baby slaves, a decision that had stung him. Apollodorus looked him up and down, noted his red wiry hair and had turned to his assistant and said, "I don't think we need any more of these do we? What can they do?"

What can they do? Alex was brave, loyal, eager, and keen. It wasn't fair. There were no glamorous banquets for him, no tending to the emperor and empress, no high level intrigue, no affair with a top official. Just a long life of delivering pointless messages to petty administrators.

Sabinus had not forgotten Alexander. In fact the boy had been in his thoughts for some days; he'd been impressed by the boy. Generally Sabinus had no time for imperial slaves. He found them ill-bred, with a snobbery ill-suited in a patrician, let alone the lowest of humanity. But Alexander had shown none of that attitude; he was untainted by what Sabinus considered the corrupt elements of the palace and so eager, so keen to please, so mouldable, thought Sabinus, who saw himself as a pedagogue of Roman virtue. That Alexander would never progress beyond messaging was one of life's brutal inequalities, thought the prefect.

How it must rankle to see others less suited rise higher and higher; see those whose only talents were in sating the emperor's depravity be exalted and honoured. How they must burn with bitterness, with envy, seething away at the system. And then a thought struck the prefect as suddenly as a heavy shower from a blue sky: what if they could be mobilised?

Alex, depressed, shuffling along the corridor was alerted by a cry of, "Alexander."

He looked up to see Nymphidius Sabinus, feeling a sudden thrill that he had remembered his name. The prefect attempted a welcoming smile; it did not fit him naturally.

"I have an assignment for you, Alexander, if you would like to follow me."

Alex stood to attention with difficulty, excitement coursing through his veins, struggling to keep a smile from breaking out. He knew Sabinus wouldn't forget him. It had been a test, to see if he were trustworthy, to see if news of his first mission had leaked. It hadn't and he'd passed. He'd proved himself.

Sabinus gave what he hoped was a reassuring smile. "I was very impressed by your work for me the other day."

"Thank you, sir," responded Alex, the corners of his mouth twitching upwards.

"Very impressed," Sabinus reiterated, noting Alex's pink hue of excitement. He really was perfect.

"I would like you to undertake some further work for me, Alexander. Important work, crucial to the well-being of the empire. Why don't you sit." He gestured to a chair. Alex looked shocked. As a slave he was used to standing. Nobody had ever asked him to sit before. He did so carefully, right on the edge of the seat.

"Do you like being a messenger?"

Alex flushed, trying to gather his thoughts. He supposed the correct answer would be, "Yes," but something about Sabinus' intense gaze made him answer honestly.

"It is not as thrilling as I had hoped."

"Few things are," symphathised Sabinus. "I imagine many people would believe that being Praetorian prefect is glamorous."

That was certainly Alex's belief.

"Not the case," Sabinus disillusioned him. "Much of my day is spent filling in forms." He gestured to the scrolls that littered the room. "For the bureaucrats. They do like their petty details. So I oblige," he sighed. "Tell me, Alexander, do you get to deliver messages outside the palace?"

"Never."

"That surprises me. You seem a very able young man. It is a shame that Phaon's so busy that he can't spot talent."

"It is rather quiet at the moment," Alex shared. "All the incoming post is being diverted to Epaphroditus."

"He is the emperor's private secretary. It is important that he is kept informed."

Alex flushed and looked down at his feet.

"Of course, Phaon and Epaphroditus are very close. They are related after all."

This was news to Alex, whose head snapped up.

"You help family, that is the natural order of things. It is just unfortunate for those who lack such connections. It makes it difficult for them."

Alex was transfixed: nobody ever spoke like this. He had lost count of the number of times he had heard the phrase, "We're all Caesar's family."

As if they were all equal. Tell that to the sweeper Onesimus or the cross-eyed Demetia, both of whom skulked in the slave complex with no hope of ever getting out, of ever being able to save for their freedom.

"I like to talent spot, Alexander. I like to promote those I feel are up to the job, no matter what their background. I don't expect anything in return, no 'special' favours. Just loyalty."

He looked directly into Alex's eyes. Alex found himself unable to break the stare. Sabinus could see into him, he knew what his most secret thoughts and feelings were, and he understood, he even sympathised. This, for Alex, was a revelation.

"Do you think you could give me your loyalty, Alexander?"

Alex couldn't speak. He gave an emphatic nod instead.

Nymphidius Sabinus, Praetorian prefect, had asked for him by name, had talked personally to him, wanted his loyalty. Alex didn't care what the job was, he would have done anything for Sabinus at that moment.

FOURTEEN

In retrospect, Epaphroditus recognised it had been an inopportune moment to raise the matter of the senatorial meeting with the emperor.

Nero stood in the centre of his bedchamber, arms outstretched as his slaves anointed his naked body with oil. "Why do I want to meet some old senator windbags?" he asked, jiggling his left leg with irritation. "Juba, you are practically basting me. I said a light layer to make me gleam."

He aimed a kick at the crouching Juba, knocking him over.

"The senate needs to be informed of the Vindex situation and how Verginius Rufus is about to demolish this upset," said Epaphroditus, neatly avoiding words such as rebellion, revolt, uprising, and insurgency.

"Vindex?" snapped Nero, glaring at Epaphroditus. "The Vanquished Vindex. Jupiter's great white bull, Epaphroditus, I don't have time for this!"

He kicked at Juba again.

"Your divine self seems agitated," soothed the secretary.

"Yes, well, so would you be. Apparently the moon is in … what is it?"

He clicked his fingers at a bearded soothsayer who stood festering in a corner.

"The moon is in her essence," the beardy one said.

"No, I don't know what it means either but apparently if I screw her now, there's a good chance she'll produce me an heir. Have I got that right?"

"Yes, Your Imperial Majesty."

"So you see. I am very busy."

Clearly some brave soul had informed the emperor of the unlikelihood of Sporus conceiving, and the Empress Statilia Messalina was back in imperial favour.

"Do I gleam, Epaphroditus?"

"Irresistibly."

Nero gave a, "Hmm," and gazed downwards. "Thing is, I don't really fancy it today." He wrinkled his nose. "But moon and essences …"

"And sometimes an emperor must do things he does not wish for the greater good of Rome and her empire."

Nero gave a tight smile. "Nicely put. You always did have a nice way with words. Hmm," he said, looking downwards again.

He clicked his fingers at Sporus who crawled across the floor spider-like, kneeled before Nero, and took the imperial member in his mouth.

Epaphroditus kept his eyes firmly above waist level. "The day after tomorrow?" he suggested.

Nero threw his head back, expelling a small gargling sound as Sporus worked at his task with enthusiasm.

Epaphroditus stood, silently awaiting an answer.

"OK, OK that's enough."

Sporus shuffled backwards, wiping his mouth on the back of his hand. Nero looked down and then back up, smiling at Epaphroditus.

"The day after tomorrow?"

"Whatever, whatever."

Nero strode past him, the body slaves following at a quick step, walking through the door that connected his room with the empress' quarters. Epaphroditus heard him shout, "Lay her out. I'm ready to shoot."

Which was an image that stayed with him for the rest of the day.

As for the meeting itself, Epaphroditus had yet to make up his mind whether it had been an unequivocal success or a total disaster. Philo had done his job well, putting together a senatorial deputation that included a couple of Nero's playboy pals, a geriatric jellyfish of a statesman, and Regulus.

All four wore togas but Regulus' looked as if it had grown from within him. Epaphroditus found it hard to imagine him in anything casual. He probably slept toga'd up. His inclusion on the list was there to prove that Nero had nothing to hide. This pesky little upset was so harmless that the emperor was happy to discuss it with his most outspoken critic (yet living) and answer any questions. The others were mere dressing for this key consultation. No, the guest list was perfect.

Where it had fallen down was the timing, which was his department. He wasn't going to beat himself up about it, though. Who would have thought to check the delivery schedule for the day? And why would anyone have thought it necessary to inform him about the delivery of a water organ? And how was he supposed to know that water organs were Nero's newest and greatest passion? Nero's passions were so numerous it was impossible to keep track of them all. And water organs? Why water organs?

Nero had been so obsessed with his new water organ that the Vindex situation had been summed up thus:

"Vindex the Vanquished? I wrote an ode about him, you know. I am setting it to music. Do you think the water organ has the right ambience?"

Then, seated behind the organ he had attempted the first stanza of "The Vanquished Vindex", the water organ all but drowning out his reedy singing voice, which was a bonus for all concerned.

This tiresome demonstration, complete with cries of, "You hear the difference in sound when I twist this tap?" proved just how lightly the emperor was taking the Gallic revolt.

On the negative side, Nero had once again proved his lack of leadership capabilities. Which would not matter had there not been a rival, more credible claimant. Epaphroditus scanned the message again; it did not improve on the fifth reading. According to his informants, Galba had fortuitously escaped the Greek-speaking, poisoned dagger-wielding assassin sent to Spain. Faced with an emperor wishing to dispose of him, Galba had thrown in his lot with Vindex.

Epaphroditus rubbed his forehead with the flat of his hand. He could feel a headache coming on.

And where was Philo? He was late yet again.

Philo was walking through the grounds of the new palace, which would have surprised Epaphroditus since it was in completely the wrong direction for his office.

The encounter with Straton had deeply shaken him and he was plagued by dreams of a nature that had him writhing in his sleep, awaking sweaty and trembling. Ever since that collision he had used ever more elaborate routes to avoid the overseer, never taking the same course twice and keeping constant vigil of his surroundings. This had dramatically increased the length of time it took him to get to work, hence his persistent tardiness.

Today's journey would involve entering the new palace gate, cutting across the extensive grounds and nipping through the subterranean tunnel that linked the two palaces. He wished he was wearing socks, as the grass was wet with early morning dew and his toes were distinctly damp. Wearing his brown tunic, he intended to camouflage himself against the scenery should the worst happen and he run into Straton.

The gardens were rather beautiful at this time in the morning, Philo thought. The sun reflecting on the lake and glistening off the shell-studded grottos that framed the water. In the distance he could see thickets of trees clumped by the edge of fallowed fields. He could almost believe himself in the country, he mused, a task several hundred gardeners worked extremely hard to achieve.

Calvia had once hosted a magnificent banquet in these grounds with small boats drifting across the lake's surface. They moored at a floating raft where a huge marquee had been erected for the dinner. A selection of notable animals were let loose for the guests to marvel at: antelopes gently sipping at the lake's edge and giraffes peeking out from the woods.

However, once darkness had fallen the party had degenerated, much as these occasions always did. Nero and Tigellinus were caught in a debate which raged during much of the evening, the question proposed: was it possible to tell a virgin merely by sight?

Nero claimed it was. Maidenly virgins had a blush, a special state of being that was perceptible to the eye. Tigellinus argued the opposite, that there were those who were so skilled in deception that they could play the shy virgin when in reality they were defiled in every orifice.

Inevitably there could only be one way to settle such a dispute. Huge bets were made by the excitable young dandies always in attendance at such functions. The stakes by the close were twenty million sesterces that it was possible to determine a virgin by sight, and seventeen million on the opposing view.

The ensuing line-up was an intriguing mix of imperial slaves and the daughters of particularly high-born citizens, given up by their parents to be debauched without protest. The participants were arranged in a line, firstly clothed and then unclothed, for the judges' deliberations.

Contestant number one was a quivering pout of a girl, the daughter of a notable senator who stood rigidly throughout the proceedings. Nero held her chin and lifted it gently upwards. The girl looked into his eyes and then quickly glanced away.

The emperor turned to the gathered crowd. "She trembles," he announced.

"But", stressed Tigellinus, "does she tremble from innocence or does she tremble because Daddy's about to discover that his little girl is not so pure."

This was accompanied by much drunken laughter as the senator stared straight ahead, showing no reaction.

Nero snapped at an attendant standing behind the girl, he untied the ribbons that held her dress together. It fell to her ankles in one movement displaying an immature body that had yet to bud. She struggled to cover herself but the attendant had hold of her arms and all she could do was buck and bend, causing more laughter. Nero considered her, smoothing a finger along her flat stomach and dipping into her belly button. She shuddered.

"Virgin," he stated with confidence and then invited Tigellinus to inspect.

The prefect had a different tactic. Lifting up his tunic he displayed his erect member to the girl. Her eyes opened very wide. Pointing his erection at the crowd, who automatically took one very large step backwards, Tigellinus decried, "I concur with our imperial master and humbly request him to settle this matter."

The girl's legs were kicked apart by the attendant as Nero made his approach, the blood that dripped down her legs afterwards granting a point for each of them.

Next up was Lycia, part of the imperial household. As a member of the emperor's harem, the chances of her being intact were astronomically slim. However, to Philo's surprise, Nero seemed not to recognise her and after an inexpert fumble he declared her a virgin. Tigellinus took the honours this time, he held up his clean fingers to demonstrate the verdict. Two points to one.

Girl number three was another slave. She shook dreadfully and bit her lower lip so hard, blood trickled down her chin. This excited the emperor and he took her quickly without stating his decision. Nobody objected to this blatant rule breaking and Nero awarded himself an extra point. Two points each.

You couldn't mistake the breeding of Regula, tall with well-formed shoulders, a high carriage, and a large aristocratic nose that over-shone her otherwise plain features. She was unmistakably her father's daughter.

Senator Regulus stood grim-faced, his teary-looking wife clinging to his arm. Regulus held his hand over hers tight, partly for support but also, Philo suspected, as a warning not to cause a fuss. Though the mood was jovial, there was a heavy presence of Praetorians who wouldn't hesitate if they felt the emperor threatened.

Regula appeared unafraid, bold even, looking straight at the emperor. Nero stroked his chin. "Very tricky," he pronounced. Tigellinus took a swig of wine, wiped a hand across his mouth and let forth an enormous belch before saying, "Posh slut. Used and abused."

Regula didn't blink, she continued to look regally haughty even as Tigellinus broke into a crude soliloquy on her alleged proclivities. Philo, keeping his eyes on Regulus, saw the man flinch at every lie told about his daughter. Nero noticed it too because staring directly at Regulus, he said lightly, "Let the guards decide this one."

Guards plural.

Philo never found out who won the bet. For just as the Praetorians stood forward, with it has to be said some eagerness, there came a familiar rasp in his ear. "Enjoying the entertainment?"

A thumb and forefinger gripped the back of his neck and he was marched out of the marquee to a more private space.

His overriding memory of the banquet was neither that particular Straton unpleasantness nor the virgin competition. It was the next morning as he sat by the lake watching the sun rise, feeling sorry for himself. He was nibbling at a leftover cake when from the skies a large bird swooped down, landing before him.

The bird was the strangest creature Philo had ever seen, for it had two long sticks for legs and was possessed of a pinkish hue. Philo watched, goggle-eyed. The bird regarded him with similar suspicion, its head tilted at an angle.

Eventually they grew used to each other's presence, the bird's head straightening. Philo placed a piece of his cake in his outstretched palm. The pink bird considered the offering and then, taking a gangly step forward it took the crumb directly from his hand. It was a moment that Philo treasured close to his heart as a point where he felt he had almost been happy.

He walked past that point of the lake now, worrying about the time, fretting about a particular report he had to write, and generally tearing himself to pieces about things that were not actually his fault. He had reached the tail end of the pillared colonnade that ran a clear mile to the entrance chamber of the new palace when he heard voices.

Dipping behind a pillar, he peered discreetly round it to see Onesimus and Juba talking in hushed whispers.

Philo's instincts told him that this scene was all wrong. Onesimus was the ferrety boy who swept the slave complex and Juba was one of Nero's body slaves, so far above his companion in status that he shouldn't even be acknowledging him. They certainly should not be chatting as equals.

They were walking towards him so Philo slid behind the pillar and stood rock still, his back pressed against the marble. As they came closer, he could just about make out their words.

"There's a lot of us now," Onesimus was saying.

Juba didn't reply for a while and when he did, Philo could hear the tenseness of his tone. "Look, if this ever comes out."

"When the time comes …" began Onesimus but was interrupted by Juba who told him,

"I'll do my bit, obviously."

As they were passing Philo's pillar, he clearly heard Juba say, "It's a weird world when I have to deal with your sort." Which was the sort of contempt Philo expected from Juba.

When they had passed and were a safe distance away, Philo slid out from behind the pillar. He was disquieted by the scene he had witnessed. Why was Juba dealing with Onesimus' sort? What was he going to do for Onesimus? And who were there a lot of?

He should report this to Epaphroditus but he wasn't sure how to word it. There was nothing concrete to pin on either Onesimus or Juba and their conversation was so vague as to be unintelligible. For all he knew, they were arranging a romantic tryst.

Unlikely, but then so were a lot of the slave relationships that raged for a brief, bright spark. No, he would hold off, he didn't want to look foolish, and Epaphroditus had reprimanded him more than once for his lateness. He would do a little digging of his own and see what he could find out before putting together a report based on solid facts to present to his superior.

FIFTEEN

Nero had cancelled all of his official duties. This had gone entirely unnoticed by most of his staff, who undertook their daily tasks in ignorance of the blow their master had been dealt.

The most powerful man in the known world sat reading an unfurled scroll, quivering and emitting small cries each time he read a phrase that displeased him, of which there were many. He glanced up at Juba, crying, "But this is—?" or, "But why would—?" and many times, "I don't understand—"

The document he was reading was the combined speeches of Julius Vindex, and a fine example of well-honed rhetoric they were. There were some doubts as to their authorship. Supposedly delivered to the barbarian Gallic tribesmen, it seemed unlikely that such nice turns of phrase would have inspired their revolt.

Somebody had clearly expanded on Vindex's themes for a wider readership; a readership familiar with their Livy and Cicero. Despite their literary pretensions, the tone was distinctly accusatory, and every accusation, every crime was laid solely at Nero's feet.

He has despoiled the whole Roman world by his spendthrift ways, bankrupting the treasury that noble Claudius filled. Why, he never wears the same clothes twice! But that is not the most shameful part, for I have seen him curled and dressed as a woman heavy with child.

"That's not true, not true at all! I have never worn women's clothing. Juba, have you ever seen me dressed as a woman?"

"No, Caesar."

"No you haven't. Because it is not true."

His list of crimes are numerous. His first was the murder of the noble Emperor Claudius, who had adopted him as his son. Oh, should a father ever have such a son!

"That wasn't me. That was Halotus, the food taster! I had nothing to do with that."

Next was his stepbrother Britannicus, who was poisoned at a public banquet. His own sister forced to sit and watch her brother die. So blatant were the miscreants of this terrible murder.

"But that was mother!"

And what should I say of poor Octavia, compelled to be his wife and how that act should lead to her dreadful end.

"She killed herself. She was of an extremely melancholic disposition. I was concerned for her. The doctors all said she could do with a break, so I sent her to the coast. How was I to know she would open her veins?"

Privately Juba marvelled at the emperor's talent for self-delusion, remembering very clearly the day Nero, or rather Poppaea, had ordered the death of Octavia. He said nothing though, just shook his head sadly as if gobsmacked by such accusations.

116

"Oh, this is dreadful, quite dreadful," cried Nero. "Do you know what he accuses me of now? Oh, it's horrid, just horrid." Nero went back to reading.

Juba, unseen, gave a small, satisfied smirk. An exotic looking man, darker in colour than most and possessed of a pair of startling blue eyes, he was both incredibly vain, treating his thick hair with a vast array of ointments and products, and a terrible bully. There were few in Nero's close circle who had not suffered Juba's caustic put-downs and vicious attempts at rape. The empress' dressers were absolutely terrified of him and worked out complicated schedules to ensure they could protect each other from his assaults.

Aware of the fear he induced, he thrived on it, eyeing up simpering maids and whispering promised indignities to them. He'd formed an ardent desire for Mina since taking up her position as keeper of the towel, developing a complicated fantasy life that involved ever more depraved acts inflicted upon her. As a member of Nero's inner sanctum, he was never short of inspiration and incorporated many of the emperor's favourite pastimes into his virile fantasies. These were made all the more vivid by his inability to consummate them. For Mina, protected up high by that undeservedly lucky bastard Epaphroditus, Juba suffered a repressed lust that no sobbing slave girl could ever sate.

At this moment he was replaying a particularly favourite scenario of his and paying very little attention to the emperor's distress. He was familiar with the Vindex scroll, as Sabinus had given it to him to pass onto the emperor, saying,

"I feel it is important that His Imperial Majesty be informed as to the depth of public feeling against him. And if you want to add in a scurrilous tale or two of your own devising, I shall not object."

Juba nodded and took the scroll, reading it on his way back to the emperor's chambers, smirking at the level of venom Vindex was directing towards Nero. There was nothing in it that was untrue, for Juba had been feeding stories from the emperor's private life back to Sabinus for months. The prefect himself was most likely the author of the Vindex scroll; it certainly rang with his own peculiar priggishness.

The part Juba was most proud of was the passage that caused Nero the most distress.

"Oh, dear gods! Have you deserted your most obedient servant? How can he say this? Oh, Juba, the things he says about our dear Sporus."

Juba shook his head sadly once more and added a tut.

"He calls him an animal, a creature of neither male nor female parts. That he has offered his every orifice for defilement to all in the palace from the guards, the treasury officials, the gladiators, the grooms, the gardeners, the secretaries, and most shamefully of all, to the Empress Statilia Messalina who is forced to endure his violations as the entire court watches on at this poor noblewoman's degradation."

OK, so it wasn't all one hundred per cent true.

You may well ask what Juba hoped to gain from such a betrayal. Sabinus, ever savvy to the baseness of his fellow man, had offered Juba exactly the right price. He was bought quite easily when Sabinus agreed to his appointment of breaking in the young female sex slaves. It was a noble position and one Juba could not wait to start.

"We can't tell him," whined Nero. "He would be crushed, absolutely crushed if he knew what lies were being said. Crushed. They can say what they like about me." Nero slammed his huge hand onto his heart. "I can take it. An emperor is much maligned, but one has to rise above it."

By forcing the gossips to open their veins and then stealing all their property, thought Juba.

"Oh my poor Sporus." A solitary tear ran down his cheek.

Juba was not moved. He was twitching with gleeful anticipation for the next paragraph, which was wonderfully dismissive of Nero's lyre playing.

Once the rage had subsided at the expense of one ornate glass vase, a bronze mirror, and three feather pillows, Nero was very clear in his instructions.

"Get Epaphroditus here NOW! I want to know why he has kept this from me!"

The Emperor lobbed the scroll at the secretary. Epaphroditus lifted up an arm to protect himself. It bounced off his elbow and landed on the floor at his feet.

"What do you say?" yelled Nero.

The emperor was quite beside himself. A blob of spit hung to his bottom lip, his face a dangerous shade of red, his fists rhythmically clenching and unclenching.

"Caesar?" asked the secretary calmly, his hands linked behind his back.

"I said, what do you say? What do you say about the information you have wilfully hidden from me. What do you say about this deceit?" Nero glared, his eyes flashing with anger.

"Caesar, I have never knowingly deceived you. You are misinformed."

"He tells me I am misinformed," said the emperor to no one in particular, pacing the length of the room.

As he paced, Epaphroditus' brain whirled. There was clearly some plotting occurring, some bastard trying to discredit him. He looked down at the scroll at his feet, recognising the seal instantly. So this is what had upset the emperor.

"Caesar, I come with news."

"You come because I sent for you, Epaphroditus. That is why you come."

The secretary was not to be silenced, adding quickly and firmly, "Julius Vindex has failed to bolster his army of untrained Gauls and his attempt to take Lugdunum has failed, for the town is firmly Caesar's. Verginius Rufus is marching down from Lower Germania with his legions right now. Vindex will

119

not be able to withstand the assault from Caesar's soldiers. He is defeated. The revolt is at an end."

This barrage of information disarmed Nero, his mouth opening and closing without sound.

"I have arranged for a ceremony of gratitude for the temples and the senate. Perhaps some honour for Rufus, he has proved himself able and loyal."

"The legions?"

"Loyal to Your Imperial Majesty, as ever they were."

Behind his back, he crossed his fingers and offered a silent prayer to the gods that he would be proved correct.

The emperor found his voice. "He says such awful things about me," he whined. "He says I have bankrupted the treasury."

Epaphroditus shook his head. "Not true, Caesar. We are making great progress on raising funds."

"And that I am a wasteful spender of public funds."

"Perhaps Vindex does not realise how expensive a business being emperor is. The people demand these huge spectacles and a good emperor must give the people what they want."

"And he says," he took a big gulp, "that I killed dear Claudius, Britannicus, and Octavia."

"That is an imprudent falsehood."

Nero looked up at his secretary with tear-filled eyes, his body quivering beneath the voluminous dressing gown, podgy feet poking out at the bottom.

"It is all in hand, Epaphroditus?" he asked, his voice filled with doubt.

"It is, Caesar. Verginius Rufus is a fine soldier," he stated with a great deal of confidence that he did not feel.

Nero, placated, attempted a smile. "Answer me honestly, Epaphroditus."

"I always have, Caesar."

"Tell me, am I a good lyre player?"

Epaphroditus affected incredulity. "Caesar, you have spent many years in a painstaking cultivation of the art."

"I have, haven't I?"

"How could one fail to be a good player after such a length of study?"

It was a good question and one Epaphroditus had wondered about for years.

Nero gathered himself together. "I am very good. I am a great artist. So if that is a falsehood then all those other horrible accusations are falsehoods too."

"That would be the logical deduction, Caesar."

"It would, wouldn't it."

Nero thought for a moment and then said, "Do you think we could help Rufus in his duty? I could arm my concubines with shields and swords, like Amazons. Vindex wouldn't be expecting that."

Epaphroditus maintained a neutral expression with difficulty. "I shall send dispatches to Gaul immediately."

"Good, good," Nero bounced up and down, restored to his usual amiability. "Have you heard the new water organ, Epaphroditus? It plays a lovely note."

Having no wish to be dragged into one of Nero's prolonged recitals, he quickly said, "I'd best get on with these dispatches."

Nero looked a little disappointed. "I suppose so. Another time."

"Another time," agreed the secretary. "Could I borrow Juba for a moment?"

Juba followed Epaphroditus out of the door. Here they bumped into Sporus. Epaphroditus narrowed his eyes to avoid the sheer dazzle. The eunuch was decked out in an ankle-length silver gown with solid gold collar, a fabulous spiky tiara matched by a pair of drooping pearl earrings. The look was finished off by some impossibly high shoes and a diamond set into each of his toenails. The secretary was impressed.

"The emperor is in low spirits. Go suck his cock or something."

A twinkly eyed Sporus asked innocently, "Is that an order, sir?"

"Consider it so."

Sporus minced his way into the chamber. Epaphroditus turned his attention to Juba. "Follow me."

When they were settled in Epaphroditus' office, Juba sat on the stool Philo usually inhabited, the secretary asked him, "Who gave the emperor the Vindex scroll?"

When Juba didn't answer, he asked, "Was it you?"

"No," protested Juba.

"You can tell me the truth here and now or I can arrange for Scaveous to extract it from you." Scaveous was the head torturer at the palace. Epaphroditus saw the panic in Juba's eyes at the mention of his name. Like most bullies he was a physical coward.

"Well?" asked Epaphroditus impatiently. "Did you give him the Vindex speeches?"

"Yes," Juba admitted, hanging his head down to avoid Epaphroditus' green-eyed stare.

"I ask myself, why you would do that?"

Juba had no answer for that, continuing to stare at the floor.

"Were you thinking to ingratiate yourself with the emperor? You knock him down and then pick him up and he is pathetically grateful to you. Is that it?"

No answer from a cowed Juba.

"Have it your way. I'm warning you not to mess. The situation is delicate, the emperor is delicate. Do your job and stay out of anything that does not concern you. Understood?"

"Understood," muttered Juba.

Epaphroditus stuck his head out of the door and gave a command. Moments later a tumbling gait could be heard. Juba's head snapped up and panic filled his eyes. Straton stood in the doorway, his bulk filling the space. He hitched up his belt and unlooped a whip from it.

Epaphroditus addressed the overseer, "Ten lashes should do it."

Then he left Straton to do what Straton did best.

SIXTEEN

Sabinus was disappointed in Icelus. He expected a great man such as Galba to own a much higher class of servant. Icelus with his bald head and delicate features did not meet with the prefect's approval. Hearing his high-pitched voice, Sabinus felt a shudder of revulsion, assuming him to be a eunuch.

Sabinus loathed eunuchs as the living proof of the degenerate times into which Rome had sunk. It was said, and it was certainly something Sabinus had shared with his troops, that noble young men were putting themselves under the knife to ensure a place at Nero's court. No longer was ability, breeding, or talent a requisite for position. Instead, young men of good families competed to prove which of them was the most defiled. Men selling their bodies as common prostitutes for a handful of asses, propositioning even senators at the baths in the most brazen of fashion. And these animals were promised elevation by the emperor!

They were meeting secretly in the house of an unconnected third party. If anyone saw him meeting with Galba's freedman, then the game was up and the usual measures would be taken. Sabinus had no intention of opening his veins for Nero's pleasure and financial gain.

"My master wishes to know if everything is in place." Icelus' long fingers wound round his wine cup.

Sabinus took a sip of his water and watched Icelus carefully. "It is," he stated with soldierly minimalism.

Icelus had expected more information than this and pointedly said, "I am to report back."

"Your master should be less worried about my end of the bargain. If I were him, I would worry about Verginius Rufus. A most pernicious soldier."

"An irrelevance," dismissed Icelus, alerting Sabinus that he was not up to speed with the dispatches. "My master is keen to hear of your plans," he reiterated.

He looked nervous. This was not an unusual response to Sabinus' presence. Even the palace gladiators had been known to stumble when the prefect entered the viewing area. It was, in a way, a terrible shame that he was uninterested in sex. The sight of Sabinus attempting to court some fair maiden would have been well worth seeing. You could have charged an entrance fee.

Right now his unblinking stare and brooding silent demeanour was doing much to undermine Icelus, who fumbled with his cup, knocking it over and then fussing with the clear-up. This, to Sabinus' mind, was what distinguished the freeborn from the slave. The prefect clicked his fingers behind his head and a slave came running.

Icelus gave Sabinus a tight thank-you smile. "Your plans?" he insisted.

Another heavy silence. If it had been anyone else sitting opposite him, Icelus would have walked. He was a freedman of a distinguished senator; his time was uniquely valuable. But his master needed Sabinus as an ally, so he waited. Finally, once Sabinus felt he'd diminished the eunuch's ill-deserved self-importance, he said, "Are in order. We have yet to agree a bonus."

"A bonus?" queried Icelus, who contrary to Sabinus' thoughts did in fact sport a complete set of testicles.

"For my guards' assistance."

"You want my master to bribe the Praetorian Guard?"

This was exactly the wrong thing to say, puncturing as it did Sabinus' delicate opinion of himself as an upright Roman citizen.

He slammed down his cup. "You insult me."

Icelus waved his hands. "No, no, not at all."

"My guards", began Sabinus, "will be taking a huge risk for your master. They will be putting their lives on the line for your master."

So am I, thought Icelus and I'm not expecting payment. He wasn't about to get into an argument with Sabinus though, he was far too valuable and events were far too progressed for niggles now.

"How much?" he asked.

Sabinus named a figure. Icelus kept his features frozen: Galba would not agree. Yet to the prefect he replied, "Agreed," figuring they could sort it out at a later date, when Galba was emperor and Sabinus was not quite so useful. It was a technicality, nothing more. Of all the disastrous decisions that were to be made in the next eighteen months, this was the absolute corker.

Of course neither Sabinus nor Icelus were aware of this and Sabinus marched off in that brisk fashion of his, sure that they had a deal. His plans were going enormously well. The key was to attack on two fronts: this was where all those previous plots had failed.

It was all very well recruiting the top echelon of the senate to your cause, but utterly pointless if you had no palace contacts. Though Sabinus greatly admired Brutus and Cassius, their assassination of Julius Caesar had been similarly ill-planned. They thrust thirteen knives into the dictator and then proclaimed there was liberty. It was not their fault, they were noble and proud, they believed in the inherent rightness of the Roman mob.

Sabinus had no such illusions: the mob needed control. Sabinus, with command of the Praetorian Guard, was in the perfect position to exercise that control.

On his recommendation, Icelus had approached Senator Regulus, a man whom Sabinus had great respect for having suffered greatly under the tyrant. The senator had proved worthy to the cause and his persuasive powers with his own class could be relied upon.

The prefect himself was tackling the palace end. He had been correct in his assumption. The palace slave complex was swarming with malcontents; ignored and sidelined and ready for conversion to the cause. Sabinus cherry-picked them using what persuasion was necessary, targeting the maligned and overlooked from amongst the staff. Those, in other words, who had the most to gain. They idolised him as their benefactor and swallowed his words until they too were declaring death to the very man they belonged to.

The emperor's confidence was beginning to flag. For every positive that Epaphroditus and his ilk provided, Sabinus had a negative fed into his weasly brain. Slowly he was being eroded. It would not take much to push him over the edge. For Nero was above all things a coward. Cocooned in the palace, the emperor was due a bucket of cold water. Let him see how the people really saw him. A matricide, a murderer, and a pervert!

SEVENTEEN

Epaphroditus was not having a good day. First there had been the depressing report from Gaul. Then there was the emperor's wobble which he managed to smooth out, only to find that this was the first of many wobbles. Every time he sat down to work, another messenger would arrive with an urgent request from the emperor, and each time Nero was steadily more unhinged.

"We should expel all the Gauls from Rome, don't you think? They are going to be in on it and they're just waiting for the signal and then they'll kill us all in our beds. We should execute them first. Can you look into that?"

"I am going to Gaul. No, don't protest. I am going. When the troops see their emperor and see him weep before them ..."

"We could use the elephants. The ones from that show last year, we could ride them to Gaul, across the Alps. Like Hannibal. Vindex would never expect that. Poppaea could sit on the trunk dressed up like an Indian. I can just see you in a turban, you'd look so sweet. Get Calvia to design an outfit."

And so on, Epaphroditus nodding to each wilder suggestion and smoothly throwing in a "True Caesar, but—", and "Perhaps as an absolute last gambit, Caesar."

It was clear that someone was feeding him information and it wasn't Juba because he was lying face down recovering from Straton's attentions.

All of which was most troubling. Epaphroditus felt like an aqueduct engineer, fixing one leak only for another to spurt. Philo took the brunt of his frustration. When showing up hours late, Epaphroditus had given him the bollocking of a lifetime. This ceased to alleviate his restlessness, if only because Philo looked so utterly wretched by the end of his tirade that he felt immediately guilty.

Kicking around his office in between visits to Nero, the beleaguered secretary considered the situation. As he saw it, it all hinged on Rufus now. If he defeated Vindex, then Galba was finished. Galba had a single legion. Without Vindex's Gauls, they were mere fodder. Surely the Spanish legionaries would have to be mad to go along with such a suicidal plan?

No, they would melt away, leaving Galba exposed for justice. A general amnesty for the rebellious legions and more importantly a whopping big bonus should ensure the army's future loyalty. A series of thanksgiving games complete with sacrifices to the gods and the emperor in full imperial regalia to impress the mob. A sober address to the senate.

Of course there would have to be deaths. Somebody had to be blamed and be seen to be blamed. Vindex, no doubt killed in battle, was no good. Neither was Galba: his age and distinction could elicit sympathy. A quiet assassination was the best option for the Spanish governor. Epaphroditus would have to look closer to home for his sacrificial victim. Regulus?

A brief purge of the senate would fill up the treasury nicely and compensate for the battle expenses. It could be handled. Life would continue as normal and with any luck the empress would do her wifely duty and produce an heir.

However, should Vindex be on the winning side ... Epaphroditus shook his head, attempting to dislodge that thought. Should Vindex prevail, the pernicious forces in the city and the palace would gather themselves together behind Galba.

The frustrating thing for Epaphroditus was that there was absolutely nothing he could do. He was helpless until the next dispatch filtered in.

He decided to go work off his irritation with Mina, walking past Philo without comment.

Sometime later with Mina's naked body lying beside him, he contemplated retirement. He could just jack in the whole thing, spend more time with his family. Have a hobby, growing really small rose bushes or weaving baskets. He could still keep Mina, perhaps he could purchase her from the palace?

Mina gave a lazy smile and ran her hand down his arm. "Has that calmed you?" she asked.

Epaphroditus clasped his hands behind his head and stared at the ceiling. His dreams of gardening gloves and familial harmony dissolved. He could never give it up. He was the emperor's servant, no matter what happened. Although Nero was undeniably nuts, Epaphroditus realised he was rather fond of him.

He had style, you couldn't deny that, and the court was a lot more lively these days. It was a great time to be an imperial freedman. With an absurdly generous emperor, you could find yourself at the end of the day up by a seaside villa, a dozen slaves, and two bags of denarii just for complimenting Sporus' slippers. Epaphroditus had done very well for himself.

That, however, wasn't why he decided to stick by Nero. It was an old adage fed down to the slaves that they were part of Caesar's family. Epaphroditus actually believed this. He was born and raised in the palace. He had known Nero from a baby, to a tottering toddler, to a spotty adolescent emperor. He was family and you didn't desert family.

So to the end, and oddly that was calming. Expelling a long breath, he turned onto his side, casting a lascivious glance across Mina's fine body.

"More?" she asked. "You cannot be serious."

He took hold of her hand and guided it downwards to prove just how serious he was.

There was situated on the old palace side of the Palatine Hill a dwelling that had once been the Emperor Augustus' private home. In comparison to subsequent imperial buildings, it was modest, though acres larger than any average plebeian home.

As well as some pleasant rooms, it housed on the first floor a secret cupboard. It was secret for what it contained rather than its actual existence, for there was a door for all to see, though most passed its inoffensive wooden exterior without thought. It was kept permanently locked and only a handful of people knew of its wondrous interior.

Philo was proud to be one of those who held the knowledge; possessing a key to this room, which he kept looped on a chain round his neck. He fished this out now and put it to good use.

His terracotta oil lamp cast a warm glow on the shelves that ran up the walls to ever increasing heights. Shutting the door behind him he plonked the lamp down and scanned his eyes across for what he needed. Five shelves up, far too high for him to reach, was a box marked "styli". For this was the legendary stationery cupboard.

Generally such needs were catered for by Jason in supplies; catered for and hotly controlled. If one lost one's stylus set or tablet or scroll of papyri, one had to devise a bloody good reason why such a careless fool should be allowed another.

In the latest round of budgetary meetings, harsh cuts had been employed. Not on the entertaining side: five new gleaming golden chariots for the emperor had been effortlessly passed off as essential purchases; nor on the rebuilding of the palace, which had lost a wing or two in the Great Fire, nor even on the fabulous banquet that Calvia was proposing and which she had costed up as requiring two million sesterces.

No, the necessary cuts had to be made more mundanely. Miltiades from the treasury slashed the stationery budget by eighty per cent, which inevitably led to near hysteria over whose ink pot was whose and a series of punch-ups in the scribes hall. However, it was recognised that some souls should be allowed to avoid such low-class bargaining and they were allowed unfettered access to *the* cupboard. Philo was one such soul.

He pulled over a stepladder and was balancing on the top, reaching over to the stylus box when he heard the door open. Turning his head he was greeted by Straton's bulk filling the small space, pulling out his whip from his belt and grinning, eyes fixed firmly on him. Philo just managed to grip onto the shelf before his knees gave way.

He sat later that night bent over a series of figures, attempting to add them up, trying to make back the hours he had missed that morning. He had been staring at them for perhaps an hour without getting any nearer to a solution. Something dark was shifting at the back of his mind that he did not wish to address, so he stared at the figures, which danced in front of his eyes.

Eventually even he could not ignore it. What Straton had done to him. No, he corrected himself, what he had *let* Straton do to him. Because that was the difference now.

When he was a slave, whatever happened to him could be written off. He had no choice but to submit. That took away responsibility. People understood that. That's why freedmen were still accepted into public life, because everyone understood you had no choice. There was a faint distaste associated with having been a slave but the intelligent freedman could overcome this, could command respect. Like Epaphroditus.

Philo wanted nothing more than to be like Epaphroditus. To have people ask for his opinion. To be listened to. To be respected. Except no one could respect him now.

What would his boss have done, Philo wondered, deciding that Epaphroditus wouldn't have even got off the ladder. He would have told Straton to get lost or something of that ilk. He wouldn't have meekly climbed down when Straton growled the order at him. Would not have stood in front of the overseer, fiddling with his fingers and feeling his heart flutter. He certainly would not have done any of those other things Straton demanded and Philo lacked the courage to deny.

He threw down his stylus in distress and rubbed his tired eyes. Moving gingerly in his chair he winced as he pulled his tunic away from the damaged area, the wounds stinging. The misery rolled up inside him. This sort of thing wasn't supposed to happen to him now. Not now he was free!

Shoving his arithmetic onto the floor, he banged his head on his desk and sobbed his heart out. Which as far as dramatic gestures go was wholly pointless. Firstly because there was no one to witness it, and secondly because when he had composed himself, he would only have to pick up his filing off the floor and place it back on his desk.

EIGHTEEN

So, what of Julius Vindex, last heard of marauding about Gallia Lugdunensis with 100,000 Gauls crying "Death to the tyrant!" while Verginius Rufus marched down towards him with some very mean German legionaries?

Surely there was some great battle, some bloody skirmish, some absolute bloodbath betwixt Vindex's untrained barbarians and Rufus' killing machine?

Well, no. At this very moment, Vindex and Rufus were sat either side of a low table on which were displayed a plethora of tasty canapés. A wine slave was in attendance to fill their cups, and the mood was distinctly non-combative.

Vindex was describing with great intensity what had led him to such extraordinary steps as to besiege his own provincial city. His hands flew in the air as he emoted the depth of his feelings.

"You must see, Rufus. You must see that the emperor is a joke. A joke."

It continued late into the night, a version of Vindex's stirring rhetoric that had inspired 100,000 happily Romanised Gauls to fling off their togas, don the traditional patterned trousers, and run truly berserk through the paved streets where they usually did their daily shop.

"So," began Vindex, slapping his palms on his thighs. "You with me?"

A dazed and quite drunk Verginius Rufus found himself nodding.

"Excellent," smiled Vindex. "You are a great man, Rufus. History will know that!"

Rufus left enthused with not only hefty quantities of wine but also a dash of Vindex's adventurous spirit.

The next morning was a different story. Sitting up in his bed, his head more than a little stupefied, Rufus ran over the previous night's events.

Vindex made it all seem so plausible and unobjectionable. Nero had to go and he, Julius Vindex with Rufus' help would ensure just that. In the damp morning gloom it did not seem quite so obvious, or benign. It was treason.

Verginius Rufus possessed a nice house, a nice wife, an assortment of delightful children, and a career that was moving nicely upwards. All that could be swept away, all that he had worked for his entire life. And for what? For the excitable Julius Vindex, less of a man with a plan and more of ratting terrier let off its lead.

Rufus reflected bitterly on his stupidity as his slave assisted him with his toilet. Palace spies were everywhere. Even in this backwater you were not safe. It was said that Epaphroditus knew more about the secrets of men's hearts than their own wives. News of Rufus' foolish act could be galloping across the Alps right now.

"Sir!"

It was his tribune, a lanky aristocratic specimen serving his standard five years, after which he would decamp back to civilisation and dine off tales of barbarian warriors and golden-haired priestesses.

"What is it?"

The tribune cleared his throat, "The men have had a thought—"

This was not an auspicious opening; legionaries with a working thought process were a menace to all.

"About this Galba fellow. Well, who is he? We've never heard of him. Why should he get to be emperor? He hasn't even got a decent province!" protested the tribune, his soft cheeks flushing. "The men are all agreed that you, sir, would make a much better emperor."

The tribune smiled in an attempt to ingratiate himself with his superior. "Galba's only got one legion, sir, and we are three legions. We will win."

Rufus, noting the tribune's self-satisfying smirk, felt sick. "We will win?" he breathed. "We will win? For how long, tribune? Until the governor of Lower Germania decides that he has three legions too and enters the game? Until the eastern legions club together with their own candidate? Until the hills and valleys of the empire are littered with bodies? Jupiter's White Bull!" he spat hotly rubbing at his sore head. "This madness ends now! Tell the centurions to prepare their ranks for battle. Julius Vindex must be stopped!"

News of Julius Vindex's demise reached Rome in June. The slave whose misfortune it was to deliver the news to Nymphidius Sabinus left with a black eye and the prefect's roar ringing in his ears.

Sabinus paced his small office. This was not right. This was not supposed to happen. Vindex was to triumph over Verginius Rufus, leaving the way free for Galba to officially declare himself emperor. He rubbed at his large jaw. All the work he had put into turning the workforce, plotting and planning. Everything was in place! His guards were poised to take control. Sabinus was ready, itching to take control! What now?

To these ends he sought out a pale and panicked Icelus, the freedman as shocked as the prefect by this turn of events. Would Rufus be seeking out his master right now? He'd defeated Vindex's superior forces easily enough; there seemed little chance for Galba and his sole legion. And here he was under house arrest, surrounded by soldiers who might receive the order to execute him at any moment. Icelus was in a grim and dangerous situation. The prefect insisting, "What now?" at him was not improving his mood.

Wiping his sweating brow, Icelus murmured, "I don't know. I won't receive orders for weeks, even if a messenger is en route. By then we could all be dead." And then he gulped, his eyes moistening. "Oh, Great Jupiter! Spare me!"

Sabinus was disgusted by this mental collapse, his jaw clicking back into line. He leaned forward placing a palm on Icelus' trembling knee.

"We carry on," he told him. "Everything is in place. We act. Now. Tonight."

Icelus' eyes widened, his lip wobbled, "Sabinus I don't—"

He was cut off. "Listen to me. Word will be sent to Epaphroditus that I was here."

"But you told the soldiers you were examining the security arrangements, to see if your guards could assist."

"Epaphroditus will not believe that."

Icelus was flummoxed by this palace doublespeak.

"We need to act quickly. If events are satisfactory, then the legions will have no choice but to fall behind Galba. Even Verginius Rufus."

He said this with such certainty that Icelus did not dare contradict, nor raise any of his very real worries. Sabinus stood, pulling down his skirts and promising Icelus, "I will not let that invert rule one day longer."

NINETEEN

The party was to be a celebration of Vindex's defeat. There were to be two parts. An elegant reception for all the best people with fabulous canapés and an exclusive wine list. No tightroping elephants, camel chariots, eunuch parades, or peculiar sex games. That was for the latter part of the evening when all the good people had gone home to bed. It was a compromise.

Epaphroditus had requested a fully restrained and tasteful evening all the way. A chance to invite the top quarter of the senatorial class and prove to a still wobbly Nero that they were all wonderfully decent and not assassins in waiting. Coupled with a chance to show the nobs that the palace was not the corrupt, decadent court they believed it to be, and wasn't it wonderful that Nero was still emperor.

Unfortunately this idea was shot down by a committee of Nero, Tigellinus, Sporus, and Calvia as being just too "dreadfully dull". The only way Nero could be persuaded to act the genial host was by the promise of the later debaucheries.

"What do you think about inviting Icelus?" Epaphroditus asked Philo as they pored over the guest list.

"Galba's freedman? Isn't he under house arrest?"

"At the moment. His presence at our soirée could project a powerful message that the emperor has nothing to fear. It could bolster confidence."

Philo pondered, "It is fairly common knowledge that he is under arrest though, sir."

"True."

Philo dared an opinion, "Also sir, would it be wise to let him mingle? We might bolster confidence in the wrong direction."

"Very true. Let's scrap that idea."

"Regulus?"

Epaphroditus winced. "I seem to recall the last palace event he attended had an unfortunate end. I hear the young lady never fully recovered."

"His daughter?"

"Unmarriageable," Epaphroditus put brutally.

They went back to the list, discarding several names with a strike of Philo's stylus. After several hours' consideration they were left with a list of worthy but dull senators and equestrians.

"Well, let's hope one of them has a flighty wife to enliven proceedings."

"Who's consorting the emperor?"

"The empress, definitely the empress. I want Sporus locked in a cage until the second party."

"Sporus is the more calming influence on the emperor," suggested Philo. "In his current mood …"

Epaphroditus waved a hand. "I know, I know. You're right, but with this lot," he gestured to the finalised guest list, "our young eunuch friend represents everything they despise in the emperor. Unfair, I know. Frankly I'd have Sporus at every event: he's witty, charming, supreme at small talk, and pleasant on the eye. What more could you ask for from an empress?" He raised an eyebrow and Philo gave a tight smile.

Epaphroditus had noticed of late that Philo seemed out of sorts. Quieter than usual, more subdued. Putting this down to woman trouble he said, "Why don't you come along to my do? As a guest, no note-taking allowed. Bring Teretia."

"Teretia?"

"Why not? She's probably never been to a palace event before."

Philo, thinking literally, informed his boss, "Unlikely. Her father works in the building trade, a foreman I think. Though I believe he is very high up in the Viminal branch of the Builders Guild."

"Well there you go, it will be an experience for her. I'll arrange a litter for the pair of you. Make a proper night of it."

Philo took this to be an order, and later while sitting at the kitchen table, he told Teretia and her family, "My boss would like Teretia to attend a party he is organising."

Pompeia put her spoon down carefully. "A party? At the palace?" she asked, her husband reaching over and squeezing her hand.

"In the old palace," Philo told them, oblivious to Teretia holding her breath beside him. "There is a large courtyard with a big fountain. They are going to hold it there."

"Your boss, Philo," began Teretius tentatively, "what is it that he does at the palace?"

Philo, blowing on his soup, replied casually, "He's the emperor's private secretary."

"And yourself, what is your role?"

"I'm his secretary."

There was a silence as the family absorbed the astonishing fact that their unassuming lodger was the emperor's private secretary's secretary.

"You'll be coming though?" Teretia burst out.

Philo nodded over his bowl. "A litter will pick us up and drop us off."

"A litter," breathed Pompeia. "Fancy, husband. A litter."

141

Teretius shook his head, impressed. "And what is this party for? Is it your boss' birthday?"

"Oh no. It is for the emperor."

There followed an awed silence. It was Teretia who spoke first. "The Emperor will be there?"

"Oh yes, and the Empress Statilia Messalina. It won't be that fancy a do, just a small gathering of senators and palace staff."

"And the emperor," repeated Teretia staring at the wooden table for fear that if she met her parents' eyes she would simply brim over with excitement and squeal.

"And when would this party be?" asked her father.

"Tomorrow night." Then, sensing an atmosphere, "It is OK, isn't it, sir? Sorry, I didn't think. I should have asked you privately as the head of the family. I should have come to you first. I am so sorry. I have upset you."

Philo was upset himself. He'd blundered into this good family and broken every protocol regarding the head of the household. Why couldn't he do anything right?

Teretius, noticing his distress, leaned across the table and patted his arm. "Philo, son. I would be delighted if you escorted my daughter tomorrow night."

TWENTY

The brief for Calvia was an unusual one. Epaphroditus had sent a memo and underlined the words tasteful and civilised five times. Calvia sent one back querying what civilisation he wished her to ape, accompanied by a series of suggestions on a Babylonian theme. That little Indian boy was then sent with a careful list of directives to repeat. Each one of which Calvia considered a thwart.

"The later events can be all your own," Philo concluded.

This did little to cheer her as she complained later to the Empress Statilia Messalina.

"It is hardly the appropriate opener for one of my events! A fest of polite conversation!"

Statilia had laughed.

They were unlikely friends. Calvia the elder by some fifteen years and inhabiting a role that involved providing infidelities for Statilia's husband. Calvia never expected them to get on. Still mourning Poppaea, she felt Statilia to be a poor imitation. An admittedly pretty girl, with wide-spaced dark eyes and a cute snub nose, but lacking the vitality of the previous empress. She had deigned to be polite but professional.

However, women were in short supply in the top echelons of the palace and Nero's new bride had latched onto her as her only equal. Calvia discovering that Statilia was possessed of a droll sense of humour regarding what she referred to as "her situation".

Where Poppaea held a vicious and indiscreet tongue, Statilia was the very essence of composure, waiting until the doors had firmly shut before divulging her secrets to Calvia.

They were sat together in Statilia's bath, up to their necks in water, petals floating around them.

"I do dislike these," said the empress playing with a petal betwixt thumb and forefinger. "They get caught in my hair and take an age to brush out. Perhaps I shall keep them in for your party."

"Like Daphne transforming into a tree to escape the horny Apollo," suggested Calvia.

"But who will be my Apollo?"

Calvia smiled wickedly at Statilia. "The emperor has golden hair."

The empress dipped her mouth beneath the water to disguise the laugh, sending bubbles to the surface.

"Gods," she swore under her breath as she bobbed back up. "He once tried to serenade me into bed when we were first married. Plucking at his lyre and singing me some awful ditty about Aeneas and Troy, I think. After four verses he put his hand on my thigh and told me in all seriousness how lucky I was to be in the presence of such artistry."

She pulled herself out of the bath slightly, looking back over her shoulder to check who was there, spying only Mina standing some feet away, a towel laid across her arm.

Statilia slid back down and whispered to Calvia. "You can't be too careful. They all spy on me, you know. That one," she aimed a thumb backwards, "is Epaphroditus' latest piece."

Calvia lifted herself up to assess Mina. "Undoubtedly. She's got the look."

"Creamy skin, long eyelashes, brown eyes," listed Statilia.

"Small but oh so rounded breasts," supplied Calvia.

"Young enough to be his daughter."

"Yet bearing a certain resemblance to his wife."

"Poor thing."

"Aphrodite or your towel girl?" Aphrodite was Epaphroditus' wife.

"Towel girl," replied Statilia, who retained the aristocratic habit of never learning the slaves' names when a, "You boy," or, "You girl," would suffice. "Little does she realise how soon she will be discarded. Detestable man. You know he has my father's house?"

Calvia did. Statilius Taurus had constructed a stunning villa on the Esquiline Hill, a previously unfashionable district. The home was large enough to rival the palace itself. But it had been the gardens that had attracted imperial envy. Hundreds of acres of woodland, water features, and flowered terraces renowned for their beauty and a peaceful retreat from the city's swarming streets.

Statilia's father had intended to open them to the populace, perhaps to garner support for a coming election, or perhaps just because he was a generous, kind man.

Emperor Claudius, under Agrippina's machinations, was persuaded that Statilius Taurus was competing to outdo the emperor for the people's affection. The grounds and house were confiscated and shortly after the old emperor's death they were discreetly handed over to Epaphroditus. A reward which had garnered much palace speculation.

"Aphrodite is coming tonight," Calvia informed the empress in an attempt to distract her mind from her family's misfortune.

"So it is a sophisticated soirée. I thought you were joking."

It was well known that Epaphroditus kept his wife away from the palace social scene. If Aphrodite were attending, it truly must be a dull, sensible affair, Calvia feared.

"I have a lovely gown for you, Empress. Very modest, elegant. It'll suit you perfectly."

"What's the *thing* doing?" asked Statilia, meaning Sporus.

"Hidden away until later."

"When it will crawl out of its lair and infect my husband, no doubt."

"Rather it than you."

"Too true," agreed the empress.

That was the difference between Poppaea and Statilia, thought Calvia. Poppaea had fought for her position, had tried every art to secure Nero. She hungered after power and hung onto it with talons.

She would never have spoken so harshly of her husband, for she knew that without him she was merely insignificant. In contrast Nero had personally sought out Statilia as possessing the correct qualities for his third wife: namely she was high-born, young, and presumably fertile.

That she was intelligent need not be a disadvantage. Her family unable to refuse such an offer, Statilia found herself fulfilling a role she hadn't asked for and definitely didn't want.

"Which Praetorian prefect is on duty?" asked Statilia.

"On duty would be overstating it but Tigellinus is attending the latter part of the evening."

"Shame," sighed the empress. "I was attending a function last nones and I could not help but notice what fine calves Nymphidius Sabinus possesses."

Calvia lifted her eyebrows and shifted in the water, splashing the empress. "Really?" she exclaimed. "You surely cannot want to go there?"

"Why not? Of all the temptations on offer ... I think," and here she lowered her voice, keeping an eye on the immobile Mina, "it's that uprightness of his. I want to bend him, corrupt him. Do you think he's a virgin?"

The reply was instant. "No."

Calvia Crispinilla, mistress of the wardrobe, had lived an interesting life, which may have included a past dalliance with a certain square-jawed man in possession of a fine pair of calves. She was not going to admit to such youthful indiscretions, however. So she smiled enigmatically and told her companion, "I would not waste a fine gown on him, Statilia my dear."

The empress absorbed this good advice and shouted out, "You girl. My towel!"

Which kicked Mina into action.

Pompeia was out straight after dawn to visit her elder sister to discuss *the* outfit. Her attempt to extract information from Philo regarding the dress code had not been terribly helpful, Philo divulging only that it was not formal enough for togas.

Pompeia Major was surrounded by an assortment of children and grandchildren, who most unhelpfully all seemed to be hungry at exactly the same moment. She was dishing out bowls, assisted by her middle daughter Phibia, when her sister burst into the crowded space clearly in some sort of a tizz.

"Sister, what is it?"

"Teretia's going with Philo to a party at the palace tonight and the emperor is going to be there," Pompeia Minor said very, very quickly.

"Jupiter Greatest and Good," her sister declared. "What's she going to wear?"

"Exactly, sister, exactly."

Pompeia Major grabbed a miscellaneous son and told him to assist his sister, before making a hurried exit with her younger sister.

"I thought he was one of those clerks. I knew he was salaried, sister, and well placed but I had no idea."

They had escaped what Pompeia Major called "the brood" and settled themselves down at a local cookshop. Pompeia

Minor lowered her voice, somewhat pointlessly since they were the only customers. "The emperor's private secretary's secretary."

"Fancy," mouthed Pompeia Major, glancing up to check her surroundings before lowering her voice and saying, "The emperor's private secretary's secretary lodging with my sister," and then, sensing an incongruity, "I don't mean to offend, sister, but surely they pay well at the palace and if this young man is so highly placed, I do wonder why he lodges on the Viminal. No offence to you, sister, for your home is lovely. Teretius has done well for you there."

He certainly had compared to Pompeia Major's husband Phibius, a useless sot of a man who, after knocking her up nine times and knocking her about many more, wandered drunkenly into the road one night and was promptly knocked down by a wagon cart.

"I would have thought a man of that standing would find rooms on the Esquiline, maybe even the Palatine. That's where their sort live."

"No offence taken. I have been thinking the same thing. He is very prompt with the rent, so there's no trouble there." A thought struck Pompeia Minor: "Sister, you don't think it's because of Teretia?"

Being close siblings, Pompeia Major picked up the thread instantly. "He fell in love with her," she stated, confident in her argument. "Because who wouldn't fall in love with your Teretia. She is lovely. And the only way he could get close to her was to take your spare room. You said he was shy."

"Very shy. He barely dares speak."

"He wouldn't dare approach her on the street like some local lad."

She loaded the "local" with contempt; both sisters held a low opinion of the neighbourhood boys.

"So he lodges with you so he can get to know the object of his love slowly. Feel more comfortable with her and when he is at ease and sure of her affections towards him, he will make his move."

"That does make sense."

"Of course it does, sister. It's a fact, that's why."

"I wonder when he will make his move?" murmured Pompeia Minor, who was yet to notice any great signs of love in Philo.

Perhaps where he was from they did things differently. Pompeia's knowledge of palace ways was scant. Her only information came direct from her lodger.

The two Pompeias turned their attention to the matter of *the* outfit.

"What sort of party is it? It's not one of those orgies?"

"No, of course not," protested Pompeia Minor. "It is a small gathering of senators and palace staff," she said, quoting Philo.

Pompeia Major considered. "Nothing flashy. Teretia is enough of a beauty to carry off a simple garment."

"But elegant."

"Oh, definitely elegant. I have that fabulous necklace that Phibius' mother gave me."

"The gold and glass one?"

"That's the one. Now what is Teretia's best colour?"

"Blue," said the proud mother without delay. "To match her eyes."

"Perfect for the necklace then, the beads are blue."

Some hours of discussion later, they hit the dressmakers.

While the sisters were out, Teretia had been holed up in her room all morning with strict instructions not to lift anything in case she broke a nail. Not to cook anything in case of an accidental burn, and not to leave their home, because all kinds of terrible things on the Viminal streets could ruin her complexion.

149

Left with little entertainment Teretia sat on the edge of her bed in perfect deportment, as instructed, and indulged in a series of increasingly romantic daydreams all concerning her parents' lodger. These had the benefit of keeping her mind occupied from the terrors that gnawed at her.

Teretia knew only the life of the Viminal Hill, and although her parents had instilled in her a sense that she was destined for higher things, this was to be her first entry into such society. She was increasingly nervous that she would make an error.

She knew fine ladies ate reclined on couches but whenever she had tried this it gave her terrible indigestion of a noisy sort. What did fine ladies talk about? How would Teretia converse with them, she who had never been to a party before? What if they looked down on her? What if they wouldn't talk to her at all? She felt an overwhelming need to chew at her nails as her worries bubbled inside.

Hearing the door to the apartment bang, Teretia popped her head round the door. It was her father. His expression melted on seeing her distress.

"Teretia darling, what is it?" He held open his arms and his daughter ran into them, bursting into loud sobs on his shoulder.

He smoothed her hair gently. "Don't upset yourself, love. What is it?"

"I don't want to go to the party," she wailed.

"Hey, hey. What is this all about? You were all excited last night. What's brought this on?"

Sitting her down gently, he took her soft hands in his.

"Oh, father, I'm going to muck it up."

"Muck what up?"

"Muck up the party. I won't know what to say and everyone will think I'm, I'm … stupid. And they'll have better dresses than me and they'll think I'm common and a stupid pleb."

Her father hugged her close. "Now then young lady, you are being very silly. Your mother is out getting you a dress right now and you know that she will do you right. Besides, sweetheart, Philo is going to be there. He'll make sure you're alright."

Teretia looked up at her father with hope. "Really?"

"Of course. He'll introduce you to the right people. He's an important man at the palace. He'll see you right. He's a good man that Philo."

The good man from the palace arrived home to find the apartment bursting with people. Surprised, he weaved his way past Phibia and an assortment of Teretia's relatives, hanging onto his satchel, trying to avoid physical contact.

"Philo, my son," called Teretius, who had found a quiet corner away from the gaggle of women to nurse an amphora of wine. He tipped a beaker towards Philo as an invitation.

"Who are all these people?" Philo asked, placing himself on a wooden stool.

"That's my sister-in-law and her eldest son is the curly-haired moppet beside her. That's my brother Gaius, he's a silversmith, and his wife and their children."

Philo was fascinated. "And the little ones?" he asked, pointing to a trio of boys who were bombing round legs in some complicated game of chase.

"Two belong to my cousin Cornelia. The mischievous looking one with the gappy teeth is my great-nephew Milo."

He handed Philo a drink. "You have much family, Philo?"

Philo stared into the bottom of his beaker and gave a small shrug.

"Are your parents still living?" Teretius gently persisted.

It was a question Philo was unsure how to answer, bringing up all kinds of issues such as sex selections and breeding programmes that were never discussed outside the slave complex.

Teretius took his quiescence as grief and he patted him gently on the shoulder in a supportive gesture, changing the subject from one which was obviously very painful to his lodger.

"Teretia is looking forward to this party. She's been giddy all afternoon."

He looked around and then lowered his voice so that Philo had to lean forward to hear.

"You're a good lad, Philo, I know that. Respectable."

Another pat on the arm.

"But you hear these stories, about the emperor and the like."

Philo shifted slightly under his gaze.

"We're men of the world," continued Teretius, "but Teretia, she's very young, innocent. I would hate her to be exposed to any dubious palace elements."

Philo shook his head quickly, "No, no, of course not."

"I hope that you will take care of her." The voice was friendly, however the intent was clear.

"It is really not that sort of evening."

Teretius being a man of the world couldn't resist asking, after a quick scan of the room reassured him his wife was not present: "Have you ever, erm, attended that sort of evening?"

Philo squirmed under his landlord's interested gaze.

"F-f-for work," he stammered.

He would have felt even more uncomfortable if Teretius had managed to ask his next question, which was luckily deflected by Pompeia rushing in and declaring, "Here she comes!"

The collective aunts, great-aunts, cousins, and nieces took a joint intake of breath. The male relatives were nudged to attention. A girl entered the kitchen and it took Philo a moment to recognise that it was Teretia. Her blonde hair was teased into a crown that arched in plaits across her head, ringlets pulled out onto the nape of her neck. It was very clearly based on a bust of Poppaea. The make-up was not as extreme as the late empress; Teretia's eyes were left naked with just a faint blush on her cheeks and lips. She wore a necklace of interlocking gold chains interspersed with blue beads and a gown of the lightest blue that clung tastefully to every delicious curve Teretia possessed. The effect was startling. The aunts let forth a long, "Oooh." Teretia fiddled nervously with the choker, shy from all the attention.

Philo, sipping at his wine, became aware that all eyes seemed to have switched to him. There was an expectant silence as the family willed him to say the appropriate words.

"Erm," he cleared his throat before saying quietly, "You look very, erm, nice."

Though not quite the proclamation that was desired, it was judged adequate and Philo found himself at the centre of some well-meaning elbow nudges, a series of people telling him he was "one lucky fellow", and the recipient of a hearty slap on the back from Uncle Gnaeus, which, still tender from Straton's ministrations, almost caused him to pass out.

TWENTY-ONE

Calvia had done a good job, Epaphroditus had to admit; the courtyard looked wonderful. With the ferns and trees that had been brought in, the guests were transported to a forest glen, the gently bubbling fountain in the centre, the couches decorated with crawling ivy, the wine waiters in flower garlands.

"The entertainment," began Calvia. "Flute girls will play through the meal dressed as nymphs."

Epaphroditus raised an eyebrow.

"Don't worry," she snapped. "They will be suspiciously well-dressed nymphs. There will be a short display of leopards. Muscus has been working very hard on this and I have to say that it is worth seeing. The emperor is insisting on some sort of recital."

The secretary groaned.

"I have managed to talk him down from a full performance of one of his own compositions to a short piece on the new water organ."

"Supreme diplomacy," he congratulated her.

"We will wheel it out here," she pointed to the fountain, "in between the final two courses."

"The piece?"

"No idea. All organ tunes sound the same to me. I did request no vocal accompaniment stressing that it would ruin the woodland illusion but that I cannot guarantee."

"Don't worry, I shall arrange for someone to leap up the moment he opens his mouth and cry that, 'Caesar's voice will melt my heart, I cannot endure its final notes without weeping, and I fear I shall dampen the mood by such a show of emotion.' Some mush like that. And afterwards?"

"Why are you thinking of attending, Epaphroditus?"

The secretary gave her a narrow look as Aphrodite returned from inspecting the rural idyll and linked onto his arm.

"It is looking lovely, Calvia," she said. "The butterflies are a masterstroke."

"Hopefully they shouldn't land on the food. Pretty but disease-ridden, so my sources tell me."

"Oh, what a shame," responded Aphrodite.

She was a tall woman, slightly overhanging her husband and so straight of poise she resembled an elegant column. Now in her forties, she could easily pass for ten years younger, a tiny curve to her stomach the only sign of the children she had born. Statilia and Calvia were correct, for there was a similarity between her and Mina's features. However, Aphrodite radiated refinement in a way that Mina did not. She had enjoyed a decade of freedom and it had polished her.

"You are looking well. We haven't seen you at an event for a while, Aphrodite my dear."

"The more recent ones have not been to my taste, shall we say."

As an insult, it was delivered with style.

Calvia gave a tight-lipped smile and, unafraid to deliver a low blow, replied, "My remits are certainly challenging. But I gain the greatest satisfaction in seeing my guests' enjoyment. The Saturnalia festivities were a particular success. I won't bore you with the details; no doubt you've heard it all from your husband, though you yourself were indisposed."

She was rewarded by the venomous look Aphrodite threw at her husband, who protested, "I didn't go. I swear I didn't go."

Calvia glided away, suppressing her desire to cackle and savouring her triumph, nodding with approval at two slaves who were meticulously winding ivy across a wooden arbour.

She was heading to berate the butterfly keeper regarding his singularly white creatures when she had clearly stated she wanted a rainbow of colours, when a damp cloak of gloom spread across her shoulders. Such a sudden loss of spirit could only have one cause.

"Sabinus," she said to the prefect, who lurked in the shadows by the entrance to the palace. "I did not think you were on duty tonight. But of course you are never off duty are you?" she sighed. "Do you parade in your sleep? Shout commands? Have erotic dreams about your guards? All those hard thighs and tight calves?"

He didn't respond, but then she never expected him to. Sabinus didn't do small talk.

"If you have come for the party—"

"I have not," he interrupted briskly as if such social enjoyment were beneath him, "I have come to check on the security arrangements."

"Shame," commented Calvia. Then, gazing over to where Aphrodite and Epaphroditus were kicking into the elaborate hand gestures that indicated the onset of a row, she decided she may as well enjoy herself with the prefect too.

"Of course the premier entertainment comes when the sun sets. I have some wonderful performers arranged. Erotica is proving to be most supple. She enacts a move that I have rarely seen so well done. She is able to simultaneously climax five men by use of her feet, hands, and various orifices. They tell me that the sensation of curved toes on the penis is far more stimulating than mere fingers and that the sight of a woman so well

157

used by so many men has been known to cause spontaneous ejaculations among the audience."

If Praxiteles, that celebrity of sculpture, had ever wished to carve a study in disgust, he could not have found a better model than Sabinus at that precise moment. He looked like he had swallowed a particularly tough piece of excrement.

This amused Calvia immensely and, unable to resist, she threw in her final barb. "An interesting sexual position. We call it the Nymphidia after its inspired creator."

Calvia watched the veins in his arms tense and bulge. His jaw stiffening as a flash of red worked its way up from his neck. He was so prickly, so sensitive, so easy to wound.

"You are a filthy whore," he spat between his teeth.

Calvia smiled. "I know I am. A filthy, disgusting, degenerate whore who uses her depraved mind to think up disgusting practices for the emperor to experiment with. It pays extraordinarily well."

"I despise you."

"I should hope so. I have worked very hard to make it the case. I couldn't bear to have you slobbering affection all over me again. It was tedious enough the first time round." She offered him a sickly smile. "But I must go, my dear Gaius. I have a flock of dull-coloured butterflies to unleash."

She waggled her fingers at him in a cheery wave. "Do say hello to your lovely mother for me. Such a shame she retired. I have never met a more inventive whore. The things she could do to a man." She raised her eyebrows right up her forehead. "Such calibre!"

Sabinus glowered at her, he radiated, he near burst into flames. He clenched his jaw shut so tight it dislodged a tooth. Calvia grinned. "Till later, my dear."

He stood still, the only movement the clenching and unclenching of his fists as he struggled with his composure. He was a man of reason, a man of sense. He would not lower himself to Nero-style hysterics. Let that bitch think she had bettered him. Tomorrow their time would be at an end and Calvia Crispinilla, that disgusting mistress of the wardrobe, would awake to find a team of his guards outside her bedchamber.

That thought cheered him, causing a thin smile to break out. He glanced around at the developing party. The slaves rushing back and forth with plates, Epaphroditus arguing with his wife. They were dead. They were all dead. Cleaned away for the new era. The era of Galba and of Nymphidius Sabinus.

TWENTY-TWO

"Dite, please," Epaphroditus pleaded, using her pet name and massaging her wrist gently with his thumb.

Snatching her hand back she stressed through gritted teeth, "You know how I feel about orgies."

He dared to reach up, tucking a strand of hair behind her ear. "I didn't go, Dite. She's stirring."

"I know what goes on at those orgies. The whole empire knows what goes on. If you were involved in any of that—"

"I wasn't there. Honestly, I wasn't."

She was too angry to look at him so he took careful hold of her arms and pulled her towards him. After a brief resistance she gave in and leaned her head against his. Using a thumb he caressed the back of her neck and told her in a voice meant for her alone, "I wasn't there. I didn't go. You know me and you know I wouldn't do that to you."

Frankly, he would have lifted her up, carried her into Calvia's arranged foliage and made gentle love to her the way she liked, if he'd the time. As it was, he had mere seconds to achieve domestic harmony before the guests started to arrive.

"Dite, don't let her ruin your evening. She's a spiteful cow and she is trying to make trouble. I promise you on the lives of our children that I wasn't there. You can ask Philo when he arrives, we were working late together."

Aphrodite raised her superior chin and appraised her husband. He looked at her seriously, raised her hand to his lips and kissed it tenderly. She was mollified but not totally appeased, warning him, "If I find out you're lying …"

"Epaphroditus, chum!" cried an exuberant Tigellinus, drink already in hand. "It's amazing isn't it? I keep expecting some heathen savage to burst out of the trees."

He took a large sip of his oversized goblet and continued thoughtfully, "Sort of thing Calvia might have lined up for later I suppose but with some dusky savage woman, grass skirt and bare knockers ready to be wrestled to the floor and … Hello, is this your wife?"

"Claudia Aphrodite, Ofonius Tigellinus. Tigellinus, my wife Aphrodite."

"Charmed," said Tigellinus attempting a polite smile but failing to stop his eyes wandering down her frame. Epaphroditus stepped in front of her, obscuring his view.

"I thought you weren't coming."

"Why would you think that?" slurred the prefect.

"Because you weren't invited."

"Wasn't I? I go to everything, it's my thing. Besides, I'm the pre-, pre-, pre-, the soldier thing. I look after the emperor."

Some help you'd be in an actual battle, thought Epaphroditus as Tigellinus propped himself against a tree and engaged Aphrodite in conversation. Possessed of a similar palace pedigree to her husband, she was more than capable of dealing with Tigellinus' crude attempts at charm and listened to his drunken ramblings with patience.

"Well, I think you are right. It is a shocker that my husband failed to invite you. I find that he has many failings."

She shot Epaphroditus a look that informed him that their previous discussion was merely paused.

It was not an auspicious start to the evening.

There were further troubles to come. A good third of the guests invited failing to show, sending slaves with their apologies. Not a good sign. It had once been the case that nobody dared turn down a palace invitation, explaining why so many well-bred and decent citizens were to be found at the more disreputable and unpleasant orgies. They should be rushing to show how happy they were that Vindex was dead. Epaphroditus did not understand their reticence. Surely they knew attendance was compulsory? Still, he could deal with such disloyalty tomorrow.

He handed Tigellinus a refill of his goblet, figuring he could move him along from rowdy drunk to comatose before he caused any trouble.

"Aaaphrodite. Such a pretty name. Tell me, Aaaphrodite, how did you come to marry that miserly paper pusher? When there are so many, many more worthy men to be found."

"Charmed, I'm sure," said Epaphroditus handing his wife a drink.

Tigellinus leaned on his shoulder and told him, "No offence, chum. No offence at all. But you have to say, it is a question. It's definitely a question …" Tigellinus' head turned and then his mouth dropped open, turning to Epaphroditus with some urgency. "Tell me that piece is part of the entertainment."

Epaphroditus followed the direction of the prefect's somewhat unsteady gaze to see a dapper Philo in a blue tunic and a nervous-looking Teretia staring at her surroundings with wonder, clinging tightly to her escort's arm.

"Oh my word! Is that Teretia?" Aphrodite asked, her jaw dropping in similar fashion to the prefect's.

Epaphroditus smiled, "It is indeed. Come say hello."

And then when Tigellinus straightened himself up, they both cried horrified, "No, not you!"

Epaphroditus grabbed a serving girl by the hem of her tunic, hissing in her ear "Distract him. Discreetly," pushing her towards Tigellinus.

The slave girl proved fully up for the task and it took a mere flash of a nipple for her to pull in the prefect's attention. He followed her, tongue hanging out as she gestured him over to the foliage with an enticing hair flick.

"Philo," smiled Aphrodite, greeting him with a kiss on each cheek and giving him a quick hug, for she was exceptionally fond of him. Philo flushed slightly and gave her a shy smile. Aphrodite demanded to be introduced to, "this lovely girl."

Teretia was mute as the elegant woman grasped her hands and told her how pleased she was to meet her. The man with her, whom she recognised as Philo's boss, the emperor's private secretary she reminded herself, smiled at her politely and asked her if she wanted refreshments. She opened her mouth to speak and then closed it again as she realised she did not know if she wanted a drink and then she couldn't think of anything to say to these nice people.

Flustered, she fiddled with her necklace, her face colouring. She was going to make a fool of herself, she just knew it, she shouldn't have come, she wasn't meant for this life. She was from the Viminal.

A passing slave displayed a silver platter of morsels. Aphrodite picked up a honey cake and told Teretia. "Try one of these, they are very tasty."

The slave stood patiently as Teretia dithered, finally picking up a cake and nibbling a corner.

"Nice, yes?" Aphrodite asked.

"It is sweet."

Philo, looking around said to Epaphroditus, "There are not enough couches."

"There have been cancellations. Phillipius and Senex for starters. Not good. Not good at all."

Aphrodite gave a large sigh. "Oh dear. Teretia, I think they are going to talk work, why don't we go sit down and leave them to it?"

Teretia threw a desperate look at Philo. She really didn't want to be parted from him, he was her anchor in this strange world. Philo, already into a full discussion on the implications of Phillipius' and Senex's absence, missed Teretia's silent plea altogether. Aphrodite gently led her to a couch where they sat down, Teretia upright, her hands nervously playing on her lap as she peered over to Philo.

She really was the sweetest thing and they made a very cute couple. However, Aphrodite was troubled by Philo's nonchalant attitude towards his guest. It was clear that he hadn't explained to her anything about the evening or given her any introduction into how she should behave, which Aphrodite found shocking.

After putting the girl at her ease by some gentle questioning about her gown and how she had got her hair to sit in that amazing style—Aphrodite confessing her own coiffure was a wig and lifting it a little to prove it, causing a giggle to escape from Teretia—she brought up some important housekeeping matters.

"They will start serving dinner shortly. Everyone will recline, even us women, for the palace maintains a modern style of dining. The slaves will bring it round and you just help yourself. Another slave will stand with a water bowl so you can clean your fingers whenever you need to. If you are puzzled by any of the food, just ask me."

If this sounded like an instruction manual, it was kindly delivered and relieved Teretia of many of her fears.

"And when the emperor and empress arrive," continued Aphrodite, "you must not look at them directly, you must cast your eyes downwards. If they should address you, you can raise your eyes but be respectful."

"Of course," agreed Teretia almost overcome by the thought that the emperor might address her personally.

Aphrodite gave her arm a friendly squeeze, telling her, "You'll be fine. I am sure you will have a wonderful evening."

Twisting her hand, looking at the butterfly that had landed there, she said to Aphrodite, "Oh, it is wonderful already."

TWENTY-THREE

The emperor, regally dressed in purple tunic and toga, a laurel wreath balanced on his limp curls, chewed at a nail.

Lysander slid in. "They are ready for you, Caesar."

"I'm not going," replied the emperor.

This flummoxed Lysander since it fell outside his job remit of general announcements. So he repeated with a little more emphasis this time round, "They are ready for you, Caesar."

"I said, I'm not going."

Lysander made panicked eye contact with Juba who let loose a lopsided grin and shrugged. Lysander slid out again and wondered what he should do. Perhaps he could wait a few minutes and then make his announcement again? The emperor might have changed his mind, not implausible, for Nero was an indecisive sort, which was why he had a whole army of advisors telling him what he should do.

Lysander waited, acutely aware that there were a great many people outside in the courtyard depending on him. He waited as long as he could bear before sliding in again.

He opened his mouth to speak but making eye contact with Juba again, the body slave slowly shook his head before mouthing "No" at him. The emperor, still playing with his fingers, did not move his gaze from the floor and did not look as if he were intent on going anywhere.

Epaphroditus was rather enjoying the decently dressed flute girls when a slave sidled up to him and discreetly whispered in his ear. Whatever was said, it was not pleasant, for his features dropped and he gave an audible sigh before getting to his feet. Philo made to move but Epaphroditus held up a hand, "No, you stay, enjoy the show."

He kissed Aphrodite on the cheek.

"Trouble?" she asked.

"Let us hope not," he replied, straightening up and following the slave into the palace.

Lysander jumped upon the secretary. "He says he's not coming."

And then he confessed, because Epaphroditus was the sort of man who inspired confidences, "I didn't know what to do."

He was patted reassuringly on the shoulder. "You did well Lysander. Go explain to the empress that she will no longer be required tonight. But don't explain why. Let us define it as 'technical difficulties'."

Lysander nodded, pleased to have an order to follow and shot off to obey.

"Caesar," Epaphroditus addressed the emperor quietly. "Your guests are waiting for you."

The emperor did not look up. "They are not my guests. They wish me ill. They wish me dead."

"Not so, Caesar," smoothed the secretary.

Nero raised his head. He wore an amused smile, its line bitter.

"I hear that Galba is calling himself emperor and that the western legions have declared for him. I have expected you to inform me of this all day. Yet you have not. No doubt it is all part of some wily slave scheme of yours."

Epaphroditus didn't much like being referred to as a wily slave, but he kept his poise.

Nero was not done though. "Are you hoping to throw your lot in with Galba? Is that it, Epaphroditus? You have a right to be worried: if I fall, you come tumbling down with me. No doubt you remember the fates of Narcissus and Pallas, my stepfather's freedmen. Who can blame you for wanting to avoid that? I certainly don't. I don't blame you at all," he spat, his temper rising.

"Caesar, I am your loyal ally as ever," protested Epaphroditus when he could get a word in.

"Loyal? Loyal? You talk to me of loyalty? When you have lied and lied to your emperor."

Nero was on his feet now, yelling. "Oh, everything's fine, Caesar, all under control, Caesar. The legions have declared for Galba! They are marching here right now!" His voice broke. "Marching here to murder me!" He sunk back into the chair before collapsing into tears.

Epaphroditus bent down and knelt before Nero, looking up at his wet face. "Caesar," he said gently. "Vindex is defeated. Galba's mad venture will crumble before him. I am loyal to you as ever and I am not alone. The eastern legions are at your disposal and there are plenty of people out there right now who want to see their emperor. You need to be strong, Caesar."

"I am not going out there," sniffed Nero.

"Just a show of face, Caesar."

"Show of face? How can I show this face?"

He looked straight at his secretary who had to admit it didn't look good, red puffy eyes and a trembling upper lip. He made a daring suggestion and prayed to Jupiter, Juno, Apollo and the whole damn pantheon of gods that he could pull it off.

"Perhaps it would help Caesar, calm Caesar, if Poppaea accompanied him tonight?"

Statilia threw the shoe long and hard, and straight at Lysander's head. It hit him smack on the forehead, knocking him backwards.

"My FAMILY are out there!" she screeched. "And you are telling me that I am no longer required!? Is that what you are telling me, boy?"

Lysander, rubbing between his eyes, repeated the message that Epaphroditus had given him. "Empress your presence is no longer required tonight. Apologies."

"Tell me, boy. Why exactly am I not required?"

The hapless Lysander shook his head. "I do not know Your Imperial Majesty."

Statilia strode across the room. "Because *it* will be there?" she suggested. "That creature playing empress on the arm of *my* husband in front of *my family* and *their* friends. Is that it, boy?"

"Technical difficulties, Your Imperial Majesty."

"Technical difficulties!? TECHNICAL DIFFICULTIES!"

Statilia was furious. She was a proud woman projecting a high level of dignity and class. High-born, she accepted that infidelity was a part of marriage. Men had their needs and it could be a relief to a wife that she need not fulfil them all. She could stomach that her husband's ardour was aroused by a eunuch, for they were pathetic creatures and what else could they do but serve sexually. She could even tolerate *its* presence at internal events.

But for it to be introduced as Nero's wife to a party of her class and her own family while she was the one hidden away, was a humiliation too far.

"You tell Epaphroditus", she instructed Lysander, "that I have spent many hours preparing for this party and that I shall be attending."

She turned to one of her attendants with a smile. "Go fetch towel girl. I want her assisting me tonight."

Philo was halfway down the corridor when he realised he was being followed, alerted by a clipping trot behind him. He turned to see Teretia lifting up her skirts and attempting to keep up with him. Seeing him halted, she upped the pace.

They had been reclined on couches, Aphrodite having whispered some useful tips for aiding digestion to Teretia, listening to the flute girls play a sprightly tune. Aphrodite having been called away by an acquaintance, Teretia and Philo were left alone. She'd been building the necessary courage to lean over and talk to Philo, when a slave knelt in front of him and delivered a message of evident importance, since he shot up instantly. Teretia, terrified of being left alone in such unfamiliar surroundings had simply followed him.

Philo, oblivious to the social faux pas and outright cruelty of abandoning his date so abruptly, wondered what to do with her. She would never be able to find her way back to the party alone through the complex palace layout and there was no time to take her back. His only option, therefore, was to take her with him to fetch Sporus. He slowed his pace for her, she twittering alongside him happy enough, though he was not paying much attention, plagued as he was by two particular thoughts. First, he was acutely aware that Sporus, though only a slave, had an annoying habit of doing the absolute opposite of what you asked and, for some reason he didn't fully understand, he didn't want to look foolish in front of Teretia.

Second, he had a vague memory of promising his landlord that he would not expose Teretia to anything that might dent her innocence. Philo doubted Teretius would be amused if he knew that he had introduced his daughter to the emperor's transvestite eunuch lover.

Sat on the floor, dressed only in a loin cloth and tiara was Sporus. It had been a deeply frustrating night. Annoyed with being excluded from the festivities, he trounced off to moan to

171

Alex only to find Alex was nowhere to be found. Which was most irritating, for Alex's role in their friendship was to be readily available whenever Sporus was depressed, angry, gleeful, or exuberant. This flagrant disregard of the known rules was most aggravating.

So he sloped back with nothing to do, nowhere to go, and no one to talk to, for even Mina was otherwise occupied with the empress. Devoid of his usual entertainments Sporus resorted to painting his toenails, lining up in rows a series of little bottles to test in front of him.

He was holding his leg out, foot pointing upwards, considering whether green was really his colour, when he was rudely interrupted.

"Get up, you are needed," Philo ordered him.

The eunuch was astonished. Philo, quiet timid little Philo had just near commanded him in a most ungracious manner.

Lowering his leg he jiggled his toes. "What do you think? I've got a different colour on each toe. I am hoping to discover my definitive shade."

"Calvia is on her way," Philo stated sternly. "You will get ready."

Sporus was determined to do nothing of the sort, insulted as he was by Philo's attitude. Of course when Calvia got there she would drag him up by his hair and whack him with the tongs. But until then, he was not going to be pushed about.

"Juno, Philo, what's got into you?" he asked, opening another tiny bottle and considering the glint on the brush. "I am not decided on green. I think it makes my toes look gangrenous. Not an attractive look."

The words slipped out of Teretia before she could stop them. Bewildered by Sporus' high voice, flat chest, and general alien appearance, she enquired wide-eyed, "What are you?"

Sporus was not offended, for he felt himself unique, and noticing Teretia for the first time he was transfixed. He allowed her his most beguiling smile.

"I am a Sporus," he told her. "But pray, what are you, sweet creature?"

She giggled. Philo felt himself bristle. "Just get up Sporus."

Looking from Teretia to Philo and then back again, Sporus gawped. Gods! Was this the girlfriend? Surely not? Mina had said she was a stunner but that description did not do her justice. She was precious.

Testing his theory, he danced to his feet and taking Teretia's delicate hand gave it a cheeky flick of his tongue. The expression on Philo's face was proof enough.

"I am simply delighted to meet you," he gushed. "And I apologise for my poor attire. Philo will confirm that I am usually so much more clothed."

"I like your crown," said Teretia.

Sporus removed the tiara and handed it to her. "Keep it if you like. I have so many."

Teretia, tiara in hand looked at Philo for permission. Seeing no answer, "I cannot accept it," she told Sporus, handing it back. "Really I can't."

"Oh, let her keep it," cried Sporus. "If you are going to bring her to these receptions she's going to need a tiara." Switching his attention to Teretia he told her conspiratorially, "Everyone *needs* a tiara."

Teretia blessed him with such a sweet smile that Sporus decided to add it to his own repertoire.

"Don't be mean, Philo. It doesn't suit." He sat on a couch cross-legged and invited Teretia to sit beside him.

Finely tuned to any slight discomfort that he might take advantage of, Sporus told the scribe, "Now don't blush, dear. I'm just offering the lady a seat. I am only being polite. I am not going to wheedle all your secrets out of her and I certainly wouldn't be indiscreet enough to let slip anything regarding pink roses."

It passed Teretia by completely, distracted as she was by the gorgeous bejewelled diadem that she inexplicably now owned.

173

Philo, however, recognised pink roses to be a veiled reference to the time Mina had appeared in his office with a bunch of said flowers for the vase that sat on the far shelf.

He had, he felt, politely helped her get the vase down to install the bouquet. She had beamed a thank you at him and then, fixing her eyes determinedly on his, unclasped her dress and let it fall to her ankles. Mistaking his stupefaction for hesitancy, she had proceeded to fling herself at him, forcing him into a corner and delivering the kind of passionate kiss that would have turned most men's knees weak.

He had thought that nobody knew of that incident, assuming that Mina was as embarrassed as he was, especially since she had taken up with Epaphroditus so quickly afterwards. Obviously not, as Sporus waggled his eyebrows above Teretia's head, raising his little finger stiffly and then letting it droop. A gesture that brought back that moment in all its mortification.

If Sporus knew, everyone knew. Philo cringed inwardly and replayed every word spoken to him in the last few months for innuendos or puns. He wished he could think of some witty retort. Instead he resorted to peevishness. "If you don't want to attend, I suppose Statilia Messalina could become available."

Sporus leapt to his feet. "That bitch!" he swore.

Teretia gave a small gasp at this sudden change in demeanour.

"I apologise wholeheartedly for that language. I hope that I have not offended your delicate sensibilities," Sporus offered.

Teretia, who though shielded by her parents, had nonetheless grown up on the Viminal, told her new friend, "Not at all. Is she really a bitch? The empress?"

Sporus rolled his eyes. "The stories I could tell. But I won't, for I am discreet and one does not wish to speak ill of a lady. No matter how evil a cow she may be."

This was the mere starting point for a whole series of imprudent confidences which would have flowed from Sporus had not Calvia swept in with a gaggle of assistants and a pair of tongs clasped decisively in her hand.

"Do not fuck me about," she warned Sporus, waggling the tongs at him. "I have no time at all but they expect miracles. So I provide." She clicked her fingers and two assistants made to pin Sporus down.

"We should go," Philo suggested to Teretia.

Seeing her new friend pinned to the bed as an assistant approached with a bowl of sizzling walnut shells, she exclaimed, "Oh, Philo, they're going to torture the Sporus. Stop them Philo. I couldn't bear …"

Her eyes filled with tears, hands clenched in front of her mouth in distress.

Sporus, hearing the commotion raised his head and told her cheerfully, "Don't upset yourself, sweetie. I am fine. It is just my beauty regime. It may be torturous but it is worth it. Believe me."

And when she maintained her anguished expression, he shouted out to Philo, "Give her a hug for Jupiter's sake, man."

An awkward Philo froze. Calvia, passing by, gave a heavy sigh, took hold of his arm and physically draped it across Teretia's shoulders, who immediately folded into him for comfort.

Laughing, Sporus let his head fall back. Calvia loomed over him with an eyelash curler.

"You'd better arrange to be present when they screw, otherwise it'll never happen."

"It'll never happen with that one, period," stated Calvia, moving in and holding Sporus' eye open.

"They're for his legs; to take the hair off," Philo explained as they made their way back to the party.

Teretia was maintaining the attachment and though his arm ached terribly, he wasn't sure whether he should release her or not. She didn't seem as if she wanted releasing, huddled into him, her head slightly resting on his shoulder. Though she was a little calmer, he could feel her small body convulsing slightly as if repressing some great emotion.

"Really he's fine. You'll see later when he escorts the emperor. Are you alright to go back? I could get the litter to take you home."

Teretia raised her head. "No, no," she said hurriedly. "I'm fine, honestly. I am just being silly."

"You weren't to know," consoled Philo, for she looked so unhappy.

She stopped and turned to face him, his arm dropping from her shoulder. Holding onto his hand she told him, "You've been so kind to me. And it's been such a wonderful evening." She did not tell him about her churning stomach and terrible anxiety.

She was building up to a romantic conclusion, readying herself to step on her toes and kiss him, when Philo ruined the moment by commenting. "It's not over yet. We haven't had the leopards."

TWENTY-FOUR

Lysander, head pounding from Statilia's horribly accurate shoe attack, had taken all he could for one night and legged it. Epaphroditus, therefore, had no idea that Statilia was set on attending until there was a burst of trumpet and she made her grand entrance. He immediately began a scan of the area for the announcer, whom he determined was most deserving to be Stratoned.

As if that were not enough to keep him occupied, he spotted Mina standing behind Statilia, who shot him an alluring, melting gaze. Which would have been great and certainly arousing had his wife not been standing next to him at the time.

Aphrodite was an intelligent woman, and even if she had not caught Mina's suggestive eyes, the quick flash of panic that ran across her husband's countenance would have alerted her. He smoothed it away and offered her the smile he utilised whenever he was about to suggest something he knew she would object to.

"Darling, I need you to head off Sporus. If the two empresses were to meet ..." He pursed his lips to indicate the severity of the situation.

Statilia was off in party mode, genially greeting her guests, Mina walking behind her, holding the precious serviette, transmitting to Epaphroditus the eye signals she employed when they were in public to suggest a liaison.

Epaphroditus gently turned Aphrodite so that her back was facing the empress.

"It is of the utmost importance," he insisted.

"I am not Philo, you cannot order me around."

"If Philo were here, of course I would ask him. But time is of the essence, Dite. Sporus and the emperor could be on their way now. It is a very delicate political situation."

"In which case, why don't you head off the emperor? That is your job after all."

She glared at him, daring him to continue his lies. They had for many years instituted a don't ask, don't tell rule in their marriage. This didn't mean, however, that she would tolerate the physical presence of the unspoken, even if it were only a slave girl.

"If time is of the essence, why are you dallying? You should be off preventing disaster. Don't worry about me. I shall be fine. I shall seek out Teretia and warn her against the evils of marriage."

Epaphroditus abandoned the strategy, "What do you want me to do?" he asked quietly in absolute seriousness.

Aphrodite told him, "I want you to kiss me as if we were alone."

Epaphroditus nodded: if she wanted to mark her territory, it was fine by him.

Mina desperately willed Epaphroditus to look her way. The empress was busy chatting and she figured this was a good opportunity for them to sneak off for some horizontal or maybe vertical exercise.

He was in intense conversation with some woman whose back was to Mina, a senator's wife no doubt. It would explain why Epaphroditus was looking so serious, for everyone knew those high class ladies were deadly dull: one only had to work for the empress to know this. Though she was a little more kindly disposed towards her boss since she had promoted her to keeper of the serviette for the evening. Serviettes were much lighter to carry than towels and they enabled her escape into civilisation.

Tingling with excitement, she glanced over to see her lover take the snooty woman's face in his hands and deliver her a long, lingering, passionate kiss. Mina, forgetting seventeen years of slave training, openly gawped.

Breaking the connection, Aphrodite, slightly breathless asked her husband, "Truthfully, did you go to the Saturnalia orgy?"

Epaphroditus looked directly into her eyes, hand resting comfortably on the small of her back. "No, I did not." Then, catching a familiar glint in her eye, he asked. "Are you just a little turned on?"

"Don't push your luck," she warned him, but her voice was light.

He angled his head slightly "Do you fancy …?"

"Don't you have a diplomatic incident to prevent?"

"After," he suggested. "Philo and Teretia seem to have sloped off to find a quiet spot. I don't see why we shouldn't."

Aphrodite was about to reply when everything seemed to happen at once. A shocked Mina had dropped the crucial serviette, bending over to pick it up just as Tigellinus, who after his romp with the serving girl had fallen asleep under a fake tree, came blundering out of the foliage and tripped straight over her.

It was a singularly unfortunate accident, since the empress swung round and was in exactly the correct position to see her husband walk under an arched arbour with Sporus in Poppaea mode hanging off his arm.

It is fair to say that everyone in that courtyard took a collective intake of breath. Epaphroditus was wincing even before the two empresses' eyes met across the green landscape.

Nero, who on entering appeared almost cheerful, froze at the sight of his wife (the official one). He silently removed Sporus' fingers from his arm. Statilia Messalina drew every essence of her superior breeding upwards. If looks could kill then Sporus was crucified and his body thrown to the dogs.

A disorientated Tigellinus pulled himself inexpertly to his unsteady feet; Mina lying on the floor in a ball, the imprint of Tigellinus' boot distinctly visible on her back. Noticing the statue-like guests he declared loudly with arms outstretched, "No harm done. I'm fine."

Then even he picked up on the tense atmosphere. Turning his head one way he saw Statilia, then turning the other way spotted Sporus. Diplomacy had never been Tigellinus' strong point. It was difficult to know what his strong point actually was, each positive aspect to his nature being anchored down firmly by the negative.

He laughed hard and loud before saying. "Come, come we're all friends here. I think we can all agree that you're both a pair of stunners tonight. Blinder." Adding as an afterthought, "Though I know who I'd do," and giving Statilia what he felt was a charming smile.

The empress gave a shudder of revulsion.

Sporus was hurt; he was far prettier than that cow! Nero had so often told him so. Stung, he disguised this by assuming Teretia's sweet smile and linking his arm into his husband's. Which was the catalyst for an astounding sight. Namely that of the empress, lifting up her skirts and running full pelt for her rival.

There was much discussion later as to who won that particular bout. Statilia certainly got a good slap on Sporus before being pulled away by a combination of Phaon, her mother, an aged senator, and two Praetorian guards. She sank her nails into Sporus' arms as they dragged her off the squealing eunuch. Looking down at his bloodied arms he was outraged.

That bitch had attacked him in public! He complained loudly to Nero.

The emperor appeared to vacillate, caught between Statilia who was struggling with her holders and screaming every obscenity she could think of at Sporus, and the eunuch who was giving as good as he got, and being a slave had a far more colourful vocabulary than she. The emperor shot Epaphroditus a pleading look.

The secretary gestured for the soldiers to release Statilia.

Standing in front of her, he told her quietly. "Empress, if you could remember you are in public."

Statilia looked daggers at him, "Oh, I am aware of that. Remove the creature or I shall kill it."

Epaphroditus did not doubt her sincerity. Sporus was escorted out protesting vigorously. The more outraged he became the higher his voice until only the dogs of the Palatine Hill were privy to his thoughts.

Statilia walked over to her frankly terrified husband and took his arm.

"Darling," she said, "I want to introduce you to these wonderful people," leading him off to chat with the understandably stunned guests.

A group of slaves busied themselves clearing up the fauna the empress had dislodged and Tigellinus gave an almighty belch before confiding in Aphrodite.

"Girl-on-girl action. You can't beat it."

In the litter on their way home Philo was subject to a babble of questions from Teretia, which he attempted to answer the best he could.

Wasn't the emperor handsome? Why did they make him look so jowly on coins?

Philo didn't know but coin portraits were very fiddly so perhaps a larger image was easier.

How did they get the leopards to stand up like that?

Some sort of training, Philo supposed.

What is a Sporus?

Which he neatly sidestepped by claiming it was a palace job title for a personal attendant.

Eventually she quietened down and in the rocking motion of the litter she rolled into him. Looking down at her, he saw that she was fast asleep, the pink tip of her tongue poking out between her lips. She looked like a rather beautiful water nymph, he thought.

Alex was sitting on his bed scribbling frantically on a tablet when Mina burst in. He quietly stashed the tablet beneath his thin mattress before she noticed.

Her eyes were bloodshot, she had clearly been crying and on seeing him she wailed, "Oh, Alex!" She threw herself into his arms and sobbed noisily on his shoulder.

He hugged her close and stroked her hair until the sobbing ceased and all he could hear was a sniff or two.

"Do you want to tell me about it?" More sniffs and then the whole story came tumbling out.

Privately Alex marvelled at Mina. What did she think was going to happen? Did she imagine Epaphroditus would marry her? It was a ridiculous thought. Mina wouldn't be freed for another thirteen years at the absolute minimum, and by that time, Alex wasn't sure how old the secretary was, but he would most probably be dead.

He didn't say any of this but something in his expression must have betrayed at least some of his thoughts for Mina said, "What are you looking at me like that for?"

"Like what?"

"Like I told you so. Like so ruddy superior."

"You knew he was married. You knew from the beginning."

"Oh, thanks for the sympathy, Alex."

"I am not sure what I am meant to be sympathetic for," he confessed. "That the married man you've been diddling is proved to be married?"

"In front of everyone!" interjected Mina hotly.

"In front of everyone who already knew he was married. I don't understand why you are so upset."

"I'm sorry to have bored you, Alex. I stupidly thought we were friends."

She got up to leave.

"When was the last time we spoke?"

Mina, confused, replied, "Gods! I don't know."

"Bit one-sided this friendship of ours, isn't it? You get upset, so you come find me to have a moan at. In between I may as well not exist."

"That's not true," protested Mina.

"Yes it is. It's the same for Sporus. He strolls in here when he wants to whine about Juba or the empress or the ugly dress he is being made to wear."

"But that's what friends do. They listen to each other's problems."

He looked at her seriously, "So what are my problems, Artemina?"

She thought for a moment before realising she had no idea what was bothering Alex these days. "You hate your job," she provided.

"Actually, I love it," he contradicted her, and there was a glint to his eyes which Mina had never seen before and which she wasn't sure she liked.

TWENTY-FIVE

One hour before dawn, the soldiers who had been guarding the home of Icelus deserted their positions. Mounted on a horse, Alex handed the freedman a tightly sealed scroll. Icelus gave him a narrow smile.

"Don't look so miserable, Alexander."

"Good luck, sir."

"And you, Alexander."

The senate, convened unexpectedly, watched as Regulus, heavy-eyed but determined stood before them and gave the speech of his political career.

Teretia, lying in bed, heard the thump of boots but she was in that period between sleep and wakefulness and simply incorporated it into a vivid dream she was having.

In the room opposite, Philo, in the throngs of his own dreams twisted and writhed, tangling himself in the sheets.

Across the city in a very nice house on the Esquiline, Epaphroditus lay in casual slumber next to his wife, an arm draped across her stomach. Squeezed in between them was their youngest son Rufus, who fidgeted periodically with thumb resting comfortably in mouth.

Dribbling from the side of his mouth, Tigellinus had yet to experience the all-time killer hangover that was waiting to hit him, or the painfully stiff neck incurred while sleeping curled up by an ornamental fountain.

His partner prefect was far more alert, armour buckled on tight and as shiny as Apollo's smile. Nymphidius Sabinus sucked air through his teeth and straightened his back. His slave, Ephos, handed him a scroll which he scanned one final time. Pushing back his shoulders he strode purposefully into the Praetorian camp, and ended a dynasty.

TWENTY-SIX

Nero rolled over. His throat was dry. He hung out an arm and clicked his fingers, moulding his hand ready for the receptacle. After a moment his sleepy brain registered that he had not received his water. He clicked his fingers again and waited. Nothing. Odd, thought the emperor, slowly opening his eyes. He sat up in bed.

"Juba, water. Juba? Ambrose? Phidias?"

He looked around. There was no one there. Thinking his body slaves were asleep, he hung over the bed and looked at the floor. No one.

Nero Claudius Caesar Augustus Germanicus was thirty-one years old and had never been alone in all that time. Not even when defecating or engaging in intercourse. Pulling his sheets up to his chin he cried, "Guards! Guards!"

But no one came.

When Nero burst into his small room, Sporus' first thought was, "But I'm a mess!"

He had gone to sleep after the party in full make-up and slightly teary. His sheets were smeared with colours and Sporus knew his face must have a similar blurred appearance. So he gave a small screech before covering his face with his hands. Looking through his fingers he saw Nero standing still, pale and shaking.

"Husband?"

Nero silently pointed to the door. Sporus stuck his head into the corridor, looking one way and then the next. He was going to turn back and ask Nero what had frightened him so, when he spotted what it was. Or rather what it wasn't.

There were no Praetorian guards. Not one.

In the slave complex there was the general hum of breakfast. Those who had been present at the previous night's event gleefully divulged the details, with just a hint of embellishment. The empress had stabbed Sporus through the arm, Tigellinus had vomited in the fountain (true that one, but it had occurred much later and not in front of the renowned senator as claimed), Phaon had copped off with Calvia, Ambrose had been whipped for dropping a goblet, and so forth.

Mina played with her bowl of gruel, squelching a spoon in and out, ignoring all attempts at conversation.

"Come on, Mina, you were there last night. Is it true? Did the empress try to murder Sporus with Tigellinus' sword?"

"No," said Mina briefly and to the point.

One of her room-mates, Daphne, sat down next to her.

"I thought you'd gone," said Mina.

"They wouldn't let me."

"Who wouldn't?"

"Mina, there's guards on the door. They wouldn't let me out."

Mina put down her spoon. "Guards?"

The word spread quickly round the refectory, slaves leaving for duties returning as pale faced as Daphne and all with the same story. There were Praetorians on the exit and they weren't letting anyone in or out.

"What does it mean?" Mina asked Daphne, thinking that it at least got her off morning towel duties.

188

Daphne chewed her lip but was prevented from answering by Lysander, who plonked himself down. Mina was drawn to the egg-shaped lump between his eyes.

"Paris just asked one of the guards why we're not allowed out." He paused for effect. Daphne was prepared to take the bait.

"What did he say?"

"Didn't say a word. Just knocked him down. Blam! One punch."

Daphne gave a small gasp. Mina couldn't resist any longer: "What happened to your head?"

Lysander touched a finger to the lump and winced, "Aren't you worried?" he asked Mina, bypassing her question. "There are soldiers on the door; they're keeping us cooped up here together. Doesn't bode well. Does not bode well at all," he concluded.

He was an announcer, which lent a deathly emphasis to his rhetoric and a tendency to self-importance. Daphne burst into tears, Lysander flitting off to the next table to inform them of Paris' fate.

What had seemed at first an oddity, a slice of weirdness to enliven the day, grew more sinister as time passed and they were still unable to leave. Lysander had not exaggerated, if anything he had downplayed. Paris was laid out flat on the floor being attended to by one of the doctors. Nobody dared make another approach to the guards. Even the overseers seemed on edge.

"You know what's happened, don't you?" said Daphne. "One of us has killed one of the imperial family. That's why we're being kept here."

Lysander, sat at another table, mouthed one word at them both: "Secundus."

The air chilled.

Pedanius Secundus had been the city prefect. A cruel and vicious man, he'd been justifiably murdered by one of his own

189

slaves. An ancient law was invoked and all 400 of his household slaves had been crucified. Mina was far too young to remember this incident but it lived on as a folk tale among slaves.

At the mention of that name, Mina shivered. The bravado dripped out of her. It made perfect sense: why else would they be imprisoned like this? It could be going through the law courts right now. How long would it take before the sentence was passed? How long did they have?

She looked around for Alex but couldn't see him. Beside her Daphne was in tears again; several others were too. The doctor attending to Paris stood up and shook his head sadly. It was then that the guards marched in. Mina was suddenly very frightened.

Epaphroditus, ignorant of events at the palace, was enjoying a leisurely breakfast with Aphrodite. As it was a warm morning they had moved the furniture out into a courtyard garden, sitting opposite each other beneath a fig tree. The older children were with the tutor, Aphrodite hearing their chorused grammar lessons with pride. Baby Rufus sat happily gurgling on Epaphroditus' lap, his father feeding him pieces of melon. A nice, calm domestic scene; one to be treasured, for Epaphroditus' long hours meant such occasions were rare.

"You need to have a talk with Philo," said Aphrodite handing him a bowl of dates.

"Do I?" he asked absently, attempting to interest Rufus in a grape.

"About Teretia," prompted his wife.

"A sweet girl. You didn't like her?"

"I loved her. She's perfect for him. Does he realise this though?"

Rufus grabbed hold of the edge of the table and attempted to pull himself up. "You think Philo's messing her about?" Epaphroditus asked, thinking what an unlikely scenario that was.

190

"No, of course not. He doesn't possess the necessary intrigue. They're not sleeping together."

Epaphroditus raised an eyebrow and, wrestling Rufus back into position, asked, "She told you that?"

"No. But it's obvious."

"Rubbish. She's a peach."

"Just because you'd dive into bed with her—"

He ignored the implied accusation. There had been some strong words spoken the previous night regarding Artemina. "She adores him. Have you seen the way she looks at him?"

"And the way he looks at her?"

Epaphroditus scanned his memory and identifying the missing piece replied, "Ahh."

"Ahh indeed. If you could talk to him."

"And say what? Dite, you can't force these things."

"Just give him a bit of a nudge."

Her husband looked sceptical.

"She's so perfect for him," she pleaded. "It would be a terrible shame if she slipped through his fingers. If you could use that persuasive power of yours."

Handing a wriggling Rufus to a slave, he told her, "OK, OK. I shall endeavour to open his eyes. But I warn you, he doesn't react well to that sort of pressure."

Aphrodite caught on immediately. "Is this where you tell me that you didn't have Philo removed from the breeding programme because it was interfering with his work?"

"No," he replied carefully and then opening up a little, "You know what he's like. He is so hard on himself and it is a lot of pressure on a guy. I don't think you girls appreciate that."

"Don't we now?" said Aphrodite popping a grape into her mouth.

"You know you've only got a set time and bloody Straton or whoever is peering through the grill and banging on the door to hurry you up. He begged me to get him out of it. He was practically in tears. So I pulled in a few favours."

This was a somewhat edited version of events; Epaphroditus having promised a distraught Philo that he wouldn't tell a soul exactly what had occurred.

"Which is precisely why you need to encourage him with Teretia," she insisted. "He needs someone gentle."

Privately Epaphroditus agreed with his wife. He'd heard his assistant's name linked with a number of girls over the years but this appeared to be mere wishful thinking on their part, for Philo was quite a catch. Though far from being a great hunk of a man, he was pleasant looking with rather sweet features and an unstudied helplessness that made women want to tuck him up in bed and darn his socks for him.

Teretia, as well as possessing a radiant goodness that made you weep to think it would ever be corrupted, seemed a practical girl. Her gentle and kind nature was perfect for intimately easing out the nervy anxiety that inflicted Philo in regard to women, and no doubt she was fully capable of keeping him in clean tunics and ensuring he was properly fed.

"I will employ subtlety and eloquence. And we'll have them married by the end of the summer."

Standing up he kissed the top of her head.

"Have a good day."

He knew something was up the moment he approached the palace. His home backed onto the grounds of the new palace. Entering by his usual route, he was struck instantly by the quiet. Usually there was a hum of slaves rushing around, entering and exiting, delivering messages, pursuing purchases from the local traders, exercising the horses, and undertaking a million different tasks that needed doing. This morning the new palace grounds were completely empty, the only noise the sound of the birds.

Approaching the main entrance, Epaphroditus noted the absence of guards, feeling his scalp tingle. The entrance hall with its colonnades and marble statues looted from Greece was similarly empty. There were no major domos, no clerks with appointment tablets, no directionary slaves, no security presence of any sort.

Whatever had happened, it had been extremely efficiently executed. His footsteps echoed, sounding ridiculously loud as he made his way along empty corridors, through room after room devoid of inhabitants.

TWENTY-SEVEN

The guards positioned themselves along the walls, leering at the huddled slaves who stared up at them with terror. Mina gripped hold of the sobbing Daphne.

A tribune standing at the head of the refectory, flanked improbably by Juba the body slave, narrowed his eyes and yelled, "Be quiet!"

Daphne bit her lip trying to hold back the tears. The tension was killing Mina. "Get it over with. Please get it over with," she silently implored, her lips moving.

The tribune cleared his throat. Mina's heart stopped, waiting for him to speak. Even Lysander, who loved a good drama, looked terrified.

"This morning," he began, "the senate signed a declaration ratifying Gaius Servius Sulpicius Galba as emperor."

Around him, slaves looked at each other in shock.

"Gaius Servius Sulpicius Galba is at this moment marching from Spain to accept the imperial title. Gaius Nymphidius Sabinus has assumed control of the city at this time."

The tribune rolled up his scroll and gestured to a soldier. The command was audible to all.

"Separate the men from the women."

Mina and Daphne exchanged panicked looks and clung together. The guards waded in and began roughly pushing the slaves around. Husbands and wives, mothers and sons, cousins and friends were dragged apart screaming. There was no one to help them, to protect them.

Their father, the genial Nero, was gone, the powerful freedmen and women of the palace were absent, and the overseers who, though brutal, had a duty to maintain the market value of the stock were being treated just as contemptuously by the guards. They could do what they liked.

Mina, seeing Erotica being dragged backwards by her hair had a pretty good idea of what was going to happen.

The women were herded into a single room and forced to squat on the floor. Mina watched the guards walking among the cowering, whimpering slaves, lifting a chin up to examine each before making a decision, the girl dragged off by a wrist or an ankle before being returned crying some time later. I won't make it easy for them, she promised herself, and I'll fight and fight.

Juba was in his element. He watched smugly as his fellow slaves were rounded up, enjoying their terrified expressions and screams. Under the guise of wheedling out troublemakers, he managed to settle many personal scores by directing the guards to efficient batterings.

It was a shame that Epaphroditus wasn't there. Juba was thirsty for revenge after the whipping he had taken at the secretary's orders. No matter, he would have to gain satisfaction by proxy. He approached the tribune with his suggestion. The latter shrugged and said, "Why not?"

Tingling with excitement Juba strode into the dormitory. The women looked up at him, most with contempt. Juba stared back at them: they were his now, Sabinus had promised. He scanned their faces and saw the one he wanted. He wrenched up her chin with his thumb, telling her, "I'm going to really enjoy this."

Mina glared back defiantly.

The emperor's private bedroom lay untouched, a sheet twisted on the floor, the only sign that something significant had taken place there. Hearing a clatter of feet, Epaphroditus shot behind a door, pressing himself against the wall, moderating his breathing to an undetectable level. The feet stopped. Epaphroditus could hear their owner's heavy breaths and then a curse. Recognising the voice he slid out from his hiding place.

"Phaon."

"Epaphroditus."

Phaon handed him a light scroll instructing him to read it. It was a declaration. Phaon had found it pinned to the senate door.

"Can you believe it?" Phaon asked him. "Fucking Sabinus! Treacherous goat!"

It explained the efficiency of the operation, thought Epaphroditus, with some admiration for the prefect. It must have taken months and months of planning; the attention to detail was impressive.

"Do you think they've killed the emperor?"

"I doubt it," said the secretary. "If they had, I am sure it would have made it as an appendix: 'The death of the tyrant'."

"So where is he?"

"Good question. Shall we try and find an answer?"

Realistically there were only a few possible locations. Nero was escorted everywhere. His personal knowledge of the palace layout was sketchy; he would head somewhere familiar.

They started with his private quarters, discussing as they went what they should do when they found him.

"The East is loyal. If we could just get him to Ostia, buy him a passage," suggested Epaphroditus as they opened wardrobes and checked under beds.

"Surely Sabinus will man all the roads out of the city."

"Well, I wasn't intending on smuggling him out in garland and purple striped toga."

"Why do you think he did it? Sabinus?"

"Oh, I imagine he sees himself as Brutus, removing the evil and depraved king. No doubt we shall hear some wonderfully pompous and ponderous speeches in the coming days on such a theme. He is not here, where next?"

Phaon considered. "Empress' quarters?" he suggested, which made them both smile.

"Sporus?"

Phaon gave a curt nod. "Worth a try."

Mina fought like she had never fought before. She bit and scratched and screamed, Juba struggling to pin her wrists down with one hand while using the other to lift up her dress. She kicked her legs wildly, writhing beneath him, hindering his rape attempt. Frustrated, he thrust an elbow downwards catching her on the side of her head and dazing her.

Juba took the opportunity this offered him, pulling his tunic over his head and prising her legs apart with his knees.

This was going to be great; he had dragged her off to a quiet room so that he could spend the whole day enacting all those fantasies that kept him amused during the last few months.

She was better than he imagined, tight and sweet. Mina's renewed struggles egged him on and he fastened onto a breast biting hard on the nipple, hearing her yell, feeling her splayed legs kick beneath him.

He was on the brink of the best orgasm of his life when something tight grabbed the back of his neck. He was lifted up and slammed face first against the wall. Running a calloused finger down a whelp on Juba's back, Straton rasped in his ear, "Didn't we meet earlier?"

Juba, nose squashed against the brick, felt the spittle hit the back of his neck.

"You got permission to fuck that slave?"

An arm hooked round Juba's neck, Straton repeated the overseer's mantra. "You don't damage the merchandise."

With Juba's throat stinging from the effort of speech, Straton decided to make his point physically by pounding Juba's head into the wall, the hooked arm holding the stunned slave upright as his knees buckled. Pressed against Juba's naked back, the overseer decided to start his day off on a high. Feeling something distinctly stiff pushing into his spine, the slave squeaked, "You can't."

Which made Straton chuckle. Because he could.

The words tumbled out of Juba at speed. "I'm working for Sabinus. Sabinus rules Rome now. Nero's dead."

Thumping Juba's head into the wall again, Straton turned to a cowering Mina, her fingers grasping at her ripped dress, for confirmation. She gave a small nod.

The overseer processed this astounding information. The emperor had fallen. Likely Epaphroditus would fall also. Philo, his Philo, worked for Epaphroditus. That put him in an extremely dangerous situation.

The thought of Philo being hurt upset the overseer immensely. Straton had worked his way through an awful lot of special friends over the years but he liked Philo best of them all. Philo was small and neat, polite and willing. Every whip scar on Philo's back was a link for Straton to a wonderful memory of the time they had spent together.

It was unfortunate for Juba that he was the personification of the threat posed to Straton's beloved. Grabbing a fistful of hair, Straton slammed Juba's head against the wall five times with force. The slave hit the floor and did not get up.

Straton rubbed his hands together. Turning his black eyes on Mina, he asked, "Emperor's dead?"

Mina nodded, her body racked with shaking. "There are soldiers on the door."

"Interesting," mused Straton. Then, gazing down at Juba's body, the blood spreading beneath it, he asked sparingly, "He important?"

Mina gave a slightly hysterical laugh before answering, "Not now."

He'd been one of Nero's body slaves. Nero was dead. Which negated his value. Having belatedly recognised Mina as one of the empress' attendants, Straton figured he could bargain his way out of a penalty. He offered Mina a hand. She looked up at him in terror, so he took hold of her and lifted her up with surprising gallantry.

"Put you somewhere safe," he told her.

"There are guards everywhere," she protested. "You'll never get out."

Straton removed a cudgel from his belt and grinned.

TWENTY-EIGHT

Standing outside the door to Sporus' room, Phaon and Epaphroditus could hear a wailing within.

"You think?"

"I doubt that it is Sabinus," replied Epaphroditus dryly.

He pressed a palm against the door: it didn't move.

"On three. One, two, three."

They slammed shoulders against the door: it gave way, a quick kick allowing them entrance. Sporus, seeing the door break, screamed and clung to Nero.

The emperor, trembling, cried, "Forgive me, Mother!" before frantically retracting that near confession on sight of his servants.

"Caesar," said the secretary, rubbing his shoulder. "We're going to get you out of here."

He stated it with such confidence that he nearly believed it.

They moved Sporus and Nero to a room with an intact door, Epaphroditus leaving Phaon as a guard.

"Keep them positive."

Phaon gave a tight smile. "Who is going to keep me positive?"

"It will all be fine. Trust me."

Then addressing the emperor, he said, "I am going to arrange transport. I will be back. Phaon will take care of you until my return."

Nero, still in his nightgown, gave Epaphroditus a teary look. "Can Poppaea come?"

A deflated Sporus, exhausted from all the crying, gave a small resigned smile before saying quietly, "I'll not leave you, husband."

Straton was counting on two things: firstly Sabinus' ignorance of the slave complex and secondly the brutal lust of the guards. He knew that given the order to pen the slave workforce in, they would be unable to resist taking advantage, fucking animals that they were. Distracted by the goods on offer, they would be sloppy and it wouldn't occur to them that there could possibly be more than one exit and entrance to the slave complex.

Straton knew the complex better than anyone. It was how he applied the near mythical trick of appearing directly behind any slaves the moment they broke the rules.

Sticking his head round a corner he gestured back to Mina to approach; she moved swiftly to his side. He noticed she was in some pain, an eye was already swollen shut and her chin a garish yellow bruise. But she was determined to keep up with him, which showed grit. Though Straton held a poor opinion of women, this one had impressed him. It also made their escape far more achievable, for she was clearly as resolute as him.

They were headed for the far eastern corner of the complex and a door that led out into the grounds. It would be far easier to run round the side of the old palace than risk the corridors where the guards were likely to be patrolling or the tunnels which were likely to be heavy with moving soldiers. Epaphroditus' office was situated towards the forum frontage of the palace that had been built by Caligula. There was a side door that, if they were lucky, they could sneak through and then rescue Philo. Or that was Straton's plan anyway.

The male slaves were being kept in the refectory, herded together in the space where some hours earlier they had queued for breakfast. Knees bent, fingers laced behind his neck, Lysander stared at the floor; his thighs and calves were burning but he did not dare stretch. The guards stood around the wall were waiting for any such violation and enacting boot-led punishment for those that tottered from their position.

Occasionally, bored of their compliance, they would kick one over for their own amusement. They were also suffering from a ticking impatience. The deal was that there would be a swap over of duties and they could hear their comrades readily enjoying the women as they stood guarding the males.

The male slaves were silent; lips were bit hard, drawing blood as they heard the women scream and cry. Not that they had been spared that ordeal: the more attractive younger boys had been picked off early on. They had yet to return. Lysander, raising his eyes slightly, saw a darting movement from the entrance.

Straton pulled his head back against the wall. "Men there," he told Mina.

"How are we going to get across?" she asked, pointing to the other side of the wide entrance. "They'll spot us for sure."

From within the refectory they heard the guards shouting orders: to keep still, to hold their positions, to look straight ahead.

"You moved!" a guard yelled and there was a thump followed by a yelp and then a laugh from the soldiers. "Can't keep still this one, perhaps he needs a bit of action to wear him out, like." Another group laugh. "Anyone fancy him?"

Mina gave a wince. "Bastards," she whispered to Straton.

The overseer nodded in agreement, his face grim. They were messing with the merchandise, damaging it. He gave another darted glance into the room, noting a Praetorian grabbing hold of a young slave by his ankles, laughing at the upside-down boy's struggles. There were perhaps thirty others stood around the walls amused by this scene, the male slaves squatting, knees bent, stared at the floor with wide eyes and pale faces.

Animals, thought Straton and calmly pulled out his whip from his belt. He gestured for Mina to stay put and held up three fingers.

"Run on three."

With the boy's cries in his ears as the guards shook him, Lysander bit his lip.

"Stay calm, stay calm," he told himself mentally, then catching another movement in the corner of his eye, he dared to raise his gaze again.

It was not until later that Lysander worked out what had happened, so quickly did it occur. Straton had whizzed into the entrance cracking his whip and catching the guard on the ankle, tugging him over before dashing to the other side of the door.

The guard pulled himself to his feet dazed. One moment he had been standing up holding onto the boy's foot and the next he was face down on the floor.

"What happened?" he asked his colleagues bewildered, noting the red bleeding slash on his foot.

They shrugged, "You slipped I think," said one.

Pressed against the wall Straton grinned and then counted down his third finger. Guards distracted, Mina ran. Lysander caught the blur of white that sped across the entrance, silently cheered by the fact that someone had clearly escaped and willing them to get help.

Epaphroditus had a mental checklist: horses, wagon, a good proportion of the imperial treasury to aid the escape, and disguises for Nero and Sporus. He debated furiously with himself as to whether Sporus made a more convincing boy or girl.

Rounding into the stables he spotted a figure slowly brushing the mane of a chestnut stallion. Epaphroditus froze.

Tigellinus turned round slowly and rewarded him with an engaging smile.

"Beauty isn't he? Only three years old and such a gorgeous creature."

"Tigellinus, I need your help. Can you loan me some guards?"

Returning to his task Tigellinus began brushing down the stallion's back.

"Sabinus controls the guards."

"Yes, but you must be able to secure a few. Two even," protested Epaphroditus. "For the emperor's safety. He is going to the eastern provinces."

Tigellinus did not look up. "It's over."

"Rubbish. There are eleven legions in the east. All loyal. How many has Galba got?"

"The senate has made Galba emperor."

"It can be undone."

The prefect gave a short bark of a laugh. "I don't think so."

"He's your emperor."

Tigellinus shook his head and moved onto the horse's legs, lifting up a hoof for inspection.

Epaphroditus, indignant and uncomprehending, protested, "But he's your friend. You've drunk with him, laughed with him, fornicated with him." Then realising his poor choice of words altered it to "alongside him".

"It has been an adventure, I'll give you that," replied the prefect with a slight smile.

Epaphroditus was by nature a calm, considered man. He rarely lost his temper but right now he felt the anger bubble up inside him. "You coward," he spat. "You fucking coward!"

"A living, breathing coward," said Tigellinus, placing the horse's hoof down gently.

"Sabinus runs Rome now. Do you seriously believe he'll let you live? I imagine his first act as commander-in-chief will be a general purge of all those who have upset him."

"I think not." Tigellinus looked the secretary in the eye. "Have you heard of Titus Vinius? Stupid question. Of course you have, informed man that you are. Vinius is Galba's right-hand man and confidant. I saved his daughter's life once."

Epaphroditus gave a bitter scoff.

"Don't look so shocked, even I have had my moments of gallantry. Vinius was most grateful, remains grateful. So you see, Epaphroditus, I am quite safe."

He turned back to the horse, running a hand down its snout with warmth. Epaphroditus was speechless.

TWENTY-NINE

Calvia Crispinilla had been lucky. When the soldiers burst into her palace rooms set on arresting her, she was waking up alongside a handsome, young charioteer somewhere on the Caelian Hill. She was gloriously stretched across his taut chest, allowing him to nibble at her ear, when a messenger arrived with the news.

Calvia was up and dressed in seconds. "Sabinus you say?" she enquired of the messenger.

"Nymphidius Sabinus has gained control of the city, madam," he confirmed.

Calvia gave a tight smile. "Well, I guess I had better get out of the city then. After breakfast, naturally," she concluded, sizing up the charioteer once more.

Over on the Viminal Hill another breakfast was taking place. Teretia was recounting in great depth and detail everything she had witnessed the previous evening to her enthralled parents. Literally everything. From the litter ride over to the Palatine, to the guards on the gates who had let them in, "Without even asking who we were because Philo is so well known at the palace," she said proudly.

The object of her adoring affection missed the devoted look that was thrown his way, being more concerned with his porridge and certain other matters that were weighing on his mind.

Pompeia and Teretius listened with awe to Teretia's expansive commentary, though the issue of the tiara had been much discussed. Pompeia worried that her daughter had not obtained it in proper fashion, Teretia hotly stating that she had. They managed to gain Philo's attention long enough to conclude that Sporus owned a great many tiaras and was free to give one away if he liked, even if it were a piece of jewellery that was worth the equivalent of a near decade of Teretius' wages. Teretia happily placed the tiara back on her head and tucked into her own bowl of porridge.

Breakfast over, Philo trudged down the Vicus Longus, past the side of the slum Subura region, fretting over the Mina situation. He'd endured a restless night, waking with a cold blast of horror in the sudden realisation that the conversation he'd passed with the kitchen girls the previous week regarding the wilting properties of celery, had not been about salads at all!

He shrank with embarrassment, recalling how he had attributed their giggly state to an unusually high level of job satisfaction. So it was with a far from glad heart that he trudged his way towards the Forum of Augustus.

Aside from the mortification, which was Philo's default mood, he was feeling distinctly peevish towards Mina. It was most unfair of her to launch herself at him in such a manner. He hadn't been prepared at all. No man faced with such an assault on his most intimate area could respond in a ripe celery way.

She should have offered him a warning of her intentions before enacting them so violently, thought Philo, utterly ignorant of the three-month campaign of heavy flirtation that Mina had directed at him with all the drive of a Delphic chariot champion (one wearing a low-cut dress with bosoms heaved upwards).

Really Philo would have preferred a memo detailing what her intentions were towards him, how she wished him to respond, and with a clear deadline set for his reply. That was the civilised way of doing things. He wouldn't have been so shocked that way, so stunned, so utterly surprised that his natural reaction to a naked Mina pressed up against him and grabbing hold of his penis was sheer panic.

He thought it dreadfully unfair of her to tell people about what had happened or rather what hadn't happened.

Her roving hand discovering that the seduction was having no effect; she had looked at him, hand still in place, with a mixture of confusion and embarrassment. What had he done? He had run away. Slinking back to the office later, he walked straight in on Mina and Epaphroditus embroiled in a far more heated embrace.

With these thoughts tumbling round his brain he near sleep-walked through the city, paying little attention to anything around him, walking past the trotting bands of guards and pushing his way through the shocked crowds gathering in the forum to read the senate's declaration.

He meandered up the Palatine Hill, failing to notice any of the things that had so concerned Epaphroditus. It wasn't until he actually entered the palace gates that he realised something was wrong and any thoughts of Mina and his humiliation were dashed right away.

Straton dipped a head into the kitchens, Mina flat against the wall beside him. There were two guards standing by a bubbling cauldron, one picking at a loaf of bread, the other absently stirring the pot.

"Crap," swore Straton.

Still there were only two of them. The overseer liked those odds. Taking his cudgel he slammed it against the wall with a thud. Mina looked aghast; he put his finger to his lips.

"What do you think that was?" Proculus asked Lucullus.

Lucullus shrugged and then, rubbing a piece of bread between his fingers, commented, "You know this is better quality than the gritty stuff they serve us."

Straton smiled. Talk about sloppy. Idiots. They thought slaves meek and pliable, ever ready to be ordered and organised. Straton had worked with slaves all his life and knew them to be as wilful and destructive as any other being. He handed Mina his cudgel, pulling his whip from his belt again. Leaning over he whispered, "Go for knees. I'll do rest."

It was a pure Spartacus moment. Straton, flexing his whip, caught the handle of the cauldron, tipping its steaming contents all over Lucullus. Taking her cue from the overseer, Mina sped in and with all her might, whacked him on the knees. He fell with an oomph. A quick slash to the face distracted Proculus long enough for Mina to fell him too. Straton grabbed her elbow and dragged her past the moaning guards to safety.

Still clutching the cudgel she turned to Straton bright-eyed. "That was entirely satisfying."

Chuckling he confided, "Why I became an overseer."

Running through the morning damp grass they made their way along the outside of the old palace. In the peaceful grounds it was hard to believe what was occurring inside. Mina tried not to think about it too much, tried not to worry about Alex and Sporus. Particularly Sporus: had he been with the emperor when it all began?

Straton, agile as ever, was encouraging her onwards, informing her, "Not far now."

So far they'd evaded the attention of the guards placed on the major entrances, Sabinus seemingly forgetful about the less obvious points. Reaching the door that led into the corridor on which Epaphroditus' office sat, they hit one final impediment.

Onesimus stood determinedly in front of it, holding onto a sizable double-headed axe.

"You'll not leave," he said, sniffing. "You have to stay. Until Sabinus says you can leave."

He clutched the axe handle and regarded Mina with ferrety eyes.

Still enthused by the casual violence she had meted out to Proculus and Lucullus, Mina cried, "Oh, come on! What do you care whether we go through that door? It is hardly going to affect Sabinus' master plan. He seems to have thought of everything."

"Them's the rules. Sabinus' rules. He is a good master you will find. If you obey that is." Onesimus narrowed his eyes, licking his thin lips, pulling the axe to his chest. "You'll not pass," he said, and Mina could tell that he meant it.

He would fight like a growling terrier to the death: it would be bloody, it would be drawn out. The noise would certainly attract the attention of any passing guards, who would despatch them to a quick death. They were stuck.

Straton watched this exchange with amusement. He calmly walked over to Onesimus. The slave pointed his axe at Straton's stomach, a look of grim determination on his face. Straton looked down at the weapon. He batted it aside with his palm.

"YOU WON'T PASS!" yelled Onesimus, sweat forming on his brow.

He took the axe in both hands and waved it one way, then the other. An action Straton watched with interest, his black eyes following its sweep. It was a good axe that, sharp and swift. Straton rather fancied it in his collection.

Onesimus took another sweep. Straton waited until the axe was at its full left-hand trajectory before he drew back his head and nutted him.

The affect was amazing. Onesimus instantly fell to the ground with a crash.

Offering a hand to Mina, Straton helped her over the prone body, before going back and prying the axe from the unconscious slave's fingers. You never knew when it might come in useful.

Straton stuck his head round the door. The corridor was in full commotion, angry freedmen demonstrating loudly at the guards.

"This is outrageous!"

"How am I supposed to work without any workers?"

"What do you mean I cannot enter my own office?"

The guards were doing their best against the army of irritated administrators, though they were beginning to look somewhat worn at the pernickety questions and barrage of strongly felt tutting. Straton signalled to Mina, she slipping through the door and viewing the scene with some wry amusement.

"Think one of them will go nuts and attack the guards with his stylus?" she asked smiling.

Straton grinned and then added gruffly. "You be safe."

Which could have been a statement of fact or a pleasant parting wish. It was difficult to tell with Straton.

"Thank you," said Mina with some feeling, for her adventure ended, she was beginning to wobble a little again.

He inclined his head towards her and departed down the corridor, where to, Mina had no idea.

She stood among the complaining freedmen and harassed guards, took an enormous breath and then let out a scream at full volume. There was silence and a series of shocked looks from the assembled huddle.

"The guards are killing the slaves!" she shrieked with high drama, her swollen eye and bruised face seeming to prove this extraordinary statement.

The angry freedmen turned back to confront the guards with murder in their eyes.

THIRTY

Epaphroditus gave up on the wagon idea. With no help available, he wouldn't have the slightest idea how to rig it up. They had no chance of getting to Ostia either. Evidently Sabinus had predicted this plan, the secretary discovered while hiding behind a door and overhearing two passing guards discussing the port blockade.

Which left what? The senate had turned. The Guard had turned. Within the palace Epaphroditus had no idea who remained loyal or who, like Tigellinus, had lost heart.

Which left whom? The people, thought Epaphroditus. The people adored Nero. If he could get the emperor to the forum, a personal plea to the mob against such treachery might well work. The Guard would be shamed into line.

Epaphroditus had no idea what Sabinus had offered them, but he was more than happy to match it. The senate was populated by vacillating cowards; they were irrelevant. Any slaves who had conspired with Sabinus, he would have personally crucified: that should snap the workforce back into line.

He began to feel almost optimistic, right up to the point where he spotted Sabinus' latest proclamation nailed to a door. Skipping the paragraph describing "this brave new era" and the more scandalous lists of Nero's supposed proclivities (Epaphroditus could well imagine Sabinus' stylus dripping with distaste, poring over this catalogue of misdeeds), he got to the main thrust.

There was a substantial reward on offer for the capture of the deposed emperor, whereas those found to be harbouring Nero would be considered criminals and treated as such. Epaphroditus tore Sabinus' words from the door and ripped them into tiny shreds. It was over.

A call of, "Sir," snapped his head upwards. It was Philo moving down the corridor in some haste. Epaphroditus gave him an affectionate smile.

"What news?" he asked.

Philo looked at his boss: he was pale, his face taut, lips tight.

"There are guards stationed outside your office, sir. They only let me out because I said I needed the bathroom. I was questioned by their tribune as to your whereabouts."

"Not harshly, I hope."

Philo shook his head, "I couldn't tell them anything. The emperor?"

"Best you not know," sighed Epaphroditus. "I need you to do something for me."

"Anything, sir, you know that."

"I need you to get word to my wife."

The thought of Dite and the children at home oblivious to his plight made his heart contract. "Tell her ..."

Tell her what? Tell her that he was betrayed on all levels. That the world had gone mad. That he was glad to have known her. That she had made him unreasonably happy all these years. That there was no one he would have rather been with.

In the end he settled on, "Tell her I'll be home as soon as I can."

"Where are you going?"

Epaphroditus gave him a tight smile. "I am going with the emperor."

Philo looked close to tears. Then remembering that he had promised Aphrodite he would talk to his assistant and fearing this would be his last opportunity, Epaphroditus added, "Go home to Teretia. She likes you a great deal."

Embracing briefly like soldiers, they parted.

It took all of Epaphroditus' persuasive powers to convince the emperor that they had to leave the palace.

"I am not going out there. They want me dead! They want their emperor dead!"

"Caesar, we have to move now."

Nero shook his tear-streaked face.

"Sabinus has men in the palace looking for you," he insisted.

"All the more reason to stay put. They won't find me here."

"Sabinus is a soldier, he is logical, he is methodical. He will have men systematically searching room by room. They will find you, Caesar."

"Then why move if they are going to find me any-way. I would rather die here with Poppaea than in a ditch en route."

Sporus, on mention of his likely death wailed. Nero patted his head. "Poppaea, love, please don't be upset. It is better that we die together."

Sporus wasn't so sure of this; falling into a panic he couldn't catch his breath, drawing in great lungfuls that didn't quench. Phaon, seeing his distress, gently untangled him from Nero's arms and led him quietly out.

Epaphroditus sat down beside Nero. "Caesar, we have to move."

"There is no point in moving."

"They will cut you down here, Caesar. They won't be con-cerned with the niceties: they will cut you down with swords.

215

They won't make it quick. They won't make it painless. It will be bloody. It will be brutal."

The emperor swallowed hard.

"Unless", Epaphroditus threw in, "their orders are to capture you alive. Perhaps Sabinus wants the honour personally. He could make Caesar grovel to him, prostrate before him. He has a cruel streak. He could make Caesar suffer greatly."

Another hard swallow, Nero's shoulders shaking. Epaphroditus broke protocol. Touching the emperor for the first and only time, he took Nero's hand and held it tight. Eventually the shoulders ceased to quake. Staring at the floor, the emperor said quietly, "Very well. Let's go."

Phaon had taken Sporus to a nearby bathroom, setting about his task with speed. The eunuch let himself be manipulated as Phaon trimmed down his beautifully manicured nails, scrubbed the polish off his toe nails and roughly wiped all traces of make-up from his face.

He held his arms up as requested as his feminine nightgown was replaced with a rough brown tunic and his slippers discarded for hardy boots of too large a size for his small feet. Fetching a pair of scissors Phaon hacked off Sporus' soft hair.

The eunuch held his curls in his palms, detached from all. This was happening to someone else, he told himself. It was all a dream, a particularly nasty and vivid dream. He would wake at any moment with his curls intact and his world just as it should be.

Phaon took hold of his hands and pulled the rings from his fingers. A lip wobbled as the ruby ring Nero had given to him on their wedding night was removed.

"OK, all done," said Phaon, helping Sporus' feet into the unfamiliar boots.

Phaon returned with a small boy, an attractive boy, for even with his head shaved and dressed in a drab tunic, his charms were evident, but it was a boy who was pale and trembling and very, very frightened.

The emperor took one look at this apparition and with some annoyance asked, "What have you done to my Poppaea?"

"I am sorry, Caesar, but it is necessary," Phaon apologised, before handing a similarly dull tunic and cloak to the emperor, who looked at them with utter disgust.

THIRTY-ONE

hilo sat at his desk, staring into space and worrying. The conversation with Epaphroditus weighed heavily on his mind. His boss had been melancholic, which was most out of the ordinary, and Philo feared that Epaphroditus was resigned to not returning. This was most distressing to him, for he revered Epaphroditus. Which was why it was so important that he delivered his message to Aphrodite. However, given that there was a guard outside the door who seemed reluctant to even allow him toilet breaks, he had no idea how to accomplish this mission.

Then there were those words on Teretia. He had taken them to mean that she was in grave danger and he was becoming increasingly frantic for her safety. What if there were a riot? Once the news regarding the emperor's demise leaked out, that was a distinct possibility.

What if there was a riot while Teretia and her mother were out shopping? He knew they did this every morning, for their evening meal was always preceded by a list of bargains obtained that day.

What if some lout spotted Teretia? She was, Philo recognised, an attractive girl and attractive girls were often on the front line of all kinds of nastiness. He didn't like that thought much. She'd been rather sweet to him at the party, chatting to him as if he were someone worth talking to, and she'd got on famously with Aphrodite. Philo liked Aphrodite immensely, which was why he was so desperate to deliver his message, riot or not. He couldn't sit here all day: people were depending on him. He packed up his satchel decisively.

The guard on the door gazed down at him. "You got the squits, boy?"

"I thought I'd go home."

"You thought you'd go home? Why would you think that?"

"I haven't got anything to do."

The guard, a gleaming example of the species, queried, "Well, what do you usually do?"

"I take notes."

"Can't you do that?"

Philo hopped from foot to foot, itching to move. "Not really. There aren't any meetings."

"Why not?"

He wondered whether it was politic to point out that it was the guard's commander Sabinus who had deposed the emperor, caused his boss to flee, closed down the palace, imprisoned the workforce, and generally inhibited Philo's day-to-day workload.

"Very quiet day," he said. "I'm just twiddling my fingers in there. It just seems a bit of a waste." Which he felt was a reasoned argument.

"No," replied the soldier.

On a usual day this would have been enough to send him scurrying back to his desk. This, however, was no usual day for Philo and he was briefly tortured by an image of Teretia running from a group of drunken youths armed with cudgels and intent on mischief.

"Why not?" he asked impatiently.

The guard, aggrieved at being questioned, replied stiffly, "Because I have orders."

"Which are?"

"To keep an eye on you."

It astounded Philo that Sabinus thought he was worth keeping an eye on.

"Won't that be rather dull?"

Privately the guard was very much in agreement. He felt he'd got the bum deal. While his colleagues were hunting down the fugitive emperor or enjoying some luscious slave girl, he was stuck here minding this little fellow. It was demeaning. But a good soldier followed orders, however crap they may be, so he replied, "Them's my orders."

"You could come with me?" he suggested.

After all what harm could it do? The message to Aphrodite was of no interest to anyone but her and if he were to be wandering around the city, it might be handy to have a Praetorian guard with him.

"To your home?"

"I have to see my mother first. At a time like this, she'll be worried about me."

The guard nodded: he had a mother after all.

"And then I live on Viminal. You could come with me, keep an eye on me while enjoying some of my landlady's vegetable broth."

The guard considered. His orders were nicely vague; they didn't say anything about imprisoning the little chap in the palace, just making sure he didn't get up to any mischief. That could be stretched. Besides, he felt like some fresh air, it was nearly lunchtime, and he liked the sound of that broth.

"Alright then."

One good thing to be said for having a guard by your side was that people didn't half move out of way. Philo had never moved with such speed and ease through the crowded city streets.

The guard, who had confided to Philo that his name was Gracchus, sneered his way through the mob that had gathered outside the palace. Clearly word had leaked out that something big had happened. The assorted Roman citizens having come for a good gander, peered at the palace trying to discern the happenings within.

There were catcalls for the emperor to come out and the odd obscene ditty sung out loud. The stony-faced Praetorians on the gates were not giving anything away, their tribune telling the mob bluntly to, "Bugger off home," if they knew what was good for them.

A youth contingent, for whom Praetorian baiting was a popular sport, lobbed turnips from a safe distance, melding into the crowd when the furious recipients of their bowling skills came looking for them. An old woman pawed at Philo, entreating him, "Where is the emperor, love? Is he ill?"

Philo shook his head before Gracchus pushed the woman away. She fell backwards and there was a general mutterance about "Bloody guards" before a fresh chorus of that popular song *The Whoremongering Praetorian* rang out.

"Where's your ma live?" Gracchus asked, ignoring the hostility aimed his way.

"Esquiline."

Gracchus had imagined Philo's mother to be a small, wrinkled, grey-haired old Indian lady. So the appearance of Aphrodite was a surprise. He found himself mentally calculating whether it were even possible that she had given birth to him, concluding that it was, but only just.

She didn't resemble him in the slightest, being tall and honey-skinned, a direct contrast to Philo's darker complexion and undersized stature. He must take after his father.

"Mother," said Philo nervously indicating the guard with his head.

222

Aphrodite gave a short nod to show she understood and gestured for them to join her round a small circular marble table.

"So what brings you to my house so early in the day, son?"

Philo looked at Gracchus for permission. The guard, hand submerged in a bowl of nuts left on the table, told Aphrodite, "The emperor has been deposed. Galba is emperor now."

Aphrodite's hand went to her throat.

"No need to worry, madam," Gracchus reassured her. "Your son is in no danger. Sabinus wants no bloodbath. It has been a very smooth transition."

Finding her voice she asked coolly, "If it is so smooth why does Philo need an armed escort?"

"Just following orders, madam."

Philo stood up. "We should go," he said, Teretia playing on his mind.

Gracchus, who was rather enjoying Aphrodite's hospitality, sighed, "I hope the food is as good at your place."

Philo embraced his faux mother, whispering Epaphroditus' message to her, "He'll be back as soon as he can."

"Should I worry?" she whispered.

Philo had no suitable reply for this.

THIRTY-TWO

Straton found the antechamber that functioned as Philo's office deserted. There did not seem to have been any kind of disturbance, tablets neatly piled up on the desk, scrolls arranged in ordered pyramids, which was reassuring but the freedman was not there, which was worrying. Philo wasn't much of a fighter: if the guards had come for him, he would have meekly followed them. Straton had always found Philo very compliant.

He pottered around for a bit, picking up a scroll here and there and lining up Philo's styluses. When unable to bear the emptiness and Philo-shaped space any longer, he paced away to the office of his superior officer.

"Bust your way out, did you?" asked Felix.

Straton shrugged.

Felix scratched his beard, a red bushy specimen grown to compensate for a gleaming bald head and to balance out a prominent nose. He was a barrel of a man, rivalling Straton for sheer bulk, with thick red knuckles and possessed of the sort of explosive temper that had flattened Carthage.

His remit was slave placements. If you wanted a boy or girl to keep you warm at night, a juggling Parthian for entertainment, or just someone to order your thoughts for you, Felix was your man. He had an expansive knowledge of the slave workforce and their talents, or lack of. In order to ensure the success of his placements, Felix had one other sphere of authority: he was in charge of the teams of the slave overseers. He was also the only man who could control Straton, though even Felix had to take the odd morning off.

Cracking a stylus in two, Felix glared at his overseer and asked, "Go on, give us the gen. What the fuck have the guards been up to?"

Straton gave some thought to his answer, summing it up in one eloquent word croaked with vehemence: "Bastards."

Felix kicked a table leg. "Bloody Sabinus. I tell you if there is any damage to the goods, it is coming out of his budget."

"Body slave down."

Another kick to the table. Felix had begun his career as an overseer and had never lost that overseer tendency to express emotion outwardly, physically and violently. It was just as well the slaves were locked away, for any in the vicinity would have been in line for a good kicking.

"Which one?"

"Blue eyes."

"Gods, Juba? Can't say I ever liked the fucker but he's worth 30k at least. What happened?"

Straton moulded his features into what he hoped was a look of innocence with maybe a hint of sadness at the demise of valuable merchandise.

"Bastards," he explained.

"Fucking Sabinus," swore Felix with real anger, his face reddening. "You know he banned his troops from visiting the city brothels? Claimed it was unsoldierly behaviour. So then he goes and lets them mind fresh cunt. What does he think is going to happen? I curse that fucker, I really do. I am straight down the temple tonight and I am going to curse that fucker right good. You just know that in nine months time we'll have a race of hooked-nosed, ugly little blighters on our hands. You'll help me examine the goods later? I want a full list of injuries."

Straton nodded.

"Good, good. Apparently I will be allowed to visit them once the emperor's found."

"Emperor not dead?"

"Apparently not. Rumour has it Epaphroditus has squirrelled him away. There's three horses missing. Suggests they've left the city."

Straton's attention was piqued by the mention of Epaphroditus. "Philo?" he asked casually, trying not to betray himself.

"He exists within a five-pace orbit of Epaphroditus so I imagine he went too. Are you hurt?" Felix asked, catching a flash of pain across the overseer's face.

Straton pointed to his throat, though the pain was in truth much lower and much more deeply felt.

Senator Regulus was adamant. "A trial is the proper solution. Expose Nero's crimes to the statute books for all posterity."

Sabinus shook his head sternly. "If only that were possible. I share, as you know, your great belief in the rightness of Roman law. It is what distinguishes us from the barbarians. But these are difficult times. Regrettably the uneducated view Nero with favour: give him a public platform and it can only inflame their passions."

He sneered that final word, as if such things were alien to him, distasteful. He saw himself as above the base human nature, free from the bindings of lust and anger. He was logical, practical, dealing in pure reason. His reason was telling him that a quiet assassination was the best course.

Regulus did not agree, which was disappointing, for Sabinus had great respect for the senator and he had hoped that Regulus would see the superiority of his argument.

Sensing Sabinus' obstinacy, Regulus said, "This is all moot until the emperor, sorry former emperor, is in custody. Is there any news?"

"The reward should motivate. Epaphroditus is unaccountably absent from his post, as is Phaon. I have people watching both their homes for movement."

"And Galba?"

"Icelus is en route with the senate's declaration. He should reach Spain just past the ides. It is glorious is it not, Regulus? I wonder if this is how our ancestors felt in the golden age, at the foundation of the republic. There is much to sort out, though. Galba will not find it easy. Too many of the best people have been corrupted by the invert: they forget their duties, their honour, and their discipline. The mob have been indulged. That must stop. Our legions at least stand proud but vice is insidious and they must be taught to resist. For too long the Roman has been ruled from the bottom up; the greedy, deceitful slave holding sway over matters of state. With the proper help, Galba can overcome this. He is a great man, from the best of families. It will be an honour to stand shoulder to shoulder with him."

There was an underlying irony to this honestly felt speech. Gaius Nymphidius Sabinus, Praetorian prefect and patriot, hater of those sinister, dabbling slaves, had narrowly avoided that very status by a mere ten days. A heavily pregnant Nymphidia finally receiving her just reward for her many services rendered.

228

THIRTY-THREE

Alex liked the Praetorian camp, marvelling at the discipline, every guard knowing at any given moment where he should be. As a slave he recognised the order but the guards marched off with enthusiasm to their duties, no incessant moaning or trudging of feet or slap of the overseer's whip to encourage them.

Alex was proud to be an honorary member of their corps. For some weeks he'd been facilitating orders between cohorts, dashing across the city from the palace to the camp, to Icelus, to Regulus, and back again. He'd never felt more useful.

The guards had grown familiar with him and he'd become a kind of mascot to them. He was an eager sort and they had challenged his ability to learn in a way the palace never had, teaching him the correct method of buckling a shin guard, how to polish a breastplate, the best way to keep their plumed helmets from moulting, how to count the correct number of paces in a march.

Alex had lapped it all up and they had applauded and slapped him on the back every time he mastered a new skill. Alex discarded his long-held messenger ambitions: now all he dearly wanted was to join the Praetorian Guard. Sometimes he even slept at the camp, curled up on the dormitory floor;

nobody at the slave complex noting his absence. He liked them all but his favourite was Antonius Honoratus.

Honoratus had singled him out for praise, was apt to take him aside in the mess for conversation, and had specifically employed him as his own personal messenger. Honoratus' attraction to Alex was entirely innocent. He had in his youth once been married (highly illegally, for soldiers were banned from nuptials) to a flaxen-haired Thracian. In Alex he saw the son they would have had, had she lived. An honest, earnest boy whom he would have taught to throw a javelin and whittle wood, both skills he passed on to Alex, the slave showing much promise in his carpentry attempts.

Sat beside Honoratus, polishing a sword with great care in the special way he had been taught, Alex asked, "Have you ever met Galba?"

Honoratus, holding his own sword upwards to examine his work replied, "Have you ever met Nero?"

"No. I know lots about him though."

"Well, Alexander, Galba is nothing like Nero."

"So you have met him?"

"I served under him in Africa. Hand me that cloth will you?"

Alex did so, querying, "What was he like?"

Honoratus smiled. "You ask a lot of questions."

Grinning, Alex replied, "Only because you never answer them."

"Something that you learn in the army. No man was ever crucified for saying too little."

Alex absorbed this homily, determined to make it his motto.

Another guard approached. "Sabinus wants to see you, Alex," he was told.

Sabinus found Alex useful. Though distrustful of all slaves, he had managed a near, grudging liking for the boy, especially on viewing his tribune's affection for Alex. Sabinus entrusted him with a series of important duties. Indeed, without Alex, deposing Nero would have been far more difficult, particularly communicating and coordinating with Galba's men in Rome.

Alex was perfect for the role, near invisible within the palace complex, he also fitted right into the city streets. He could move with ease between the two and always completed his assignments with prompt efficiency. The mission that Sabinus had in mind now required that same level of invisibility.

"I have orders for you, Alexander."

Alex gave him the official Guard salute that Honoratus had taught him.

"There is a villa four miles outside the city gates. I take it you can ride?"

Alex nodded, failing to add that he was rather a novice in that particular skill.

"You will observe this villa for any unexpected visitors. Should Phaon or Epaphroditus arrive— I take it you know who they are?"

"Yes, sir."

"Good. Should they make an appearance you will bring me word back here immediately. Do you understand?"

"Yes, sir," replied the slave in a monotone that disguised the excitement that bubbled within him.

He had caught the subtext. It was he, Alexander, a mere messenger slave, who was to hunt down the emperor!

The journey had not been enjoyable. Nero had taken fright at the crowd outside the palace. A ragged-looking pleb seeing their horses had cried, "They are going to save the emperor."

This had set off a commotion, attracting the attention of the Praetorians present, only a quick kick to the horses saving them.

Though Epaphroditus had stressed the need for silence, Nero had talked incessantly all the way. Dwelling on past glories, he mourned his tour of Greece.

"I should have stayed. I should have never come back to this cesspit. The Greeks appreciate my talent. They recognise my artistry. How many prizes did I win?"

Epaphroditus, distracted by a passing wagon, muttered, "Many."

"Many, many prizes. I swept the board. Do you remember the Olympics? Wasn't that glorious? When I won the poetry competition at the Olympics, the only man ever to do so in all of history!"

The secretary sat on his horse beset by a gnawing fear. The road was busy; it would only take one word, one "Caesar" accidentally spoken, one person to note the saggy jowls that seemed so familiar, and they would all be dead. Thoughts of Aphrodite and his children filtered through his apprehension.

He was supposed to be finding a suitable husband for his eldest daughter, Silvia, but he had vacillated, unwilling to let her go. She was so dear to him and privately he disliked the idea of some man pawing at her. They both wanted a freeborn husband for Silvia, to lend respectability and remove the stain of slavery from the family. An advantageous marriage could secure her brothers' futures also.

Barred from public office by his freedman status, Epaphroditus was determined his sons would rise straight to the top. He had money enough to buy votes, but good connections were needed. A patrician marriage could provide this and pave the way for excellent marriages for his other girls.

Of course, none of this would happen if Sabinus were to have him killed or if he died with Nero. His estates would be confiscated; Aphrodite would be reduced to penury.

It was at this point that Epaphroditus decided he would live. No matter what it took.

THIRTY-FOUR

Alex, laid out flat in the grass outside Phaon's country villa, pondered. He viewed the emperor's demise as inevitable: a tyrant could only rule so long by fear alone. Eventually the good Roman citizen would rise up against such barbarity. Such had been the case throughout history.

As for Epaphroditus, Alex could not be sorry for him. The man had schemed and plotted his way to the top, now he had simply come unstuck. Mina would mourn a little for him but she was young and she would get over it. He would help her, be her support, just as he always had.

With one exception, he was determined to tell her how he felt. Honoratus had told him of his dead wife, of how he'd defied the law to wed her, suffering the brutal army punishment which confined him to barracks for days.

Yet as Honoratus told it, he never regretted his marriage, even though he had spent such a short time with his flame-haired wife. To Alex, who possessed a strong romantic streak, this was an inspiring story. If one had to suffer for love, then he was prepared to do so. It couldn't be any worse than the daily torment he endured as Mina regaled him with intimate stories about her lover.

He heard the horses before he saw them. Flattening himself in the grass, using a hand to shield the afternoon sun, he saw three horses stop at the end of the road that led to the villa. Even from this distance he recognised Phaon and Epaphroditus. They helped a sturdier figure down and a smaller, slighter boy.

The sturdier figure seemed in some distress, though he could not hear the words. Epaphroditus' gestures clearly indicated that he was attempting to mollify the fatter man. The four walked down the drive, but they did not enter the villa's main entrance but rather moved round the side, passing through thickets of shrubbery, the secretary holding back the branches for the others.

They paused suddenly, the fatter figure gesticulating wildly. Epaphroditus took off his cloak and laid it on the ground. The fat man walked over it with a satisfied nod of the head. Alex watched them make laboured progress, Phaon carrying the boy on his back. Once they were out of sight, he sat up and dashed off to pass on the message that the emperor was found.

They had tried to enter the villa discreetly, for Epaphroditus knew Sabinus would have well-placed scouts. Nero did not do discreet. The insistence that a cloak be laid down for him was just the first of many delays.

Phaon had told them of a tunnel that would offer them unseen entrance. Nero refused to take it claiming that he would not go underground before he died. He whined as they pushed aside brambles: they were scratching his legs making them most unattractive. There were thorns in his cloak: would Phaon please get them removed. He didn't like the look of this villa: how did he know that this wasn't a trap they were leading him into. They were going to abandon him here, leave him to his fate, desert their Caesar like the traitors they were. Oh, how woeful his situation was.

Epaphroditus, who had spent his life serving ungrateful masters, bit back his irritation with ease, dishing out smooth pleasantries which the emperor batted aside with increased hysteria. Sporus, clinging to Phaon's back, looked around anxiously as if expecting an ambush at any time. At one point he looked directly at Alex's position but did not see his friend lying in the grass. The messenger similarly failed to recognise his old room-mate away from his usual court splendour.

They finally gained entry to the villa, Phaon disappearing to find his slaves. Nero crashed on a mattress, pulling his cloak over him and pointedly not looking at either Epaphroditus or Sporus.

"I suppose you expect me to die here, on this filthy bed. Like a dog! Oh, how that befits Caesar!"

It was a somewhat confused metaphor: did dogs usually go to die on a mattress? Epaphroditus let it pass, giving a shaken Sporus a gentle squeeze on the shoulder.

The little eunuch looked up at him and mouthed, "I don't want to die."

The secretary nodded and mouthed back, "Trust me."

He had very quickly worked out that if they could get Nero to go first, they all had a chance of surviving this.

The emperor moaned and cried on the mattress.

"Caesar," whispered Epaphroditus.

"How ugly and vulgar my life has become. This is no credit to Caesar, no credit at all."

"Caesar, please try to calm down."

The emperor sobbed loudly, turning his back to the secretary. Phaon returned, showing Epaphroditus two daggers. Sporus pushed himself backwards into the wall, staring with horror.

"Caesar, my slaves tell me that there are horses on the main road," Phaon told Nero's back. "It is the cavalry come to take you to Sabinus."

"Caesar, it needs to be now," Epaphroditus entreated.

"Caesar is not ready," came the reply.

"Caesar needs to ready himself quickly."

"I will tell you when I am ready," came the sharp retort. "I need a little something to wet my mouth."

"I'll get some water. Give me a hand, Sporus?"

Phaon handed the daggers to Epaphroditus, who examined their points, and led off Sporus.

"You alright, little one?" Phaon asked the eunuch kindly.

Sporus shook his head. "I don't think I can be there when it happens," he said, voice trembling. "I couldn't bear to see him …"

Tears ran unstopped down his cheeks.

"Sporus, he is going to need you there, to give him courage. You wouldn't want him to die without at least one person who loves him?"

"No, that would be awful."

Sporus followed Phaon quietly, staring at his feet. They looked decidedly odd to him, covered as they were in thick boots. He hadn't worn boots for years, certainly not since he became a eunuch/part-time woman.

He wondered if Nero recalled his actual status. He called him Poppaea all the time now; he hadn't been fully Sporus in the emperor's presence for months. Nero would talk eloquently about the plays they had attended, races they had seen, games they had played. Except they hadn't, because that had been the actual Poppaea. Sporus hadn't been there. Although he adored the light being shone on him and was fully dedicated to the role, if he were being entirely honest with himself, he was starting to find it disquieting.

The most troubling aspect of it was the visit by the bearded Greek doctor who talked with him about "completing the procedure" and meandered at length about caterpillars and butterflies. Calvia deciphered it for him later with typical bluntness: "He wants to cut off your cock."

236

Sporus had a vivid recall of his first "procedure" and could think of nothing worse than enduring that agony again. Besides, he was very fond of his penis and had been intending to hang onto it until his death, when they could pickle it, put it in a jar, and display it on a plinth in the temple of Mars Ultor for all he cared.

He would beg if necessary. He wasn't proud. If he wanted something badly enough, he would grovel and cry like the slave he was. He had been known to greet the emperor like an Eastern king, lying prostrate on the floor, kissing his toes and spouting a ton of florid panegyric that he made up on the spot. He'd got the odd kick in the mouth for it, but on most occasions it had secured him an indecent amount of favour.

He wondered what would happen to him now. Would Galba require a catamite? Sporus could dance a little and hold a tune nicely, skills he was happy to fall back on if necessary. If he survived the night that was.

"Epaphroditus," said Nero quietly, still facing the wall.

"Caesar?"

"Was I, was I a good emperor?"

"The best."

"I did try. I tried so very hard to inject some artistry, to raise the cultural bar. To show the people …" He broke down before continuing, "To show the people that their Caesar loved them as they loved him. Did they love me, Epaphroditus?"

"Undoubtedly."

"Yet here I lie," he said in a small voice.

Phaon and Sporus returned with refreshments.

"Caesar, I have water, a little bread."

Nero turned over, sitting up. Phaon handed him the water. He took a sip and winced.

"Nero's bitter brew," he said with a tight smile, refusing the bread.

"Come, Poppaea, weep a little for me."

Sporus, seeing Nero so humbled, did not need any encouragement, falling into a fresh bout of sobs, cuddling up to the emperor.

Nero held out his palms with a resigned look. Epaphroditus handed him the daggers. Sporus buried his face in Nero's chest, determined not to watch.

Trying the point on one of his fingers he said, "One of you should go first, to prepare the way for me."

The colour drained from Phaon's face. Sporus buried himself deeper into Nero. Epaphroditus' brain whirled as he answered calmly.

"We need to ease your way at this end, Caesar. To ensure it is quick, painless. Besides, I think that Caesar could not bear to see his Poppaea die."

Nero, hugging Sporus tight, replied, "You know me so well. She will follow though. You will ensure that her final moments are dignified. And then you will follow."

That was an order. The secretary nodded, noting Sporus' shoulders beginning to shake.

"Where should I?" Nero held a dagger to his throat.

"Your breast, Caesar, through the ribs," suggested Phaon.

They assisted the removal of his tunic. Nero held the dagger over his breast. Taking several deep breaths, he pulled back his hand and went to stab. Epaphroditus felt his heart stop and restart again as Nero halted the dagger at the last point, bursting into tears and crying. "Oh, I can't do it. I can't do it. This is no credit to Caesar, no credit at all."

They were alerted by the sound of hooves and then a series of loud bangs.

"Caesar," implored Epaphroditus.

"I can't do it, I can't do it."

"I'll hold them off," Phaon said, dashing to his feet.

"No," said the secretary. "Stay here."

238

"Epaphroditus, I have to delay them. If he should fall into their hands."

"Wait," he told Phaon.

Turning to Nero, he put his hands on the shaking emperor's shoulders. He looked directly into Nero's watery blue eyes.

"Let me help you," and when the emperor did not reply, "Please, Caesar. Poppaea will follow, you will not be without her long."

Phaon's head twitched at the sound of running feet.

Nero handed Epaphroditus the dagger. Embracing him, the secretary stabbed Nero straight in the chest. Nero gave a grunt and fell back onto the mattress, his eyes wide with shock. Epaphroditus did not hesitate, taking the second dagger he pierced the emperor's throat. A gargling sound, and then silence. Sporus gave a loud shriek and threw himself onto the body of his husband.

The door flung open revealing a group of dusty-looking Praetorians.

Bloody dagger still in hand, Epaphroditus told them, "You are too late. The emperor is dead."

PART II

NYMPHIDIUS SABINUS
SUMMER AD 68

"I must dwell on him for a moment—for he was to be deeply involved in Rome's imminent calamities"
—Tacitus, *The Annals of Imperial Rome*

THIRTY-FIVE

One week later, Spain.

Since an assassin had been sent to eliminate him, Gaius Servius Sulpicius Galba had taken refuge within the comforting protection of his Spanish legion's barracks, waiting to see how Vindex's revolt played out.

He was a tall man, though slightly stooped now with age. A long face with cavernous cheeks was overwhelmed by a large hooked nose, above which sat grey, calculating eyes. A distinguished presence, he dispatched orders with one harsh look from his patrician face, recalling the strong men of the republic. Galba, however, was no republican.

He was assisted by two of his staff members, Titus Vinius and Cornelius Laco. Vinius, a man of action, squarely built with a strong jaw and fair eyes. Laco, the legal advisor, epicurean, soft, devious, and developing a sizeable paunch. Galba hoped to use such contrasting personalities to offer him both positions on any decision.

A laudable aim, though it was rarely successful: Galba usually caught between his bickering advisors. Such was the situation now: they were discussing what to do if Icelus' machinations in Rome failed.

"We march to Rome!" Vinius was advocating.

"And do what?" said Laco, picking a pip from between his teeth. "Ask Nero to kindly relinquish his throne?"

"He'll take fright before we even reach the Alps. If Icelus' reports are true, he's a wobbling mess already. We just need to push, threaten."

"How very noble," drawled Laco.

Vinius scowled. "And you would—?"

"Rome is no matter," he began, earning a scoff from Vinius. "The forces of the empire are here in the provinces. Whoever succeeds here," he tapped a finger on the table, "has Rome for the taking."

Vinius shook his head, "Laco, you cannot be serious! We need to take the city. The legions will only fall behind the man on the throne; they respect the trappings of power. They won't follow any dirty-mouthed commander."

Laco's response was a dry, "They will if he pays them enough."

Vinius began to protest angrily but was halted by Galba barking, "Enough!"

The advisors ceased their bickering. Galba stroked his chin slowly as his grey eyes narrowed. He was seventy-one years old and this was his strength. He had lived through the reigns of Augustus, Tiberius, Caligula, Claudius, and now Nero. He had served all five of those emperors in a series of increasingly exalted positions and he had been careful.

One learnt not to be too flashy, too obvious, too successful. Above all he had learnt never to outdo the emperor. Such a lesson had enabled Galba to extend his considerable wealth without attracting imperial envy.

He had viewed the current emperor's rule with a sceptism few were old enough to possess, for Galba had served Caligula. He remembered in graphic, bloody detail what had happened to Nero's uncle and he noted the nephew slowly alienate the army, the Praetorians, and the senate. Well, there was only one way this was headed.

Except that when Caligula had been cut down, there was his doddering, slobbering uncle Claudius to take over: a blood member of the imperial household linking all the way back to noble Augustus.

There were no blood members now: Nero had casually executed the lot of them. Not one single drop of Augustus' blood remained. Nero was the last of the Julio-Claudians.

When Julius Vindex had written to him proclaiming him the only candidate to replace Nero, Galba had been flattered. And then on closer inspection and the words of Vinius and Laco (who on this sole subject could agree), Galba decided that Vindex was correct. He was not only the best candidate but the only one. No one else could match his record for government service. No one else could match his pedigree. Galba would be emperor.

A soldier marched in briskly and barked, "Icelus, sir."

Icelus? Galba stood up behind the desk. Vinius and Laco took up similar positions, tense, anticipating. Either the freedman had been forced to flee for his life or it was done.

Icelus would have liked to march in efficiently. However, seven long days on a horse made this improbable and he limped in with a wince to be faced with a trio of tense faces.

"Well?" said Galba before he'd even reached the desk.

Icelus gave a pained smile. Handing Galba a scroll he said, "It is done."

Unable to take his word, Galba broke the seal and hurriedly scanned the document; his advisors watching him nervously. Eventually he sat back in his chair and smiled.

"Good work, Icelus."

Vinius and Laco found themselves releasing a breath.

Galba pinched his long chin between his fingers. "You will need orders to take back. Tell the senate ..." He looked up at Laco.

"Tell them he accepts their offer. How is Rome?"

"Edgy," admitted Icelus. "Sabinus seems to be in control, though."

"Good. But is he to be trusted?"

Icelus pondered. "For now. He wants 30,000 sesterces for each guard."

Vinius laughed. "Is he mad?"

"Quite possibly," admitted Icelus. "He is certainly a unique man. I have stalled him so far."

"No matter yet," said Laco. "It can be dealt with later."

"I don't like the sound of this," fretted Galba. "He could be a liability."

"Troops first," Vinius suggested. "Let's go cheer them up with the news that they are going to Rome."

"Are they?" drawled Laco, bringing up their previous squabble. "Surely there are things to be dealt with here."

"Such as?"

"All those governors who failed to heed our cause. They were short-sighted. Do we want such men to hold high positions?" he appealed to Galba, who nodded.

Laco continued, "Nero failed to secure loyalty in the provinces. We'll not make the same mistake. They shall be tried."

"No trials," insisted Galba, his large nostrils flaring. "I will have no grandiose deathbed speeches for the masses."

Vinius raised a quiet point, "Tigellinus?"

"Yes, yes," waved Galba. "You have repaid his favour, he is safe."

"Thank you, Caesar," smiled Vinius.

Galba gave a taut smile at that last word.

"Sabinus?" asked Icelus.

"Is useful", said Laco, "for the time being. I suggest, Icelus, you go make nice to him."

Icelus shot him an annoyed look. "Could I have a drink first? A bath?"

Vinius slapped him on the back. "Not an army man are you, Icelus? We've been fighting for weeks, not a bathhouse in sight."

Galba was scanning the scroll again, a smile playing across his thin lips as his advisors joshed. Eventually he interjected, "You may rest, Icelus," and pointed to a couch. "You may leave," he told Vinius and Laco. "There is much to do."

They nodded and departed, beginning to argue already on what should be accomplished first. Galba turned his attention to his freedman. "So it is done!"

"Yes, sir."

Galba smiled again, "You did well."

"Yes, sir."

"You will return to Rome tomorrow."

Icelus winced, shifting his sore buttocks, but there was to be a pleasant conclusion as Galba stated, "Tonight you stay with me."

THIRTY-SIX

Felix was not happy. In fact, it was fair to say he was steaming. He sat behind his desk fuming as his scribe read out the list of injuries to his stock.

Straton stood beside him: he was not fuming, he was exhausted. He'd spent the last eight days assisting with the cataloguing, holding down traumatised slaves so that their wounds could be noted officially. It was back-breaking, dull work without any of the benefits of casual violence usually associated with his job, accompanied as he was at all times by two administrators posing as independent witnesses.

The death toll had been five; Straton watching with unease as Juba's corpse was examined. The scribe attributed this demise to a "violent blow, which caved in the subject's skull", Straton allowing himself a small smile as the hated guards got the blame.

Felix banged a fist on his desk. "I am 100k out of pocket."

Straton doubted this. Excepting Juba, the departed had been fairly low-level slaves: a pan washer, a middling attractive catamite, a couple of seamstresses, and a flautist.

"I've had to write off half my concubines for the next month at least. The catamites haven't fared much better. Just as fucking well Sabinus ain't got no use for them—fucking dry balls. I am going to see him right now."

The chair scraped back across the floor. Felix was on his feet, rolling up his sleeves, ready for a fight. Straton didn't move.

"You're coming," Felix told him. "Don't look at me like that. What else you got to do?"

Actually he'd hoped to visit Epaphroditus' old office to see if Philo had returned. He was becoming increasingly concerned for the little freedman. Unwilling to divulge any of that, Straton shrugged and followed Felix out.

Sabinus, elbows on desk said, "You are telling me that my guards have abused their position?"

"Too fucking right I am," replied Felix, wound as tight as a ballista. "Tell him," he said to Straton, then remembering his overseer's limitations continued, "No don't tell him, we'll be here all day. He has been up all night with the merchandise. Right fucking mess."

Since assuming power, Sabinus had not made any noticeable changes to his office. It was still as barren as ever, the sole furniture a utility desk and chairs. The only décor was a small bust of a man, which to the overseer's beady eyes seemed vaguely familiar, and a depiction of Cato the Younger looking sternly down. Much like Sabinus was now.

The prefect allowed Felix to rumble on before holding up a palm mid-rant, stating calmly, "You are wrong. My guards are disciplined. Given an order, they follow it. There were no orders issued to commit the acts you claim."

Felix spluttered, giving Straton an incredulous look. "I have witnesses, Sabinus. I have fucking documentary evidence."

He dropped the scroll on injuries onto Sabinus' desk. The prefect did not touch it.

"I should look closer to home for your culprits," he said, shooting the accusation straight at Straton. For once Straton was innocent and faintly offended. The only goods he'd touched in recent days were Juba and Onesimus and neither of them had been particularly entertaining to Straton's tastes.

Sabinus stood up. "Besides, they are only slaves."

He didn't so much as dismiss his visitors as abandon them. Marching out briskly, leaving Felix and Straton staring at his vacated chair.

"Cock," said Straton.

"Too true," agreed his boss. "Know what his problem is?"

This was quite an opening. A discussion of exactly what Sabinus' problem was could happily fill several hours.

"No fucking charm. If we had brought this to Epaphroditus, he'd at least have given us some smooth blarney before doing dick all."

Straton nodded at the truth of this and then pointed to the shelf.

"Caligula," he rasped.

Felix followed Straton's chubby finger to the small bust. He peered, scrunching up his eyes. "So it fucking is. Well that bodes fucking well, don't it?"

Felix aside, who on a matter of principle disliked everyone, Nymphidius Sabinus was not endearing himself to the palace workforce. The carnage his guards had committed was not easily forgotten. It led to an uneasy atmosphere, for who knew when Sabinus might decide to let his troops loose again.

Then there were the slaves who had colluded with the guards. Yes, they had received their promised promotions but they were empty honours, ostracised as they were by their furious colleagues. Onesimus and the others who had assisted Sabinus learnt that to be highly placed and ignored was just as painful as their former lowly status; with the added humiliation of lacking the skills necessary to perform those new roles. Nobody was in a hurry to illuminate them.

If the palace was uneasy then so was the city, held as it was under Sabinus' nailed boots. Notices had gone up officially banning guild meetings, weddings, and gatherings of any

251

kind. The theatres and circuses were shut and a strict curfew was in place that all had to be indoors by the set of the sun.

Though this was only a temporary measure until the events were more settled, rumours flowed that the closure of the bathhouses and bars was a permanent edict. Sabinus' well-known dislike of anything "fun" gave this story legs.

Protests were erupting daily outside the palace calling for the return of Nero. Flowers, cakes, and small devotional objects were placed in front of the great doors by loyal citizens. Sabinus had them removed, yet the next day there were even more. The prefect put this down to Galba's absence. The mob wanted, needed a figurehead. Once Galba was in Rome these silly little stunts would cease. In the meantime the guards suppressed dissent with their usual skill.

Placing down a small clay representation of the god Apollo (for he was a lyre player just like the emperor), Teretia was accompanied by her father and Philo.

She wiped away a tear. "It is so sad," she told them.

"To think, love, you saw him the night before it all happened." Teretius hugged her close to him.

"And he was such a nice man. So kind."

Philo, who'd witnessed Nero sign an awful lot of death warrants over the years, maintained his silence, unwilling to disillusion them.

"Don't you worry, love. We all went down the temple, didn't we, and asked the gods to give him safe passage. He'll be in the Garden of Hesperides right now."

Teretia gave a sad nod.

"So there is no need to get upset, for the gods look after their own. He'll be reunited with Emperor Claudius and Empress Agrippina and the Empresses Octavia and Poppaea."

Not usually given to sarcasm, Philo couldn't help think what a happy family reunion that would be; imagining Nero caught between his two deceased wives: the virtuous Octavia and the wanton Poppaea. It had been an interesting spectacle in life; in eternity, it would be quite something. Then dismissing those thoughts as disloyal and feeling guilty for thinking badly of the recently deceased emperor, he told them, "I had better go in."

"We'll come in with you, son, make sure you're alright."

Though Teretius possessed the strong shoulders of a builder, Philo didn't fancy his chances against a cohort of Praetorians. His own personal Praetorian, Gracchus, had thankfully left his side once news of Nero's death was received. A relief, since Philo was loath to spend another night kipping on the floor of his own room while the guard took the bed. As Gracchus was the one with a sword, Philo could not complain. The guard also snored, loudly and persistently.

Philo, lying on his back, feeling the floor boards vibrate with each snort from Gracchus, wondered how vigilant the guard actually was. He was reminded of the days when he shared a room with Lysander, who the night before an important engagement would intone his announcements, Philo lying awake listening to: "Nero Claudius Caesar Augustus Germanicus, Pontifex Maximus, Father of his Country, Holder of the Tribunician Power, Holder of the Consular Powers. Imperial Majesty I present unto you … Imperial Majesty …" until despairing of ever sleeping, he would dress and wander off to his office for a bit of light filing.

He didn't have any filing here, but he couldn't bear the noise any longer. So he grabbed his satchel, slipped out of the door, and padded barefoot to the kitchen. Opening the shutter, there was just enough morning light to see and he settled himself down at the table, pulling out the minutes of a meeting he'd been revising before his world had exploded.

He was correcting a grammatical error when he heard a shuffle. Looking up he was overcome by the vision that was poised in the doorway: Teretia, sleepily rubbing her eyes, her golden hair tied in a single plait and cocked over one shoulder.

She was dressed in a flimsy summer nightgown and as it was a sticky night, it clung to every curve she possessed; revealing in clear definition two pink, very hard nipples. The stylus shot straight out of Philo's fingers across the table.

Squinting, she asked confused, "Philo? Is it breakfast?"

He shook his head distractedly, mouth hanging ever so slightly open.

Sitting down beside him, she asked, "Are you sad about the emperor?"

He didn't think he was particularly. It wasn't as if he really knew Nero. He'd stood in an awful lot of meetings with the emperor. He'd attended many of the same events. Yet he had never actually spoken to him, nor had Nero directly addressed him, not even so much as a, "You boy," though the emperor had on occasion made reference to him as Epaphroditus' Indian boy, a geographical error that made Philo wince every time he heard it.

If Teretia hadn't been looking so half-dressed, he probably would have told her this. Instead he responded with a non-committal shrug, which he hoped made the point as well.

"And your boss?"

He had been trying not to dwell on Epaphroditus. At the mention of his name, his shoulders sagged.

"Oh, I am so sorry."

She looked at him with concerned, kind eyes. Faced with such compassion, Philo found many of his worries slipping out.

"I just can't see how he can survive this. There are soldiers looking everywhere for the emperor. I can't see how he will get away. Sabinus hates Epaphroditus. If he should capture him …"

She didn't ask who Sabinus was. She didn't even question why he should hate Epaphroditus. She just listened, squeezing his hand when he stumbled over his words, so quickly did they roll from his tongue.

"And I don't know how I could break it to Aphrodite if, if he, if he should be—" he rubbed an eye with the heel of his hand. "If he should be dead," he completed finally.

Facing up to it, making it true.

Teretia watching him suffer, thought her heart might burst. He looked desolate. She wanted to help so badly, to offer a small amount of comfort in these dreadful times for him. She knew there was nothing she could say that would achieve this, for though Teretia was young, death was not new to her: there had been all those brothers and sisters she would have so liked to meet.

There was no platitude that would bring Epaphroditus back to him. Instead, she instinctively reached across and held him in her arms. Philo happily relaxed into her embrace and because she was so nice, so kind, so sweet, he had found the tears rolling down his cheeks and he near sobbed all over her.

Later he was to squirm when he remembered this scene, not just because he felt there was something inherently pathetic about a grown man crying on the shoulder of a young girl, but for what happened next.

It was as he was calming down, Teretia supportively stroking his back, that she inadvertently touched one of his more tender Straton-induced weals. A shot of pain rushed through his blood and, adjusting his head slightly, he accidentally glanced straight down her cleavage: a truly glorious sight which caused him to spontaneously disprove all those rumours that flourished about him.

He flew backwards on the bench, grabbing his satchel and pulling it in front of him with a speed not seen since Statilia had gone all out for Sporus at the party. Teretia, looking as surprised as Sporus had when clocking the empress running towards him, had said nervously, "Philo?"

Hoping that her widened eyes were the result of his sudden movement rather than at what had been poking at her navel a moment before, Philo hastily told her that he was very tired and must go back to bed. He fled to his room, diving under his blanket, satchel still in place.

Walking through the palace with Teretius at his side, he was acutely aware that he had crossed a line by becoming sexually aroused whilst in an embrace with his landlord's nightie-clad daughter. It was exactly the sort of behaviour that would get him evicted.

"This is, erm, where I work," he told his landlord.

He opened the door, half-hoping to see Epaphroditus waiting to berate him for his abysmal timekeeping as usual. Feeling crushed when the room was silent, empty, he walked through to the adjoining office, just in case.

Teretius gave a low whistle as he marvelled at the opulence of Epaphroditus' former office and then, being a builder, mentally dissected how much it must have cost. Philo checked over the desk, hopeful of a message from his boss telling him what he should do.

All he found was a to-do list, and a series of unsigned invoices. Seeing his distress, Teretius asked, "Do you want us to stay? Because we can, if you want us to."

"No, it's alright. Things have to get back to normal."

Whatever normal was.

He walked them to the door. "You know your way out?"

"We'll be fine," Teretius assured him. "You just take care, son."

Teretia stood on tiptoes and gave him a small peck on the cheek. Philo cast a nervous look at his landlord. Teretius didn't seem to mind, giving him a friendly wave on their exit.

Standing behind his desk, he decided to finish off his filing and then start on the agenda for the usual morning meeting that probably wasn't going to happen. Hearing a noise and thinking it was Teretius returned, he began, "Really, I am," before coming to an abrupt halt when he saw who it was.

Straton was gazing at him as if he were the most precious jewel in the empire. Philo found himself enveloped in a fierce hug, Straton running his paw of a hand through his hair and muttering what Philo assumed were endearments. In-between smothering kisses the freedman pleaded, "Not here. Please not here," keeping one frantic eye on the door.

The overseer was too overjoyed at his return to comply.

THIRTY-SEVEN

Where most were keeping their opinions to themselves and their heads distinctly down, the former Empress Statilia Messalina was fully prepared to show the Praetorian prefect and de facto ruler of Rome just how unimpressed she was by him. She rewarded him with her haughtiest, stoniest glare. His fine calves were of no concern to her now.

"Do you come to tell me I am a widow?" she asked.

Sabinus, ever so slightly uncomfortable at being in a woman's private area, stood by the door gleaming in full uniform, his helmet held under his arm.

"It was necessary for reasons of state. I am very sorry, madam."

"No you're not. You're not at all."

Though she knew Nero must be dead and though she had never even liked her husband, she nevertheless felt a tiny stab of sadness at his demise. Swallowing her emotion, she glared straight at Sabinus, asking, "And what did my husband ever do to you?"

"He was a despot."

"Who promoted you beyond your worth, offering you his loyalty and trust. Look how you have repaid his kindness."

"I would not expect you to understand politics."

"Because I am a woman."

"Because you are a woman," he agreed.

"What does politics have to do with imprisoning a free woman?" she persisted, determined to strike blows on behalf of her deceased husband.

"You are not my prisoner."

"There are guards on the door."

"They are there for your safety."

She burst into laughter "Really? Who is threatening me, Sabinus? Aside from yourself."

"I am no threat to you, madam."

"We are talking in circles," she said, feeling her irritation rise: why wouldn't he just say what he meant? Devious, duplicitous, traitor. "I wish to leave the palace. There is no place here for me now. I shall return to my family."

"No," said Sabinus, meeting her eyes for the first time.

This fazed her, for she broke the connection pleading, "But why? I am nothing. A consort to a dead man."

"You have proved yourself a good consort."

"Is that a compliment?"

"Consider it so. It is a role that few women have inhabited successfully. Livia, perhaps. The rest have been disappointing." He curled a lip. "Claudius' Messalina; Agrippina; Caesaria; Poppaea."

Statilia began to feel uneasy. Sabinus, still stood a safe distance from her, continued on his theme. "A good wife is hard to find. So few measure up to the necessary standards. It would be a shame to lose one who in most categories is more than adequate."

The empress was definitely uneasy now, shifting on her couch.

He came over and sat opposite her, engaging her with an intense gaze.

"You are from an excellent family, you know how to behave in public, your private life is unblemished, and you are attractive in countenance."

He listed this as if drilling his troops. There was no emotion in it, no flattery. He was stating the facts as he saw them: nothing more, nothing less. He took hold of her hand, examining it in his own.

For one barmy moment, Statilia thought he was going to propose. He quashed this by stating: "Galba is unmarried. He will be looking for a wife to continue his line. You have yet to prove your fertility but you are within childbearing age. A more attentive husband will sow you."

Statilia's eyes opened very wide in response to this extraordinary speech. Noting her horrified expression, Sabinus continued, "Galba is a good man. He has none of the vices to which you have been subjected in recent times." He reassured her, "He will treat you well. With respect."

Statilia Messalina had endured two disappointing marriages. She was not looking for a third.

"Nymphidius Sabinus, I intend to return to my family home, where I will live a private life as a widow. I do not wish to marry Galba. You are not my father: you cannot compel me into matrimony."

Sabinus let go of her hand, "But it is a great honour."

"That I do not seek."

"It is your duty as a woman to produce future citizens. You have no other purpose," he babbled, so surprised was he by her rejection.

She stood up. "You offend me."

This threw him completely. "Offend you? I have the greatest admiration for you. For all that you have endured with dignity."

"Get out!"

Sabinus stood up, aware that Statilia's attendants were staring at him with awe. Mina was particularly taken: she had never seen Sabinus anything but composed.

"Madam."

"I said get out!"

"Empress," he accidentally interjected, which was the opening she had been waiting for to deliver her sting.

"No, not empress. You murdered the emperor and then mere days after his death, you dare to come here and tell me it is my duty, my purpose, my very point of being to open my legs for the man who has usurped my husband's rightful position. How dare you? Get out!"

In all his years as a soldier in some of the most dangerous spots on the edge of civilisation, Nymphidius Sabinus had never retreated. He had stood firm as slingshots raced past his ears, as arrows plunged into his shield, and as hundreds of naked Britons ran full pelt at him. Faced with Statilia Messalina in full outrage, he retreated.

He justified his humiliating exit by telling himself that she was a hysterical woman, unable to listen to reasoned arguments. The best recourse was to let her calm down of her own accord. Once she had considered his words, she would realise what a great compliment he was paying her and what an honour it would be for her to accept Galba as a husband.

Sabinus was not lying; he genuinely did have a deep admiration for Statilia Messalina. He knew, as the whole palace did, the degrading activities that Nero had forced her into.

That she was able to hold onto his arm at public functions for the entire world to see and behave exactly like a loving wife should, was testimony in Sabinus' eyes to the empress' great strength of character.

He cast her as one of those great Roman women: the Sabine women who stood between their warring husbands and the men who had defiled them. Cornelia, the mother of Gracchi, that epitome of womanly virtue. The vestal Claudia Quinta, whose chastity was proven when she pulled a barge holding the likeness of the goddess Cybele along the river Tiber. That sort of bird.

He would never admit it to himself, for he felt himself above such emotions, but Nymphidius Sabinus had just the tiniest crush on the empress. In another life they would have made a good match, for they both had a strong sense of duty and a similar grim obstinacy, as well as a noted attraction towards each other. In this life Sabinus' ignoble background prohibited him from pursuing such an alliance and his own peculiar nature inhibited him from seeking the comforts of any woman.

He stomped back to his office. She would agree. He had timed his offer ill, he could see that now. Once she had time to think about it, to mull, she would agree. He sat at his desk, pulled out a blank scroll, and began penning yet another missive to Galba.

Mina took the delicious story of the empress and Sabinus back to the slave complex. Here it was embellished, embroidered, exaggerated, and added to considerably. Hearing the tale back, Mina was amused to learn that Statilia had shown her displeasure by kneeing the prefect in the groin and that he was currently being treated by one of the doctors for a displaced testicle.

The atmosphere in the slave complex had improved markedly over the past week. Not that it was forgotten, for the black eyes and staggering gaits were very much evident, but they had developed a black humour about it, which had raised spirits.

The elder concubines started it, regaling the injured girls with some graphic descriptions of their past partners. Notably, old Emperor Claudius with his twitching head and the globules of spit that formed in the corners of his mouth. Thalia revealed that at the moment of orgasm, the late emperor's eyes would cross. A number of the concubines squealed with recognition, and the younger girls couldn't help but laugh.

A new phrase entered their vocabulary and it was found to fit all kinds of situations. "Better a guard than a Claudius!"

Even Mina's own rape was added to the jokes. Juba's death immediately afterwards being put down to her staggering sexual prowess, and she was nicknamed "the cunt of doom". Mina rather liked this. It didn't heal her bruises and it didn't stop the terrifying dreams that haunted her but it did make her smile and she used it as a threat whenever she could.

Like everyone else when news of Nero's death leaked out, she assumed that Sporus and Epaphroditus had perished too. She tried to find Alex to tell him, but he was not in his room, his room-mate Anacreon admitting that he had not seen him since the night of the party.

Mina, sitting down on Alex's bed, had asked, "You don't think …?" finding that she couldn't finish the sentence.

"I don't know what to think," said Anacreon. "All I know is that he has been really secretive of late and I have barely seen him for weeks."

She remembered her last conversation with Alex. He had been quieter than usual, preoccupied. He was not one for keeping secrets, at least not from her. They told each other everything, they always had. She couldn't even ask Sporus if he knew what had been bothering their friend.

Poor Sporus. She felt his loss keenly. The world seemed much duller without him. She, Lysander, and Daphne snuck out one night and held a small ceremony for him. They each read a eulogy, pouring a libation of wine into the ground and sacrificing a small cat (for it was the only creature they could catch) for the eunuch.

Mina, closing her eyes, saw her friend at his magnificent best. Dazzling, beautiful, and practising his smile number five, which he saved for public occasions. The three of them marched back arm in arm, sharing anecdote after anecdote, dissolving into giggles.

And though Sporus had always claimed he wanted golden chariots ridden by the most handsome men from each of the empire's provinces, an elephant, thirty quick-stepping giraffes, and a thousand wailing mourners for his funeral, Mina hoped he would have enjoyed their small send-off.

THIRTY-EIGHT

Philo awoke in unfamiliar surroundings. His sleepy mind tried to make sense of it. He wasn't in his room at the Viminal. The bed was far too comfortable. Opening an eye, he saw a large, hairy arm draped across him. He lifted it carefully and returned it to its owner. Not carefully enough. Straton opened his black eyes and gave him a lazy smile. "Morning."

After Straton had fully expressed his joy at Philo's survival, he told the freedman in his usual sparse way, "Look after you. Protect you."

Then he carried off a chair and positioned himself outside the door to Philo's antechamber. Sitting at his desk, Philo could see the bulge of the overseer's arm by the frame. He wasn't clear exactly what he was being protected from, given that the only man who truly terrified him was sitting outside the door armed with a cudgel.

Left alone in his little office with no work to do, Philo was unable to concentrate and was plagued with thoughts of Epaphroditus and poor Aphrodite, widowed and alone. He knew he must visit her, though what he would say, he had no idea. What could he say to ease her grief?

He felt it too, for there was no one that Philo admired more than Epaphroditus. He was the best of bosses and, Philo felt tentatively, a friend too. He was often invited to that elegant Esquiline house for supper; Epaphroditus and Aphrodite always showing great concern for him, even helping him with his freedom fund when it became clear that Felix's valuation of him far outstripped his savings.

Epaphroditus had laughed. "Philo, you are the highest placed scribe in the palace. You're fluent in nine languages, two of which I had never heard of until I employed you. Your Greek is so good that you corrected the Athenian assembly for misuse of a past participle. They use your script writing for the youngsters in the imperial training school to emulate. Of course you're worth fifty thousand sesterces. Personally I'd pay double for you. There are flashy buggers out on the Caelian Hill who pay fifty thousand for a mere meat carver."

Memories such as these flickered through his mind until he worked himself into a fresh pit of misery, picking at the edge of his desk, splintering his fingers. Eventually he could hold it in no longer and he broke into a bout of sobbing. This sniffling elicited the attention of Straton, who turned his bristled head into the room. Seeing Philo so distressed, he was immediately over.

One thing to be said for Straton was that he did not ask questions. Kneeling before Philo, the overseer had growled with some concern, "Stay."

Philo, consoling himself it would at least take his mind off his troubles, meekly followed him to his quarters.

Swinging his feet out, sitting on the edge of the bed and rubbing his eyes, he felt ten times more miserable than he had the night before. Epaphroditus was still dead, Aphrodite still a widow. He would now have to face a series of well-meaning questions as to where he had spent the night, and he was beginning to suspect that the overseer's interest in him was more than merely opportunistic.

Straton dreamily traced a scar down his back, leisurely following its path from his shoulder to the dip of his buttocks. Philo flinched out of the way, abruptly jumping to his feet and announcing, "I've got to go to work."

"Had no breakfast."

"I'm not hungry." A statement that was instantly disproved by a loud rumble from his stomach.

The overseer chuckled, getting up and throwing on a tunic. He pushed Philo gently back onto the bed by his shoulders, telling him, "Wait here," returning with a steaming bowl of porridge and two spoons.

Sitting on the edge of the bed, Straton's intense glare on him, Philo abruptly lost his appetite. The overseer tried to encourage him to eat but he felt distinctly sick and handed the bowl back untouched. He felt even sicker when Straton, in his sparse way, suggested that he knew just the thing to bring on his appetite and began to nuzzle playfully at his neck.

Aphrodite had endured a terrible week. She had barely slept, jumping at every noise she heard in case it was him, in case it was news. He promised he would be home. He wouldn't have said it if he had not believed it himself. She clung to that thought, even after Philo brought her news of Nero's fate.

She refused to imagine life without him. They had known each other their whole lives near enough, since they were children. Amusing in a way, his insistence that you couldn't force Philo and Teretia together, when that was exactly how they had met, thrust together by Apollodorus' grand vision.

She remembered their first meeting with clarity. She was truly terrified, sat in a corner hugging her knees, when a boy was shoved in before the door was firmly slammed shut behind him. The boy, who turned and looked at her with interest, was of medium height, slim with neat brown hair, his only truly stand-out feature was a pair of unusual green eyes. Aphrodite pushed her back further into the wall, shaking and willing it to be over quickly.

He was utterly unlike the others though, sitting down a comfortable distance away from her, he introduced himself.

When she didn't answer this, Epaphroditus began an amiable monologue, touching on such subjects as the impracticality of white for the palace uniforms, the results of the previous day's chariot race, and how he felt there was really so little meat on a dormouse that it was hardly worth roasting one.

Eventually she felt she had to interrupt. "That overseer will be back," she warned him. "He will expect to see you mounting me."

"I assumed you didn't want to. Your body language screams resistance."

"That wouldn't stop most."

"True but you look like a scratcher to me. I value my skin. I try to take care of it." He stroked his own sleek arm.

"And when the overseer returns? What do you think he'll do to your lovely skin?"

"So you agree that it's lovely," he said smiling, showing a set of white even teeth. "Now that is progress. You looked like you wanted to murder me when I came in."

She unfolded her legs. "You'd better," she told him, and began to lift her skirt.

He leaned forward and placed his hand on hers. "Don't," he told her. "We can fake it."

"Fake it? Are you mad? How can we fake it?"

Epaphroditus divulged his plan. "He is going to look through that grill and all he's expecting to see is a pair of heaving buttocks and hear grunting. I'm prepared to provide the buttocks if you provide the grunts."

He was so confident, so sure of success that she found herself agreeing. They worked out the best position to affect the illusion and when Straton looked through the grill, as predicted, he saw exactly what he expected to see, a pair of slaves going at it like dogs.

Having no interest in such sport, he slammed the grill shut and shuffled off to check on the next couple. Meanwhile Aphrodite and Epaphroditus straightened themselves up.

"Told you that would work."

And they shared a conspiratorial smile.

That memory cheered her spirits. Epaphroditus would not want her sitting in the house in this gloomy light, he would not want her wallowing in misery. He would want her to fight for him.

She called to her slave, "Callista, help me dress. I am going out."

The guard on the door, a soldier with a mean-looking slash to the face, looked down at the little group: Callista carrying Rufus, and Aphrodite holding onto two other little hands. Aphrodite had worked out her strategy carefully. She'd known Sabinus for many years and was fully aware of his traditional views on women, and their functionality. Aphrodite therefore brought her three youngest children with her to remind him that she had more than fulfilled her womanly duties.

She deliberated hard over which of the children should accompany her. The perfect number was three because once you delivered a successful trio of children, the Roman state considered you worthy enough for a tax break. As regards to personnel, she decided on Rufus, Claudia, and Julia. They were the cutest-looking of her brood. Rufus was at that endearing baby stage when everything was a puzzle or a joy, Claudia was a little girl brimming with happiness, and Julia had dark curls that Aphrodite felt were particularly pleasing. Rufus, Claudia, and Julia were also the most likely to behave.

Her teenage daughters Silvia and Faustina could not be relied upon to be polite to the prefect and were likely to fall into some complicated and bitter row of their own. Her son

Pollus was going through that difficult, brooding period: a time of life Sabinus might well recognise but was unlikely to be charmed by.

"Aphrodite Sabina to see Nymphidius Sabinus," announced Callista loudly.

Aphrodite's other name was not Sabina, it was Claudia, but this small lie would allow her access to Sabinus as a supposed relative.

Proculus pulled at the neck of his breastplate as he was rewarded Aphrodite's most devastating smile.

"May we enter?" she asked, adjusting her dress so that she would not offend Sabinus with any accidental flashes of flesh.

Proculus moved his spear aside without any questions. "Of course, madam," he replied, throwing her back a charming smile of his own.

Lysander was lounged against Sabinus' door waiting for someone to announce. He was bored. People came to see Nero all the time, which gave him ample opportunity to impress with his pleasing baritone and correct pronunciation of all those tricky client king names. Nobody wanted to visit Sabinus. Lysander did not blame them. He'd only worked for Sabinus a single morning and he'd never felt more depressed.

Hanging around Nero's rooms, there was always the chance to eye up some gorgeous dancing girl, enjoy the sports that Nero so liked, and snare some of the delicious canapés that whizzed by.

Sabinus didn't do anything. He just sat at his desk writing, occasionally yelling at a guard (but without the entertaining hysterics that Nero employed), and then at intervals of precisely two hours (Lysander knew this for he was timing the prefect by the water clock that stood dripping on a plinth), he went for a stroll and came back again. Presumably for the latrine, Lysander assumed, thinking how typical it was of Sabinus to have ordered his bowel movements into a fixed schedule.

He hoped that Galba was more interesting. Otherwise he might have to rethink his career. Seeing Aphrodite and her brood approach certainly perked him up.

"Hello, it's Lysander, isn't it? Please could you announce Claudia Aphrodite really quickly so he doesn't have an opportunity to object?"

Lysander sensed a plot. "Certainly can. Can I announce the moppets too? Please? It would really make my day."

Aphrodite gave Lysander a smile. "They are Claudia, Julia, and Rufus."

Lysander bent down and shook their little hands. "Nice to meet you."

Claudia ran forward and attached herself to one of Lysander's legs. He smiled down at her and ruffled her hair.

Sabinus was finishing off his note of felicitations to Galba when the announcer slid in and said in double time, "Claudia Aphrodite and her children, Claudia, Julia, and Rufus."

Aphrodite entered smartly on the beat of the last syllable.

"Nymphidius Sabinus," she greeted him with an injection of fake warmth.

He looked at her suspiciously as she settled herself opposite him. Callista standing discreetly behind with Rufus, Aphrodite pulled Claudia and Julia onto her lap. They gazed up at Sabinus with Epaphroditus' green eyes.

"How can I help you?" he asked briskly, angry at being surprised in such a manner.

She forced a smile at him. "I seem to have misplaced my husband. I thought if anyone might know where he is, you would. I hear you are an important man now."

Sabinus tried to discern how much truth there was in her words. He had never been much good at reading women and she was an ex-slave, duplicitous and grasping as all her kind were.

"I am afraid I cannot help you," he told her bluntly.

Trying to keep her voice even, she asked, "Because you do not know or because you wish to torture me and my children?"

She hugged her babies tight.

Emotion did not move Sabinus, he felt it unnecessary and irrational.

"That is all I can say. If you will excuse me, I have other duties to attend to."

"If you will release his body," she said, unwilling to let him go. "It would be the decent thing to do."

She saw the confusion cross Sabinus' face. Aphrodite felt her heart quicken. He wasn't dead. Her husband was alive.

THIRTY-NINE

After that first night, Epaphroditus knew he was not going to be killed. There was no reason why, if those were their orders, the soldiers would dally in their task. For a long time he couldn't fathom why Sabinus would spare him. In his place, Epaphroditus would not have hesitated to have the prefect executed. In fact many a dull day had been enlivened by imagining that very scenario.

He did not like Sabinus and the feeling was mutual, their relationship coloured by the secretary's past dalliance with the prefect's mother. Epaphroditus would personally maim any man who touched his daughters and assumed this worked the other way. Which was why he couldn't understand his continued mortal existence.

Eventually he worked it out. Sabinus was waiting for his orders from Galba. A typical soldier, Sabinus would not move unless commanded to. Which was useful because it meant that someone else was yanking Sabinus' strings. Someone who might be more lenient towards the former secretary.

Epaphroditus had read up on Galba. There seemed little to him. He certainly would never have expected the Spanish governor to undertake such an audacious coup. Still, the guy had survived the reigns of Tiberius, Caligula, Claudius, and now Nero. That had to take some nous. Or good advisors.

Epaphroditus knew that behind every great man were a series of better men telling him what to do. The secretary knew of three such men attached to Galba: his freedman Icelus, Titus Vinius, and Cornelius Laco. He was interested to meet all three of them. They might well be the cleverest men in the empire.

He was being held along with Phaon and Sporus in Phaon's wine cellar, which was some consolation to the freedman who could at least keep an eye on his precious vintages.

"I knew I shouldn't have bought this house," he grumbled to Epaphroditus. "When I handed over the coins, a black bird flew overhead. It was a bad auspice and I should've paid attention."

He kicked out a foot, hitting an amphora which wobbled, and then threw himself forward and caught it before it hit the floor. He hugged it to his chest and gently placed it with the others, which lay propped against the wall. Running a hand across his brow he exclaimed, "Phew! Falerian. Cost me a small fortune."

Epaphroditus, lounged against the wall, crossed his ankles. "Perhaps we could crack it open now," he suggested lightly.

"Not a chance. I am saving it for a special occasion."

"For the emperor's memory?"

"More special than that."

This made Epaphroditus laugh, a moment of levity before his mind turned to more serious matters.

"Sporus," he addressed the eunuch in a whisper, keeping one eye on the grill in the door.

Sporus was curled in a ball gently sobbing, his small body shaking.

"Sporus," repeated Epaphroditus, placing a hand on the eunuch's shoulder. "Sporus, listen to me. You have to listen to me."

The sobs subsided slightly and he rolled over facing the secretary with red eyes.

"When they question us, you must keep silent. Do you understand?"

This was quite a request. Sporus chatted animatedly even through sleep.

"I am going to pass you off as a mute scribe. Sabinus will no doubt have a warrant out for you."

Sporus' wet eyes opened very wide. "A warrant—?" he managed to squeak out before Epaphroditus put a finger to the eunuch's lips.

"Silent, yes? Your voice gives you away."

So far the guards had failed to recognise Sporus' significance. The eunuch, through no fault of his own, was apt to be used as an example of Nero's unsuitability to reign. If Sabinus wanted to make a point about the new regime's moral code, Sporus would be a useful propaganda tool.

Behind the finger, Sporus nodded, his body shivering with fright.

"Good lad. Try to get some sleep."

Sporus curled back to face the wall.

Phaon, sat next to Epaphroditus, whispered in his ear. "What do you think of our chances?"

Epaphroditus gave a yawn, stretching out his arms. "Grim. But then they've often been grim."

Phaon nodded. One did not get to such palace positions without facing a fair amount of peril along the way. Palace politics were deadly. As the previous imperial secretary and head of the messengers section could attest.

Epaphroditus sat back and rested his head against the wall, letting his brain whirl through a dozen potential survival tactics. Something would occur. That he was positive of. He was not going to die like this. And certainly not under of the orders of that dry-balled, humourless excuse for a man, Nymphidius Sabinus!

In fact the politicking for Epaphroditus' life was already taking place. Aphrodite did not rest. Her husband may be alive, which was truly wonderful, but he was not with her. There seemed little point in going to see Sabinus again. She would appeal to a higher authority. One with the necessary power and influence to release her husband.

A broad-shouldered, muscled, black slave wearing only a loin cloth escorted her through frescoed rooms. He did not speak to her, so she assumed his presence was mere decoration. There were a lot of decorative slaves in this house; all male and all similarly under-attired. As a decent, married woman Aphrodite was not sure where to look.

The black slave passed her on to a huge bare-chested man with long hair entwined in Gallic style tresses, a gold torc encircling his thick neck, and wearing nothing but patterned trousers.

"My mistress is ready to receive you," he said in perfect Latin with no trace of a foreign accent, Gallic or otherwise.

She was led through to a pleasant lounge, the walls white and airy with a frieze of dancing nymphs; painted panels depicted scenes from Roman history with a graceful hand. Her hostess was resting on a low couch, one shapely leg held in the air, another muscled he-man massaging it with long strokes. On seeing her guest, the leg was lowered, the masseur dismissed with a wave of the hand.

"Aphrodite, how wonderful to see you."

She was kissed on both cheeks by a woman, who though her hair was streaked with grey and her face lined, retained her exquisite beauty.

"Nymphidia Sabina," replied Aphrodite warmly.

Nymphidia arranged herself back onto her couch completing the manoeuvre with a grace that made Aphrodite feel awkward and gangly in comparison. She gestured to the trousered slave.

"Bring some refreshments, my dear, will you?"

A most unusual way to address one's slaves, the look that passed between Nymphidia and her Gaul suggesting to Aphrodite that the slave was more than mere property. Gazing around the room, she noted four other skimpily clad male slaves standing to attention. Did Nymphidia own no slave girls?

The Gaul returned with a tray of drinks, which he placed on the table.

"Thank you, Hercules," said Nymphidia, and then when the slave departed, she confided in Aphrodite. "Well, what else could I call him? He is an absolute hero!"

This made Aphrodite smile for the first time in many days.

They exchanged pleasantries, Nymphidia asking after her children's health, which was the opening she needed for her request.

"Of course they desperately miss their father."

Nymphidia, taking an elegant sip from a glass goblet, asked innocently, "Why, where is Epaphroditus? Not another fact-finding trip to Greece?"

"No, your son has him under arrest."

"Gaius?" Nymphidia put her drink down. "Are you sure?"

"Positive. I went to see him yesterday. Nymphidia, please could you talk to him? He will listen to you."

"Gaius must have his reasons," she insisted. "These are strange times. Perhaps it is a short-term measure until events calm down."

"I just want my husband back," Aphrodite pleaded, and then swallowing her pride, added quietly, "I know that you were once close. I would hope that you remembered him fondly enough to help him when he really needed it."

Nymphidia met the younger woman's eyes unabashed. "I cannot promise anything but I will talk to him."

Aphrodite grasped her hands, "Thank you, Nymphidia. I will not forget this."

The older woman gave a gracious smile. A smile that had ensnared emperors and princes. "I am sure it is all a terrible misunderstanding."

Sabinus did not like his mother visiting him at work. She was a distraction to his men. Even Lysander announcing her arrival had a look of lust in his eyes. Not surprising really when Nymphidia swept in, a vision in a pink chiffon dress. It was cut low on her chest, highlighted by the large heart-shaped pendent that hung between her breasts. She was wearing a dark wig styled fashionably, which took years off her age. She could easily have passed for Sabinus' sister.

Jaw clenched shut, Sabinus saw Lysander's eyes run down his mother's perfect figure.

"Dismissed," he barked.

Lysander backed out graciously, his eyes fixed greedily on Nymphidia. His day had definitely improved!

"Gaius," she embraced him tightly.

"Mother, what are you doing here? I have things to do."

He shuffled a few scrolls on his desk to illustrate the point.

"That is not much of a welcome."

She stroked his arm. He muttered an apology.

"Now that is better, darling. Can I sit? You don't seem to have much furniture," she commented as she lowered herself into one of his sparse chairs. "I could loan you something more comfortable. I imagine you will have lots of visitors now."

"Not really."

"Am I the first?" she asked, bright-eyed.

"Mother, I am very busy. I can come by the house later, for dinner."

"Hardly much point when you never eat anything I put in front of you."

"I don't like rich food, you know that."

Nymphidia regarded her son, reflecting that he had never progressed beyond the sulky adolescent that had caused her so much anxiety.

"You should marry. A wife would make sure that you ate properly."

Sabinus furrowed his brow. "I do not wish to marry."

"Now that you are in such an exalted position, I am sure I could find you a nice girl."

Sabinus fiddled with his sleeve. "I am very busy, mother."

"Very well, I shall not keep you, darling. Aphrodite came to see me today," she told him, watching his expression carefully. "I gather she spoke to you."

"It is state business. She had no right to speak to you about it."

"She is worried about her husband."

"He is unharmed."

"Why are you holding him? I would have thought Galba would welcome a man like Epaphroditus into his administration. He has many talents."

Sabinus bristled, an action not lost on Nymphidia.

"Darling," she sighed. "Let him go."

He turned his back to her, fussing over his desk. "I will not have you interfering in the business of government."

"My father, your grandfather, was private secretary to both Caligula and Claudius. I was serving the state long before you were born. I am not some silly woman you can patronise."

"You are my mother. It is unseemly."

"Who got you this job?"

She saw his shoulders tense, heard him say quietly, "I hope I have made a success of it."

Standing up, she hugged him from behind, assuring him, "Of course you have, darling. I knew you would. It is why I suggested you for the position."

That and she desperately wanted him home. He was her only child and for all his faults, she loved him intensely. The years he was away had been torture for her. Devouring his short missives for greater meaning and suffering daily agonies as she read palace reports of battles, skirmishes, and casualties.

When the prefect position became unexpectedly vacant, Nymphidia seized the opportunity. Though powerful in her own right within the complex palace network of alliances, she still required a high-placed sponsor to support her machinations.

Midway through a particularly vigorous sex act, she whispered, "Do something for me …"

Epaphroditus, standing behind her, his head buried in her hair, hands grasping onto her breasts, replied extremely positively, "Bona Dea! Anything, anything …" lapsing into a protracted groan.

It was a highly effective tactic and had been employed by Aphrodite in the past to acquire amongst other items: a rather nice dining set, a holiday by the sea, and the promise that he would explain to the children where babies came from.

Nymphidia secured his recommendation by offering favours of a type guaranteed to hold his interest. Sabinus, successfully installed, she tactfully extracted herself from the liaison. Remaining on good, but purely platonic terms with the secretary.

"It was Epaphroditus who endorsed your appointment. This seems a poor way to repay him for his kindness."

The shoulders tensed again. She stroked his hair as she had when he was an unhappy child.

"Gaius," she soothed. "I know you want to do the right thing here. You wouldn't deprive his children of their father."

He snapped his head away from her hand. "Why not? You deprived me of one."

"Not this again. We are not talking about this now. You will release Epaphroditus," she stated, and then seeing him open his mouth to protest continued, "You will. Or I shall go see Regulus and Senex and Phillipius and whoever else it takes to get this thing done."

Sabinus, painfully aware of the intention behind his mother's words, gave a curt nod.

"Good." She kissed him on the cheek.

He flinched, much like when he was eleven and she had done so in front of his entire class at school. Which would have been embarrassing enough except she went one step further, rushing to pick him up without changing, offering his class-mates a valuable insight into just what a palace prostitute wore to work.

FORTY

Antonius Honoratus listened to their request with respect. He was impressed by their continued loyalty to the dead emperor and their desire to dispose of his remains reverentially. Sabinus had drilled into them how tricky and cowardly the imperial workforce was. Honoratus had no reason to question this, for Sabinus had grown up at the palace and was surely correct in his assertions. However, having met Alex and now these three loyal servants, he was beginning to wonder.

Their scribe was a bit off though, curiously shaky. Honoratus was a good tribune who cared for his men and could spot panic in the eyes of a battle virgin prior to engagement. This scribe looked like he was about to face a thousand screaming Gauls.

"I am sure Nymphidius Sabinus would not deny our request. It is rather hot and the flies …" Epaphroditus finished off his smooth rhetoric.

"No, I imagine not," replied Honoratus. "It shall be so. I shall organise my men to build a pyre."

A small noise escaped from the scribe.

"I thought he was mute."

"He is unable to form the necessary words. I have tried to train him out of his grunts, they can be most off-putting. A dignified silence is what is required, I have told you before."

He gave Sporus a light cuff round the head.

Honoratus, infected with a growing suspicion was interrupted by the arrival of Alex.

"News from Rome, sir," he barked, like the soldier he wished to be.

Honoratus broke the scroll's seal and scanned the contents. Looking up he told them, "You are to be released. The city is secure. You may take the emperor's body back to the city."

"Sabinus says that?"

Honoratus smiled. "No, I do. A discreet funeral, mind."

"Naturally. Perhaps he could lie with his father's side of the family," suggested Epaphroditus.

The Domitius family tomb lay near the imperial mausoleum on the Campus Martius. It was a compromise Nero would have hated. But Nero wasn't there to argue. It would do.

Honoratus noted Alex's eyes drawn towards the scribe. "Something wrong, Alex?"

Alex wasn't sure, there was something familiar about the slave but he couldn't work out what. He shrugged.

"What did you say his name was again?" Honoratus asked Epaphroditus.

"Philo, my scribe," said the secretary, and then realised that he had made a terrible miscalculation.

If he had not quite recognised this dull approximation of Sporus, Alex was well aware that this was not Philo. He told Honoratus this, whose genial expression hardened.

"You know this man's scribe? And this is not him?"

"No," replied Alex. "That's not Philo."

To be fair to Alex, he was caught in an awful position with very little time to consider his actions. Epaphroditus was giving him a glare that contained a thousand threats. Phaon was looking similarly annoyed. The scribe was shaking and throwing pleading glances in his direction and Antonius Honoratus, who had taken Alex under his wing, taught him to whittle, and generally made him feel useful for the first time in his life, asked him gently, "Who is it, Alex?"

He looked once more at the scribe and in that moment of recognition, the word fell from his mouth before he could stop it.

"Sporus?"

"Honoratus, you are a reasonable man."

Probably the only reasonable man in Rome, thought Epaphroditus, who wasn't going to lose his one chance to reason with a reasonable man. "He's a child. A boy. What possible danger can he be?"

"Sabinus' orders were very clear," Honoratus told him. "The eunuch was to be captured. To be held."

"For what purpose? I cannot think of a single thing Sabinus could want him for."

They were sat in what was Phaon's study. Honoratus had taken it for his office and toned down the sexually lurid murals, covering them with blankets and hiding the enormous statue of an excited-looking Zeus going for it with a swan. Honoratus looked very comfortable. He did not look like a man who would change his mind. He was a soldier. Epaphroditus found them annoyingly literal.

"Do you have children?" he threw in casually, though if any of his children had turned out like Sporus, he would have had them exposed on the Tarpeian Rock.

"No," replied Honoratus.

An answer that gave Epaphroditus little to work with. He debated moving on to nephews, maybe a favourite cousin, before deciding that for once honesty might be the best policy.

"I will lay it out to you straight."

"That would be gratifying."

"Let me take Sporus with me. I'll keep him out of sight. You can tell Sabinus he died with Nero. Everyone's happy."

Honoratus was baffled by Epaphroditus' definition of laying it out straight. It seemed to involve a large amount of subterfuge and deception. He pointed out the flaw. "Sabinus would not be happy."

For Epaphroditus that had been the key benefit of his plan.

"Sir," came a small voice at Honoratus' elbow.

"Yes, Alex."

"Epaphroditus is right. He is no threat."

"You know this eunuch? More than by sight?"

Then seeing the internal conflict played across the slave's face, Honoratus said gently, "Alex?"

"He is my friend."

A sentiment that Sporus definitely did not share, locked in a small dark pantry, soldiers leering at him through the window. They were curious about eunuchs, a fact they had more than demonstrated earlier, Sporus bruised from their rough hands pinning him down as they made laughing bets as to how much of his genitalia remained.

He sat hugging his knees, rubbing the tears from his eyes. Every time he closed his eyes, he saw his beloved husband bloodied and dying. He should have killed himself after Nero. He should have gone with him.

The emperor would be waiting for him, not understanding why he wasn't there. He was a coward. What was he going to do with this life he had preserved? It already seemed much duller without Nero. The colours of the world muted. He would never know such glamour, such fun again. He should have killed himself when he had the opportunity.

Hearing the door open, he did not bother to look up. No doubt it was more people come to prod and poke him.

"Sporus, I have vouched for you. Honoratus is letting you go. You are going back to Rome."

Sporus didn't move.

"Did you hear?" Alex tried again, "You are free."

"I suppose," said the eunuch quietly, "this is where you have been these last few weeks. Playing with your soldier buddies." He gazed up, shooting Alex a withering look. "Oh, you even have a little sword."

Alex's hand went to the blade at his side. Honoratus had given it to him in case he met any bandits on the road.

"Sporus, you can go. I vouched for you as my friend."

"You are no friend of mine."

"Sporus?" Alex sat in front of him. "What's wrong?"

A bitter laugh escaped from the eunuch's lips.

"You knew! You knew this was going to happen and you didn't warn me. You let me walk straight into this absolute disaster."

"I couldn't say anything," Alex protested. "It was classified."

"You are supposed to be my friend."

"I am. I vouched for you. I saved you."

"Well, thank you very much. I am so grateful to you, Alexander." He shuffled sideways so that he did not have to look at the messenger.

"Sporus, don't be like this," pleaded Alex. "I am sorry I didn't tell you but I couldn't. You must see that. If the details had leaked out before …"

"Then your buddies might not have been able to murder my husband," supplied Sporus.

"He wasn't your husband. You're a man. You can't marry another man. You were his slave. Like I was his slave. But we're free now of the tyrant. You won't have to perform such duties anymore, don't you see?"

Sporus was stunned. He had taken it as a definite that Alex thought exactly as he did. That he was fully in agreement that puce was a dreadful colour, that Statilia Messalina was a bitch from the depths, that to be eunuchised was to be blessed, and that his own conquest of Nero was altogether thrilling.

That Alex apparently did not see Nero as Sporus' great love was a shock. That he saw the deceased emperor as some kind of monster was incomprehensible. Nero was his husband. Was. Sporus was now a widow and his friend, his best friend in the whole world, had let it happen.

He looked at Alex's freckled face, "You are so deluded."

"Sporus, we're ready to go."

Epaphroditus stood in the doorway, arms crossed.

Sporus brushed himself down. Alex pulled at his arm. "Sporus, I'm sorry, OK?"

The eunuch flinched away. "No, not OK. It will never be OK."

FORTY-ONE

The refectory was packed for the usual breakfast squabble. Mina, bowl in hand looked around for a seat, catching sight of Daphne waving her over, a gesture she ignored having spotted a much less crowded position.

Straton sat on his own, as always, with five seats available either side of him. They would remain empty no matter how many slaves crowded into the room. They would eat on the floor or lean against walls rather than occupy those seats. Mina, taking a deep breath, walked over and plonked herself opposite him. The overseer looked up in surprise.

"Cunt of doom," he rasped with amusement.

Aware that near-on the whole room was watching her with the sort of awed anticipation the race crowds held for a really big chariot pile-up, Mina said in a soft voice, "I didn't tell anyone it was you."

Straton nodded a thank you and concerned himself with his food, a portion that was at least five times the normal allocation.

"Mina," hissed Daphne with urgency, gesticulating wildly.

She turned, and addressing Straton began, "That thing you did with the whip, flipping the cauldron over and that guard."

Straton gave her a narrow look, wondering where this was leading and irritated that she was blocking his view. He liked to spend breakfast tucking into his grub and randomly assigning evil leers to anyone who accidentally glanced his way.

"I was wondering if you could teach me how to do that?"

"Why?"

Meaning, why would he do that as opposed to why did she want to learn.

Mina took the second interpretation. "It was cool, amazing."

She then threw in a phrase guaranteed to prick the ears of any overseer. "I thought it might increase my value."

Whip skills in an attendant of the empress? Straton didn't think so. Not with the current holder of the position. It was the sort of thing Poppaea or Agrippina would have got off on. But then Straton recalled Nero enjoying the spectacle of female gladiators: maybe Galba would too.

"You don't say much, do you?"

Used to such disparaging comments from Felix, for nobody else dared to speak to him, Straton automatically pointed to his throat.

"Oh. That must be very frustrating, being unable to express yourself."

Straton slammed a fist into his palm causing several slaves on nearby tables to jump. Mina didn't move, but, rather, asked with a smile, "What if you want to say something nice, though?"

He forced out a throaty chuckle and replied, "Don't."

She had in fact hit upon a lone vulnerable spot beneath Straton's thick hide.

Since Philo had spent the whole night with him, Straton had been aware that there were things he wanted to say to the freedman. He expressed himself as physically as he could but was nagged by the thought that it wasn't enough.

He hit upon the idea of buying Philo a present. To show how much he cared, to speak the words he couldn't. He had racked his admittedly meagre brain for the perfect gift, settling on a book. Philo was always reading and carried round a whole satchel of scrolls and tablets with him. Plus Straton recalled that he had once won a prize for Greek composition at the imperial training school. So he shuffled down the Via Sacre, money safely deposited in his boot, towards one of the emporiums that sold those mysterious objects.

The shop assistant took one look at Straton and decided he wasn't worth the effort. He lounged at the back of the shop filing his nails.

"Wanna book."

"They're all labelled," the assistant said, waving a limp hand.

Straton followed its direction, staring helplessly at the cubbyholes of scrolls with their peculiar scratched figures beneath. Turning back to the assistant, he rasped, "Greek book."

He didn't look up, concentrating on a particularly tricky corner. "They're all labelled."

"For friend," Straton persisted.

"They're all labelled."

Straton debated picking one up, handing over the money and taking it with him. But what if it wasn't right? What if the words were all wrong?

What if they contained words that he did not want to say to Philo?

"Nice book."

The assistant looked up and sighed before repeating his mantra. "They're all labelled," and returning to his nails.

Mina would have said he was frustrated by his inability to articulate, Felix would have thought it typical of his carelessness and fined him accordingly. Whatever it was, Straton found his limited patience tried. In a move of astounding speed, the hapless assistant found himself pinned against the wall with his own nail file pressed against his throat. He stared terrified into Straton's black eyes.

"Wanna book," he said with a heavy dose of menace.

If he hadn't been using his hands to restrain the lad he would have cracked his knuckles to emphasise the point.

The assistant was miraculously converted to his cause. Regaining his salesman persona, he told Straton, "We have a lot of books, sir. Everything you could possibly require."

He nodded enthusiastically. A little too enthusiastically, for he jolted Straton's hand, which stabbed him in the neck with the file.

Straton had enough experience of arterial blood to know that you skipped out of its way pretty darn quickly, especially if you were wearing your second-best shopping tunic. The assistant flailed around for a bit, crashing into displays and shelves before collapsing in a gurgling heap on the floor, the nail file pointing upwards.

Straton gave him a kick. "Bollocks," and made a hasty exit before the vigiles turned up.

"Will you teach me then?" Mina asked.

"If you do summat for me," he replied, giving her a lecherous glare.

Mina raised an eyebrow: if Straton wanted "summat" of that nature from her he would have just taken it when he had the opportunity during their adventure.

"You want me to look scared for the audience?"

"Got reputation to maintain."

She gave a wicked smile then pushed the bench back, gave a truly horrified look before scurrying off head down, flinging herself next to Daphne and bursting into exaggerated tears.

Straton was secretly impressed. Burying the desire to applaud, he let loose his nastiest grimace on all the eyes that were on him. He ran a red tongue across his lips. The refectory collectively shuddered and there fell absolute silence. Which was exactly how he liked it.

Down in the bowels of the palace, in a dark, damp dungeon of a room, two imperial slaves were stood contemplating a lit torch that was resting in a sconce on the dripping walls.

It was all in the wrist. Straton demonstrated by pointedly flicking his whip with a floppy wrist and then with the strengthened variety.

Mina goggled as he flipped the flaming torch from its bracket towards them, effortlessly catching it in his free hand. She ducked instinctively. Straightening up, she clapped with enthusiasm, bouncing on her feet.

Straton bowed and then handed her the whip. He set up a clay beaker on a chair. Standing behind her, he took hold of her wrist and pulled it back. "Snap it. Quick like."

Mina flicked the whip, smacking the side of the chair and knocking it clean over.

"Sorry."

Straton shrugged. "Not bad."

He set up the chair again and nodded. After ten goes, Mina finally managed to hit the beaker. Knocking it to the floor where it cracked into pieces. She punched the air with a yelp and looked to her mentor for approval. Straton gave her the thumbs up and chuckled, "Lesson over."

Mina sat cross-legged on the floor, and then regretted it since it was cold and just a little bit slimy. Rubbing her hands on her dress, she asked, "Sooo, what's this something I can do for you?"

"Book."

"A book?"

"Book as present."

Mina struggled to understand. "You want a book? To give as a gift?"

"For friend."

Mina wasn't aware that Straton had any friends. She'd never seen anyone with him voluntarily. Those in his vicinity tended to be held in a tight neck-lock.

"Special friend," he elaborated.

"Ahhh," she said, trying to keep her expression neutral. "You want to buy something nice for your special friend."

Straton nodded. "Book."

"What sort of book?"

"Greek."

"Greek author or translated in Greek?"

This baffled the overseer who looked at Mina imploringly, willing her to understand.

"What about poetry?" Seeing his blank expression, she continued, "It is perfect gift material for special friends. Catullus, perhaps? He is not Greek but he wrote some wonderful love poems."

Love poems? It seemed to express the necessary sentiment. "Good?"

"Very good," Mina told him and then leapt to her feet. "Hang on a mo, I have some. I could show you."

He looked worried.

"Or I could read them to you," she suggested, realising it was unlikely that he was literate. That seemed to cheer him, so she sped off.

"Now then," began Mina cross-legged on the floor, scroll unfurled in front of her. "I have two poems here. They are very different in tone. I will read them both out and you decided if either suits. OK?"

Straton, leaning against the far wall nodded.

She took a deep breath and in her very best reading voice read:

> "Please, my sweet Ipsithilla,
> my darling, my charming girl,

tell me to come to you after lunch,
and (if you give the word) help me by seeing
that nobody bolt the street door,
and that you don't decide to go out,
but rather stay at home and make ready for us
nine consecutive fuckifications.
If there's any chance, give me the order right now;
for I am lying down on my back, fed full,
banging through my cloak and tunic."

She finished, put the scroll to one side, and looked at Straton. The overseer considered; he liked the word "fuckification", it summed up the act quite nicely for him. Nine times though? That was quite a feat even for a man of Straton's virility, and who was this Ipsithilla chick?

Seeing his confusion, Mina said, "No need to decide yet, here is the second one:

Juventius, if someone allowed me to carry on kissing
Those honeyed eyes of yours,
I would kiss them right on to three hundred thousand
nor would I ever think that I was going to be sated
not even if the crop of our kissing
were denser than the dry ears of corn."

Straton was silent. He was unexpectedly moved by this strange thing of poetry. How did this Catullus fellow know that all he wanted to do was cover Philo in kisses and that no matter how many times he did so, it wasn't enough?

"What do you think?"

Straton wiped a stray tear from his eye. "Beautiful."

Mina was touched by his emotion. "It is lovely. I am sure your friend will be moved. If you like, I could copy it out for you."

Straton looked confused so she explained, "I can get a smaller roll of parchment and copy the words all neat and nice.

Oh, and I could do a pretty border round them." She sketched a rectangle with her finger on the floor to demonstrate. "I am good at drawing. It will make a really special gift."

"Thank you."

"It might take me a little while, though," she warned him, "to do it properly. We could continue with these lessons in between?"

She was a good bargainer and he couldn't help but grin as he spat on his hand and shook hers with a frighteningly firm grip.

FORTY-TWO

It was an odd sort of funeral. There was neither procession nor the traditional banquet. There were no flute players nor professional mourners; just the three of them, and Honoratus with that ginger boy who claimed friendship with Sporus.

They seemed unlikely friends to Epaphroditus, but then the secretary's idea of a friend was someone who could do him a favour. If there were nothing to be gained, Epaphroditus failed to see the point of such bonhomie.

They were stood around the funeral pyre, Honoratus and Alex keeping a respectful distance as Epaphroditus, Phaon, and Sporus watched the flames burn. It was not the funeral Epaphroditus had planned for Nero, but then he had not expected the emperor to die so soon, so young. It was a shame, a terrible shame.

Epaphroditus wiped a stray tear from his eye, caused by the smoke rather than any great emotion. Phaon was similarly stoic. Stood between them, Sporus wept openly, howled, and threatened to throw himself on the pyre with his beloved; a clearly empty threat, since he made no attempt to get any nearer to the flames.

"What will you do with him?" Phaon asked over Sporus' head.

Epaphroditus gave a thin smile. "I have the perfect place to hide him."

"Which is?"

"Aha, it is genius," said the secretary, maddening his companion by refusing to elaborate.

He draped an arm across the eunuch. "Come Sporus, it is done."

Sporus looked up, his eyes red from all the crying, his body trembling with emotion. "He was such a good man, such a good husband," he cried.

"Of course he was," soothed Epaphroditus, leading him towards the wagon. "He was a great. We'll never forget him, will we?"

"Never, ever, ever," promised Sporus.

Alex opened the door of the wagon and was treated to an evil glare from the eunuch, who walked up the steps of the wagon without comment, throwing himself into its interior and breaking into a new bout of sobbing.

Bastard, he thought, utter bastard. If Nero were here, if his beloved husband were alive with him now as he should be, then he would whisper magic in his ear, spread joy with his body, and get the utter bastard crucified. Just wait till Mina heard what he'd done!

Epaphroditus sat next to him and closed the wagon door. It didn't occur to Sporus that he wasn't going back to the palace. Which was just as well, because if he had known where Epaphroditus was taking him, they would have never got him in the coach in the first place.

Epaphroditus stood outside his house sniffing at his tunic. He hadn't changed in all his time in captivity. His chin was bristled and he no doubt looked as crumpled as he felt. He shuffled past his doorman wearily, waving away questions as to his well-being. He trundled through the elaborately decorated public rooms designed to impress visitors, through to the slightly more sedate private area, which lay to the far side of the large cultivated courtyard that sat in the middle of his impressive home.

He was navigating past the shrine to the household gods which was packed with small offerings to the lares and at least ten lit candles that one of his slaves was poised by to ignite should they go out, when he heard a whine.

"Daddeeeeeeeeeeee."

Julia tottered towards him clutching a doll.

"Daddy, Gaia's arm's fallen off."

She handed him the doll and then the arm.

"Oh dear," he said, picking up his daughter. "Shall we make her better?"

Julia, nestling into him, gave a nod and began happily sucking her thumb.

Aphrodite, laid out on a couch, stared at the ceiling. There was still no news, not even from Nymphidia. What could she do now? Who could she appeal to? There was no point addressing Sabinus or his mother again: evidently Nymphidia had failed to persuade her son.

Would she have to wait until Galba reached Rome before her request would be heard? That could be months away. Longer even. She did not think she could bear this torment much longer.

"Mummeee."

"Not now, Julia," she said without moving, her thoughts gloomy.

"Mummeee," little fingers grabbed at her arm. "Daddy says he can make Gaia better."

She shot up into a seated position. Epaphroditus stood holding the doll.

"Do you have some yarn and a needle?" he asked casually.

Jumping to her feet, she threw her arms around him, kissing him on both cheeks before pushing him away. "You stink!"

Later in their bathhouse, as she scraped the dirt off his back, he told her about the funeral.

"It was quiet, dignified, and respectable, so bearing absolutely no resemblance to the man. Shame really, we've had a proper send-off planned for years. It would have been spectacular. I had the elephants in training."

Aphrodite filled him in quickly about events in his absence. He laughed very hard when he found out who had saved him.

"Gods! That has got to grate on Sabinus, his mother intervening. Good old Nymphidia."

"You will stay away from him, won't you? I don't trust that man."

He lifted an arm so she could scrape down his side. "I am Nero's private secretary. Nero is no more. Which I guess makes me unemployed."

Overjoyed, Aphrodite gave him a kiss on the back of his neck. "There have been lynchings in the city of those perceived to have benefited from Nero's reign," she warned him.

Epaphroditus gazed at his gleaming black marble bathroom. "All the more reason to keep a low profile." Then, changing tack, "Tell me something good. Has Rufus spoken his first word? Any news on potential suitors for Silvia? And please tell me Philo and Teretia have done the deed."

"The short version of that is no, no, and no." She lifted up his other arm. "The longer one is that Rufus babbles away all day long but nothing intelligible so far. No doubt it will be Dada like all the others." She slapped him playfully on the back. "Silvia tells me she does not favour Martinus anymore: my words not hers. Hers were rather stronger. I don't know what he has done but he has fallen all the way from Adonis to sardine."

"I have to agree with her there. I always found him sly."

"Nonsense, he is perfectly presentable. But we will not force it; tomorrow he could be her Mr Perfect. You know how changeable she is. As for Philo, he has been here rather a lot, checking how I was and offering what scant news he had on you."

"Very kind of him," Epaphroditus approved.

"I thought so. Really he has been very sweet. I did ask him how Teretia was and he looked stunned at the question. So there is nothing going on there."

"Juno! What is it going to take?"

She began work on his shoulder blades. "It can be your retirement project, matchmaking Silvia and Philo. Separately," she added hastily.

Epaphroditus was surprised that she thought him retiring. He had seen it more as a temporary survival tactic. He did not disabuse her yet. She was so sunny and it cheered him to watch her smile.

When he had been at his lowest moments, holding the bloody daggers or attempting to reason with that tribune, it was the image of that smile that kept him positive. But then, that was how it had always been. Children stowed safely away, sitting comfortably naked with his wife as she washed him, he felt perfectly content.

FORTY-THREE

The humiliation of his mother's interference weighed heavily on Sabinus' shoulders. Epaphroditus, that fawning courtier, that sly slave who'd meddled his way to the emperor's side, whispering malice into his ear. Acting as a gateman preventing those good men, those noble senators, from access to their emperor!

It shouldn't have been that way. In fact it hadn't been that way in those early years of Nero's reign. Then the young emperor had wise old Seneca as his advisor, tempered by Burrus, the Praetorian prefect. Sabinus greatly admired Burrus. The role of prefect had a dubious lineage but Burrus had been an upright sort, just and fair. Sabinus felt he had emulated this example, unable to recognise his own failings. It would never have occurred to Burrus to overthrow the emperor. He truly was a loyal servant.

Indeed, Sabinus, so keen to show his metal, to distinguish himself, had allied himself more with the likes of Macro, the prefect who had colluded with Caligula to remove the Emperor Tiberius, rather than the kindly, honest, loyal Prefect Burrus.

Sabinus, however, was not given to introspection and given that he now controlled the city, nobody was going to dare point this out to him either. Right now he was brooding over Epaphroditus' survival. He deserved to die. If he were to rebuild the glory of Rome, the old order had to be removed entirely. Sabinus had already made several "removals".

A few undercover Praetorians had whipped up a mob against Nero's former bodyguard and ex-gladiator Spiculus. Shouting how he had abandoned the emperor to his fate was enough to secure Spiculus' death, crushed beneath the statue of the man he had deserted.

Aponius, the informer, was repeatedly run over by wagons until his cries ceased. Polonius, the court poet, simply torn to pieces by furious hands. Epaphroditus should be with them, his body thrown into the Tiber with his fellow slaves. But his mother … Sabinus bit his lip. His mother was not a woman to cross. She was irritatingly strong willed, quite unsuited to her sex.

The issue of Epaphroditus could wait. Sabinus had more weighty matters to attend to first. He fiddled with his toga, his attendant assisting him with its draping.

"Antonius Honoratus," announced Lysander, pulling apart each syllable in an attempt to jolly his role up.

"Ahh, Honoratus. What do you think?"

Honoratus eyed the crisp white toga with the purple stripe that ran down its hem; a stripe that signified a rank that Sabinus did not and could never hold.

"I am addressing the senate," he told the tribune. "I thought the armour would unnerve them."

It wasn't Sabinus' armour that unnerved people. It was his grim jaw and his twisted personality.

"The toga is more assuring," he continued. "They need to know that this is no military endeavour, that the power lies with them. As it should," he concluded.

Honoratus was about to speak when Sabinus said, "I am merely their conduit until Galba reaches Rome."

"How long will that be?"

Sabinus had no idea. He had received no word from Galba yet. But Spain was a long way away. Icelus was no doubt en route with words from his great master. To Honoratus he said crisply, "Confidential, as I am sure you will appreciate."

Honoratus nodded.

"Was there something you wanted, Honoratus?"

"Tigellinus," began the tribune.

Sabinus stiffened.

"We found him at his country estate. He even opened the door for us. Roaring drunk of course."

"Of course."

"What did you want to do with him?"

Sabinus' lips twitched into a smile of sorts, as a series of joyful images floated before his eyes. Honoratus noted the unusually cheerful expression on his superior's face. "Sir?"

Sabinus snapped back to attention. It was tempting, very tempting but he was above such petty emotions as revenge. He was just, he was fair, and he was honest. All the things Tigellinus was not. Nymphidius Sabinus straightened his spine, kicking his attendant away.

"He is freeborn. Let him be trialled as such. Let them all hear the crimes that man has been responsible for, the depravity he has immersed himself in. Let them all hear! And let them cast their judgement on that man!"

He waved an arm with pointed finger that stabbed the air on each point. He composed himself with several deep breaths, fiddling with his toga again, his attendant rushing forward to fuss.

"The senate will be expecting me," he mumbled, his face still red, and then to Honoratus he spat: "Keep my esteemed colleague under guard. Let him fear for his future!"

Tigellinus was not fearing for his future. He was very much living for the moment. That moment involved being waist-high in his bath, flanked by two of his more voluptuous slave girls. They were helpfully refilling his goblet and feeding him scraps of chicken, which he tore at with his teeth from their fingers. He was also drunk, very drunk. His arms, laid over the shoulders of the luscious Doria and Cleothera, were the only things preventing him from slipping into the water and drowning.

It was a very comfortable house arrest.

A weary Alex dumped his bag on his bed. Anacreon, lying under a blanket, opened an eye.

"Oh, you're back," he said before rolling over.

As room-mates they seldom crossed paths. Anacreon worked on the lighting team night shift, ensuring that any-one rambling after hours didn't walk into a wall and that the palace orgies were light enough to be titillating but dim enough to hide any hairy nastiness. The only time they spoke was to tell the other to: "Shut up, I'm trying to sleep."

It was utterly unlike the relationship he had enjoyed with his previous room-mate. He sat on his bed and rubbed a calf. He didn't even know where Sporus was now, since Epaphroditus had taken responsibility for the eunuch's safety, spurning Alex's entreaties to help.

"I think your sort has done quite enough already. We wouldn't want you running off telling tales to the boss," Epaphroditus had said with fury. "Do let me know how you enjoy working for Sabinus. Such a reasonable man."

Sporus, standing beside him, had given Alex a look of sheer venom. It bored into him and he hung his head in shame.

Sporus would get over it. They had argued many times over the years; you couldn't be friends with Sporus without quarrelling. He was prone to temper fits and took offence at the most innocent remarks. Alex was forever having to apolo-gise for his actions whether he had erred or not, soothing the eunuch's delicate sensibilities. It could be rather tiring but when Sporus was on top form, dazzling with gossip, ready to banter, he was the bestest friend Alex could ever have wanted.

He would calm down, Alex thought. Emotions were running high. There had been a revolution after all. Anacreon snoring softly, Alex decided to go find Mina.

Mina's whip technique practice was slightly hindered by the fact that she lacked an actual whip. Straton being firmly opposed to arming the workforce, she was reduced to working on her wrist action. Snapping an imaginary strap, observed from the doorway, looked extremely strange.

"What are you doing?"

Mina spun to see Alex. Her eyes opened wide and she ran and flung herself into his arms. Kissing him with joy she asked, "Where have you been?"

Gladdened by such a greeting Alex grinned, and then looking at her properly he asked, "Mina, what happened to your face?"

She prodded her still-swollen eye. He was her dearest friend but he hadn't been there when the guards had raped their way round the complex. You had to be there to understand, so she replied, "Nothing." And then abruptly changed the subject. "So where have you been?" And then changed it again by whining, "Sporus, gods, poor Sporus. I can't bear it, Alex. Do you think he suffered? You know what a wimp he is, he cries over a broken nail. I couldn't bear to think he—" she broke off.

He took her hands, looking her straight in the eyes. "I am sure it was quick and stylish and dramatic and everything he would have wished for."

They shared a smile. "We had a little ceremony for him, Daphne, Lysander, and me. You should have been there."

There was a faint accusation in her tone.

"I was away delivering a message. I didn't know about all this till I got back."

Mina looked at him. "But you don't deliver messages outside the palace."

"I've been promoted," he said proudly. "I'm Nymphidius Sabinus' personal messenger."

"You're working for the GUARDS?" screeched Mina. "Why are you working for that scum?"

Alex was hurt. He'd feigned joy at each one of Mina's elevations: why couldn't she be happy for him?

"It is a good job."

Mina eyed him suspiciously. He looked just like Alex, a stung Alex, but Alex nevertheless. Her best friend Alex.

"Sorry, sorry," she apologised, discarding any momentary doubts she possessed. "It's just everything is so messed up. The poor emperor, and the empress is stuck in her rooms and they won't let her leave. And Sporus is gone, gone. And Epaphroditus ..." she trailed off again. "Do you think I should send a note to his wife, to offer my condolences?"

"No," said Alex definitively.

Mina tossed her hair over her shoulder. "You're right. It is inappropriate. She must feel ... I mean I feel awful and we were only together a few months. He was such a fine man, Alex. He was so good to me. I mean most men, they care nothing for your pleasure but he always took the time and he didn't have to. He was an absolute god in bed."

Alex who didn't much like straying into this territory said, "What were you doing when I came in?"

This distracted her from her lament over her lost lover, for she gave a full smile and told him excitedly. "Alex, I have hot, hot, hot gossip but you *cannot* tell. Otherwise it could limit my life expectancy significantly."

"You can trust me."

"Seriously, you have to swear."

"Consider it sworn."

She rocked on her heels. "If only Sporus was here, he would lurve this one."

He gave her hand a supportive squeeze.

"Of course, no way would he keep it quiet, it would be right round the palace by tomorrow, so perhaps it is good that he is not here."

"Oh just dish it, Mina."

She leaned forward with an exaggerated gesture. "Straton has a *special* friend."

"I imagine he has a lot of special friends on a daily basis, all pinned down and struggling to get away."

"No, this is different. I am helping him with his romance. I am copying out some Catullus for him to give to his friend."

"You are helping Straton? Mina, are you mad? The man is insane."

Mina waved that away with a florid motion. "He is insanely in love. It's rather sweet."

"Straton sweet?" Alex was open-mouthed. "You can't hang out with Straton. He's dangerous, he'll hurt you."

"Bollocks he will. Aren't you curious as to who his special friend is?"

"I assume you don't know otherwise it would have been the key component of your gossip."

"At least pretend to play along, Alexander."

"OK, OK, Artemina. That fat bird who works in the tannery?"

"Reading poetry? I think not," Mina dismissed.

"I don't know then. I can't imagine Straton with anyone. I always saw him as more of a sexual menace than a lover."

"Intriguing isn't it?" said Mina before happily lapsing into a prolonged speculation, Alex batting away her more ludicrous suggestions.

If he felt any guilt at deceiving her into thinking her friend and lover were dead, he pushed it aside, justifying his actions as crucial for Sporus' safety. As for Epaphroditus, he wanted him excised from Mina's mind, telling himself it was for her own good. The secretary did not care for her, no matter what she thought. It was better this way.

FORTY-FOUR

Philo wasn't sure. He bit his lip as Felix outlined the main duties of his new position.

"Doesn't Sabinus already have an assistant within his corps of troops?"

"Not up to the fucking standards his pseudo-imperialness is demanding," was Felix's reply, which did little to allay Philo's worries. "Fucking Praetorians can't even spell consortium let alone minute one. Besides, you've been at a loose end since Epaphroditus departed."

Philo winced, protesting, "Not true, I've completely reorganised the office."

"How many times?" asked Felix wryly.

Philo shuffled his feet, admitting, "Seven. But this time is the best yet, it is simpler to find the relevant files. I may pass my method onto the scribes hall."

"Yeah, whatever. Anyway, this is your new assignment," stressed Felix, handing him a blank wax writing tablet and a new stylus. "And if you can get that fucking bloated wineskin down to a coherent paragraph, I'll be fucking impressed. Now out! Get to it!"

Philo exited hastily with his new stationery. Outside Felix's door he reflected on how little he wanted this job.

It was Philo's observation that Nymphidius Sabinus was a man who relished control. This was a positive attribute when dealing with the guards, who needed a good whack into line and a steely eye on their activities, especially when Tigellinus had been so neglectful of his position.

However, in the running of the city, Sabinus' pedantry was an impediment. Those high ranking and experienced freedmen were not used to endless memos demanding updates. And since Sabinus had moved into the palace, he could show up at any hour. Pity the poor fellow who wasn't poised at this desk when the prefect materialised expecting immediate action.

Lysander had complained vociferously to Philo that Sabinus made him recite his whole day's announcements first thing in the morning to check their suitability. "Like I might accidentally slip in a profanity or mispronounce a name! As if! I am a professional!" he had preened.

It did not sound promising. What motivated Philo was not money (which he didn't understand) or glory (which his quiet modesty did not attract), but rather the satisfaction of a job well done. Even as a lowly filing clerk in the scribes hall, he exacted a great deal of pleasure from an afternoon spent wiping the dust off a room full of ancient writing tablets. By the time Philo had finished, they were not merely clean, they near sparkled; and you would never have known that some of them dated back sixty years to old Augustus' time.

The Praetorian prefecture was essentially a figurehead role, a physical representation of the emperor's security. Yet Sabinus had mucked in like a common legionary, running the troop's manoeuvres and exercises himself. He busied himself with the minute detail of shift patterns and personally concerned himself with the disciplining of errant guards. Philo imagined that any work he produced would be checked and double-checked and then altered by the detailed prefect. Which was no fun at all.

Philo couldn't imagine Sabinus encouraging him to make suggestions like Epaphroditus had. Nor could he imagine that Sabinus would be as good company. So he shuffled his way to his new job as the personal secretary to the most powerful man in Rome, all the while thinking that he would much rather be reorganising his files for the eighth time.

His new job did not have an auspicious start. Sabinus gazed down at his new secretary and said briskly, "You're not Greek."

Philo was used to such prejudices. Why anyone thought that just because you happened to hail from Corinth or Argos you should be any good at shorthand was a mystery to the freedman. He had met plenty of Greeklings who couldn't even cross-reference!

Yet fashion dictated that the best secretaries were Greek. The few in the palace who shared Philo's looks tended to be used as mere decoration. That he had managed to avoid this ornamental fate said much about Philo's skills and talents.

He handed Sabinus the scroll Felix had given him. It wasn't sealed; Felix rightly assessing that it wouldn't occur to Philo to open anything that wasn't addressed to him. Just as well, for it contained a succinct paragraph on what Felix considered Philo's particular talents. Sabinus read:

> Philo is a clever little sod. Has Greek and all that fuck-
> ing fancy stuff. He was a top little prize winner at school
> and has worked apparently successfully as an assistant
> private secretary.
>
> Philo is easily cowed and responds well to bullying.
> He has no known vices due to being limp-dicked, which
> will not hinder his work.

"You'll do," stated Sabinus, pointing to a small wooden desk to the side of his own.

315

Philo scuttled over and settled himself down, pulling open a drawer and filling it with his spare stylos.

"You will come with me," barked Sabinus. "There is a meeting."

The meeting was being held in the former home of the Emperor Augustus. A modest building in comparison to the rest of the palace complex but still a huge house that could fit Teretius' and Pompeia's apartment into it many times over. The room was painted with alternate red and yellow panels, fake arches and columns painted on to simulate depth, a jug apparently balanced atop a frieze. There were three chairs placed. On two sat Senators Regulus and Senex. Sabinus placed himself on the third facing them, Philo's keen eye noting that this chair was a thumb higher than the other two.

Sabinus sat in his higher chair, toga draped artfully around him, his arms resting on the chair's arms, hands gripping the ends.

"It has come to my attention that certain decrees have been sent by the senate to the provinces," he stated.

"That is the standard procedure," said Regulus.

Sabinus affixed them with a glare. "The standard procedure has always been that senatorial documents are stamped by the emperor before being dispatched."

"The emperor is in Spain," pointed out Regulus.

Sabinus' face clouded and he stated with rock firmness, "I am aware of that. But until the emperor is in Rome all decrees will come to me for approval. That is what will occur."

Leaving no room for debate. The senators were silent. Sabinus, assuming this to be agreement, forced a smile. "Good," and then yelled "Slave!"

Philo, who had been quietly taking notes, stared about the room before realising the command was meant for him.

"You will write down these words. It is a decree," said Sabinus, keeping his eyes on Regulus and Senex. "Edict of

316

Gaius Nymphidius Sabinus. I hereby decree that all passes of transport must have my seal for them to be valid. Any passes stamped with alternative seals will be void and passage refused. Have you got that?"

"Yes, sir," responded Philo, noting that Sabinus had abruptly dropped his title of Praetorian prefect.

Apparently his mere name was all that was needed now.

Looking up, Philo noted what Sabinus failed to: a shared glance between Senex and Regulus. They did not look happy.

The slaves placed the desk down against the wall and stood back. Straton, fingers on chin, considered and then pointed to the other wall. The slaves held back their sighs, for it didn't do to upset Straton, and moved it again.

"Hey up!" In bounced Mina, sticking her head round the door and snapping an imaginary whip into the room.

Straton grinned and pointed a toe at the floor. "Would have landed here."

"What I was aiming for."

The slaves looked at each other with surprise. Nobody spoke to Straton like that. The overseer, spotting this, gave one a quick kick to the back of the knee and told them, "My whore."

"Oh absolutely," said Mina cheerfully. "It is a tough job but someone's got to do it. Tell me, what depravity do you wish to inflict upon me today?"

She plonked herself down on the end of his bed.

Straton's quarters had been a revelation to her. She imagined he spent his evening in some dark hole, with torture implements lining the walls and a series of quivering naked slaves queued up ready for him to practise on. In fact his space was distinctly feminine. A large four-poster bed complete with shimmering white curtains sat in the middle of the room, its covers carefully matched to the pastel walls and the delicate glass vases that stood respectfully on plinths. A huge chandelier hung from the ceiling, its lamps lending the room a muted, near romantic light.

If you cared to look more closely, though, you would note the scratch marks on the floor that had to be caused by finger nails, the tiny flecks of blood that were just visible on the walls, and the thick leather straps that were belted round two of the bed's wooden posts. Mina tried not to dwell on such matters; it put her off her training.

"What think?" asked Straton pointing to the desk.

It was a light mobile model with a folding chair and a beautifully laid out stylus set.

"Lovely," Mina appreciated. "For your friend, I take it?"

The overseer nodded with evident pride. Here Philo could work, write his letters and that, and Straton could make sure he ate by bringing him snacks and enough to drink. He liked to watch Philo write his letters. When the freedman was concentrating hard, he would poke a small pink tongue to the corner of his mouth, which the overseer found particularly endearing.

Straton ran his hand down the joints, "Good?"

"Very good," smiled Mina. "Your friend will love it."

Straton gave a satisfied nod. "Lesson."

Mina jumped off the bed. "I have been practising my wrist technique like you showed me. Shall we get started?"

"Not here," frowned Straton running a hand across his new desk. "Might damage."

FORTY-FIVE

The rumour that Mina was sleeping with Straton flew round the palace in record time. In fact it was near general knowledge before she'd even finished her whip lesson.

"I saw them walking down the corridor the other day and I thought they were just, like, walking down the corridor but they must have been off for a lovers' rendezvous," said Erotica, flicking her hair back over her shoulder.

"Daphne, you're her room-mate, is it true?"

"No, of course not," said Daphne, running a hand over her pregnant stomach and chewing her lip.

Erotica leaned forward. "Go on, there is something going on, isn't there?"

"No, no. She has been absent a lot recently, though," Daphne admitted before interjecting a "but" to Erotica's triumphant expression. "She is probably just spending her time gossiping with Alex."

Ligia stuck her head round the door. "It is true," she hissed. "Anaxagoras saw her following him into one of the dungeons last week. Phemonides saw them having a conversation in the queue at the refectory. And Lysander says they've been at it since the emperor died."

"It's not true," Daphne protested somewhat wanly.

Alex was also fending off stories about Straton and Mina.

"It is not true," he told Lysander.

"Alex, Alex, Alex," condescended the announcer. "All the evidence says yes."

"What evidence?"

"There are witnesses who have seen with their own eyes them entering secret chambers together and then re-emerging later bright-eyed and with a certain spring in their step."

"Straton with a spring in his step? Don't make me laugh."

"Witnesses, Alex, witnesses."

Ligia popped her head round the door. "Daphne says Mina goes missing for hours at a time and refuses to say where she's been."

Lysander gave Alex a look of such irritating smugness that he responded before thinking. "OK, OK, so she's been spending a lot of time with Straton. But they're not having some sordid sex session. She is just helping him with—" and then he stopped.

"Helping him with what?"

Fabulous, thought Alex. There was no way he would repeat what Mina had told him about Straton and his love life. You didn't talk back to Straton. You didn't upset him. You didn't even look at him. And you didn't do any of the hundreds of small slights, like happening to be in front of him in the breakfast queue, that he found personally offensive.

Revealing for general consumption the overseer's softer, more private side was the sort of offence that would strip Alex's back down to the bone. So he sighed. Promising himself he would make it up to Mina later he replied, "Nothing, nothing."

"Aha!" cried Lysander triumphantly.

"This is HUGE!" cried Ligia and sped off to spread the word.

At a late night meeting, Apollodorus and his scribe worked their way through the list of slave girls of the right age and mix to be entered in the impending set of the breeding programme. They were reviewing the list of girls who had been excluded from the previous set. There were many reasons why this might be the case: they could have been pregnant (illegally in Apollodorus' view), diseased, or a request could have been entered for their removal.

Artemina's name had a big fat star next to it and a footnote stating it was at the request of Epaphroditus. Apollodorus was about to wipe out the star with the flat end of his stylus when he queried:

"Artemina? Is she the one?"

"Oh yes," smiled his scribe.

Apollodorus put his stylus down. "Let's keep her off. I want to see what a son of Straton looks like."

Mina trudged back to her room despondently. Her lesson had not gone as well as she had hoped. She was disappointed with her performance. During her practice sessions with the imaginary whip, she had a near-perfect aim. Armed with the real thing she found she was a great deal less accurate. Straton in his limited way, assured her that she was doing well but she left feeling extremely frustrated with herself.

She had hoped to excel at it, to actually be good at something that wasn't holding a towel for hours at a time.

Stomping into her room she found Daphne quietly repairing a dress. "Mina!" she exclaimed, throwing aside her needlework. "Oh gods! You wouldn't believe what Erotica told me."

Mina, who loved a good gossip above all other pastimes, flopped herself down. "Goody. Spill. I need cheering up."

They were interrupted by a small contingent who invited themselves in, taking up space on the two bed rolls. Lysander took on the role of spokesman. "Artemina," he began gravely. "We know."

321

Stretching herself out, she replied enigmatically, "Do you now?"

He sat down beside her. "Yes, we do, and we want you to know that we are all here for you and that the best thing you can do is to get it all off your chest."

"Oh, Mina," cried Daphne "Is it true?"

"Is what true?"

Erotica got in there first. "Is it true that you and Straton are having sex?"

"Me and Straton?" asked Mina, swallowing her shock and catching Alex's apologetic shrug.

She gazed round at the small party. There was such interest, such hope, such gleeful anticipation that she felt she couldn't disappoint. Throwing back her head she cried, "Oh, I cannot deny it any longer. It is true. Straton and myself are indeed enjoying a rare and blissful union."

Erotica swore under her breath, Daphne squealed, Lysander inhaled near all the oxygen in the room, and Alex crossed his arms giving Mina a disapproving glare.

Erotica was the first in with the question. "Bona Dea, Mina, what's he like in bed?"

Mina, suddenly struck with a horrifying image of Straton in the buff, repressed a shudder and replied wistfully, "It is like the tale of King Minos' wife."

To a room full of uncomprehending faces.

"You know the story."

"Don't think we do," said Lysander.

"King Minos on claiming his throne promised Neptune that he would sacrifice a white bull in his honour. But it was such a fine bull that he decided to keep it instead. Neptune, mad at such defiance to the gods, got his revenge by inducing Minos' wife Pasiphae to fall in love with the bull. Unable to control her lecherous feelings, she had a craftsman construct a wooden crate fashioned in the shape of a cow so that she could consummate her vile passions. One day she had the crate taken into the fields and she lay within, waiting and waiting. The bull, noting the strange creature examined its form and, as bulls will, mated with it copiously. And from this union, the Minotaur was born! Well it's like that but without the crate."

Even Erotica didn't want to delve any deeper into that one.

"Gods, Alex, what does it matter?"

"It doesn't bother you that the whole palace believes you to be screwing Straton?"

They were walking hurriedly through the old palace to get to their designated positions, heading for the long colonnade that led to the new palace. Alex was struggling to keep up with Mina.

"No, why should it?" she threw over her shoulder at him. "I know it is not true, what does it matter what anyone else thinks?"

"What if Straton finds out? How do you think he'll feel about it?"

"He'll never hear about it. Who would dare tell him?"

Stopping to catch his breath, Alex shouted at her retreating back. "They'll think you're a whore!"

She stopped, turned, and walked back towards him thunderously.

"You are an attendant to an empress. That's a big deal, Mina. All this stuff, it diminishes you," he told her.

"It diminishes me," she repeated. "How wonderfully clear your world is, Alex."

"I know what dignity and respect are."

She laughed. "Dignity and respect, he says. We're slaves."

"That has nothing to do with it!"

"Maybe not for you it doesn't. You are given your message, you take it, you deliver it. Hurrah for you, Alex. It's different for me. Since Epaphroditus died, I have no one to protect me, Alex. I am open to all kinds of crap out there every single day. You have no idea what it is like."

He was silent.

"Sporus would have understood. He knew what it was like, a pawing hand. Being dragged off just because you happen to be in the wrong place at the wrong time and some lusty senator fancies a scratch before his meeting. A middling freedman clerk who can't get his missus to put out."

Alex attempted to interrupt her rant. "Mina."

"So what if everyone thinks I'm banging Straton? Maybe they'll lay off me. Who would dare to cuckold Straton?" she told him, before swishing off down the corridor in a high fury.

FORTY-SIX

It had taken but a morning for Philo to dislike working for Nymphidius Sabinus. Philo had always considered Sabinus an odd man. Up close these oddities became more pronounced.

Whereas working for Epaphroditus involved a great deal of collaboration and brainstorming, Sabinus would sit at his desk apparently brooding then break into dictation with such abruptness that Philo would leap in his chair.

Dictation was pretty much all he got to do. There wasn't even any filing since Sabinus kept his meticulously ordered cabinet permanently locked. His one attempt at some light dusting had been thwarted by the prefect snapping, "Stop fussing like a woman, slave!"

Which was another grating aspect of working for Sabinus: he insisted on addressing Philo as "slave" no matter how many times he politely corrected him.

And then there were the other comments. His tirade on the palace employing foreigners when there were honest freeborn Romans needing work. His determination that Galba would cease to ship "them" in. And his paranoia that good Roman values were being corrupted by Eastern ways. All delivered with a knowing glare at his assistant.

If Philo disliked being addressed as slave, he was even more sensitive about being described as Eastern. Now that he was free, Philo was a full Roman citizen with two new Roman names and all the advantages and prestige that citizenship bestowed on him. He felt fully Roman and he was hurt by Sabinus' habit of addressing him as if he had the chalked feet of a foreign import.

Epaphroditus would not have treated him so meanly. Epaphroditus had encouraged Philo, had rescued him from the scribes hall, had drawn him out from his shyness, teaching him everything worth knowing about the palace. Philo did not believe that he would learn anything from Nymphidius Sabinus. It would be much better for everyone if he were redeployed.

"Not fucking good enough, Xagoras. Not fucking good at fucking all!"

Xagoras attempted an interruption with a, "Sir—" but Felix just yelled over him.

"Fucking goods was laughing at you Xagoras! I told you to give him a fucking whipping and he comes out fucking smiling! I would call that a fucking failure of the first fucking order! I'm starting to forget why the fuck I ever fucking employed you. You are fucking useless! I knew I should have got fucking Straton onto this!"

Felix became aware of a movement in his peripheral vision which distracted him, allowing Xagoras to get out almost a whole sentence.

"But Felix, he was on public duties. I couldn't—"

Felix pointed a finger literally in his face, prodding his nose. "You've been fucking told! Now get back to fucking work! I've got business."

The business was Philo, who was lurking by the door frame, waiting for a suitable moment to interrupt. Xagoras willingly departed, with a sharp kick up the bum by Felix's hobnailed boot hurrying him along.

The head of slave placements expelled a breath that drained the red flush from his cheeks, then said, "Come on in, Philo. Take a seat. Tell me what you fucking want."

For the fierce-tempered, foul-mouthed Felix, this was excessive politeness. He sat down behind his desk and pointed to the chair in front of it, telling Philo, "Well, sit the fuck down."

Philo sat down so abruptly his buttocks hit the wood forcefully and he squeaked with pain.

Felix waited a whole heartbeat before yelling, "Get the fuck on with it!" with such velocity that Philo jumped in his seat and his buttocks were subject to a second bruising.

"I need to be redeployed," he said unsteadily, eyes crinkled with anxiety as he awaited another explosion from Felix.

Felix surprisingly did not blow; he did, however, raise those red bushy eyebrows and breathe, "Fuck me, Philo. That's a good fucking job that is. Why the fuck do you want redeploying?" He seemed to ask with genuine interest.

"I don't ... I'm not sure ... I just think ... We don't, ermm, meld. Sabinus and I. We don't meld."

"Sabinus don't meld with no fucker. That's his fucking tragedy. It's why he's a fucking frigid, friendless fucker."

"We don't work well together," pressed Philo gently. "Epaphroditus always said that an assistant was the out-stretched arm of his superior. I am not Sabinus' outstretched arm. I'm more like a ... a ... a wart on the end of his nose. Not of any purpose but always in vision."

Felix scratched at his beard. "It's a good job we never made you fucking court poet."

"He doesn't even like me!" protested Philo.

Felix leaned back in his chair and folded his arms across his wide chest. "Yes he fucking does."

Philo blinked in shock, shaking his head. "No, he really doesn't Felix. He hates me. He is very mean to me."

"See them there."

Philo followed Felix's finger to the large pile of tablets on the end of the desk. "That there is Sabinus' complaint list."

Felix reached over and picked a tablet off the pile, flipping open the cover and reading, "The waiter who delivered my lunch today is unacceptable. He has a lazy eye and his movements are sluggish. I suspect he is of louche morals."

Felix rolled his eyes, placing the tablet down and picking up the next one in the pile. "He scratches in inappropriate places in public."

He snapped the cover shut and picked up another, "Too scruffy."

And another, "Clearly inverted."

And another, "Voice is too loud."

And another, "Behaves like a slave ought not to."

And another, "Too slow."

And another, "Irresponsible and irregular."

The pile was still stacked fifteen tablets high. Felix's eyes met Philo's.

"There ain't nothing in there about you. He likes you. Or at least he fucking tolerates you. He ain't tolerating anyone else, he's got through eight announcers already."

Philo winced, rightly anticipating Felix's conclusion. "So I ain't fucking redeploying you! Now get the fuck out!"

He left Felix feeling ear-blasted and dejected. Returning to Sabinus' office, Philo was appalled to find the prefect standing by his desk rummaging through his satchel. Epaphroditus would never have violated his private possessions!

"What are you doing?"

Sabinus was unmoved and apparently unaware of the gross transgression he was committing. "I am looking for that message," he said and continued to look through Philo's satchel.

328

"I gave it to Alexander as you requested," squeaked Philo, deeply distressed to see his beloved satchel being so manhandled by someone who had no right to do such a thing.

Sabinus pulled out a scroll and placed it on a desk and then pulled out another object, balancing it on his hand.

"What's this?" he asked staring at the small, bronze figure.

"It's mine!" cried Philo.

"It is a monkey."

It was not a monkey it was Hanuman! Hanuman who had led the monkey army to rescue Princess Sita from the demon king Ravena's clutches. Hanuman who was the embodiment of heroism and bravery. Hanuman who was Philo's protector in a scary world.

"I don't approve," he stated, handing the object to an agitated Philo. "You are in Rome now. You should not cling to such Eastern ways."

He stressed the Eastern with a sneer. "You should integrate or go back," making it clear which was his preferred option.

Philo gave Hanuman a small kiss on the top of his head by way of an apology for being so grossly treated and returned the heroic monkey to safety in his satchel, bending down and stashing the satchel far beneath his desk and out of Sabinus' clutches. The prefect viewed this scene with a sneer.

"You will pack up your things."

Philo, head beneath his desk, stood up promptly and stared at Sabinus' grim face. He was being sacked. He'd never been sacked before. Wasn't it marvellous! Good old Hanuman! Philo knew he wouldn't let him down. The monkey god would be getting a whole saucer of milk and at least three puddings that night, decided Philo.

Of course Felix would combust, but Philo could take his foul-mouthed tirade if it meant escaping the company of Nymphidius Sabinus. Perhaps Felix would redeploy him to the treasury. Philo liked adding things up. He found it much easier to deal with money scrawled onto a ledger than those strange coins in his hand. And there were some nice offices in the treasury.

Philo's inner joy was comprehensively crushed when Sabinus explained in his usual monotone, "We are moving. This office is no longer suitable for my position."

What position Sabinus imagined he held was open to interpretation. He had ditched the Praetorian uniform and appeared solely in tunic and toga. He did not call himself the emperor's private secretary or even advisor. He did not give himself any titles. He was simply Nymphidius Sabinus and he was to be obeyed. His authority came from the 10,000 guards who owed him their loyalty and whom he, or at least Galba, owed 30,000 sesterces each.

Sabinus had yet to understand that there was no money to give out. The treasury was empty.

FORTY-SEVEN

U nlike Philo, Alex adored working for Nymphidius Sabinus. The barked orders that so intimidated the freedman thrilled Alex; messages had to be delivered that moment, speedily, and the return message back with Sabinus in ever decreasing amounts of time.

Alex had never needed to count the hours before. He rose like most of the city with the sun and retired when he was told to. Other than that he measured the passing of time by how hungry he felt. Sabinus' deadlines had introduced Alex to the world of the clock. The prefect had a water clock placed outside his office and Alex had learnt to read the figures painted on its round disc so that he could judge if he had made his target.

Alex rose to such challenges; the narrowing targets motivated him for the first time in his messaging career and he strove to satisfy Sabinus. Of course the prefect did not give praise lightly, if ever. But Alex correctly recognised the lack of harsh words from Sabinus denoted his satisfaction with him.

After hitting his first eight target times, one involving a long hike to the far corner of the Oppian Hill side of the palace grounds and back again to the forum side, Alex was finally promoted to externals. How he smiled at that first adventure into the city streets with Mina, getting lost like that! How stupid!

Given a chance to learn, Alex soaked up knowledge like a bum sponge, memorising the key landmarks that allowed him to find his destination wherever he was in the sprawling limbs of Rome.

Alex's increased responsibilities were also taking his mind off his fight with Mina, which he still bristled over. He couldn't understand why she would allow herself to be demeaned in such a manner. The things people were saying about her!

Alex had already got into a fight, bruising his knuckles on Anacreon's jaw after he had asked with a grin if Alex knew what position they did it in, since he couldn't fathom how Mina could stretch her legs wide enough to accommodate Straton's bulk. There would be many more gags like that.

Alex couldn't stand it and he particularly couldn't stand the way Mina just laughed them off. So they were slaves: it didn't mean they couldn't have respect for themselves at least. There were ways through the system that didn't involve debasing yourself.

He gazed at the rows and rows of death masks that lined the walls of the atrium where he sat. He was delivering a message to a consul, an actual consul! Sabinus had instructed that he must only give the scroll to the consul himself, which had led to Alex blagging and bragging his way past seven different types of household slaves so far.

Eventually he had been taken to see some sort of secretary, or so Alex deduced from his ink-stained fingers, who had promised he would hand the scroll personally to his master.

Alex had folded his arms and attempted a Sabinus style glare, telling the secretary, "It is for the consul alone. I shall wait until he is available."

Which Alex hoped would not be long since he had a two-hour target to hit. Then he had been shuffled into this atrium.

The consul was a disappointment. He was a small rotund man, fleshy of cheek, and nothing like the noble erect creature of birth that Alex had expected.

"From Nymphidius Sabinus, sir," Alex had barked, handing over the scroll.

The consul's eyes narrowed, a tension appearing in his shoulders. Such was the power of that name. Alex came to recognise those who feared Sabinus the greatest. They rushed him through, sat him down, and provided him with refreshments as they vocalised their respect for the prefect. Words Sabinus was keen to hear repeated on his return.

The fat little consul did not utter any such words. He snatched at the scroll, sighing heavily as he read.

"A response, sir?"

The consul gave a tight smile. "Only one. Tell your master that though it is unfortunate that he is unable to attend the senate, the convening will still go ahead as it has for 300 years and he can read about it in the annals like everyone else!"

Nymphidius Sabinus' new office was surprisingly located in the new palace, the very building he had raged about so much. The room was a former lounge that had been used for some of the more intimate and depraved of Nero's parties, a circular space with a pearl-studded ceiling and a marble floor in contrasting shades of greens and yellows.

Sabinus justified this luxury by declaring that he had reclaimed the space for the good of Rome. What was true was that he had reclaimed a much larger desk for himself and an entourage of attendants who flurried round him, to his displeasure and annoyance.

He was not happy with Alex either. The messenger, who had grown accustomed to the brisk nature of soldiers, kept his expression deliberately neutral.

"How can the senate meet if I am not there?" he asked rhetorically. "I ratify all motions. There is no purpose to their convening if I am not there. You, slave!" he addressed Philo. "You will note this down word for word."

Epaphroditus nearly choked on his wine. "He's disbanded the senate?"

Philo nodded, helping himself to a date. "He claims that due to the unrest in the city, he cannot guarantee the safety of individual senators."

Epaphroditus tapped his fingers on the arm of his chair. "Ten thousand guards cannot protect six hundred senators. That is a sad indictment of his own troops. Is he mad?"

Philo pondered before asking with curiosity, "What was he like before?"

Nymphidia maintained her son was sensitive. Working for Sabinus' grandfather Callistus, Epaphroditus had been a prime witness to the prefect's awkward progression from fretful baby to tormented adolescent.

There were, he knew, *incidents* leading to Sabinus being removed from the exclusive tutor his grandfather paid for; Nymphidia utterly unable to bear her only child's misery. Epaphroditus sympathised and took the rewards from Nymphidia such concern earned.

Callistus insisted the boy needed toughening up and apparently the Roman army had done just that. The delicate boy, who had been such a worry to his mother and such a disappointment to his grandfather, returned from the legions altogether different and about as sensitive as a wall.

Philo chewed at the inside of his cheek, saying quietly, "He's not seeing things correctly. There have been lynchings in the city. Sabinus thinks it is because they were Nero's men but it's not. It's because they didn't protect Nero from him."

"Sabinus' problem, among many problems, is that he truly believes in his own righteousness. If he were capable of even the slightest flexibility—"

A leader couldn't run a city of over a million inhabitants, let alone an empire of many more millions, without being able to anticipate his audience and modify his voice. Sabinus' confidence in his own rightness and his unbending superiority had never earned him friends in his private life, let alone on the public stage.

"He's treating you alright though, Philo?"

Philo laced his fingers together; he did not appear very happy. "He's a bit abrupt," he admitted. "I'm not sure he even needs an assistant. He likes to do everything himself."

Of course he did, mused Epaphroditus. Sabinus would have no advisors, no helpmates. The only voice he listened to was his own.

"Still, Galba will be in Rome shortly," he injected cheerily.

Philo went, "Mmm," pressing his lips together tight.

There were tales of provincial officials being dispatched without trial under Galba's orders.

"Hello, you two," said Aphrodite, appearing in the inner courtyard, a red shawl wrapped around her shoulders.

She walked behind her husband and kissed him on the top of his head. Epaphroditus reached back and clasped her hands.

"How are you, Philo? Feeling better?"

Philo flushed and fidgeted on his chair. "Yes, thank you. It was a bit of a shock, that's all."

Philo, on receiving a note from the widow Aphrodite asking him to visit her, had trotted over to the Esquiline unsuspecting. He was shown through to this courtyard and there stood Epaphroditus. Alive. Very much alive.

Philo was flabbergasted. He staggered backwards as if hit in the face with a shovel, shocked stupefaction playing across his features. His eyes darted back and forth in confusion until clearly some kind of internal battle had been won and he finally believed what he was seeing was indeed true. Then he burst into tears.

"I told you I should have warned him first," Aphrodite chastised her husband, "But you would have your moment."

"It's fine," assured Philo, "I'm fine. Absolutely fine."

He tried a smile: it came out rather wan.

Aphrodite settled herself down beside her husband. "How is Teretia?"

The first few times she had asked Philo this question, he looked thoroughly perplexed. Now he accepted that this was a standard question he was expected to answer and he replied, "She's pickling."

Epaphroditus raised an eyebrow. "Pickling?"

"Her and her mother. They are pickling the summer fruits so that they can enjoy them all year round. There are jars all over the kitchen. And spoons."

"Well, that's nice," attempted Aphrodite, though she had never pickled in her life and it had never occurred to her to question her slaves on how they provided summer fruits in the winter. "You should bring her here for dinner, shouldn't he?"

She elbowed Epaphroditus who instantly concurred, "Oh, absolutely."

"That is very kind of you but I don't think it would be proper," was Philo's odd response.

Epaphroditus got in first, "Proper?"

Philo turned his attention to the arm of his chair, which suddenly became uniquely fascinating. "It would not look very good to her husband if she were to go to a dinner party with another man."

"Teretia's married?" gasped Aphrodite.

"Future husband," corrected Philo.

"Teretia's betrothed?" she gasped again.

"Well, no," conceded Philo. "But I believe they must be looking for a husband for her. Teretius has mentioned several times to me that he has a large dowry saved."

I bet he has, thought Epaphroditus.

"I wouldn't want to jeopardise any marriage arrangements by ill rumours." Philo was unaware that for the past four months the palace gossip trail had linked him so firmly with that girl that a birth announcement was imminently awaited.

Epaphroditus placed a restraining hand on Aphrodite's arm before suggesting lightly, "Perhaps you could run it past her father first. Make sure it was proper?"

Philo fiddled with a sleeve. "No, I don't think so. I'm very busy with work and Teretia's busy with her pickling."

And what with Straton wanting him in his bed seemingly every night, Philo had very few free evenings. Not that he vocalised this but his troubled expression was put down by Aphrodite to a wistful longing for Teretia, and by Epaphroditus to the trials of working for Sabinus.

FORTY-EIGHT

"**Y**ou should sort it out with her."

Alex's head snapped up from the sword he was polishing and looked at Honoratus.

"You were thinking about that girl."

"I was not."

"Alexander, whenever you think of her you make this face," Honoratus pursed his lips and furrowed his brow, exaggerating Alex's jerky polishing movements. "I can always tell."

"I do not look like that."

Honoratus laughed. "Alex, please sort it out with her. If only for the sake of that weapon."

Alex looked down at his sword, the surface was smudged uneven. "Oh."

"Sabinus will have you on fifty squat thrusts if he sees that. Here, let me." Honoratus took the sword from Alex and began polishing it with a rag in smooth, long motions along the blade.

"I don't think she'll listen to me. She's proper mad and when Mina's mad—" he pursed his lips again, remembering a past quarrel which had resulted in severely bruised nipples.

"I have faith you can win her round," commented Honoratus, not looking up.

"I just don't understand how she can let people say those things about her!" complained Alex. "Because she's not like that, not really."

The Mina he knew was funny and brave. She was resolutely loyal to her friends. Always the first to put a supporting arm round you or to cheer you out of a gloom. He wanted everyone to know that Mina, his Mina, not the girl who was supposedly putting out to the gross overseer.

"Be open and honest with her. But not too honest," suggested Honoratus with a wry smile. "Calling a girl a whore is not the best way to win her heart."

Alex flushed bright red but registered the point, and when his sword was shiny to Sabinus' standard, he sought out his friend.

Hanging on to the door frame he asked, "How is your fake romance with Straton going?"

Mina, laid tummy down on her bed with an open scroll resting on a board in front of her, replied, "The one you don't approve of?"

"Yes, that one," said Alex, daring to enter and sit beside her.

She looked at him, her face softened, and she smiled, a dazzling Mina smile. He was forgiven.

"I feel it has added a whole new intriguing facet to my character. Even the empress asked about it," she told him.

"She didn't?" Alex dutifully replied with an infusion of shock.

"She did," smiled Mina, sitting up and tucking her feet underneath her. "She wanted to know if we were using contraception since she felt a pregnant keeper of the towel would be an unpleasant sight in her entourage."

"What did you say?"

"I said that yes we were, and then made up some bull about a special concoction of herbs and oil that was foolproof for preventing babies."

"I find it astounding that people actually believe that you and Straton …"

"Felix doesn't," confessed Mina. "He grabbed me the other day to tell me that he didn't believe a word of it. I told him it was all true and he said that I was not Straton's type."

"He has a type? I thought he would be more of a snatch and grab whatever was on offer type."

Mina fidgeted and then lowered her voice the way she always did when she had something of interest to report.

"So Felix says to me, and this is a direct quote though I have expurgated the swearing: 'Look here, girl. I've mopped up the messy consequences of Straton's little passions for years and there is no way that you are one of them. You have three factors against you.'"

"Which were?" asked Alex, who had mentally added a "fucking" every four words into Felix's reported sentence.

"Apparently I am too feisty, too tall, and too female."

"The Catullus poem was addressed to a young man," Alex pointed out.

"Indeed, that's what I thought. It narrows the field a bit." She picked up the scroll. "What do you think?"

Alex took it from her and admired the neat calligraphy and the drawn figures of naked, leaping satyrs that ran round the border. They were a happy bunch, with erect phalluses which they used to balance wine cups on or worry Maenaeds. Alex followed their antics down the side of the scroll to the bottom where they rode a series of exotic animals, chasing after the fleeing Maenaeds. On the right-hand side, the Maenaeds were comprehensively run down and ravished in a glorious riot of entangled limbs, spouting cocks, and general mayhem.

Had Mina possessed the slighest idea who her scroll was intended for, she would have definitely chosen a tamer subject.

"It's great, Mina. You are really talented."

"It took me ages. Do you reckon Straton will like it?"

"'Course, and I'm sure his very special friend will like it even more."

Mina threw herself backwards onto her pillows, "Gods, I wish Sporus was here: he would die for this one!"

Alex gave a nervous smile. "Yes, he would have," he offered smoothly. "And he would have found out who Straton's friend was in record time."

"He would have camped outside his door until the friend sneaked out. And he would have rushed in here in his clip-cloppy heels and tiara and swooned all over the bed before telling us he knew something of dire importance and making us interrogate him for answers."

Alex could almost see Sporus doing exactly that and he smiled as he said, "He would have dragged it out over an entire night."

Mina sat up. "I miss him."

Alex gripped her hands telling her, "So do I."

He assured himself that he was not lying to her. He did miss Sporus. He was just the beneficiary of an additional nugget of information that Mina wasn't.

Nymphidius Sabinus disapproved of many things: moral laxity, heavy drinking, and the colour purple. Philo was surprised to find that lunch featured on the prefect's list of complaints about the modern world.

The prefect considered lunch a sign of constitutional weakness, an opinion he was all too ready to share with the freedman, complete with a commentary on how legionary rations were fully sufficient for the body's needs. He was particularly scathing on Teretia's lovingly baked spiced almond cakes, which he considered decadent.

Such harsh words were playing havoc with Philo's rather delicate digestive system and he had taken to lunching in his old office where he could nibble away unjudged. He was nipping down the corridors now, clutching his satchel, and anticipating Teretia's tasty date salad and the supposedly decadent cake.

Pushing open the door to the antechamber, he was confronted by a stranger. He was fiddling about at Philo's old desk, manhandling a stylus box.

"Can I help you?"

The man turned. He was bald with a prominent Adam's apple and a rather tortoise-like appearance.

"You are?" he asked.

Philo, who was well trained, instantly responded to the stranger. "Philo, sir."

The man smiled, showing two buck teeth. "Nice to meet you, Philo. I am Icelus. I am Galba's private secretary and advisor."

Philo, immediately spotting an opportunity to escape Sabinus' employment, said quickly, "I am the emperor's private secretary's secretary," and then qualified this for the lost Icelus. "I am your secretary, sir."

Icelus smiled, "Excellent. I am sure we shall work together fine."

Philo attempted a smile back. It couldn't be any worse than working for Sabinus, surely? "Is there anything you require, sir?"

"I wish to call a meeting. Do you do meetings?"

Philo nodded. "I can handle the arrangements and I do the minutes."

"I am not sure that this one should be minuted."

"We have two archives," Philo explained. "One for the public domain and one definitely not."

Seeing Icelus' puzzled expression, he added, "It can be useful to have a record of what was agreed, even if it is disagreeable. Especially if it is disagreeable, people have a tendency to backtrack …" He trailed off, aware that he was dictating to his new boss.

Icelus didn't seem to mind though. "Excellent. Would you accompany me to this meeting?"

"If you want me to," said Philo, disconcerted by the request.

He was always told he had to be somewhere. Even Epaphroditus, who he felt was the best of bosses, had never requested him in such a polite manner.

"They tell me I should hold this meeting in the circular room."

"Octagonal dining room," Philo translated. "New palace."

Fiddling with his cuffs, Icelus added awkwardly, "You know where that is?" Philo nodded eagerly.

"There are other things I require."

Philo whipped out a note tablet from his satchel and waited, stylus poised.

"I thought … I rather thought that I would stay here, until Galba, sorry the emperor, arrives in Rome."

"You need rooms at the palace?"

"Yes," said Icelus, pleased the scribe understood him.

Philo scribbled away, telling Icelus, "I will arrange for a suite. There are some nice suites in the new palace. Do you need your belongings transferred? If you could give me the details, I will get it arranged. Is there anything else, sir?"

A lot of worries slipped from Icelus's shoulders. "This meeting?"

"The attendees?" prompted Philo.

"Oh, of course," Icelus went pink. "Nymphidius Sabinus."

Philo blanched slightly but noted down the name on his tablet. "Anyone else?"

"No one else. That is all for the time being. Thank you, Philo."

"I'll get onto it straight away, sir."

Icelus was about to sit down on the chair until Philo interrupted, "Ermm, sir, your office is through there," indicating the connecting door. "This is just the antechamber, my office."

Icelus went pink again. "Of course" he hedged, embarrassed. "I'll just pop through and get settled."

Sabinus paced. He failed to understand why Icelus had chosen this room for their meeting. There were perfectly serviceable offices elsewhere. The octagonal dining room with its marble inlaid floor and huge domed ceiling reminded him of Nero. It was in this room that Nero indulged his most base of activities: defiling freeborn girls; parading that eunuch. Even going so far as to penetrate it in front of senatorial officials, complete with running commentary as he thrust. Then there were those other activities that Sabinus found too distasteful to name and too disgusting to contemplate.

Around him slaves milled about, setting up tables and couches, laying out platters of food. He grabbed one roughly by the arm.

"Who told you to set this up?"

"Midas, sir."

Midas worked in the hospitality section. Since the coup that brought down Nero, he had been severely underworked. With the opportunity to wow one of the new emperor's advisors, he decided to go all out to impress.

Sabinus picked at the flamingo meat, a lip noticeably curling.

"It is unnecessary," he told Midas.

Midas, podgy in face with a mop of golden curls, held his ground.

"It is a welcome lunch for Icelus. A hello from the workforce."

"It is flamboyant."

"We would look pretty piss-poor hosts if all we offered was bread and water."

Sabinus fixed him with a glare. "Remove it."

Midas gave an audible sigh. "And the dancing girls?"

"Are not needed. Will not be needed. I shall instruct Felix to retrain them in more suitable professions."

Midas signalled to the slaves, who began to retrieve their carefully placed platters.

345

"And get Straton."

"Straton?"

"I don't like your cheek," Sabinus told him stonily.

Icelus and Philo stood to one side to allow Straton to march Midas away. Passing by, Straton gave Philo's hand a soft brush. Thankfully Icelus was too taken by the opulence of the dining room and Midas' head was firmly forced forward, so neither of them noted this little loving gesture.

Lysander, leant against a wall examining his nails, leaped to attention when he saw Icelus and gave him a florid introduction that made Philo wince.

"Icelus, good to see you." Sabinus embraced him briefly, uncomfortably. "How is our esteemed emperor?"

"Very well when I left."

Icelus was gently manoeuvred to his correct seat by one of Midas' team.

"You passed my letter on to him?"

"Of course," Icelus said, and then seeing Sabinus desperate for reply added, "He was most gratified by your words."

Which was suitably vague. Icelus was sure that Galba had not read the prefect's scroll, caught up as he was in the multitude of business that needed taking care of. His answer seemed to please Sabinus who gave a small smile. A sight so rare that Philo, sat discreetly next to Icelus, nearly dropped his note tablet. An action that unfortunately attracted Sabinus' attention; he stared, puzzled, at Philo.

Icelus, catching the look, erroneously thought he should undertake the introductions. "This is my assistant, Philo. Philo, this is the Praetorian prefect Nymphidius Sabinus."

The prefect frowned; an awkward Philo shuffled on his chair and took out his note tablet, avoiding Sabinus' gaze. Turning back to Icelus, the prefect told him, "The senate are most eager for the emperor to take his rightful place. Does he follow you?"

"There will be a delay. The emperor wishes to settle the situation in the provinces before heading to Rome."

Sabinus looked ever so slightly crushed. "Oh, I see."

"He has every faith in your abilities," said Icelus, which perked the prefect up. "He gave me some instructions."

Philo handed Icelus the required scroll. He unfurled it but did not read, paraphrasing its contents.

"The emperor thanks you for your service. He is keen for the city to return to normal as soon as possible."

Sabinus was nodding, firmly in agreement.

"He wishes the lynchings to cease instantly."

"An unfortunate business."

"He wishes no retribution to be carried out against the former emperor's associates."

Sabinus shifted slightly.

"He orders you to release Ofonius Tigellinus."

"Now hang on," said Sabinus.

Icelus pointed to the relevant section, handing it to Sabinus who read it with mounting temper.

"Tigellinus is a corrupt, malign influence," he told Icelus. "He was Nero's creature, absolute. He was an active participant and initiator of the worst of crimes under that tyrant's rule."

He would have continued in this vein at length had not Icelus interrupted him. "Those are your orders."

Sabinus was silent. He was torn. The orders were wrong but he could not yet believe that Galba could be wrong. It was a misunderstanding: the new emperor had been away from Rome many years; he did not understand what Tigellinus had been. Sabinus vowed to write to him, explaining in detail why Tigellinus had to die. Galba would follow his reason. So he nodded his agreement.

"Calvia Crispinilla?" queried Icelus.

"Fled to Africa the last I heard. A former lover, Clodius Macer, is governor. I imagine she will whore her way into his favours again."

This came out with slightly more bitterness than was intended. Philo paused with his note taking, looking up at the prefect with interest.

The discomfort Sabinus felt at revealing more than he meant to was eased by Lysander sliding in and announcing, "The noble and honourable Senator Regulus; the noble and honourable Senator Senex."

They entered, a vision in togas, and greeted Icelus much like a conquering hero. Nymphidius Sabinus they ignored entirely.

FORTY-NINE

Spain.

"He complains about your pal Tigellinus," said Galba slamming the scroll down. "At length. Is any of this true?"

Vinius, who had spent his youth with Tigellinus, did not bother to read Sabinus' accusations, admitting with an apologetic shrug. "Probably."

Galba looked to Laco. "Is this going to make me unpopular in Rome?"

Laco dodged the question. "It will make you unpopular with Sabinus, he loathes Tigellinus."

"I gathered that."

"Offer him someone else," suggested Vinius. "Sate his bloodlust, keep him sweet."

Galba looked to Laco again.

"It would look odd to single out any one person whilst allowing other more involved personages to live. Inconsistent."

Galba chewed his lip.

"Sabinus though," piped in Vinius. "He needs pacifying."

Galba vacilated, unsure which was the best course. Vinius and Laco began arguing between themselves.

"Gods, Laco, we need to draw a line between us and Nero's cronies. How are we meant to do that with them all flouncing round Rome free as ever. The senate will lose faith that we mean to change things."

"I agree, Titus, but you've ruined that by pleading for your Praetorian pal."

Galba covered his ears.

"Your Imperial Majesty, Marcus Salvius Otho."

Galba looked to his advisors.

"Governor of Lusitania," supplied Laco. "He was the first to offer you his support."

"Show him in."

Otho bounded in, offering his colleagues a smile of surprising infectiousness. He was a sturdy man with odd, bowed, hairless legs, and feet that splayed in strange directions. All of which might have damned a lesser man to longer tunics and disguised sandals. Otho, however, carried these deficiencies off by sheer force of personality, his bright eyes and thick thatch of dark hair also drawing attention away from his lower level.

"Imperial Majesty," he beamed. "I brought you a gift."

He clicked his fingers and a small group of boy slaves trotted in dressed in sparkling white tunics with gold collars. They were an attractive bunch with doe eyes and tanned limbs. Even those present whose tastes did not turn that way couldn't help staring.

"I know," said Otho proudly. "Gorgeous aren't they? I thought to myself, what could old Galba need. And then it came to me in a flash." He clicked his fingers to demonstrate the moment of illumination. "Now that you are emperor, you need a proper entourage to serve you. These fellows could be straight out of the imperial ministries. They're not because I bought them off this Jew slave trader I know. Syrian, he told me. Of course he's a trader so let us assume not. But Eastern beauties, aren't they?"

"That is very kind of you, Otho, but I don't think—" began Vinius, but he was cut off by Laco.

"Now then, let's not be hasty," he said, gazing with interest at a particularly fine-looking boy.

Galba wore a look of pure disgust. His own tastes ran to the mature man. "I have no need of such creatures. Take them away."

"You don't have to use them as catamites," Otho said cheerfully. "They can carry plates and serve dinner. Seems a waste of good bum but they can do it."

"Get them out."

"But we thank you for the thought," prompted Vinius.

"Yes, yes," muttered Galba as the boys trotted out. "Not suitable for an army camp, distracts the troops."

"Yes, we prefer them to rape the natives," jested Laco. "Helps with the war effort."

"I could send them over to Rome," suggested Otho. "Get them settled in for your arrival."

"It shall be some time before I return to Rome."

"Oh really? I heard the senate is mighty eager to meet you and get you properly installed."

"The senate will have to wait," said Galba shortly. "There is other business to attend to."

Otho, who had been going to argue, recognised a cut-off when he saw one. He closed his mouth and employed a genial smile.

"Whatever you decide to do, Caesar, you can count on me. I am 100 per cent behind you."

Yes, with a knife, though Laco. He didn't trust Otho one bit. Everyone knew his reputation. He had been one of Nero's playboy pals, indulging in every vice known to man and beast, until the friends had irreparably fallen out over the issue of Otho's wife, Poppaea Sabina. Nero, who clearly retained some fondness for his old friend, had him exiled rather than executed.

To the surprise of all, Otho proved a very successful governor, which had gone some way to restoring his beleaguered character. Laco remained unconvinced. Vinius, on the other hand, was engaging brightly with the governor, promising him many benefits for his unconditional support of their enterprise, which Otho graciously thanked Galba for with the skill of a dedicated courtier.

FIFTY

Sabinus was having supper at his mother's. She'd made a number of concessions for her son. They were sat upright either side of a long plain table. The food was similarly plain, ungarnished from any sauce that might make it more palatable. Hercules and his muscled brother slaves had been hidden away for the night. In their place were a series of wholesome-looking slave girls whom she had hired for the evening in some vague hope they would catch her son's eye.

Her appearance she was unwilling to concede on, and she wore her standard well-tailored gown with a scooped neckline revealing the bulging tops of her breasts. Her style was classic but suggestive.

Surprisingly Sabinus had not commented on her attire at all. He sat pushing a spoon into a heap of boiled asparagus staring absently at the vegetable.

"Why are you not eating, darling?" enquired his mother, leaning back in her chair so a slave girl could collect her own empty plate.

"I'm not hungry."

"But it's your favourite. I had cook make it especially for you."

No response. Nymphidia leaned her elbows on the table. "What is it, darling? What's making you so unhappy?"

She was his mother. She alone could distinguish between his usual taciturnity and the genuine moroseness that was affecting him now.

"Nothing, nothing is wrong," he murmured, pushing the plate of asparagus away.

Nymphidia waited and a few moments of silence later he burst out, "Icelus took my scribe!"

"That is very rude of him," she consoled. "I'm surprised Felix would allow such a redeployment."

"Wasn't Felix," he mumbled, still avoiding her eye.

"No? Why don't I buy you a new scribe? A better one. One imported from Greece, trained to even higher standards than the palace. Seneca once paid 300,000 sesterces for a Greek that could recount all of Plato's works. It is said it saved him having to thumb through the scrolls himself. Of course you wouldn't need that particular talent, darling, but for 300,000 I imagine they could cope with our paperwork and more besides. Let me go down to the market tomorrow and I'll get you a Greekling that will make Icelus sick with envy."

"That's not the point, mother." He looked up and she noted the distress in his eyes. "There's other things—" he tailed off, struggling to articulate his emotions. "Galba has not written to me. Not at all."

"Spain is a long way away, darling. Messages take time, there are many miles to cover."

"Icelus gets missives. He quotes Galba's instructions. I have written to him every day, mother. Every day with information on the situation in the city. I have kept him abreast of all developments. Yet he does not write. Not to me."

He paused in his misery. Nymphidia reached across the table and rubbed at his arm supportively.

"I saved his life! I saved Galba's life. The tyrant was going to kill him. I warned him. I saved him!"

"I know you did, darling," she soothed gently.

"I gave him Rome! I made him emperor. Without me—"

Nymphidia walked round the table and sat beside him. She took his hands in hers. They were large and hairy, much changed from the tiny little fingers that had clutched hers all those years ago. Different too from the elongated adolescent fingers that had twitched in distress as he had told her about the bullying he was suffering at school.

Yet he needed the same from her even now, comfort. She put her arms around him and her son buried his face away in her shoulder. Rubbing his back she told him calmly, "You don't know this is a slight. Galba may not have even received your letters."

He looked up with hope. "You think that they are being kept from him?"

"It is a distinct possibility. Are you sending them via the imperial post?"

"Yes, as normal."

"Plenty of opportunities there for interception. Icelus may be keeping them himself."

Sabinus frowned. "I don't understand."

Nymphidia had always been the more astute of the two, taking after her father Callistus. He was the dogged survivor of Caligula's reign.

"Just think, Gaius. If Icelus is the sole contact to Galba, then he reports what he likes. He takes all the glory, all your successes."

"You think that is the case?"

She squeezed his hands. "It's a possibility, is it not?"

Sabinus cleared his throat and pulled back his plate of asparagus by its rim.

"I think you are right, mother," he stated, having moved swiftly from despair back to his usual righteous confidence. "Icelus is keeping my letters from Galba. Insidious slave. But I will not let him poison that great man's mind against me. I shall send an envoy personally to speak with Galba."

"Send a gift," suggested Nymphidia. "A token of your respect. Nothing flashy, no gold, nothing ornamental: Galba is a man of simple pleasures, I hear."

"What would you suggest?"

"Furniture, well crafted by Roman citizens. Utilitarian yet with beauty."

Sabinus gave a nod to show his approval of the suggestion. "I shall send Guard Gellianus with my gift."

"Good plan, darling. Gellianus will plead your case well. Let Galba know the great steps you have taken on his behalf. He will appreciate the risks you have taken."

Sabinus bent over his plate and began spooning asparagus into that grim mouth of his.

Nymphidia smiled. "Tuck in, darling. There is boiled cabbage to come."

FIFTY-ONE

"Gosh, did you sleep here?"

Philo opened his eyes to see Teretia bent over him with concerned interest. He straightened himself up and gazed round the kitchen.

"I must have," he concurred, prodding at his cheek which had been resting on the table.

"It can't have been very comfortable."

A persistent ache in his neck confirmed that statement. He pushed back his shoulders and stretched out his arms behind his head.

"You must have got back terribly late," commented Teretia.

She stood on tip toes, retrieving a saucepan that was hung on a hook hammered into the wall. "They work you too hard at the palace. It's unjust."

Actually he hadn't been working. He had been with Straton. Lying on the bed and staring up at the ceiling, feeling vaguely nostalgic for the days when the overseer would simply march him to the nearest cupboard, perform the standard thirty-seven thrusts (which Philo would mentally tally downwards), and then let him go.

All this stroking and cuddling and fawning was deeply alarming. Philo anticipating a day when Straton would prevent him from ever leaving his quarters. He pictured a future of being buckled to the bedpost, hand–fed, and cosseted by the overseer. It was this horrifying image that propelled him, while Straton nipped off to get a bowl of nuts for them both, to make his escape.

Waiting until his tormentor was outside the door, Philo leaped up, threw on his tunic, slipped on his sandals, and legged it. He disappeared with such speed that he forgot not only his belt but also a lamp to light his way home.

He stumbled through the night peering into the darkness for any vaguely familiar shapes and consoling himself that if he couldn't see anything then he was most likely to be invisible to any would-be robbers. After what seemed like many lost hours, Philo eventually found the correct apartment block, trudging bleary-eyed into the kitchen intending to make it to his bed. Which he clearly hadn't.

He wondered, as he watched Teretia go about lighting the stove, how he should explain his vanishing act to Straton. A violent illness that had suddenly hit him perhaps?

He pulled his satchel belt over his head and laid it on the table, rubbing at the red mark on his neck where it had dug in overnight.

"What does the V stand for?" asked Teretia pointing to the golden letter embossed on the top right corner of the satchel.

"Vima."

"Vim-ma?" she pronounced hesitantly. "What's Vima?"

Philo was not given to confidences. He never felt he had anything worth sharing, but seeing Teretia's curious gaze he opened up a little.

"It's what my mother called me."

Teretia folded her elbows onto the table. "Like a nickname? When I was little, my father used to call me his sweet little honeypot." She flushed. "Rather childish, I know."

Philo smiled. "No, I think it's nice. It suits you."

That caused another flush, this one of pleasure rather than embarrassment. "So what does Vim-ma mean?"

"It's not an endearment. It's the name my mother gave me."

Teretia's forehead creased. "So you're not Philo at all?" she breathed, shocked by this startlingly revelation.

Philo featured near exclusively in her daily journal and she didn't fancy going back and correcting those frequent references.

"No, I am," he consoled. "The palace calls me Philo but my mother always called me Vima." He fingered the golden dip of the V. "She gave me this satchel when I passed my exams. So I would be a proper Roman boy."

It had been creakingly new and shiny then. The brown leather had gleamed so much he could see his face reflected in its surface. Now it was battered. The strap had been replaced several times, the buckle was cracked and dimpled. But he would not have disposed of it for any money.

Teretia, picking up some of those thoughts, said, "It is an exceptionally fine bag. Do you feel more like a Philo or a Vima?"

He pondered, concluding, "Philo I suppose. Everyone calls me Philo now."

He scratched at his arm, saying quietly, "I used to think that if I were properly Vima then things would be different. I would be different."

Vima to Philo's mind would have been taller, brawnier, and braver. Vima was everything Philo should have been but wasn't. Vima wouldn't have let Straton bully him. Vima certainly wouldn't have fled in the night to escape the overseer. Vima would have stood up to Straton. He wouldn't meekly comply with the overseer's every demand, no matter how distasteful to him. He would be strong.

"Perhaps you could be Philo on ordinary days and Vima on special ones," suggested Teretia, adding shyly, "If you liked, I could call you Vima. On those special days."

359

Philo thought about this, a cheery glow forming inside him. "I think that would be nice. Because there isn't anyone to call me Vima now."

"We could keep it alive. Keep Vima alive."

Philo smiled, his eyes crinkling. "I would like that. I would like that a lot."

Teretia smiled back with a cheery glow of her own that showed in two pink circles on her cheeks. "Now I must get on with breakfast. I won't send you to work without your porridge because you wouldn't be able to concentrate properly!" she exclaimed, heaving herself to her feet and bending down to check on the stove.

She was a nice girl, thought Philo, and then upgraded this to an exceptionally nice girl. Absently staring at her bottom as she added twigs to the fire, he dispassionately noted that was exceptionally nice too.

The cheery start to Philo's day did not last, arriving at work to find an enraged Nymphidius Sabinus in his office.

"Slave, get me Icelus. We have matters to discuss."

It was said in a tone that suggested these were matters that Philo need not concern himself with.

"He is not available."

"Make him available."

"He is addressing the senate."

Sabinus gave him a stony glare. "But that is what I do! I address the senate. Why was I not informed of this?"

"Senatorial deputations are attended by the senate, the emperor, the emperor's private secretary, and the head of the treasury," Philo told him, adding as further proof, "It is the protocol."

"Protocol? Protocol?" growled Sabinus, turning purple.

Philo quickly threw in, "Praetorian prefects are not required at these meetings."

Sabinus opened his mouth to protest. "But I am different."

Too bloody right you are, thought Philo, before reporting much more smoothly than he felt, "I could note your request to be present for the next deputation. An 80/20 split on the vote would allow it."

The prefect pointed a long finger at him. "You tell Icelus that I will see him when he returns."

"He has a very busy schedule today."

He retrieved the relevant tablet holding it up for Sabinus to see.

Fully purple, Sabinus told him, "I will see him when he returns, you slave traitor!" before stomping off.

Philo concluding that the prefect was still annoyed by his defection.

When Icelus returned, he asked, "Good meeting, sir?"

Icelus smiled. He had just about curbed the instinct to look behind him to see who Philo was addressing.

"Very productive," Galba's private secretary told him cheerily. "They are sending a deputation to northern Italy to talk with the emperor, to sort out some of these niggling little issues."

"Nymphidius Sabinus was here. He was rather put out."

"Oh dear."

Icelus fiddled with his attire, a brand new tunic with accompanying imperial purple stripe down one side. Philo had organised it for him, arranging for a tailor to measure him and show him materials ready for his approval.

He was most pleased with his assistant. The rooms he had arranged were fabulous. Extremely comfortable and fitting for his new position. He even had three personal attendants to see to his every physical need.

He could ask for any dish at all, anything his imagination touched on, and they would bring it to him hot and steaming. So far he had tried ostrich, peacock, turbot, braised deer, honey-roasted dormice. Galba had never served food like this. His tastes were plain.

Then there were the wines from every corner of the empire. They even had beer from Germania. Icelus had not much liked its bitter taste but he had given it a good chance to impress. Maybe too good, for his head was rather woolly today.

Snapping his attention back to Sabinus, he told Philo, "He won't much like what has been decided. Tigellinus' position has been filled. Cornelius Laco is on his way as we speak."

"Laco is prefect?" queried Philo in a tight voice.

"There are usually two. I understood that was the procedure. Perhaps you could stress that word when you talk to Sabinus. Also you might want to make mention of the vote: they have decided not to pay the Guard's bounty."

Icelus concluded lightly, "Galba has always been against buying men's loyalty."

Philo swallowed hard.

"I am going to write up some notes. Please do not disturb me," said Icelus as he walked into his office and closed the door.

Philo was well aware that the note taking was an excuse to sleep off the previous night's activities on the low couch he had insisted on installing. Sabinus wasn't going to like this, he wasn't going to like it at all. Still, Icelus hadn't said how he should tell Sabinus that his men weren't getting paid and that he was being demoted, had he? An internal memo was as good a way as any. He pulled out a blank tablet and jotted down a few words.

FIFTY-TWO

Nymphidius Sabinus awoke with a sudden gasp of breath, sitting up straight in sweat-drenched sheets and sporting a sizable erection. This scene would have surprised many, for the general consensus was that Sabinus didn't have a prick, and if he did, it was incapable of performing any such normal functionality having long rusted over from lack of use.

The gossips were incorrect. Nymphidius Sabinus was a man possessed of the normal male desires. Where Sabinus parted company with normality was in his superior sensibility that he could overcome such urges.

So rather than taking himself in hand as his pulsating cock twitchingly demanded, he flexed his hands, closed them into tight fists and thought good, noble Roman thoughts until he was flaccid. Then he stood, rubbed his eyes, and walked naked across the room to where a bowl of water sat on a shelf, splashing the cool liquid on his face, hearing the shouts of the guards being drilled outside.

Sabinus had not always been such a frigid man as Calvia Crispinilla could attest to, for she had once been embroiled in a rather passionate fling with the younger Sabinus.

It had been a bit of a lark for her. Agrippina one morning in court had leaned over and whispered in her ear, "What do you think, Calvy? Donkey or stallion?" indicating to where Sabinus was stood beside his mother.

Though a taciturn presence even all those years ago, he was not displeasing on the eye. Tall with broad shoulders, the fabric of his tunic pulled taut across his chest promised some delights beneath and a handsome if rather stolid expression. Calvia had definitely been interested.

"Well?" prompted Agrippina silkily. "I bet you 10,000 sesterces he's a donkey in the bedroom. Do you take the challenge?"

"Make it 20,000 and I concur. If he's a donkey now I'll make him a stallion by the ides."

And they had shaken on it with gleeful giggles.

Sabinus had taken it far more seriously, with an intensity that had begun to unnerve Calvia. Her attempts to end the liaison once the bet was settled were met with near grief from the devastated young man. He insisted that she did not, could not mean it. A line that he continued to hold onto even after she had taken up with a new lover.

Calvia was not one to soften the blow. She failed to see why she should, and faced with Sabinus lurking outside her rooms at the palace she told him in two short words what she wanted him to do. He did not budge. Sighing she told him, "Look, Sabinus, we had some fun. We spent some nights together—"

"Five," he interrupted. "We spent five nights together."

"Five nights," she accepted, and was about to begin her fourth attempt to dump him when he said.

"And seventeen times. We made love seventeen times."

Which was one thing to be said for him, Calvia supposed, he certainly had stamina and a precision that she had found not unwelcome.

"Sabinus."

"Gaius, please call me Gaius. We have no need of formality, not now. Not with what we have."

Calvia held onto her temper with difficulty. "We have nothing."

Seemingly not hearing these words Sabinus said, "We should marry."

Calvia was shocked into laughter. "Marry?" she cackled. "Are you mad? Why would I want to marry you?"

"I have money," he assured her. "I can keep a family, make a home for you and our children."

She gave a shudder at the mention of children. A cohort of grim-faced little buggers just like their father.

"And mother says she will secure me a good position at the palace."

He stated this as if the matter were decided, for he possessed strong convictions back then too.

"Nymphidius Sabinus," she stressed. "We are not suited."

"That is not true. That is not true at all. We are suited. We have proved that. Seventeen times," he added, his lips twitching upwards slightly.

Calvia realised this was his attempt at a smile. She had never seen him smile before. He did everything in the utmost seriousness.

He tried to take her hand but she held it pressed against her side. "It is ridiculous. You are ridiculous. I told you it was over last month."

"But you don't mean that," he insisted stubbornly.

"But I do. I so very much do," she replied with a bleak smile, and decided to concentrate on her most pertinent objection to the match, which she threw full speed at him.

"My family have sat in the senate for seven generations." She held up seven fingers. "My great-grandfather was consul, as was my grandfather, as was my father. My mother's family have produced senators for five generations."

More fingers were held up to demonstrate. "My family own most of southern Italy. I myself am a very wealthy woman. I am a trusted confidante of the empress. I am a friend to the emperor, to the emperor's children, to their children's bloody friends. My connections are impeccable, my lineage is impeccable. And *you*, *you* are a whore's son! How could *you* ever imagine we would marry? That I would accept you? My family, my glorious family polluted by slave blood? By whore blood? I do not think so, *Gaius*. I really do not think so. If I accepted you, Jupiter himself would strike me down dead, right here on the doorstep for even contemplating such blasphemy.

"You are nothing. You are nobody. You are not worthy to even address me, let alone sleep with me. I have been kind, I have been accommodating, but no longer. You will fuck off this instant and you will never grace my doorstep again, you will never speak to me again, and if I find out you have told anyone, anyone that we slept together, I will personally have you and your whore mother killed!"

Then she slammed the door in his face.

Two days later he joined the army, much against his mother's wishes. A devastated Nymphidia burst into a banquet and launched herself at Calvia with a howl, an offence that earned her a ban from the emperor's bed. Doubtless this had been Agrippina's aim the whole time.

Far away with the legions, Sabinus had plenty of time to dwell on his foolishness. He had been blinded by lust, just like all those men who visited his mother, with their lewd eyes and heaving grunts that seeped through the wall disturbing his sleep. How he despised them and yet he had fallen into exactly the same trap. Never again. He would not succumb: never lose his judgement, his reason, to the machinations of women.

It was not a time that Sabinus thought much about. Ironically it would be far more damaging to his incorruptible reputation that he had slept with Nero's mistress of the orgy, than for Calvia to admit to their past liaison.

He wiped his face on a towel and began to dress. Though he owned plenty of slaves, he thought it womanly to own intimate body slaves. A Roman man who couldn't dress himself? Pathetic.

His thoughts turned to his current situation. Things were wrong. They had been wrong ever since Icelus had returned to Rome; he was being excluded from events. It had been subtle at first. It was not now. A breakfast briefing he hadn't been told of, an oversight Icelus had said. An address delivered before the Guard without his permission, without even being run past him first. It was an informal chat, said Icelus. A request for a meeting to discuss the potential arrests of Nero's closest advisors, blankly ignored.

Sabinus recognised a slight when he saw it. He just didn't understand why. He had done everything that was asked of him. He delivered to Galba the ultimate prize. Without his support, without his Guard, Nero would still be emperor, singing his dreadful songs and contaminating everything he touched. Icelus was even dodging the question of the promised bounty to his troops.

This was not how it was supposed to be. Galba should be here, Sabinus by his side as his most trusted advisor, reforming Rome together. What was it Augustus had said? "I found Rome in brick and I left her in marble."

Sabinus had found Rome caked in moral shit and he was going to leave it smelling of roses. Except that nobody was asking him questions anymore, seeking his opinion, accepting his views. Regulus had not been to see him in days, was not at home when he called, no matter what time he did so.

All he could think was that his mother was correct and Icelus, that cunning, dirty slave, was somehow intercepting his correspondence with the mighty Galba, securing his own position by denigrating Sabinus. But Gellianus should now be on his way back from Spain after speaking personally to the great man. Sabinus had no doubts that the emperor had been astonished at the slights thrown his loyal servant's way. Matters, he was sure, would be settled to his satisfaction.

He had pulled his tunic over his head and was concerning himself with his belt when Alex entered with a crisp, "Sir."

"Yes?"

Alex clicked his heels together. "You asked for immediate notice when Titus Gellianus returned."

Sabinus spun round. "He is back in Rome? You are sure?"

"He is waiting in your office."

Sabinus rubbed his jaw. "Good lad, Alexander. Very good lad."

Alex preened under this compliment, a grin breaking out over his face and ruining his messenger stoic stance. Sabinus, however, did not notice this break in protocol. He was far too elated. This was it, this was the news he had been waiting for. Icelus would be punished for his degrading treatment of him; he would be restored to the position he deserved.

"Titus Gellianus."

Gellianus, a tall, sandy-haired man smiled to see Sabinus, his eyes crinkling. "Gaius," he said, arms outstretched embracing the prefect.

"Your mission?" Sabinus asked instantly, not even bothering to greet his friend.

Gellianus' smile faded. "Not good."

"You saw Galba though?" he insisted.

"Briefly."

"You gave him my message?"

"Like I said, it was brief. Sorry I couldn't deliver it in person. I handed him the written version."

"He read it, though?" Sabinus pressed with a hint of desperation.

"Passed to an assistant without opening it."

"My gift?"

"He refused it. He said he had no need of it." Gellianus opened his palms. "That is it. I was not allowed to see him after that. There seemed no point in staying."

Nymphidius Sabinus collapsed into his chair, staring into space. This was not right. This could not be. Galba was going to accept his gift. Dismiss Icelus. Send a personal message to him. Thank him for all he had done.

Gellianus, seeing him so distressed, placated him with, "Come out with me. Let's get a drink. I know you don't usually but I think you need one."

Sabinus, staring at his desk, said quietly, "I thought he was a noble man. I thought he was honourable."

"There have been executions. They were loyal to Nero, true, but not excessively so. There were no trials, no chances to appeal. Marcus Salvius Otho denounced them personally."

"Otho?" queried Sabinus. He knew Otho, he knew what Otho was. He was a degenerate.

"He is close to Galba, trusted," said Gellianus. "I have it on good authority that Vinius and Laco are fleecing the provinces they pass through. Anything movable, shiny, they have brought to them. They are very rich men."

Sabinus flinched, his shoulders sagged, his face hidden behind his hands.

"This Icelus," continued Gellianus. "Even Galba's own men despise him. They told me that he is …" Gellianus trailed off.

Sabinus looked up, his face twisted with misery. He waved a hand for him to continue.

"They say he and Galba are lovers, have been ever since he was his slave. Icelus always sleeps in his room, in his bed. It is not much of a secret."

A vein throbbed at Sabinus' temple. What had he done? He had taken the empire from one invert only to deliver it to another.

Alex was on duty outside Sabinus' office. He had one ear pressed to the wood. All he could hear was muffled voices, nothing of note. His free ear detected footsteps and he shot back into a rigid attention stance. It was Philo.

"Ah, Alexander," he said. "Can you deliver this to Sabinus for me."

He handed him a wax tablet. Alex looked down at it and then up again at Philo. "His office is right there," he said, thumbing at a door mere steps away from them.

Philo, who had no intention of being present when Sabinus read this particular message, told Alex, "Palace protocol. I'm not an official messenger, it would be inappropriate for me to deliver it."

Alex took the message and shuffled the short distance to Sabinus' office. Looking back, he saw Philo had already disappeared.

A concerned Gellianus had been dismissed. Nymphidius Sabinus paced his office, his thoughts jumbled, unstable. He couldn't accept that he had been wrong. Those words Galba had written sung with sincerity. It was that heartfelt sentiment that had echoed with Sabinus, that had brought him to the elder man's side.

They were going to reform Rome together, Galba had said. He had said. Sabinus fussed with his correspondence attempting to find the hallowed document. Failing, he threw the paperwork onto the floor.

"Message for you, sir."

Sabinus' head snapped up, his eyes lit with hope. It would be from Galba, explaining himself, thanking him for his work on his behalf, suggesting his next course. He snatched the tablet from Alex. He ripped off the leather ties and read in shock the news that he was to be supplanted. Cornelius Laco was appointed his fellow prefect and would take the senior role of the two. And then that final blow.

The money he promised his guards, the money they were owed for deposing Nero, was not going to be paid. The tone was clear: there had never been any intention of it being paid. He had been used.

Sabinus could perhaps have stomached this personal betrayal, but his men? His loyal men, his troops, his comrades? To be used and disposed of so readily, so eagerly. That was unacceptable.

Amid the turmoil that was Sabinus' mind, one thought rang out with clarity again and again. Galba was not fit to rule. What had been done, what he had done, it could be undone.

FIFTY-THREE

The drying of the empress' hair was the most exciting duty of Mina's role. Not that she participated in the gentle patting of Statilia Messalina's long tresses: as keeper of the towel she was far above such a minion's job. No, she was the one who handed the dry towels to the patters. It meant that she got to move about a bit as she deposited the wet articles with the disposer of the empress' garments and retrieved clean articles for the next stage in the process.

The empress sat in her robe, a green number decorated with entwining flowers and tied with a firm bow at the front. Her wet hair was draped behind her as two assistants patted it gently between towels. Around the room the rest of her attendants busied themselves silently preparing the rest of her toilette. Statilia, who found such rituals tedious, dictated a letter to her correspondence clerk, Cassandra, as they worked.

"My dear Calvia. What a joy it was to hear from you. Your African adventure sounds most thrilling. Certainly more exciting than my tedium. Juno, how dull things are here!"

Cassandra's stylus flew across the tablet. She was a serious-minded girl of shocking efficiency and marvellous organisational skills; Philo in a dress, if you like.

"I have come to almost miss my despised husband," continued Statilia. "At least he could throw a decent party, with your skilled assistance, naturally."

A small attendant slipped through the door and up to Cassandra, whispering in her ear. Cassandra's thick eyebrows rose slightly and her nose furrowed more. "Mistress, will you excuse me for one moment?"

"I am dictating," insisted Statilia.

"Yes, mistress, but you have a visitor."

Statilia sat up, the patters jerking behind to follow her movements. "I am ready for bed. I do not receive visitors at this hour."

"That is what I intend to tell the gentleman."

Statilia raised a hand. "Well do that. We'll continue dictation after."

Cassandra nodded and slipped through the door.

She returned a moment later distinctly paler.

"Mistress," she began respectfully, bowing her head. "Nymphidius Sabinus is in your chamber wishing an audience."

"I am ready for bed."

Cassandra, her head still bowed said, "I know, mistress, but I feel this may be a necessary audience. The prefect seems a bit …" She broke off, biting her lip.

"Well?" queried Statilia.

"Out of sorts."

"Out of sorts? What does that mean? Let us lose the tact, Cassandra."

The correspondence clerk bit her lip again. A generally calm unruffled presence, she looked distinctly agitated. A state that was beginning to infect the other attendants, who began to flap around their mistress.

"He seems rather odd. Disturbed."

"He is always odd. I don't believe I have ever met an odder man. He must have been born under a very ill alignment of stars."

"He was most insistent that he see you, mistress. He was unwilling to concede to my explanation of your routine."

Cassandra looked very unhappy with this state of affairs; she favoured a rigid routine; it was what enabled the palace to function. Odd deviations like Nymphidius Sabinus turning up unannounced at the empress' bedchamber in a clearly agitated state of mind troubled her greatly.

Statilia, noticing her clerk's distress rose. "Very well," she said, belting up her robe tighter. "I cannot promise to be civil to him."

As if she ever had been.

The interconnecting doors to the empress' private sitting room were flung open and Statilia entered with a smattering of attendants, including Mina. She figured with the empress' hair still damp, an emergency towel might be required. Also there was not a chance she was going to miss out on all the excitement.

Statilia's aim in agreeing to meet Sabinus in her robe with damp hair was to shame him for his rudeness in insisting they meet at this time of night. He would take one look at her and be cowed. And then she would give him what for! Impossible man!

He was pacing back and forth, a fist clenched to his mouth. Hearing the door, he ceased his movements and turned to greet the empress. It took but one glance for Statilia to assert that there was something very wrong with the prefect.

For starters he was smiling. Sabinus never smiled; he scowled, he frowned, he grimaced, and he glared. He did not smile. Yet here he was offering her an easy languid smile. An unnatural sight on those hard features, it sent a shiver down her spine.

And then there was his left eye; twitching in a rhythm of its own. Yet Sabinus seemed utterly unaware of these spasms, speaking with rapid words which overran themselves in confused sentences.

"Noble madam. Noble empress. I must speak with you. Important. Very important. Yes, crucial, very crucial. I have done you a most terrible disservice. A terrible thing. I must apologise. I must offer you my most humblest apologies. How could I have done such a thing, to such a … such a … Such a goddess. A high, high woman of most noble, noble blood. Blood."

Statilia threw widened eyes at Cassandra who mirrored her mistress' concerns. Mina openly boggled at this peculiar state of affairs.

"You must forgive me," insisted Sabinus, taking hold of the stunned empress' hands. "Please, madam, say you will forgive me."

He looked at her with pleading eyes, the left still twitching, the right glassy and unfocused. Had she not known better, she would have thought him drunk.

"Unforgivable, unforgivable," he muttered, staring at her hands, then suddenly unclasping them in a sudden jerk. "Impropriety," he said.

Cassandra took a step forward. "Perhaps the prefect would like to sit?"

"Would I? Would I like to sit?" he asked Statilia.

"Yes, you would," she confirmed. "You would like to sit here for a moment."

Mina and Cassandra carried two chairs forward. Sabinus sat on the edge of his, a foot tapping out a beat with increasing speed. Statilia sat opposite him, throwing panicked looks at both Mina and Cassandra.

"Forgive me, empress."

"What is it I must forgive you for?" she asked cautiously, lowering herself into her chair slowly.

He looked at her with moist eyes, rubbing a hand across his forehead agitatedly. "I made a suggestion to you, madam, some months back that I … that I realise was abhorrent. You

376

saw it, you did because you are a clever woman. An intelligent woman. You saw its abhorrence. But I did not. Because I did not know. I didn't know!"

Another twitch to his eye. This time stronger, so that it pulled at his lip also. This he noticed and a hand went up to the affliction.

"I forgive you." Though she had no idea what he was referring to.

"You see I thought he was a good man," he explained. "I truly believed that. In here." He thumped at his chest so hard that Mina gave an involuntary squeak, earning herself a warning glare from Cassandra.

"I did not realise. I did not know. I was, I was, I was, I was …" He stuck at the words, giving his chest another hard thump that surely must have bruised the skin.

"It doesn't matter," said Statilia as calmly as she could.

"But it does!" he interrupted loudly. "It matters. It matters that I was going to force you to accept that man thinking he was a good man, thinking he was a right man, thinking he was a noble man with noble aim. I was a fool. A fool." He brought his fist down onto the arm of the chair. "Say you will forgive me," he demanded.

"I have said. I do forgive you. Accept my forgiveness," she babbled, feeling her own heart beat against her chest.

Was he going to turn violent? There were guards outside the main entrance to her apartments certainly, but loyalty to their boss might impinge on their reactions. Cassandra, thinking the same, gestured towards Mina, angling her hand towards the bronze lamp stand that she was stood beside. Mina looked at the stand, she looked at Sabinus' head. She quietly clenched her fist round the stem and gave Cassandra a quick nod. The clerk shuffled towards a sideboard to be closer to a large blue glass vase, signalling with her eyes to Mina that if called for, it would be a two-pronged attack. Mina raised herself onto her toes and regretted that she didn't have her whip: if ever there were a moment for some good cracking whip action, this was it.

Sabinus fidgeted on the chair, his eyes darting from left to right, his foot tapping.

"Sabinus," began Statilia cautiously.

"Gaius. You can call me Gaius," he said. "That was my father's name. Gaius. I was named after him."

"Is that so?"

"Yes, it is. It is so. It is true. Gaius Julius Caesar Germanicus. You see Galba, Galba has less of a claim. I was prepared to relinquish my birthright, my claim, because I thought he was a man of noble character."

None of this made the slightest sense to Statilia. "Sabinus," she said carefully and then altered this to, "Gaius," when he glared at her, "I have to go."

"Go?" his head jerked. "No, no you cannot. I must explain to you. I must explain what is going to happen. You must understand why I have no choice."

"And you shall, you shall. But I need to get dressed. I am in my robe. I'm chilly."

It was mid-August and swelteringly hot, yet Sabinus did not seem to notice this incongruity, telling her, "You will return so I can explain."

"Of course I shall," replied Statilia forcing a smile. "You stay right here and I'll be back shortly."

She disappeared into her bedchamber. When the doors closed, she turned to Mina and Cassandra and breathed, "Oh my gods! The furies have taken his mind!"

Her attendants cooed in shock.

"What do we do?" Statilia begged Cassandra.

"I could fetch the guards."

"Won't they be on his side?" pointed out Mina.

Statilia looked to Cassandra again. "A madman in charge of the Praetorian Guard!" She breathed heavily. "Who knows what he'll order them to do. You heard him, he wants to explain to me why he has no choice in whatever insanity he has planned!"

Mina had a sudden flashback to the day Nero fell when the guards raped their way around the slave complex. Evidently the other attendants remembered it too since they began to panic, some openly weeping. Statilia rubbed at her arms. Cassandra remained unmoved, her lips pursed as she applied her considerable mind to the dilemma.

Unfortunately she wasn't given enough time to formulate a reasoned response because Mina got in first.

"Straton! I'll get Straton. He can nobble Sabinus and sit on him until his wits return!"

"Do it!" commanded Statilia.

Empresses by necessity are a tough breed. Statilia Messalina calmed her breathing, pushed back her shoulders, and restored her regal appearance.

"I will keep him busy until you and your gorilla of a lover return. Let nobody say Statilia Messalina did not do her duty for Rome! Cassandra, get me a draught of wine. I need a strong drink to face that loon! To think I once admired his calves!"

FIFTY-FOUR

Banging repeatedly on the door, Mina yelled, "Straton! Straton!"

The door swung open to reveal the overseer clad in a crumpled brown tunic, beltless and bootless. He appeared surprised. Perhaps it was the knocking. Nobody ever knocked on Straton's door. If you were forced to pass it, you tiptoed lest the beast awaken and drag you into his lair where a sordid and depraved fate awaited you. Or so the stories went.

"Emergency!" bleated Mina. "You're needed."

"Off duty," replied Straton.

"A real emergency," stressed Mina, jumping up and down. "You have to come. You have to come now. I promised."

She shouldn't have promised. Straton's off-duty hours were very important to him. He needed a break from all that menacing, relax his leering muscles, ease the ache from his whipping arm.

From behind the door came a crash, followed by a thump. Straton disappeared inside, returning with a thick belt strap held in his hand.

"Fell," he told Mina. "Not hurt though. OK."

He gave a little smirk, which was focused on the belt.

Ahh, so the friend was staying. Mina cursed Nymphidius Sabinus. If he hadn't gone bonkers, she could have sated her curiosity, popped her head in, and said a cheery hello. Ask the special friend whether he had liked the Catullus scroll. But the empress was waiting for her. If she failed in her task, Mina anticipated a swift demotion down to hairclip polisher.

"Please, Straton," she pleaded. "You've got to help! You have to nobble Nymphidius Sabinus. He's gone nuts!"

Straton absorbed this news blankly and with no hint of surprise.

"Get to punch the fucker?" he asked Mina.

"Absolutely. Anything necessary to disable him."

Straton grinned. "Excellent."

Straton and Mina were not the only ones rushing to intercept Sabinus. After delivering his message to Sabinus Alex had sped off to find Honoratus. Failing to find him on duty at the palace, he abandoned his post and sprinted across the city to the Praetorian camp.

There was something very wrong with Nymphidius Sabinus and Alex was concerned. It was Sabinus who had led him into the greatest adventure of his life. He owed him. Honoratus would know what to do, of that Alex was sure.

Honoratus listened to the slave's description of events silently. At the end of Alex's account he asked, "This is true?"

"Absolutely," Alex assured him. "I don't know what is up with him. He seems … he seems …"

"How, Alexander?"

"He seems … ill. In his mind, I think."

Honoratus stood up slowly, telling Alex, "I will go talk to him. You did right coming to me. You are a good lad. A very good lad."

Alex would have beamed under this compliment but it hardly seemed correct in such circumstances. So he gave a tight nod instead.

Back in the palace they found Sabinus' office empty. Honoratus began to seriously worry.

Honoratus pinched his chin. "He's not here and he's not at the Praetorian camp. Where else could he be?"

"His suite in the old palace?" suggested Alex.

"Let's go see."

They hadn't got very far when they picked up the latest slice of gossip: Sabinus had been spotted entering the empress' apartments.

"Oh, that cannot be good," groaned Honoratus.

Having apologised to Statilia for his crude attempts to marry her off to Galba, Sabinus was now most concerned to explain to her why he was taking the measures he was. How necessary they were, how he had no choice, how he had been forced into circumstances against his will.

He fixed her with his intense brown eyes, the left still twitching. A little more coherent, he told her, "This is how it must be, madam. I cannot allow this invert to rule. The situation cannot be allowed to deteriorate. I will not let what we have achieved be weakened. You understand that? Say you understand?"

It was demonstrably important to Sabinus that Statilia approved of his plans, which was troubling because she had no idea what he was talking about. She concurred anyway, taking a large sip from the goblet Cassandra had supplied her with.

"Of course I understand. I approve. Fabulous idea."

She kept one eye on the door. Where was her towel girl and that gorilla man?

Sabinus nodded and then he stood. "When I am emperor, I shall ensure you are well looked after."

Statilia's attention was very suddenly grabbed and the goblet fell from her hand. "When you are emperor?"

"It will be far easier to remove Galba while he dallies in Spain with his catamites. Once the legions hear what has occurred, they will deal with him," said Sabinus, sounding much more like himself, insanely overconfident and delusional.

"You are going to declare yourself emperor?"

Statilia suddenly realised what all those rambled sentences about "noble men who were not noble" had been about.

"It is the only way," stated Sabinus. "It is my birthright I claim."

"Your birthright?" queried Statilia, cursing herself for not paying more attention to his earlier babblings.

"Yes, my father was brother to Agrippina. Nero is my cousin and I am his sole blood heir."

Now hang on, thought Statilia; her late and unlamented mother-in-law Agrippina had possessed three brothers. Two had died without issue, executed by another rogue Praetorian prefect, Sejanus. And the third? The third had been Gaius Julius Caesar Germanicus. But that was not the name he had been commonly known by: Caligula. Sabinus believed Caligula to be his father and now he was intent on using this to make himself emperor.

If Statilia had thought Sabinus had lost his mind previously, now she was absolutely convinced of it.

FIFTY-FIVE

Cassandra was holed up with the attendants in the empress' bedchamber, all of their eyes fused to the gap in the door where they checked on their mistress' safety and Sabinus' state. A flurry of squeals announced the arrival of Straton. He grinned at the women who floated away from him whimpering.

"Gods! Pull yourselves together," tutted Mina.

"Oh thank the gods!" prayed Cassandra. "Thank Juno, Vesta, Diana, and Artemis!"

Mina sat on the edge of the bed, legs apart, hands on her knees. "What's the situation?"

"As it was, Mina. I don't think the mistress is going to hold it together much longer. I can see another shoe situation developing."

The empress' assistants all nodded sagely, familiar with Statilia's habit of flinging her footwear when annoyed.

"She's only got her slippers on, though," offered Ligia helpfully.

"Well, don't you worry, my little women. We are here to sort it. Aren't we, Straton? Straton!"

The overseer who had been admiring the empress' mahogany dressing table snapped back to attention. "Yeah," he rasped. "Right."

He pulled out a cudgel from his belt.

Cassandra's eyes widened. "You're going to hit him with that?"

"Yeah."

"Won't it kill him?"

Straton shrugged. "Might."

"I thought you were going to bring a net or something."

"Not a retiarius," said Straton with some distaste.

He despised the net and trident men of the arena. He was more of a Thracian man.

A pale Cassandra said to Mina, "I'm not sure about this. If he dies, that's bad, really bad."

"I don't think the mistress would mind."

"No, you can't go around murdering Praetorian prefects."

Straton scratched his bristled chin before assuring the panicked clerk, "Happens all the time."

"Does it?" asked Cassandra and Mina in unison.

If they were hoping for a history lesson in the ignoble deaths of past prefects they were set to be disappointed.

"Yeah, does," was Straton's only response.

Calm, efficient, dutiful correspondence clerk Cassandra ran over their options. She quickly realised that they didn't have any and said to Straton, "Do it."

Straton grinned, slapped his cudgel onto his palm and made for the door. He had just clasped the handle when a voice yelled.

"Oh no you don't!"

Antonius Honoratus, Praetorian tribune, flanked by Alex, Praetorian messenger.

"We have a situation," explained Cassandra tactfully.

"Sabinus has gone nuts!" said Mina, bouncing on her feet and waving her arms about. "He could be manhandling the empress right now!"

Though this elicited worried squeals from the attendants, it was a wholly unlikely scenario. Nymphidius Sabinus manhandling a woman? He wouldn't know which end to start with.

"We'll deal with this situation," stated Honoratus, coolly walking towards Straton. "Stand down, slave."

Straton only legitimately took orders from one man, Felix. Anything else he deigned to do had been carefully weighed up as to its "fun factor". Coshing Sabinus would definitely fall under that category, so he ignored Honoratus' order and pushed down the door handle.

"Stop!" yelled Honoratus rushing forward, sword drawn.

The attendants screamed and huddled down one end. Mina grabbed a hairbrush off the dressing table and lobbed it straight at the tribune. It missed him entirely. Flying over his head and hitting a pleasant glass vase, which did not so much smash as explode. As glass projectiled around the room, the door was suddenly flung open, knocking Straton out of the way, and there stood Statilia Messalina. She viewed the chaotic scene of her attendants crying together in a corner, her correspondence clerk wielding a lethal looking hairpin, and her towel girl picking glass out of her hair, with a long disdainful glare.

Honoratus straightened himself up and re-sheathed his sword. "Empress, we shall handle this situation now."

"Be my guest," she acquiesced a little too easily and a little too serenely.

Honoratus and Alex disappeared into the lounge and then reappeared almost immediately.

"He's not there," said Honoratus with a scowl.

Statilia, taking on the role of a genial mistress, gently patted her traumatised slaves on the head and told him stonily, "No, he's not. He's gone to finish off his coronation speech."

"His what?" blurted out Alex.

"Gosh, you are behind on the news. He's going to declare himself emperor tonight at the Praetorian barracks," said

Statilia, greatly enjoying the uniform shock she had produced in her audience.

That bossy tribune looked like he'd been slapped and the ginger boy was paler than a shade.

"But", she continued, "he's gone off to find a quiet spot to polish up his speech. He seems most determined to perfect its delivery."

"Tell me exactly what he said."

"I already have."

Statilia sat in front of her mirror as her slaves completed the hair-drying task. "He is going to declare himself emperor."

"At the Praetorian barracks?"

"As I said."

"Tonight?"

"Yes."

"What time?" insisted Honoratus.

"I don't know. When he's finished his speech. It did sound rather rousing."

Taking sympathy on the struggling tribune, Straton waded in with a rasped, "Bonkers."

"Oh, entirely," offered Mina. "He's completely lost it."

Honoratus rubbed at his chin. "He's going to declare himself emperor? It's lunacy!"

"It's more than that," piped in Cassandra with such quiet confidence she attracted the attention of the whole room.

With all agog, even the empress, Cassandra quietly and confidently and with natural efficiency outlined the disaster that was awaiting them.

"Galba is marching to Rome with the legions. If he gets here and the city has fallen to Sabinus, then they'll be fighting in the streets. Legionaries versus guards and a civilian population of a million right in the middle of it. The winners will want their reward naturally and with a whole city to sack …"

Mina shuddered. Alex shuddered. The empress shuddered. Honoratus rubbed his face with his hands. Even Straton comprehended the enormity of Cassandra's words.

"Fuckin' bloodbath," he said.

Statilia turned to the tribune and near implored him, "You've got to stop him."

Honoratus gave a sharp nod and then to Alex, "Get your fellow messengers to search the whole of the Palatine Hill. He's got to be on site somewhere. We need to intercept him before he can deliver that speech."

Alex, wide-eyed, asked, "And if we fail?"

Honoratus shook his head. "I am going to the Praetorian camp to ensure that does not happen."

"How?" asked Mina, intrigued and just a little thrilled by all the excitement.

Honoratus gave a pained smile. "I am going to give my speech first."

FIFTY-SIX

Alex did not need the lunacy of Sabinus' intentions spelled out. Even if Sabinus were Caligula's son, and that was not wholly unlikely given the stories about the prefect's mother, he was illegitimate. He could not inherit Nero's position. His status was derived from his mother and everyone knew what she was.

He may have achieved equestrian rank but Sabinus was barred from rising any further. He could not be emperor. The senate would not accept it. The people, still smarting over the loss of their beloved Nero, would definitely not accept it. It was foolish. It was insanity. Alex had betrayed his best friend to follow the stars of a mad man.

As he dashed erratically around the palace searching out the prefect, he had plenty of time to mull over his actions. As a teenage boy, Alex had a delicate self-image: he needed to see himself as heroic, as brave, as fundamentally in the right. He was beginning to suspect that on all these accounts he was flawed.

It wasn't terribly brave of him to stand behind the Praetorian Guard with all their weaponry and armour. Neither was it heroic to stand by and let his best friend be captured, nor to lie to Mina repeatedly. Alex was beginning to dislike himself intensely. Perhaps if he found Sabinus, he could make it right. Ask Epaphroditus where Sporus was, take Mina to visit him. Make everything okay again.

Antonius Honoratus was a pragmatist. His soldier's mind was weighing up the chances of Alex finding Sabinus. They were, he decided, slim. The Palatine complex was over 400 acres of space: two huge palaces complete with courtyards and cellars and store cupboards and staff areas and a dozen other buildings that served administrative functions.

Even slimmer were their chances of changing his mind should they stumble across Sabinus. He was notoriously stubborn. A useful attribute in battle, Honoratus had personally benefited from that dogged insistence, that endless fight. But now it was Nymphidius Sabinus' greatest weakness.

That slave girl had painted a truly horrific picture; a city torn apart by civil war. Honoratus could not let that happen. He could not diminish the majesty of his precious Guard by involving them in this madness.

Had they not risked everything already to replace Nero? How would it look to play that trick again so soon, without the new emperor even reaching Rome? It would look mercenary. It would undermine trust in the emperor's own bodyguard. Why should Galba trust them? Why shouldn't he just disband them?

Honoratus had to protect his men and if Sabinus were himself, he would understand that, he would approve. He would know that it was necessary for him to die. For the good of his Guard.

"I'm sorry," croaked Alex. "I looked everywhere. I tried my best."

His calves burnt, his back ached from the exertion. His face was pained, near tearful. Honoratus smiled wanly and tousled his ginger hair affectionately.

"I know you did, Alexander." He gazed into the dusk of a slow summer's evening. The crickets ticking, the moon large and luminous. A calm and peaceful night for a lynching.

Finally, in a small, discreet office overlooking the Circus Maximus, just as the sun was setting, Gaius Nymphidius Sabinus laid down his stylus. He read his great work one more time, nodding vigorously at each point. It was perfect. Rubbing his eyes, his left still twitching, he stood and stretched. It was time. He was ready.

It was fully dark when he reached the Praetorian camp. Clutched in his hand was his precious speech, the masterpiece that he had spent the day working on. In truth he did not need the written copy, for he had memorised it word for word. It was compelling rhetoric to his Guard explaining why he had been forced to take this necessary step. He was not to know that his soldiers had already been exposed to a flowing, heartfelt speech; a plea for sanity, for measure, for peace.

Sabinus gave the watchword to the sentry who let him pass unimpeded.

"Ah, Honoratus, gather the men together."

Honoratus, grim-faced, did not move. Behind him guards began to congregate.

"I was thinking of the mess hall," continued Sabinus. "A much better venue than out here on the street."

There came the unmistakable sound of swords being drawn. Sabinus glared at his troops. "I said the mess hall. That was an order!"

No one moved. "Honoratus?"

Pulling out his sword the tribune said, "I'm sorry, Gaius," and signalled to the guards behind him. They began to advance.

Sabinus' eye twitched. These were his troops, his loyal men. What were they doing? He took a large step backwards.

"Honoratus?" he asked again, the confusion evident in his eyes.

The tribune did not respond.

"Honoratus?" A final plea. "Guards?"

They walked forward, swords drawn and pointing right at him.

Finally he understood and gave a smile. A lopsided drunken smile.

"I guess I will not need this now."

He threw his speech into the air. Then he turned and ran.

He had covered 200 yards when he heard a swishing noise and there came a pain in his lower back, hot and searing. He fell forward, landing face down, an arm reaching round to the source, hearing the sound of running boots approaching fast.

Alex, hanging onto the door frame of the mess hall, saw Honoratus throw the javelin in the hope of killing the prefect quickly. It hit him in the lower back and there he had fallen. He saw Sabinus attempting to crawl away, pulling himself along by his fingers, nails clawing at the dirt.

The guards gathered round the prone figure. Someone put a foot on the prefect's back to hold him still. Swords drawn, grim-faced, they struck. The blades flashing in the gloom as they thrust into the body. Alex, gripping onto the door frame, heard a loud anguished cry and he screwed his eyes shut.

Finally someone patted him on the arm and he opened his eyes. Proculus, his sword hanging down, dripping blood, told him, "It's done."

The remaining guards sloped back, downcast, to their quarters.

In the dirt track between the buildings, Honoratus sat beside the body of Nymphidius Sabinus. The tribune held his head in his hands, his shoulders shaking. Alex ran over, crouching beside the weeping Honoratus.

"It shouldn't have been like this," said the tribune, wiping his eyes on his arm.

Alex embraced his friend, who wept openly on his shoulder.

In the mess hall the guards talked lengthily about what had happened. There was regret of course. Sabinus had been a bloody great prefect. Although, they mused wryly, they wouldn't miss those drills! A few chuckles. A few memories shared of the time Lucullus had vomited from exhaustion all over the prefect's boots. How mad he'd been! Even Lucullus laughed, though his ribs still smarted from the punishment beating dished out months before.

"Do you think we'll get a reward?" voiced Horus.

Oh yes, definitely, was the consensus. Galba would be right pleased with them. He'd reward them richly. And then came a voice of contrition.

"Yeah, but what if Galba suspects we were in on it? He was our prefect after all."

"Na. We killed him, didn't we? Saved Galba's throne."

But once spoken that doubt began to infect them. They had after all mutinied against the last emperor, Nero, abandoned their posts, and forced him to resign. What if Sabinus' actions put doubt in Galba's mind as to their loyalty? They wouldn't get their reward, would they?

They argued back and forth with raised voices and fists. Eventually some kind of agreement was noisily reached that they had to prove their loyalty to Galba.

Alex did not know how long they sat there by Sabinus' corpse. All he knew was that it was daylight and the flies had begun to gather above the fallen prefect. Honoratus did not want to leave his commander. He owed him so many debts, he told Alex. They must entreat the gods for the prefect's safe passage across the River Styx. They must perform the necessary rituals.

On this Honoratus was insistent, as he stared down sadly at Sabinus' bloody face.

Alex looked away from that dead gaze and noted the approaching Praetorians. "Sir."

Honoratus got to his feet. "Guards?" he queried as they circled round him.

Alex narrowed his eyes and stepped closer to Honoratus. The tribune placed his hand on the top of his sword ready to draw it if necessary.

Proculus took a step forward and dropped a coil of rope.

FIFTY-SEVEN

Teretia did not like the blond, shaggy-haired man. She did not like him at all. He had intercepted her in the entrance hall by a large brown marbled pillar.

"I'll deliver you to your destination," he said, and then stared at her breasts with such naked lust that Teretia had promptly knotted her shawl across them, telling him tartly, "No, thank you. I know the way."

This polite rejection had no effect on him and he pursued her down the corridor.

"You are going to need a proper announcement," he said, walking briskly alongside her. "And I am an official announcer."

"No, thank you."

"You'll never get past the security points. You'll need me to get you through."

"I have a pass, thank you."

"Yeah, but what kind of a pass? You won't be able to get out of this palace. It's a different coloured one for the new palace."

"I am not going to the new palace."

"Where are you going then?" he asked, intent on accompanying her.

Teretia jerked her shawl back onto her shoulders. "That does not concern you, sir. I do not need your help." And then she set off again at a faster pace.

The man jogged alongside her. "You can't go wandering around here on your own. It's not safe for a girl like you."

"I shall be quite safe."

"Oh no, no, no, I couldn't allow it. Not when there is a chance of ravishment. Let me take your bag."

He reached over for her basket. Teretia snatched it away and faced her harasser. "Please leave me alone," she requested politely.

He leaned against the wall and affected a nonchalant stance.

"I can't do that. I wouldn't feel right leaving you unescorted in these corridors."

His deep voice conveyed an image of torments and troubles beyond the next corridor. "I would worry for your safety, your innocence. Though we have only just met I can see that you are a very nicely brought up girl. You're a virgin right?"

Teretia's cheeks went red.

"I couldn't leave a virgin alone here. It's a status that doesn't hold within these walls. Now come, miss, let me take your arm and escort you to your destination properly." He held out his crooked arm in anticipation.

"I am at my destination," she replied, opening the door and slamming it shut.

Philo was sitting at his desk. Before him was a small cylinder-shaped scroll. He unfurled it carefully; weighting it down with a round glass ball he kept for such occasions. His eyes skimmed over the extraordinarily explicit dancing satyrs and concentrated on the words. Again.

This was his tenth reading of this particular scroll. He had taken each reading with the careful deliberation of an amateur philosopher looking for the meaning of existence.

He dissected every possible connotation of every word that was neatly inscribed on the parchment. To no avail. The meaning was clear; no matter how many times he read it, desperately searching for any other possible connotations in the verse. It was all too clear: Straton was in love with him.

Which was just fabulous. A fabulous end to what had been a trying eight hours for Philo. He worked deliberately late in the forlorn hope that Straton would get bored waiting for him, as had become the overseer's habit.

For one moment, as he cautiously stuck his head out of the door, he thought that his plan had succeeded. The corridor was empty, no sign of Straton, no sign of anyone. He could go home! Enjoy one of Pompeia's delicious meals and go to bed. Alone. For once.

Only once he was outside the door, the looming bulk of Straton had ambled round the corner, his thumbs hooked in his belt. On seeing Philo he had grinned widely, "Just in time!"

From then on matters deteriorated until the horrifying moment when Philo heard Mina outside Straton's door. A sliver of ice entered his heart. She was going to walk in. She was going to see him like this!

Philo was a lousy liar, but even if he had possessed Epaphroditus' wily tongue, he could not have come up with an alternative explanation as to why he was in Straton's quarters, lying on Straton's bed, totally naked with his wrists buckled to the bedposts.

When Straton disappeared to see what she wanted, panic had set in. He twisted his arms trying to squeeze his hands free from their bondage. She mustn't see! She mustn't know! Fully panicked as he heard the talk outside, he bucked his wrists frantically; squirming round with a jolt he had lost his balance and toppled off the bed with a crash, landing sharply on his hip. He would have cried out but his terror of Mina overhearing forced his silence; Philo biting hard on his lip, tasting blood. He wrenched his shoulder too. It burnt horribly.

After Straton had gone, there seemed little point in going home. Any tasty meal prepared for him would have been disposed of hours ago and he had simply gone back to work without enjoying any sleep at all.

So the appearance of Teretia, even flustered, red-faced Teretia was a burning sun of niceness in Philo's otherwise grim life. He threw the Catullus scroll into his drawer and rose to greet her.

"Hello." His lip twitched upwards into a rare smile.

"Oh, Philo I've just met the most awful man!" she exclaimed hotly, her cheeks turning red again.

The spectacle of Teretia in distress affected Philo in the same way it affected every other man. He was instantly outraged and desirous of protecting her from further harm.

"What was his name? I shall report him," he said firmly.

Flustered, Teretia could not remember. "He had blond hair, shaggy on top with sideburns, and he was tall and I think he had brown eyes but he was looking at me so peculiarly and I did not want to give him any encouragement. And he was wearing a white tunic. Oh, but that's not very helpful is it, because all the slaves wear white!"

Actually Philo had identified the culprit at "blond": Lysander. Who else could reduce a girl to this state in so short an acquaintance?

The acquaintance was renewed when the door was flung open and Lysander asked loudly, "Philo, who was that gorgeous big-titted freebie?" only to be faced with the big-titted freebie herself, rapidly turning red again. His former roommate had his arms crossed and, most out of character, was scowling at him. Lysander was unfazed.

"That's the one!" he exclaimed and then gave her *the look*.

The look rolled down Teretia's body. It lingered particularly on her breasts and hips. It ran down to her thighs where the fabric of her dress clung, tailed down to her pink toes peeking out of her sandals, and then reversed back up; taking in all this scenery again and settling on her face. He smiled, charmingly, running a hand through his blond locks.

Philo was familiar with *the look*. He had witnessed it performed on many of the palace girls. He supposed somewhere there might actually be a woman who was flattered by it, but right now Teretia responded in the exact same way as all those other recipients of *the look*. She shuddered. Then she unconsciously took a step towards Philo. Something akin to gallantry rose in Philo's breast.

"Lysander, I think you should go away now because you have work to do and Teretia has come to see me and she doesn't want to talk to you."

For Philo, who never lost his temper, this was a stinging retort. For everyone else, it could be described as mildly abrasive. Or meekly piqued. Lysander in any case did not notice his friend's quiet irritation. He had become stuck on one particular part of that sentence.

"TERETIA?" he shrieked, his eyes bulging. "That's Teretia?"

It was a shock. Lysander's mental image of Philo's supposed girlfriend had been of a mousy, dull, stodgy creature who liked tidying things, sharpening styluses, reading, and all those other pastimes that gave Philo pleasure. He shook his head vigorously.

"No way, no way."

He was saved from another faux pas by a dusty messenger who shoved him out of the way and hung heaving on the door frame. Lysander, rubbing his shunted shoulder, glared at him.

The messenger garbled out his news. "The Praetorians have killed Sabinus!"

Silence. Then Lysander burst out with, "What?"

Philo blinked. Sabinus dead? Killed by his own men? It didn't seem likely.

"Are you sure?" he queried.

The messenger nodded.

401

"Did you see the body?"

The messenger wiped his mouth with the back of his hand. "He's dead."

"But did you see the body?" pressed Philo with good reason.

He was still receiving eight sightings of the very dead Nero each day.

The messenger was unable to offer him the categorical assurances he sought, so he turned to Teretia and said, "I'm sorry. I should really go see if—"

"I think that is perfectly correct," Teretia assured him, flashing him a sweet smile that had Lysander itching with envy.

Philo furrowed his brow, his soft brown eyes troubled.

"Teretia, I don't think you should walk home alone. If Sabinus is dead there could be disturbances. I'll escort you home on my way to the Praetorian camp."

"I'll come too!" burst in Lysander, earning himself a scowl from Teretia now. "Someone might need announcing," he claimed and sidled up to the girl. "If there is any trouble I'll protect you. I work out at the gym every day."

He flexed a bicep. To his surprise Teretia did not feel the hard muscle, rather she squirmed closer to Philo. Overcoming her shyness, she slipped her hand into Philo's. An action that he was surprised at, but not adverse to, and he gripped her hand back.

Statilia Messalina received the news while propped up in bed.

"But I thought that tribune was going to intercept him?" she exclaimed before turning to Cassandra. "Go tell gorilla man to stand down. And get my breakfast started. I am famished!"

Then she clicked her fingers towards her sheet folders who rushed forward to perform their duty.

Straton had stood outside the empress' chamber all night, cudgel raised in happy anticipation of some bloody good Praetorian bashing. He took the news of Sabinus' demise badly. Smashing his cudgel against the wall in frustration and rasping, "Fuck it!"

Mina, curled asleep on the floor, lifted up a weary head and gazed up at him through half-opened eyes. "Is it kicking off?" she asked, yawning.

"Fuckin' guards killed 'im," moaned Straton, kicking at the door.

"Bummer," yawned Mina and went back to sleep.

FIFTY-EIGHT

It was Philo's plan to head down to the forum, past the Temple of Vesta and the Senate House, through the Forum of Augustus and onto the Vicius Longus. This would lead him up the Viminal Hill where he could drop Teretia at home and then follow the road up to the Viminal Gate, beyond which lay the Praetorian camp.

There he could ascertain whether Nymphidius Sabinus was indeed dead or whether it was just another facile rumour. Story confirmed or denied, he could trot back to the palace to inform the emperor's representative in Rome, Icelus. Who by that time should be out of bed, Philo hoped.

However, this plan was thwarted from the very beginning. Walking through the old palace doors, he could already see a crowd forming below in the forum area. This was not the usual bustle of traders, shoppers, senators, and officials. This crowd was not moving. It was still. Gathering by the rostra, waiting.

"They've heard too," Philo said to Lysander.

The announcer nodded, his expression grim. "It's too big a story to keep quiet."

Philo bit his lip and held onto Teretia's hand tighter.

"They need an official line," he murmured, and then took control. "Lysander, can you get word to the bed chamberlain that Icelus needs to rise now. Tell the Praetorian tribune on duty that they need to get more guards on the doors and some down there to keep order. I'll tell Icelus that he needs to issue a reassuring statement in Galba's name stating that everything is under control and for people to return to their homes. Then we need to—"

But that sentence was cut off by a sudden uproar from below.

There was a commotion of some sort. Philo could see a dash of citizens to the Senate House steps. He narrowed his eyes, holding a hand up to shield out the bright sun, trying to ascertain what had panicked the citizens. It was difficult to see. The forum was chock-full with temples and basilicas which blocked his view. Then he saw it. A flash of purple by the road that ran alongside the Senate House, then another. Purple plumed helmets bobbing in line, one after another. Briefly in sight and then lost behind the Temple of Julius Caesar. The perfect symmetrical beat of marching boots confirmed Philo's thoughts: Praetorians.

"It's not time for a changeover," he murmured to himself.

The new cohort was not due on duty for another four hours. The Guard was rigid in its timetable. While Philo worried about this change in the schedule, the civilians on the ground knew what they had to do. They had to get out the way of those whoremongering bastards.

There was a scatter of heads as they ran to the safety of temple steps or behind the pillars of the Basilica Aemilia or onwards to the Via Nova where the shopkeepers were already pulling down their shutters in anticipation of trouble.

Outside the old palace on the north-west corner of the Palatine Hill, Lysander, Philo, and Teretia were joined by other curious members of the imperial household who watched the show below.

"What do you think they're up to?" asked Lysander as the Praetorians lined themselves up shoulder to shoulder in front of the clear space before the rostra.

The rostra was the long flat platform where Mark Antony had delivered his famous funeral oration to the fallen Julius Caesar. Where Cicero's head and hands had been displayed until the crows picked them to pieces. And where Julia, Augustus' wild daughter, had played the prostitute, yelling out for passers-by to service her. The Praetorians had something altogether different in mind.

The citizens grouped on the steps of the Senate House were watching the marching line of Praetorians pass them. Then one of them pointed and there was another flurry of noise. Philo squinted. Between the columns of guards now entering the forum was a gap. Two Praetorians separate from the standard marching formation were each holding a line of rope, pulling something behind them.

He focused on the floppy shape that banged along the ground, jarring over the cobbles. He could make out two arms, their wrists bound with rope, and between them a head, face down. The torso from the hips down was dragging along the ground, dead legs weighted down, dead feet scraping. As they hit a loose flag stone the head flopped to one side, causing a sharp intake of breath from the imperial staff.

"It's Sabinus!"

"They've murdered the prefect!"

"We're next!" exclaimed Lysander, twitching his head round for somewhere to hide.

Philo turned to Teretia. "I think we should go inside. I don't think you should see this."

She had already seen enough. Her face was very pale. She nodded distractedly, unable to tear her eyes away from Sabinus' bloody corpse being dragged across the Via Sacre.

407

The same could be said for the crowd, who watched in silent wonderment as the line of guards in front of the rostra broke aside to allow the two Praetorians dragging Sabinus' body through. They mounted the rostra slowly, Sabinus' legs flailing at each step. The watching slaves winced on his behalf. When they reached the top, they dropped the body with a thud and took up position at either end of the rostra. The Praetorian tribune Crispinus skipped up behind them, stood at the front of the rostra, unsheathed sword in his hand and announced, "The traitor is dead! See the traitor! Long live Imperator Galba!"

The guards in front of the rostra yelled their agreement back, waving their swords in the air. "GALBA! GALBA!"

The wide-eyed civilians watching those swords waving, some still dripping with Sabinus' blood, felt they had no choice but to state their loyalty and a cry of, "Emperor Galba," rang around the forum with increasing volume.

Crispinus, stood on the rostra, smiled at the noise, glanced down at Sabinus' bloodied corpse, and gave it a sly kick.

Philo put an arm round Teretia and began to gently lead her away. "We'll go back to my office," he told her kindly. "And I'll order some snacks in and we'll just have a nice chat."

"Oh no," breathed Lysander, "Oh no, no, no!"

Philo and Teretia spun round. Philo followed to where Lysander's panicked eyes were fixed. He could see a tall, dread-locked Gaul bashing his way past the yelling guards, clearing a way through for the woman who walked behind him.

"Oh no," cried Philo.

"What is it?" squeaked Teretia.

Philo's expression was pained. "It's his mother. It's Sabinus' mother."

Nymphidia Sabina had just risen when the rumour was carried to her elegant villa.

"What rubbish!" she had exclaimed.

Her son was adored by his men. She had personally seen the respect they held him in. It was just another silly story. One of many that fed the minds of the credulous during these paranoid times. When the second messenger came with the news that Praetorians were marching en masse from their camp outside the Viminal Gate into the city, she had paused. Then she had asked Hercules to accompany her to determine what was going on.

Stood now before the lines of guards by the rostra, Hercules proved his worth.

"Let us through," he demanded.

The guard before him sneered. Hercules sneered back fiercer.

Nymphidia scanned their faces, where was Gaius? He was their commander he should be at the front.

Hercules fixed the guard with his hard blue eyes and then roughly pushed him aside. Taking hold of Nymphidia's hand, he pulled her through as he bashed the lines out of the way, moving too quickly for them to retaliate.

As they reached the bottom of the steps, Nymphidia saw the tribune holding up his bloody sword and a figure on the ground by his feet. She ran up, overtaking Hercules.

Crispinus was shocked out of his chorus of, "GALBA!" by the appearance of a well-dressed lady of certain years. He stared at her, she stared back, and then she looked down at the body by his feet. The face was covered in blood, the features battered by their journey to the forum, yet she could still recognise that large jaw. That strong nose. Those brown eyes glaring lifelessly up at the sky. Her boy, her only boy.

She fell to her knees with a crash, Hercules rushing to her side. Then Nymphidia Sabina sat back on her heels and screamed.

It was a sound of such intensity, such power, such raw grief that it cut through the patriotic yells of the guards and there fell absolute silence.

409

Of everyone who was in the forum that day, not one ever forgot that scream. Certainly not Alex and Honoratus, who had rushed down from the Praetorian camp and had just passed the Senate House when it rang out; the hairs on Alex's neck standing up, goose bumps forming on his arms. Honoratus stood dumb as he saw Nymphidia on the rostra rocking on her heels, Hercules holding her tight as she struggled against him sobbing.

Teretia too was sobbing, pressed against Philo as he stroked her hair and made soothing noises. Lysander, wide-eyed, opened his mouth several times without any sound coming out. Which had to be a first.

Icelus, belatedly joining the shocked slaves, stared down on the incredible scene below and said lightly, "Well, that solves that problem. I couldn't see Sabinus getting on with Cornelius Laco. Philo! Philo! Put down that girl. You have work to do."

Philo's arm fell from Teretia's shoulders limply to his side.

"I have to—" he began to her teary face. "I'll get a slave to take you home."

She gave a pained smile and clutched hold of his hand. "Thank you, Vima."

A shared look was broken by Icelus yelling, "PHILO! Now!"

The freedman pulled his toga back onto his arm and retreated into the palace, followed by the shocked imperial workforce.

In the forum below, the guards stood silently shamed as Nymphidia Sabina cradled the body of her only son to her breast, hugging him tight to her. Crispinus dropped his bloody sword with a clang and then motioned for the guards to disperse.

Such was the end of Gaius Nymphidius Sabinus.

FIFTY-NINE

"Thank you for coming," said Nymphidia softly.

She was soberly dressed in black, a simple bead necklace encircling her elegant neck. Pale of face, she was calm; but from the fidget of her hands, Honoratus could see this composure was hard fought.

"I wanted you to know that after what you witnessed, once the crowd had gone, I retrieved—"

He stopped, unable to find the suitable words, handing her a small urn.

"I am sorry that you were not there. The secrecy was unfortunately necessary."

Icelus had been determined that as a traitor, the proper end for Sabinus was the River Tiber. It had taken all Honoratus' pleading and an interjection from Philo noting Nymphidia Sabina's personal popularity within the palace that had secured control of the corpse.

"Galba will not approve," Icelus had said.

Reluctantly he accepted the argument that the day spent on public display was enough to show the harsh treatment any would-be traitor could expect from Emperor Galba.

Nymphidia held the urn between her palms. "I shall place him next to his grandfather."

Honoratus cleared his throat. "I served with Gaius in many battles over the years. He had my back more times than I can count. He was the bravest man I ever met and I never met anyone truer to his principles."

"Thank you."

"He often spoke warmly of you."

Nymphidia barked out a laugh. "Oh, I doubt that," she said. "You see, Honoratus, we are so very cosseted at the palace. You would not know that, but we are. Any smart child, if she or he has the necessary cunning, can rise all the way up; wield incredible power that sways the very course of the empire, gaining amazing wealth on the way. We think it matters, we believe ourselves citizens. I am a wealthy woman, a very wealthy woman. I may be sat next to some senatorial wife at a palace function and we will chat and gossip and enjoy each other's company. Yet if I were to pass that same woman in the forum, she would blank me entirely. The following week I could be sat next to her again and we will be bosom buddies. Perhaps her husband has told her to sweet-talk me: he wants a governorship and I have the emperor's ear, amongst other things." She gave a bitter smile. "But I shall never receive an invitation to their home nor would they accept one to mine. I am not respectable. I am not proper. That is why my son joined the army, to escape my reputation. To escape me," her voice broke slightly. "No talk of class in the ranks is there, Honoratus? All comrades together, nobody caring about background, nobody caring if your mother's a whore. All you care about is if the man next to you will fight, will watch your back." She broke off again, staring sorrowfully at the urn.

"I wanted to ask, madam, if I may," he began.

She looked up at him. "You want to know if Caligula was his father."

"It would lay some things to rest for me."

Nymphidia Sabina sighed gently. "I'll not deny I knew Caligula intimately but it was after Gaius was born. He knew that, he would remember. I don't know where this sudden fallacy came from."

"He was not himself at the end, madam."

"Indeed not."

"I am so very sorry."

"I don't blame you, really I don't. It is my fault, Honoratus."

Honoratus began to interrupt to protest but she spoke over him. "No, it is. I was the one who brought him back to Rome. He was happy in the army. He liked fighting, the battles. But I was selfish. I missed him. I wanted him home. And it killed him. I killed my son."

It was then that she broke down, her shoulders shaking, a wail that had built deep inside her escaping as she clutched the urn to her chest, sobbing.

"My boy, my poor boy. I am so sorry. I am so sorry."

Hercules, who had been stood impassively behind her, stepped forward and took his mistress into his strong arms. She leaned into him with an easy intimacy. There was nothing left for Honoratus to say so he took his leave of her.

Outside the front door to Nymphidia's elegant Palatine mansion, Alex was leaning against the wall. On seeing Honoratus he asked, pained, "How is she?"

"Not good," admitted the tribune, and then noting Alex's own gloomy demeanour, "And you Alex?"

The boy shrugged. "Not good."

Mina had been entirely unsympathetic, claiming that hadn't she always said the guards were brutes? It was about time he opened his eyes to what they were really like. She didn't understand nor care the deep trauma that Alex had suffered. The loss of someone he had greatly admired, whom he had willingly served, who had died in such a squalid manner.

413

Which had left Alex feeling distinctly lonely. Honoratus understood him, though, the tribune forcing a smile and saying, "Let's go cheer ourselves up, hey?" and ruffling his hair.

Alex forced out his own smile.

They walked back across the Palatine Hill, past the former homes of the great Emperor Augustus and his formidable wife Livia. They squeezed past the Temple of the Magna Mater, hearing the eunuch priests within practising their cymbal playing. As they passed the front of the temple, Alex saw the door was open. A young eunuch dressed in a traditional saffron gown, his hair tied in a ponytail, his eyes made up with kohl, stood on the steps accompanied by an older, fatter fellow priest.

Alex gave them a mere glance. The look that was directed at his back was longer and filled with hateful intensity.

"Come, sister," said the older priest. "It is time for the sacrifice."

Sporus narrowed his eyes but let himself be led back into the temple. His thoughts on one thing alone: revenge.

AUTHOR'S NOTE

It is perhaps because the years AD 68–69 are so jam-packed full of incident that the actions of Gaius Nymphidius Sabinus are given so little attention. But he was truly pivotal in the events that unfolded and without him, it is fun to speculate whether there would ever have been the infamous Year of the Four Emperors.

When Vindex began the revolt against Nero, there was no sign that he would be successful, even when the likes of Otho, the governor of Lusitania, and Galba, governor of Spain, sided with his intentions. The hardened German legions were very much pro-Nero and the emperor was extremely popular in the East. (Indeed after his death it was from the East that so many of the fake Neros appeared.) There is much scholarly debate asserting that Nero should have won. Vindex was defeated in battle, after all. So what went wrong?

It is clear from our sources that Nero moved from not taking the revolt at all seriously (the scene with the notable senators, where Nero fiddles with his water organ throughout, is historically attested) to taking severe fright. And here enters Nymphidius Sabinus, for it is he who turns the emperor's own Guard against him, causing Nero's flight and ultimately his suicide.

The question is whether Sabinus was in it with Galba or whether he saw which way the wind was blowing and turned traitor? Sabinus had done very well out of Nero. The son of an imperial freedwoman, his grandfather had been Caligula's private secretary: from slave to right arm of the emperor in only two generations.

Without Sabinus, Galba could not have become emperor. It is Plutarch who gives us the fullest account of Sabinus' behaviour in Rome whilst the new Emperor Galba travelled down from Spain. Evidently he got rather above himself, did much in the new emperor's name that could not be undone, and apparently even took Sporus as a consort! An action my fictional Sabinus would never have contemplated. This is why, according to Plutarch, Sabinus makes the rash decision to remove Galba and make himself emperor. The son of a former slave becoming emperor? Even in such interesting times as AD 68 this was wholly unimaginable. Something clearly had gone amiss with Sabinus. I decided on some sort of a nervous breakdown pushing him to this ultimate act.

But he is such a sketchy character historically (a gift to a writer) that we will never know why he acted as he did. One thing, however, is clear: it was Sabinus' actions in deposing Nero that directly unleashed the Year of the Four Emperors.

A tale to be picked up in *Galba's Men*, Book II of the Four Emperors series.

L. J. Trafford

ABOUT THE AUTHOR

L. J. Trafford worked as a tour guide, after gaining a BA Hons in ancient history. This experience was a perfect introduction to writing, involving as it did the need for entertainment and a hefty amount of invention (it's how she got tips!). She now works in London doing something whizzy with databases.

Praise for *Palatine*

'The politics of the Palatine, during the last days of Nero and beyond, are beautifully played out in a tense atmosphere of ruthless ambition and distrust. The characters are very well drawn, with hardly a shred of our own western morality; they fit into the age very believably and yet are recognisable to the modern reader. I found it to be a thoroughly enjoyable and riveting read, full of intrigue and depravity with a fast-paced plot. Great fun!'

Robert Fabbri
bestselling author of the Vespasian series

'What a great read *Palatine* is! I thoroughly enjoyed this fresh and engaging take on a well-known story: it's quick-witted, well observed, and packed with characters that stay in the mind long after the last page has been turned.'

Ruth Downie
bestselling author of the Medicus mystery series

'*Palatine* is *Downton Abbey* with teeth, a racy, entertaining, largely slave's-eye view of Nero's final months in power combining historical fact, Suetonian mud-slinging, skulduggery both above and below stairs, a touch of romanticism, and more than a smidgen of period brutality. It's well written (page-turningly so), and Trafford has a good eye for character and a good ear for dialogue, as well as knowing her stuff historically. Excellent. I look forward to the next one in the series.'

David Wishart
bestselling author of the Marcus Corvinus Mystery series

Made in the USA
Middletown, DE
02 July 2020

11817778R00239